SAUCER

THE CONQUEST

SAUCER

THE CONQUEST

STEPHEN COONTS

ORION

First published in Great Britain in 2004 by
Orion Books
an imprint of The Orion Publishing Group
Orion House, 5 Upper St Martin's Lane,
London WC2H 9EA

A CIP catalogue record for this book is
available from the British Library

ISBN (hardback) 0 75286 864 0
ISBN (trade paperback) 0 75286 865 9

Printed and bound in Great Britain by
Clays Ltd, St Ives plc

www.orionbooks.co.uk

To all those dreamers who looked at the moon and wanted to go

ACKNOWLEDGMENTS

THE AUTHOR WOULD NOT HAVE GOTTEN HIS SAUCERS OFF the ground without the generous help of two people. Gilbert "Gil" Pascal, physicist and electrical engineer, is always ready to noodle about "what if" questions. His flights of technical imagination made a huge contribution to this tale. Plots are the forte of the author's wife, Deborah Coonts, who is always ready to exercise her fine, devious mind on the author's behalf. Her contributions to this novel were essential to the creative process. A heartfelt thank-you to both of them.

The author has referred extensively to *The Giant Leap* by Adrian Berry (New York: Tor Books, 2002). Mr. Berry eloquently explains the problems future interstellar voyagers will encounter and offers some innovative, fascinating solutions.

SAUCER

THE CONQUEST

PROLOGUE

THE TRAIN EASED SLOWLY OUT OF THE BLACKNESS OF THE desert night into the spotlights. As the three locomotives hissed steam, soldiers piled off the train and rushed away to form a perimeter.

Newton Chadwick stood with the small knot of civilians under the lights looking up at the giant black shroud that covered the flatbed car behind the engines. It was huge, rising over seventy feet in the air.

A dozen workers in hard hats stripped the protective shroud off the large, circular object on the flatcar. Then they began the task of rigging a harness so that the crane permanently mounted beside the track—one normally used to handle steel girders used to construct towers to test nuclear weapons—could off-load the object onto a waiting lowboy.

The senior civilian turned and solemnly shook hands with each of his colleagues. Newton Chadwick was the youngest of the group, just twenty-two. A child prodigy, genius and physics superstar, he had been thrown out of four universities for drunkenness, antisocial behavior, lewd and lascivious conduct and, at the last institution, burning down his dormitory when an unattended still in the attic caught fire.

Newton was tall, pencil-thin and gawky, with flaming red hair and an awesome collection of freckles. His father, a wealthy distributor of soda fountain equipment, had been unable to overlook the obvious fact that the youngster bore no physical resemblance to him or any of his relatives. Blaming the boy's mother, the soda fountain magnate dumped several million in a trust fund and booted young Newton out into the unsuspecting world.

Newton's odyssey after his traumatic emancipation is beyond the scope of this work. Suffice it to say that after many and diverse adventures, he was recruited by a former professor who knew the quality of the boy's mind to assist in the examination and testing of captured German rockets and the development of American ones. The professor told a variety of well-intentioned lies to the authorities, who granted Newton an interim security clearance.

Tonight, as he stood in the Nevada desert surrounded by his colleagues, all of whom possessed a breathtaking collection of academic degrees, young Newton ignored the senior scientist's comments and stared at the flying saucer being off-loaded onto the lowboy.

A flying saucer! Who would have suspected that such a thing really existed?

"It was recovered in New Mexico, I heard," one man, a Harvard Ph.D., said. "Near Roswell, after one of these things crashed during an electrical storm."

"You don't believe that, do you?" another responded. "That's just a cover story."

"But where are the people who flew it?"

"They'll never tell *us!*"

"They're probably locked up somewhere, being interrogated."

"It's a Nazi bomber. That's the only logical explanation."

"Or Soviet."

Even at his tender age, Newton Chadwick understood that the government was perfectly capable of lying to the public, and probably had.

How the saucer came to earth and into the government's possession was immaterial. The reality was that it was right there before his eyes, a massive physical presence straight out of a Buck Rogers comic book.

The color was dark, almost as black as the night that surrounded them. The spotlights reflected from the smooth, polished surface in little pinpoints of brilliant light. The saucer was, Newton estimated, about ninety feet in diameter, perhaps a dozen feet thick in the middle, feathered toward the edges into a perfectly round, smooth leading edge. The three massive struts upon which it sat jutted from the belly. On the bottom of the struts were pads, not wheels. Protruding from the saucer's edge, covering an area of about fifteen degrees of its circumference, were four rocket nozzles, each perhaps fifteen inches in diameter. The landing gear struts and rocket nozzles were the only imperfections in the perfect oval shape that Newton could see from his vantage point.

"It's German, no doubt about it," one of the scientists insisted. "The government is trying to keep it under wraps. They don't want Uncle Joe Stalin to hear about it."

Newton thought that hypothesis highly unlikely, but he held his tongue. The German rockets that he had spent the last six months examining were much cruder in appearance than this . . . this sleek, ominous, perfectly round black shape. Neither Soviet nor German industry was capable of manufacturing anything like this. Nor was American industry—or any industrial establishment on the planet. On *this* planet.

The saucer wasn't from *this* planet! That realization crystallized in Newton's mind.

But if it wasn't made on earth, then where?

It must have been flown here. By whom?

". . . An opportunity of a lifetime," the senior man was saying. He rubbed his hands in excited anticipation.

No one responded to that. The rest of the members of the group stood mesmerized as the crane lifted the saucer onto the massive lowboy. It took ten minutes to strap it down—ten long minutes of absolute silence among the watching scientists, each of whom was lost in his own thoughts.

Finally, when the saucer was secured, the lowboy and a convoy of army trucks full of armed soldiers crept away from the lights into the darkness of the desert night.

When the remaining soldiers had disbursed and the small knot of scientists stood alone beside the motionless train, the senior man again broke the silence. "Washington wants an encrypted report of our preliminary examination by tomorrow evening. The interest is at the very highest level. We'll start at seven in the morning."

A few people muttered replies, but Newton Chadwick didn't. He was staring into the night that had swallowed the saucer.

HE COULDN'T SLEEP THAT NIGHT. THE ARMY INSTALLED the wizards in a large tent and issued each of them a cot and sleeping bag. Lying on his cot in the darkness, his nostrils full of the sage and juniper scent of the high desert, he lay listening to the whisper of the wind, thinking about the saucer.

The existence of the saucer required each person who saw it to throw out the preconceptions of a lifetime. Somewhere out there in the vast nothingness of space, somewhere far away in space and time—for Chadwick well knew the two were inexplicably linked, which was one of the great mysteries of life—there were other intelligent creatures; they had built this saucer, and it was now here . . . on earth. On this small planet orbiting a nondescript star on the edge of a humongous galaxy that wheeled endlessly on a hidden axis in the infinite void.

Newton Chadwick was a child of his place and time, and he didn't know what to make of it. Sure, he had read his share of science fiction as a youngster—and that was precisely what it was, fiction. He had seen the Buck Rogers matinee features, watched space cowboys shoot it out with aliens bent on conquest. Or worse. Mind candy for a Saturday afternoon.

The saucer changed everything. Everything!

The other men on cots weren't sleeping either. They coughed and tossed restlessly, but no one was breathing deeply or snoring. Physicists, mathematicians, working engineers—they were from the nation's finest universities and large industrial concerns. No doubt they were also wondering what they would find when they opened the saucer in the morning. And, because they were human, thinking about how the discoveries they would make would build careers and reputations.

Finally, when he could stand it no longer, Chadwick eased from his sleeping bag, stepped into his clothes and shoes, and slipped out of the tent. The night sky was full of stars, countless points of light flung carelessly into the inky blackness by . . . by . . . God?

Young Chadwick had never thought much about God. He had been dipped in religion as a child when his father and mother dragged him to church at irregular intervals, but little of it had stuck. Tonight, staring upward at the gleaming stars in the obsidian sky, he realized that if there were a God, He was a whale of a lot larger than the white-haired old man depicted on the stained glass windows of that church in New Jersey.

And there was the Milky Way, a ribbon of light that stretched from horizon to horizon, a galaxy of countless stars.

For the first time in his life Newton Chadwick felt as if he were marooned on a small island in an endless sea, confined to a tiny spit of sand, unable to escape.

One of the wizards was a slim older man with wispy white hair surrounding a tanned bald pate who habitually sucked on a pipe. He was the gloomiest of the lot the following morning, saying little in response to the excited inanities and speculations of his colleagues as they ate a hasty breakfast in an army mess tent. He ate in silence as they discussed the possibility that one of the creatures who had flown the saucer might still be in it. "Did the army open the thing?" No one knew.

Finally someone drew him into the conversation with a direct question. "I wish I weren't involved in this," he said gloomily. "I wish I were back in my lab at the university happily ignorant of the existence of that thing." He jerked his head in the direction of the hangar that held the saucer.

"What are you saying, Fred? The arrival of the saucer is the most exciting thing to happen on this planet since Christ rose from the dead."

"As I recall, the news of the Resurrection made a great many people very unhappy," Fred responded. "The saucer story will be greeted the same way. Who do you think is going to be overjoyed at the news? The clergy? Industrialists? Union leaders? The politicians? When they pause for a moment's thought—and I'll freely admit that they rarely exercise their brains for that long—the politicians are going to realize that the arrival of a spaceship flown by intelligent creatures from another solar system is going to rock civilization. May even shatter it."

"Anarchy? Are you predicting anarchy?"

Fred toyed with the remnants of his breakfast. "A man my age should probably stay out of the business of crystal ball predictions. However, I do think our report is going to give official Washington one hell of a scare. My gut feeling is we are wasting our time. We'll never be allowed to say a word about anything we see or do here today, and yet no one here will ever be able to forget it. We'd all be better off not knowing."

The discussion swirled around the table, but Newton Chadwick didn't participate. He rarely did. The senior men had careers, tenured faculty chairs and hard-earned reputations to worry about. He didn't. Newton forked eggs and potatoes, drained a second glass of milk and left the tent while they pondered the shape of the world in the coming Age of the Saucer.

THE SAUCER WAS PARKED IN A LARGE HANGAR AT AN unused air base in the desert wastes. The wizards rode for an hour on the bus to get there. One of the officers handed out a special badge to each man, who was required to wear it on a chain around his neck as if it were a set of dog tags. They were all in such a hurry to see the saucer again that they donned the tags without protest and queued up to get past another soldier, a sergeant, who scrutinized each badge even though he had just watched the officer hand them out and the wizards put them on.

As usual, Chadwick found himself at the end of the line. He ground his teeth and waited his turn.

There it was! Sitting under the lights on its legs, apparently undamaged by the rough handling it had recently received.

They found the entry hatch on the belly of the saucer quickly enough. As the rest of the group fondled the machine and examined the rocket nozzles and tried to see through the canopy into the dark interior, three of them worked on getting the hatch open. Twenty minutes later they were still at it. They would have spent the day staring at the mechanism if one of them had not kept his hand on it for about ten seconds, then tried to manipulate it. Now it opened.

"It is sensitive to heat," they cried to their colleagues as they gathered on hands and knees under the saucer to examine the mechanism. As they excitedly discussed how this minor miracle might be physically accomplished, Newton Chadwick wriggled between them and slithered up through the hatch.

The interior was dark, lit only by the overhead lights from the interior of the hangar that penetrated the canopy. And it was empty of the creatures, living or dead, who had flown the saucer. A much relieved Newton Chadwick began a hasty inspection.

There were seats equipped with seat belts. Humans, Chadwick concluded. Or humanoids, humanlike creatures. Controls, a pilot's seat, white panels where the instruments should be . . . pedals for the pilot, a stick on the right and left. And a headband. Much like an Indian's headband that he and his friends had worn in play not too many years ago.

He picked up the band and inspected it as closely as he could in the gloom. As he did so, several of his colleagues worked up the courage to join him in the saucer's interior.

"I see you're still alive, Chadwick," the senior man said acidly. Obviously the boy didn't know his place in the pecking order, but what could you expect from a youth with his credentials?

"He's our mine canary," the second man announced. His displeasure was also evident. "If there are horrible bacteria waiting in here to smite us, at least we have five minutes."

Chadwick couldn't resist. He coughed, grabbed his throat and made a retching sound. The older scientists scurried back out the hatch.

Newton donned the headband. Well, the saucer people apparently had heads about the same size as his, which was seven and an eighth in baseball caps. *Remember to insert that tidbit in the report to Washington,* he told himself as he looked around on the panel for something to make the headband do something.

Hmm . . .

"Are you alive in there, Chadwick?"

"I feel quite feverish, sir." They liked it when he called them sir. "Vision fading, coming and going."

"Get a doctor! Quickly." The call was repeated, which caused the soldiers to scurry about in a frenzied way. Chadwick ignored the commotion: He was too busy pulling and pushing the half dozen knobs and levers on the instrument panel. Surprising that there were so few. He had seen the cockpit of a four-engine airliner, which was stuffed with dials and gauges and dozens of levers . . .

Aha. The entire panel came to life when he pulled out one of the red knobs.

He stared at the white panels, which changed colors and became almost transparent. Symbols appeared.

And he saw into the heart of the machine.

The headband . . . My God!

He tried to organize his thoughts, and saw the presentations on the panels before him change as fast as thought.

It was some kind of calculator, like the Univac. He had read of it, a giant machine that filled a building and could be used to make scientific calculations. This was like that, only . . .

His mind galloped on. How does the saucer work? Where did it come from? Who flew it? He got immediate answers to these questions, although he didn't fully comprehend the information he saw.

As fast as thought.

"What in hell are you doing in there, Chadwick?"

Now the senior man crawled in. Before he could see the displays, Chadwick pushed the red power button in. The panels turned white and the humming in the compartment behind him died.

"Jesus Christ, you damned fool! Are you running this machine? What in hell do you think you're doing?"

"Trying to find out what makes it go," Chadwick answered curtly and, stuffing the headband into his pocket, turned around to study the back wall of the cockpit, which must provide access to the machinery he had heard.

What the senior man would have said we will never know, because he was joined by four of his colleagues, and they were instantly lost in a discussion of the wondrous things they saw about them.

Newton Chadwick, on the other hand, found the latches to the machinery compartment hatch, figured out how they worked and scuttled through. From his pocket he produced a small flashlight. With it on, he closed the hatch behind him. The scientists standing shoulder to shoulder in the cockpit paid no attention.

THE DISCUSSION THAT EVENING IN THE MESS HALL WAS curiously antiseptic, Newton thought. During dinner the scientists had been animated, filled to overflowing with wonder and awe at the things they had seen that day. They chattered loudly, rudely interrupted each other and talked when no one was listening. When the mess trays were cleared away and mugs of coffee distributed by soldiers in aprons, the senior man pulled out a message pad and pencil and laid them on the table before him. The conversation died there.

"What should we tell Washington?" he asked, all business.

His colleagues were tongue-tied. None was ready to commit his ideas to paper and be held accountable by his professional peers into all eternity. "We don't know enough," Fred muttered. He was the unofficial spokesman, it seemed to young Newton, who sat in one corner watching and listening.

Chadwick had said nothing during dinner. As a young man he had learned the truth of the old adage that learning occurs when one's mouth is shut. He had listened carefully to all the comments, dismissing most, and collected the wisdom of those who had a bit to offer.

He had no intention of opening his mouth, so he was startled when the senior man said sharply, "Chadwick, you were scurrying around inside that saucer today like a starving mouse. What do you think?"

Young Newton pondered his answer. Finally he said cautiously, "I don't think the Germans made it."

"Well, fiddlesticks! I think we can all agree on *that*." The senior man surveyed the faces around the table over the top of his glasses. "Can't we?"

"Maybe the swastika burned off when it entered the atmosphere," some spoilsport suggested.

They wrangled all evening. At ten o'clock the senior man left, thoroughly disgusted, and trekked through the Nevada night to the radio tent. There he wrote the report to Washington. He read it through, crossed out a sentence in the middle and corrected the grammar. Finally he signed the form and handed it to the radio clerk to encode. He took solace from the fact that the message was classified and would never, ever, be read by his faculty colleagues at the university. He paused to light his pipe as the clerk read his composition.

"Can you make that out?" he asked gruffly.

The clerk looked at him with wide eyes. "Seems clear enough, sir."

The senior scientist left the tent in a cloud of tobacco smoke.

This is the message the encryption clerk read:

"Team spent day examining the flying saucer, which appears to be a spaceship manufactured upon another planet, undoubtedly in another solar system, by a highly advanced civilization using industrial processes unknown on earth. Appears to be powered by some form of atomic energy. No weapons found. Recommend that extensive, thorough examination continue on a semipermanent basis. Knowledge to be gained will revolutionize every scientific field."

The encryption clerk whistled in amazement and went to work with the code book.

IN THE DARKNESS OUTSIDE THE SLEEPING TENT, NEWTON Chadwick sat in the sand and fingered the headband he had "borrowed" from the saucer. The magic wasn't in the headband, which was merely a fabric that contained thousands of tiny wires, each thinner than a human hair. This headband, Newton believed, was the way the pilot of the saucer communicated with the electronic brain of the machine. That electronic brain was the heart of the saucer. True, there was a nuclear reactor that used heat in a strange electrolysis process to crack water into its constituent parts. The hydrogen was then burned in the rockets. And there was a huge ring around the bottom of the ship that Newton suspected was used to modulate the planet's gravitational field in some manner.

Yet the crown jewel of the saucer was the artificial brain that talked to his brain through this headband. This headband proved that the crew of the saucer had brains very similar to ours. And there was more: Inside that device, Newton suspected, was some record of the scientific and technical knowledge that the saucer's makers had used to build it. This record was the library housing the accumulated knowledge of an advanced civilization, and it was there for the man with the wit and brains to mine it.

These older men, scientists and engineers—he had listened carefully to their comments all evening. They still didn't understand the significance of the electronic brain, nor the headband. One reason was that they had not powered up the saucer. The other was that Newton had pocketed every headband he found, all four of them.

Given enough time, they would get a glimmer of the truth. They certainly weren't fools, even if they were conventional thinkers.

Actually there were at least three electronic brains that Newton had found. He thought about them now, wondering how so much information could be packaged into such small devices. Amazingly, they weighed about eight pounds each and were no larger than a shoe box.

He was sitting there speculating about how they might work when a soldier drove up in a jeep and rushed into the tent. In a few moments he heard the senior man swear a foul oath.

"Damnation!" he exclaimed to his colleagues. "Washington refuses to allow further access to the saucer. They want it sealed immediately. We are to return to Florida tomorrow."

Newton Chadwick leaped to his feet. He stuffed the headband into a pocket as he considered.

Inside the tent Fred declared, "They've lost their nerve. I was afraid of that."

There was a jeep parked next to the one the soldier had just driven up, one that had been provided for the use of the senior man. Chadwick walked over and looked in the ignition. The key was there. He hopped in, started the engine, popped the clutch and fed gas.

IT WASN'T UNTIL AFTER BREAKFAST, AS THE SCIENTISTS packed, that anyone missed young Chadwick. A search was mounted, and by midmorning it was learned that he visited the saucer about two that morning. He had displayed his badge and was admitted by the sentries, who had not been told to deny entry to badge-holders. Chadwick was inside for only thirty minutes, then drove away in an army jeep.

Despite the protests of the senior scientist, the army officer in charge sealed the saucer and refused to allow further entry, so no one knew what Chadwick had done inside it, if anything. Neither Chadwick nor the jeep could be found. Not that anyone looked very hard. The very existence of the saucer was a tightly held military secret, and the circle of persons with access to that information was very small.

Back in Florida the scientists who had visited the saucer were debriefed by FBI agents. They would be prosecuted, they were told, if they ever discussed the existence of the saucer or anything they had learned about it with any person not authorized to have access to that information. When the senior man asked who had access, he was told, "No one."

It was all extremely frustrating. The senior man retired two years after he saw the saucer. He wrote a treatise about it that his daughter thought was fiction. After his death from a heart attack, she tossed the manuscript into the trash.

The other scientists who had gone inside the saucer that day in the desert were also forced to get on with their lives while living with the memory of what they had seen. The Age of the Saucer that they had hoped for didn't arrive. Like the senior man, they too aged and died one by one, bitter and frustrated.

As the seasons came and went and the years slipped past, the saucer they had seen in the Nevada desert sat undisturbed in its sealed hangar.

OCTOBER 2004, MISSOURI

THE SLEEK LITTLE PLANE ZIPPED IN LOW AND FAST, DROP-ping below the treetops as it flew along the runway just a few feet above the ground; then the nose pointed skyward and the plane rolled swiftly around its horizontal axis once . . . twice . . . three times.

Rip Cantrell was the pilot. The alternating sunny blue sky and colorful earth were almost a blur as the plane whipped around. He centered the stick and the plane stopped whirling.

Up he went higher and higher into the sky, then gently lowered the nose and let the bird accelerate. The plane was an Extra 300L, a two-place aerobatic plane with two seats arranged in tandem. The pilot sat in the rear seat; today the front one was empty.

With the airspeed rapidly building, Rip brought the stick back smoothly. The increasing Gs mashed him down into the seat. Fighting the increased weight of his helmet and visor, he steadied at four Gs as the nose climbed toward the zenith. Throwing his head back, he could see the ground come into view as the plane became inverted at the top of the loop. He backed off on the G to keep the loop oval. The engine was pulling nicely, the ground beginning to fill the windscreen, so as the airspeed increased, he eased the G back on. The nose dropped until the Extra was plunging straight down.

Here Rip pushed the stick forward, eased back on the throttle and slammed the stick sideways. The plane rolled vigorously as it accelerated straight down in a wild corkscrew motion. *The controls are incredibly sensitive,* he thought, marveling at the plane's responsiveness to the slightest displacement of stick or rudder.

A glance at the altimeter, center the stick and pull some more, lifting that nose toward the horizon. The Gs were intense now; he was pulling almost six. He fought to keep his head up and blinked mightily to keep the sweat running down his forehead from blinding him. In seconds the plane was level. Rip eased off on the G and pulled the throttle back to idle.

The piston engine's moan dropped to a burble, and the plane began a gentle, descending turn to line up on the runway. With the power at idle, the plane floated into a perfect three-point landing, kissing the grass.

Rip steered his craft to a stop in front of the large wooden hangar beside the runway and cut the engine. He opened the canopy, snapping the safety line into place so it wouldn't fall off, and unstrapped. Still in the pilot's seat, he took off the helmet and swabbed the sweat from his face.

One of the men sitting on a bench beside the hangar heaved himself erect and strolled over to the Extra.

"Well, whaddaya think?"

"It's okay," Rip said. Lean, tanned by the sun, he was about six feet tall and in his early twenties.

"You sure fly it pretty well," the guy on the ground said enthusiastically, cocking his head and squinting against the glare of the brilliant sun.

"Save the flattery. I'll buy it."

The next question was more practical. "You gonna be able to get insurance?"

"I'm going to pay cash," Rip said as he stepped to the ground. "Then I don't have to insure it, do I?"

"Well, no. Guess not. Though I never had anyone buy one of these flying toys that didn't want to insure it. Lot of money, you know."

"I'll walk up to the house and get the checkbook. You figure out precisely what I owe you, taxes and all."

"Sure." The airplane salesman headed back to the bench beside the hangar.

Rip walked past the hangar and began climbing the hill toward his uncle's house. It was one of those rare, perfect Indian summer days, with a blazing sun in a brilliant blue sky, vivid fall foliage, and a warm, gentle breeze decorated with a subtle hint of wood smoke. Rip didn't notice. He climbed the hill lost in his own thoughts.

His uncle Egg Cantrell was holding a conference at his farm, so the house was full to overflowing. He had invited twenty scientists from around the world to sort through the data on the computer from the saucer Rip had found in the Sahara and donated to the National Air and Space Museum the previous September. Egg had removed a computer from the saucer and kept it. Its memory was a storehouse of fabulous information, which Egg used to patent the saucer's technology, and even more fabulous data on the scientific, ethical and philosophical knowledge of the civilization that constructed it.

The visiting scientists shared Egg's primary interest, which was computer technology. He had spent most of the past year trying to learn how the saucer's computer worked. The Ancient Ones knew that progress lies in true human-computer collaboration. They had promoted computers from dumb tools to full partners capable of combining known information, new data and programs of powerful creativity and logic techniques to generate and test new ideas. In effect, the computer could do original, creative thinking, a thing still beyond the capability of any computer made on earth.

Egg and his guests were having a wonderful time. They spent every waking minute with a dozen PCs containing files Egg had copied from the saucer's computer or talking with colleagues about what they had learned.

Egg was on the porch in an earnest discussion with two academics from California when he saw Rip coming up the hill with his hands in his pockets, eyes on the ground. He had been like this since his girlfriend, Charlotte "Charley" Pine, took a job with the French lunar expedition. She had been gone for six weeks, and a long six weeks it had been.

Egg excused himself from his guests and intercepted Rip before he could get to the porch. Egg was in his fifties, a rotund individual with little hair left. His body was an almost perfect oval—hence his nickname—but he moved surprisingly quickly for a man of his shape and bulk. He had been almost a surrogate father to Rip after his real dad died eleven years ago.

"Good morning," Egg said cheerfully. "Heard the plane. Is it any good?"

"It's okay. The guy is waiting for me to write him a check."

"He can wait a little longer. What say you and I take a walk?"

Rip shrugged and fell in with Egg, who headed across the slope toward the barn. "It's been quite a year, hasn't it?" Egg remarked. Actually more like thirteen months had passed since Rip donated the saucer from the Sahara to the National Air and Space Museum. They had indeed been busy months for Egg as he mined the data on the saucer's computer, filed patent applications with his, Rip's and Charley's names attached and licensed the propulsion technology.

The money from the licenses had been pouring into the bank that handled the accounts. While they were not yet rich enough to buy Connecticut, each of them could probably afford a small county in Mississippi or Arkansas.

Having a lot of money was both a curse and a blessing, as Rip and Charley discovered. They didn't need regular jobs, which meant that they had a lot of free time. Charley taught Rip to fly, and after he got his private license they had flown all over the country, leisurely traveled the world and finally returned to Missouri in midsummer.

After a few more weeks of aimless loafing, Charley jumped at a job offered by Pierre Artois, who was heading the French effort to build a space station on the moon. One morning she shook Egg's hand, hugged him, gave him a kiss and left. Her departure hadn't come as a surprise. He had known she was bored, even if Rip hadn't figured it out.

"I sorta miss Charley," Egg said now to Rip, who didn't respond.

Inside the barn Egg seated himself on a hay bale in the sun. Rip stood scuffing dirt with a toe, then finally seated himself on the edge of a feed-way.

"What are you going to do with your life, Rip?"

"I don't know."

"Buying toys won't help."

"The Extra is quite a plane."

"Everybody needs one."

"I reckon."

"Toys won't help what's ailing you."

Rip sighed.

"You could help me with this conference, if you wished," Egg continued, his voice strong and cheerful. "They keep asking questions about the saucer—you know as much about it as I do, maybe more."

"Don't want to answer questions about the saucer," Rip

responded. "Talked about it enough. Time to move on to something else."

"What?" Egg asked flatly.

"I don't know," Rip said with heat. "If I knew, I'd be doing it."

"You aren't the first man who ever had woman troubles. Sitting around moping about Charley isn't going to help."

That comment earned a glare from Rip.

"The launch is going to be on television this evening," Egg continued blandly. A French spaceplane had been launched every two weeks for the last six months, shuttling people and equipment to the new French base on the moon. Charley Pine was scheduled to be the copilot on the next flight. Since an American was going to be a crew member, the American networks had decided to air the launch in real time. "Are you going to watch?"

"She's going to the moon and you want me to watch it on television. How should I answer that?"

Egg sat on his bale for another moment, decided he didn't have anything else to say and levered his bulk upright.

"Sorry, Unc," Rip told the older man. "My life is in the pits these days."

"Maybe you ought to work on that," Egg said, then walked on out of the barn.

"Well, it *is* a mess," Rip told the barn cat, who came over to get her ears scratched. "After you've owned and flown a flying saucer, been everywhere and done everything with the hottest woman alive, where do you go next?"

The galling thing was that he knew the answer to that question. To the moon, of course! And he was sitting here in central Missouri twiddling his thumbs watching television while Charley did it for real.

Terrific! Just flat terrific!

* * *

CHARLEY PINE HAD JUST LIVED THROUGH THE BUSIEST SIX weeks of her life. From dawn to midnight seven days a week, the French had trained her to be a copilot in their new spaceships.

Unwilling to bet lives on just one ship, the French had built four of them. Two generations beyond the American space shuttles, the French ships were reusable spaceplanes, launched from a long runway in the south of France. They carried two large fuel tanks, one on either side, which they jettisoned after they had used the fuel. They then flew on into orbit, where they rendezvoused with a fuel tank, refilled their internal tanks and continued on to the moon. After delivering their cargo, the spaceplanes returned to earth orbit and reentered the atmosphere. They landed in France on the runway they had departed from and were readied for another voyage to the moon.

Bored with doing nothing, unable to interest Rip in anything other than sitting around, Charley had instantly accepted Pierre Artois' job offer. She didn't tell Rip until the following morning. Then she broke the news at breakfast and was gone fifteen minutes later.

Sure, leaving Rip had been hard, but she was unwilling to retire at the ripe old age of thirty. Sooner or later, Rip was going to have to figure out life. When he did, then she would see. If he did.

Pierre Artois believed in maximum publicity. The French government was spending billions on the lunar mission, so he didn't miss many chances to get all the good press he could. This evening, six hours before launch, he and his lunar crew stood in front of a bank of television cameras to answer questions.

Before the press zeroed in on Artois and the French space minister, one of the reporters asked a question of Charley, who was wearing a sky blue flight suit that showed off her trim, athletic figure. Her long hair was pulled back in a ponytail. The reporter was an American, who naturally asked his question in English.

In addition to all the technical information she was trying to absorb, Charley was also taking a crash course in French. Her four semesters of French way back when allowed her to buy a glass of wine, find a restroom and ask for a kiss, but that was about it. She gave up trying to learn the names of all the people shoving information at her, and called everyone *amigo*. That froze a few smiles, but Pierre Artois said she was one of his pilots, so frozen smiles didn't matter. She was actually grateful the first question was in English, until she heard it.

"Ms. Pine, some American pundits have said that hiring you to fly to the moon is just a publicity stunt by Monsieur Artois. Would you care to comment upon that?"

"Not really," she said lightly, trying to be cool. "I've been in space before." Actually her flying credentials were as good as anyone's. A graduate of the Air Force Academy and the air force's test pilot program, a veteran fighter pilot and the pilot of the flying saucer that had made such a splash last year, she believed she deserved this job, so the sneering hurt. It also immunized her against second thoughts about Rip. She was going to do this or die trying.

The chief pilot on the first mission was a man, Jean-Paul Lalouette. He was five or six years older than Charley and seemed to share the condescending opinion of the American newspaper pundits, but he was too wise to let it show— very much. Charley picked up on it, though. She glanced at him now and saw he was wearing the slightest trace of a smile.

Lalouette and his male colleagues thought she should be

very impressed with them. The fact that she wasn't didn't help their egos. "T. S.," Charley Pine muttered, which was American for *"C'est la guerre."*

After a couple of puff questions that allowed Charley to say nice, inane things about the French people and the lunar base project, the press zeroed in on Pierre Artois, to Charley's intense relief. She took several steps backward and tried to hide among the technicians she and Lalouette were flying to the moon.

Pierre obviously enjoyed the glare of television lights. A slight, fit man whose physical resemblance to Napoleon had occurred to so many people that no one remarked on it anymore, he looked happy as a man could be. And well he should, since he was making his first trip to the moon on this flight. His journey to the lunar base after years of promoting, cajoling, managing and partially financing—from his own pocket—the research and industrial effort made this appearance before the press a triumph.

Charley Pine didn't quite know what to make of Pierre, whom she had met on only three occasions. She had watched him in action on television for several years, though. The scion of a clan of Belgian brewers and grandson of the legendary Stella Artois, Pierre struck Charley as a man who desperately wanted to be somebody. An endless supply of beautiful women, a river of money and an exalted social position weren't enough—he had larger ambitions.

Charley had devoted ten seconds of thought to the question of what made Pierre tick, and concluded that the answer was beer. Every French farmer who ever squished a grape had more panache than Pierre did. France was all about wine, and Pierre was beer. This tragedy fairly cried out for psychoanalysis by a top-notch woman—or even a man—but unfortunately Pierre hadn't bothered; like Napoleon, he had looked for a world to conquer. The French lunar expedition was his, lock, stock and barrel, and he was going to make it a success . . . or else.

Despite Artois' love of the spotlight, Charley Pine admired him. Pierre Artois was a man who dreamed large. He dreamed of a French space program, with a base on the moon as a stepping-stone to Mars, which he defined as a challenge worthy of all that France had been and could be in the future. He had fought with all the will and might of Charlemagne to make it happen. His vision, optimism and refusal to take no for an answer had triumphed in the end.

The real reason for the French space program, or indeed any space program, was that the challenge was there. The moon was there; Mars was there; the stars beckoned every night. Charley Pine believed that people needed dreams, the larger the better. Our dreams define us, she once told Rip.

What a contrast the dreamer Pierre Artois was, Charley mused, to the modern Americans. Somewhere along the way they had lost the space dream. Space costs too much, they said. NASA had morphed into a petrified bureaucracy as innovative as the postal service. These days Americans fretted about foreign competition and how to save Medicare—and who was going to foot the bill. Rip once remarked that the current crop of penny-pinching, politically correct politicians would have refused to finance Columbus. Watching Artois, Charley knew that Rip was right.

The press conference was a photo op and nothing more. One of the American reporters asked about the fare-paying passenger Artois had agreed to take to the moon, one Joe Bob Hooker, who rumor had it was paying twenty-five million euros for his round-trip ticket. "This is a profit-making venture," Artois responded. "He paid cash." He refused to say more about his passenger.

"Your wife has preceded you to the moon, has she not?"

Ah, yes—true love on the moon. No fool, Pierre knew the

media would play this story line like a harp. He glanced longingly at the ceiling, then said simply, "We will soon be together. I have missed her very much." He touched his left breast and added with a straight face, "She is the best part of me." Charley Pine nearly gagged.

After a few more one-liners for television and a pithy comment or two for the newspapers, Pierre led his crew off the stage.

Soon they began the suiting-up process, some of it filmed by a cameraman with a video camera. Then the crew boarded a bus for the two-mile journey to the spaceplane, which sat on the end of a twelve-thousand-foot runway. The bus had to travel a hundred yards or so on a public highway, one lined with the curious and small knots of protesters with signs. Apparently even the Europeans couldn't do anything these days without someone complaining, Charley thought.

She found herself beside the American passenger, a stout man in his fifties. "You the American woman?" he asked.

Hooker's color wasn't so good.

"That's right."

"Glad you're going. Nice to have somebody to speak American to."

"Right."

" 'Bout had it up to here with the frogs."

"They kept you busy, have they?"

"Like a hound dog with fleas. You can really fly this thing?"

"No. I'm a Victoria's Secret model that Artois hired when he found he couldn't afford the real Charlotte Pine."

Hooker gave her a sharp look and said nothing more.

After a glance out the window she concentrated on lowering her own anxiety level. *This is just another flight,* she told herself, just like all those flights in high-performance airplanes she made in the air force. More precisely, like those saucer rides with Rip Cantrell.

She was thinking of Rip when the spaceplane came into view. *Jeanne d'Arc.* She had explored every inch of the craft during training and spent several weeks in the simulator, yet the sight of the ship sitting on the concrete under the flood-lights, ready to fly, caused a sharp intake of breath.

She was really going to do it.

She was going to the moon!

Yee-haa!

I hope Rip is watching on television!

HE *WAS* WATCHING ON TELEVISION, OF COURSE. DUE TO the time difference, it was early evening in America when the live coverage began. A dozen scientists crowded around the television in the living room of the Missouri farmhouse with Egg and Rip.

"It'll be okay," Egg muttered to Rip, who didn't respond. He was intent on the television, listening to the commenta-tor, ignoring everyone around him.

The countdown went smoothly. There were two minor holds, for only a few seconds each, and the commentator didn't give the reasons for either.

The spaceplane looked weird with the two huge external fuel tanks attached to its side. This particular ship, *Jeanne d'Arc,* was a proven platform, with three round trips to the moon already in her logbook. Rip thought about that now, reassuring himself that everything would go well, that Charley would come back safe and sound.

Still, better than anyone else in the room, he understood the dangers involved in space flight. Not to mention going back and forth to the moon. The French lunar project was mankind's biggest leap yet off the planet, akin to tackling the Atlantic in a rowboat.

His heart was pounding and he was covered with a sheen of perspiration when the first glimmer of fire appeared in the nozzles of the spaceplane's rocket engines. The flame grew steadily until it was as bright as the sun, overpowering the television camera's ability to adjust for light.

The roar came through the television's speakers, a mere shadow of the real thing. Still, it filled the living room and drowned out the last of the conversations.

The spaceplane began moving. Faster and faster, accelerating. The nose wheel stayed firmly on the runway as the ship accelerated past a hundred knots, then two hundred. A small number at the bottom of the screen reported its increasing velocity.

At 264 knots the nose rose a few feet off the pavement. At 275, the ship lifted off. Seconds later the landing gear began retracting.

The nose kept rising, up, up, up. The ship was exceeding four hundred knots when the nose reached fifty degrees above the horizon and the autopilot stopped the rotation.

Soon the fireball from the engines was all that could be seen on the screen.

It gradually became smaller and smaller as the sound faded . . . until it was merely a bright point of light in the heavens.

The camera followed the light until it was out of sight, then returned to the tarmac. The cameraman focused on the spot where the spaceplane had begun its roll, a spot now empty.

"She's on her way," Egg said.

Rip Cantrell took a deep breath and exhaled very carefully. He surreptitiously wiped at the tears that were leaking down his cheeks. "Yeah," he whispered. "She's on her way."

INSIDE *JEANNE D'ARC* CHARLEY PINE MONITORED THE instruments as the ship roared away from the earth. To her left Jean-Paul Lalouette was similarly engaged. Her duties were to bring any anomaly she noticed to his attention. Her eyes swept the panel again, looking for warning lights, errant pressures, a gauge indication that hinted something, anything was not as it should be. Yet all was precisely as it should be, perfect, as if this were a simulator ride and the operator had yet to push a failure button.

Both pilots wore their space suits, complete with helmets, in the event the plane lost pressurization during launch. They planned to take them off after all the systems checks were completed in orbit.

The acceleration Gs felt good, pushing Charley straight back into her seat. The voices of the French controllers passing information about the trajectory and data-link information sounded clear and pleasant in her ears; the background was the low rumble of the rocket engines.

When the external tanks were empty, they were jettisoned explosively. The engines then began burning fuel from the internal tanks as the spaceplane continued to climb and accelerate.

Charley's eyes flicked to the windscreen, four inches of bulletproof glass. At this nose-up angle the night sky filled the windscreen, full of stars and a sliver of moon. As they climbed through the atmosphere the stars became brighter and ceased their twinkling, and the crescent-moon gleamed more starkly against the background of obsidian black.

She had little time to enjoy the scenery. The next task was rendezvousing with the orbiting fuel tank. She became engrossed in the problem, watching the display that depicted the spaceplane and the orbiting tank and the three-dimensional course to intercept.

When she realized that the join-up was working perfectly and Lalouette had everything under complete control, she glanced again at the moon. For some reason it seemed larger than it did standing on the surface of earth. Now it appeared as what it was, another world.

2

THE OBSIDIAN SKY FULL OF STARS, THE WEIGHTLESS FEEL-
ing, the earth hanging beside the spaceplane with storms
over the oceans and snowy mountain peaks twinkling in the
sun—Charley Pine had been here before and been forever
changed by the experience. Now she was back. She was sooo
excited . . . and just as her personal karma account began
overflowing she remembered Rip and felt the tiniest twinge
of guilt.

Yeah, so, he wasn't here! He was only twenty-three, for
Christ's sake. He didn't earn a seat in a spaceplane's cockpit;
she did! All those years in college, flying, test pilot school—
yet she wouldn't be here if it weren't for Rip.

Well, she would tell him about it when she returned to
earth. That was the best that she could do. She brushed Rip
away and returned to the business at hand, controllers and
trajectories and systems.

Charley Pine took physical control of *Jeanne d'Arc* for the
first time over the Pacific Ocean to effect the rendezvous
with the orbiting fuel cell. With the sound of her breathing
rasping in her ears and her heart thudding in her chest, she

made tiny control inputs as the spaceplane crossed the distance between the two orbiting bodies. She knew from her military flying experience and the simulator that it was necessary to check the closure rate on the instruments—not to rely on her eyes—since the rate would appear to increase as the bodies closed the distance.

With Lalouette monitoring the instruments and calling out the distance and closure rate, she flew the spaceplane into the rendezvous position and stopped all closure. Only after all relative motion had stopped did she nudge the controls enough to gently bring the spaceplane into the fueling port. The clunk of the hydraulic latches closing, locking the ship firmly to the tank, was the best sound she had heard in years. She breathed a huge sigh of relief.

"Nicely done," said a male voice, not Lalouette.

She looked around. Pierre Artois was watching. He was suspended in the cabin, floating, maintaining his position by occasionally touching something fixed to the ship. Even though this was his first journey into space, he looked quite comfortable.

"Thank you."

"If I may ask, mademoiselle, why did you accept my offer to join our expedition?"

Charley glanced at Lalouette, a working pilot who had beaten out hundreds of other applicants for one of the four first-pilot positions, and saw him glance curiously at her.

"I was looking for a flying job," Charley replied, "and you made an offer." She shrugged. Gallically, she hoped.

Artois wasn't satisfied. "I have heard that you are a part owner of the patents on the flying saucer propulsion technology that was recently licensed by Monsieur Cantrell. If true, you must be a very wealthy woman."

Lalouette's eyes widened when he heard that remark. To the best of Charley's knowledge, her ownership of a portion of the proceeds from the saucer propulsion licensing deals had not been publicly reported. Apparently Artois had done his homework before he hired her.

"That comment is going to do wonderful things for my social life," Charley shot back. "Listen, Mr. Artois. I'm a professional aviator. Flying is what I do. I'll fly anything you people own, including spaceships, as long as the paychecks cash. Bounce one and I'm outta here."

"Sounds fair enough," Artois said dryly, and shoved off.

Charley Pine shrugged at Lalouette, one of those what-can-you-do? shrugs that are popular in New York, and together the two of them began the process of readying *Jeanne d'Arc* to receive fuel as the coast of California slid under them.

IT WAS AFTER MIDNIGHT IN MISSOURI WHEN EGG CANTRELL went looking for Rip. The assorted scientists were fast asleep in every bed in the house, on the couches and on cots in a large tent a rental firm had erected on the lawn.

In the hangar, Egg called Rip's name, got a muffled answer and followed the sound. He found two feet sticking out from under his old pickup, the 1957 Dodge.

"What are you doing under there?"

"I'm about finished. Two more minutes."

Egg's hangar was built during World War II for the Army Air Corps; it and the nearby air traffic control tower where Rip was sleeping these days were the only structures still remaining from the military past. Egg had jackhammered the concrete runways years ago and reseeded them in grass. Today the hangar contained an Aeronca Champ airplane, several old farm tractors, an Indian Chief motorcycle, a Model A Ford and an assortment of antique furniture and farm machinery he had acquired at estate sales, plus numerous items he just found interesting, such as an old printing press and Linotype he purchased when the county newspaper went digital.

This old Dodge wasn't his everyday pickup, of course. He had paid two hundred dollars for it way back when, and amazingly, it still ran.

Rip crawled out from under the engine compartment, wiped his hands on a rag and said, "Okay. I'm ready to try it."

"Try what?"

There was a piece of plywood in the bed of the truck. Rip picked up a corner and let Egg see the automobile batteries underneath arranged in rows. He put the plywood back in place, flashed a grin at his uncle and got into the pickup. The engine started right up.

"The problem is power," he explained to his uncle as he revved the engine. His eyes gleamed. Egg hadn't seen him this excited since Charley left, forty-four days ago. Egg had been counting. "The engine in the pickup doesn't make enough of it," Rip continued. "I use the generator to charge the batteries, then use the batteries to power the system."

"What system?"

"Stand back a little and I'll show you."

Egg took several hesitant steps backward, and as he did the pickup lifted off the dirt floor of the hangar and rose several feet in the air, where it stopped. The nose was at least a foot higher than the rear corner of the truck, which was barely clear of the ground.

"Antigravity," Rip said, laughing. "I built a small system like the one in the saucer. What do you think?"

"Seems as if you have a bit more work to do."

"I haven't got the lift lines in the right places. Turns out it's a bit more difficult than I figured, but that's the way it goes. Life is tougher than it looks, isn't it? I'll iron out the glitches." He turned off the engine of the pickup, which had no effect on the vehicle's position in the air. "Stand back and watch me move this thing around."

Egg took several more steps backward, bumped into a tractor, and decided to take cover behind it. As he did so the truck silently moved aft toward the center of the hangar, still suspended at an odd angle above the dirt floor.

Rip tried to make the truck turn—and succeeded in slewing the nose around dangerously, almost hitting Egg's Aeronca. He got it stopped just in time. Dust from the hangar floor swirled around.

"Sorry, Unc. I'll take this thingamabob outside." With that, the truck crept forward out of the hangar. It slowly accelerated until it was moving at about the speed a man could trot. It crossed the runway, heading for the trees on the other side.

Egg could hear Rip cussing. He was saying some rather nasty words in a loud, clear voice when the truck smacked into a large tree on the far side of the runway.

There it sat intimately embracing the tree, the nose several feet in the air, the rear still sagging dangerously. Rip climbed out of the cab and jumped to the ground. He was standing with his hands on his hips staring at the damaged grill and bumper when Egg reached him.

"Another technical problem rears its ugly head," Egg murmured.

Rip shook his head in frustration.

Then the batteries powering the antigravity device began losing their charge. The truck eased toward the ground inch by inch until it was once again sitting on all four wheels.

"Darn," Rip said mournfully.

Egg couldn't help himself. He exploded in laughter.

When he finally calmed down, he asked, "Why, pray tell, are you putting antigravity rings on that old truck?"

"Actually I'm trying to figure out how to put them on the

Extra. Then I'd have a fast, maneuverable airplane that could land anywhere. We could make airports obsolete. Thought I'd start with the pickup to see what the problems were."

"Hmm."

"Yeah, I know. If I'd done this two months ago maybe Charley would still be here." He raised his hands and dropped them. "What can I say?"

The sliver of new moon had set hours ago. Egg and Rip were lying side by side in the grass looking at the stars through gaps in the clouds when Rip said, "She's on her way."

"Wish you were with her?"

"Well, heck yeah. Big adventure. 'Course, she's an older woman and all. You just knew a romance like that wouldn't work out. She's a good pilot, though."

"So what are you going to do with your life, Rip?"

"Get on with it. Nothing else I can do, is there?"

JEANNE D'ARC LEFT EARTH ORBIT WITH A LONG BURN designed to accelerate her to escape velocity. With the Global Positioning System (GPS), automatic star trackers and the small onboard computers that didn't exist in the mid-1960s when the Apollo craft were designed, the French ship was much more self-contained than the American moon ships had been. Due to the vast strides in computer technology, each computer on *Jeanne d'Arc* contained more computing capacity than all the NASA computers together had when Apollo 11 successfully voyaged to the moon.

The crew had taken off their space suits, positioned the ship in the proper orientation, checked the computer programs, locked in the autopilot and waited.

The burn, when it came, was a rush of acceleration and emotion. The trajectory they hoped to achieve was a parabola that would take *Jeanne d'Arc* to within sixty miles of the lunar surface. If the spaceplane didn't decelerate as it circled the moon, it would slingshot around it and return to earth. Tears leaked from the corners of Charley's eyes and were pulled back into her hair by the acceleration, which was designed to raise their velocity to a trifle over thirty-five thousand feet per second.

An hour later, with the engines secured, all the checklists finished and the planet slowly falling behind, Charley and Lalouette unstrapped and floated out of their ergonomically correct couches.

Lalouette gave Charley a big grin and said, "You did very well. I have never before flown with a beautiful woman." Apparently the fifty hours he had spent with Charley in the simulator this past month didn't count.

"I'm so happy for you," Charley Pine said sweetly.

"We'll get to know each other much better in the coming weeks," he said confidently.

"Down, boy. Remember the cameras." Small cameras in the cockpit were sending continuous streams of audio and video back to Mission Control in Paris. Unfortunately there were no cameras in the sleeping compartments.

Well, she had known the French were romantically challenged when she signed up for this gig. She hadn't given that aspect of the adventure much thought, though, because she had been so busy. She didn't even know if Lalouette was married. Hadn't asked, hadn't looked at his ring finger, wasn't the least bit interested. The worst of it was that the more difficult she was to conquer, the more the Frenchman would enjoy the chase.

With that gloomy thought in mind Charley Pine floated down the passage toward the head.

"JEAN-PAUL LALOUETTE SAID YOU ARE RICH. IS IT TRUE?"

The person asking was Claudine Courbet, an engineer on

her way to the lunar base for a six-month stay. She and
Charley Pine shared a tiny cabin. Neither had any say in the
pairing since they were the only women on the flight.

Since Claudine asked the question in French, Charley had
to translate the question in her head, then think of an
appropriate response. *"Oui,"* she said, not knowing enough
of the language to deflect the question.

"Some people think that explains it."

"What? Explains what?"

"Why you are here. Did you or your family agree to pay
money so you could be on the crew?"

"No."

"Someone said you probably did after they heard Jean-
Paul's story. Pierre has invested his fortune in this project.
Some say he is down to his last euro. That's why he sold a
round-trip to the American. Still, he'll never get the money
back."

"Easy come, easy go," Charley Pine said.

"On the other hand, some people said you are Artois' next
girlfriend," Claudine confided, then hurried to add, "but I
do not think that. He has a girlfriend, an extremely rich
one—her grandfather is one of those Italian car people. She
is very pretty even though her breasts are not real."

"The curse of the store-bought tits," Charley murmured in
English. "I thought he was married?"

"Oh, yes. Julie Artois. But men like Pierre also have
women friends. It is expected."

"I see," said Charley Pine, who didn't. The thought of
being some married man's mistress left her cold. She began
the process of zipping herself into her hammock so that she
could sleep. This was the first time she had tried it in the
weightless environment, and she was finding it a serious
chore. When she was in training, the French had told her all

tasks in weightless environments took more time and effort. "How do you say 'damn' in French?" she asked Claudine.

Her roommate ignored that comment. "Pierre was under extreme pressure to include a European in the flying crews or lunar team," she continued earnestly. "For political reasons, you understand. The European Union and all that. He refused to be pressured, but he had to do something since the government is investing so much in the lunar project. He would have been wise to hire a European scientist long ago and be done with it, but he did not wish to chance a breach in security. I think he recruited you to silence his critics in the government."

"Those pesky critics," Charley replied. She managed to tug the zipper home and sighed in relief. She had hated sleeping bags since her camping days as a preteen. Just when you finally get zipped in, you have to go to the bathroom. Thank God she remembered to go before she started this evolution.

Before Claudine could get started on another juicy tidbit, Charley asked, "How do you like your first spaceflight?"

That got Claudine revved up. Her husband refused to allow her to go, but she signed up anyway. This was the adventure of a lifetime; the view of the earth from space was fantastic; she had dreamed of standing on the moon looking at earth all her life, ever since she saw those photos of the Apollo crews as a child; she would just get another husband when she returned to earth. She was still chattering away when Charley drifted off to sleep.

CHARLEY PINE AWOKE WHEN CLAUDINE COURBET CLOSED the compartment door behind her as she left. Charley lay floating weightless in her hammock for a few minutes trying to get back to sleep. It was a lost cause.

She examined the compartment thoughtfully. It was not

large; every cubic inch was utilized in some manner. Color-coded pipes and conduits ran through the room against the wall that was the ceiling when the spaceplane was on earth. Emergency oxygen masks were rigged on one wall beside a fire alarm and portable extinguisher. Near the portable extinguisher was a nozzle on a flexible hose that hooked into the ship's main firefighting system.

Arranged so that she could see it while lying in her hammock was a computer screen. She reached out and turned it on. In seconds she was looking at the main systems displays. A touch of her finger brought up navigation information. Another touch gave her a camera's view of earth, a huge blue presence surrounded by the blackness of deep space. She lay for a few moments watching the night line move over the surface as the massive orb rotated.

As she watched she realized that the planet was moving ever so slowly away from the camera. This was an illusion, of course. Actually the spaceplace was flying away from the planet in free fall on a course that would put it in orbit around the moon in about seventy hours.

Her parents had divorced when she was seven. She grew up with her mother, who taught school in a Washington suburb. During the summers she visited her father, a building contractor in Atlanta. She had an unremarkable childhood, doing all the usual things that bright girls growing up in the American suburbs do. She played soccer, field hockey, basketball and baseball, giggled with her friends, went on dates, made straight As in junior high and high school—and managed to avoid the marijuana and hard drugs that many of her friends dabbled in, and some were consumed by. Was in a bad car wreck and walked away with only a broken arm. Decided she wanted to fly and worked hard to get an appointment to the U.S. Air Force Academy.

The flying had been challenging, so she applied for the test pilot program and was accepted. Moved in with a few guys along the way and always moved out after a while.

Just when she gave up on the air force, Rip and his flying saucer came into her life.

Rip Cantrell. As she watched the earth on the monitor she thought about him, about his face and smile and touch.

She had it bad. Damn!

The heck of it was that the kid hadn't really grown up yet. He was willing to lie around doing nothing—well, doing nothing but having sex five times a day and eating three meals—while the days slid past one by one, turning into weeks, then months.

She couldn't live like that.

Oh, well. She would have to make a decision about Rip after she returned from the moon. She had agreed with Artois to work for the French lunar project for at least one year, making at least three lunar flights. When she returned from the moon in three weeks, she would have a week off. She decided to call Rip and invite him to France.

That decision made, she was still too keyed up to sleep.

She unzipped the hammock, got out of it and stowed the thing, then checked her reflection in a mirror. She had two hours before she had to be back in the cockpit. She decided to explore, maybe visit with some of the other people on board and share the adventure.

Charley Pine opened the door of the compartment and launched herself slowly through it, careful not to carom off the bulkhead. She closed the door behind her.

CHARLEY PINE FOUND PIERRE ARTOIS AND JEAN-PAUL Lalouette filming a cell phone commercial on the flight deck. Artois had a small phone in hand and was placing a call to someone while the cameras rolled. Perhaps, Charley thought, Claudine was right about Pierre's financial situation.

Charley watched a few moments, then drifted back along the passageway. The chef was preparing a meal. No freeze-dried grub on this French space freighter—the crew ate French cuisine and drank small portions of wine with every meal. Preparing real food and serving it in a weightless environment was a serious challenge, but the French were up to it.

The chef offered Charley a sample of several of his creations. She used an eating utensil that totally enclosed the morsel while it was under way from a covered dish to the mouth. The food was delicious and the covered spoon ingenious, and Charley said as much to the chef, who beamed.

The cargo bay was the heart of the ship, its raison d'être. One of its doors was ajar—it was usually locked—so Charlie opened it. Containers and large assemblies took up most of the sizable compartment. Every container or assembly had to be carefully suspended and braced so that it would not move when the rocket engines were running nor drift in weightlessness. There was little room in the cargo bay for people; the passageways through the cargo reminded Charlie of the passageways in submarines—except you floated effortlessly along this one, propelling yourself with an occasional gentle push, now and then touching something to prevent impacting the sides.

She saw people near the rear of the compartment, where the heaviest items were placed. One of them was Claudine Courbet. With a flick of her wrist Charley started that way. As she neared the container Claudine and a man were working on, she saw that they had taken one of the container's panels off to expose the contents. Both had their heads inside as Charley approached.

There wasn't much room, so Charley waited until someone noticed her. Claudine and the man were conversing, in muffled French that Charley couldn't understand.

Claudine finally backed out into the passage and saw the pilot. A look of surprise crossed her face. "What are you doing here?"

"Visiting. And you?"

The man also backed out and turned his back to the container, almost as if he didn't want Charley to see inside.

"I thought you were asleep," Claudine said.

"I was. Obviously now I am awake."

Claudine nodded her head at her coworker, then started toward Charley. "Come, let's go to the salon where we can talk. Dinner will be ready soon."

"Fine," said Charley Pine, and did a somersault to get her head pointed in the right direction. A pull with both hands sent her shooting along the passageway. Claudine followed her.

FROM HER SEAT IN THE COCKPIT OF *JEANNE D'ARC,* CHARLEY Pine faced a sky full of stars. The moon was off to the right about fifty degrees. The spaceplane wasn't heading for it, but for a point in space where the moon would be when the spaceplane arrived.

She was alone in the cockpit, which was a very pleasant feeling. By regulation, one of the pilots had to be in the cockpit at all times. She and Lalouette took turns, four hours on, four hours off.

She felt as if she had lived her entire life to get to this moment, flying through space with the earth at her back and the universe ahead. It was heady stuff. *Cool,* she thought. *Super cool.* A smile lingered on her lips.

Once again her eye swept over the computer readouts presented on the cockpit multifunction displays (MFDs).

Yes, the star locators were locked on their guide stars, the radar was indicating the precise distance to the moon, and the computers had solved the navigation problem and were continuously updating it. They presented the solution in the form of a crosshairs on the heads-up display (HUD), plotting velocity through space against time to go to the initial point, which was the point at which *Jeanne d'Arc* would begin its maneuvers to enter lunar orbit. Best of all, all three flight computers were in complete and total agreement.

Absolute agreement among three individuals was only possible if those three were machines, she thought. "Not any three people alive," she muttered.

She checked ship's systems, flicking through presentations on another MFD. Hull integrity, air pressure, atmospheric gas levels, fuel remaining on board, water pressure in the lines, temps in the galley, internal and external hull temps—yes, all were as they should be, well within normal parameters. It made her feel a bit superfluous sitting here monitoring all of this, and yet the spaceplane's systems were not monitored continuously from Earth. To save money and weight, the French made their ships more self-sufficient than the old American space shuttles or Apollo spacecraft. Mission Control was always there, a valuable asset in case things went wrong, only a push of a button away on the radio, but truly, the pilots were in charge.

Charley was wearing a headset so that she could hear any transmissions from Mission Control. There had been none since she checked in twenty minutes ago. She had to check in every hour on the hour.

She pulled the earpiece from her left ear and placed it against her head so that she could listen to the sounds of the ship.

One would think that every click and clang inside the ship would carry throughout the structure, and it did, but not as audible noise. The ship was too well insulated for that. If one put a hand on the outside hull, the random tapping and rapping could be felt. One could almost imagine the ship was alive. She rested her right hand on the frame of the side window to enjoy the tiny tremors.

She was gradually coming down from the adrenaline high that had kept her wired for the last twenty-four hours. Maybe after this watch she could sleep.

She yawned. Actually, she was getting sleepy now.

Okay, Charlotte, old girl, stay awake!

The good news was that if she drifted off, any ship's system that failed or exceeded normal operational parameters would illuminate a yellow caution light and sound an audible warning. It sounded like a siren and would wake the nearly dead. A different tone would sound if one of the flight computers disagreed with the other two.

If she slept, the ship would continue on course, precisely as if she were awake, and Mission Control would give her a blast if she missed her hourly call-in. And yet, she was a professional. "I am *not* going to sleep in the cockpit," she declared out loud.

"I certainly hope not," said a male voice behind her, startling her. She had heard nothing as he came in.

She glanced over her shoulder. Pierre Artois.

"*Bonjour,*" she said, successfully hiding her irritation at being surprised.

"*Bonjour, mademoiselle.* How do we progress?"

In answer, she punched up the navigation display on the MFD and pointed to the readouts. "Zipping right along, as you can see."

"So how does *Jeanne d'Arc* compare to your flying saucer?" Artois asked as he maneuvered himself into the pilot's seat and donned a seat belt to hold him there.

Charley considered her answer before she spoke. "This

ship is nicer, more people friendly. The saucer was more of a pickup truck, designed to haul people and cargo back and forth from orbit to a planet. The saucer had no cooking, sleeping or toilet facilities. Very Spartan."

"Ah, the creature comforts. These days one expects them."

They discussed the differences for a few minutes, then the conversation petered out.

Finally Artois said, "And Madame Courbet, your stateroom companion, are you getting along with her?"

"She's very nice."

"Yes," he agreed. "Nice. Indeed."

Artois sat for a few more minutes, then unstrapped and pushed himself out of the pilot's seat with a gentle nudge. As he floated aft for the hatch he said, "I hope you have a good voyage."

"You too," said Charley Pine. She glanced back to make sure he actually left the compartment.

What was that all about? she wondered.

A few minutes later Joe Bob Hooker caromed into the cockpit. "Just like a goddamn cue ball," he said to Charley. He held himself suspended behind the seats and stared through the windscreen.

"Oh, my God! Would you look at that?" He shifted so he could look out the pilot's side window. "If that don't beat all! Who'd a believed it, I ask you that. Who'd a thought it?"

"So is this worth twenty-five mil?"

"Can't take it with you, kid. No, sir." Hooker crept forward so that he could look back over the tiny left wing at earth. Finally, when he had had enough, he slid backward and stabilized in a position where he could look at her. "It was more than that, actually, with the exchange rate and all. And the Frenchies made me pay a half million for my flight suit. They don't know it, but I'm taking it with me when I get home."

"Hell, yes."

"I'm from Texas," he continued. "Little crossroads in west Texas nobody ever heard of. Grew up without a pot to piss in. Went to Dallas right after high school and looked for something to get into. Figured cars were the deal. Everybody's always going to need a ride. Everything else comes and goes, but everybody will always need wheels. Started with a used car lot and learned the business. Bought another. Finally got into new cars. Sold my soul to the banks, but finally made it pay. Own a string of dealerships now. Can sell you any brand on the planet that's legal to sell in the U. S. of A."

"Already have a car," Charley said.

"They wear out. That's the good thing about 'em."

"So you're married?" Charley asked, for something to say.

"Third marriage," Joe Bob said with a sigh. "Cute little thing from Highland Park. Tan and toned up tight. 'Bout your age, I figure, a year older than my oldest daughter. I was the biggest bankroll available when she ditched her first husband. Loves to spend money and do the Junior League thing. She thought I was crazy to sign up for this flight, but what the hell, she's fixed for life if I don't come back, so she said yes. Get her a young stud-bucket the afternoon they tell her the good news."

"I see."

"Well, you should. You got the best seat in the house."

With that he squirmed around and launched himself aft.

WHEN SHE FINISHED HER WATCH, CHARLEY PINE CRASHED in her sleeping bag. She awoke refreshed and alert.

After another four-hour watch, during which Pierre Artois and two of the engineer passengers did a show for French television from the rear of the cockpit, she decided she could do with a bath. This task turned out to be a challenge in the weightless environment. One stripped and entered a tiny bathing chamber. A push of a button sprayed a minute quantity of water, about a pint, upon the bather from four dozen jets. When the dousing stopped, the bather scrubbed him or herself with a soapy rag. A touch of a button gave another few seconds of rinse water, which was then suctioned out of the chamber to be boiled and recycled.

Charley managed to wet her hair, which would have to do. No wonder most of the men wore their hair very short.

Water was precious. *Jeanne d'Arc* was carrying several hundred gallons to the lunar base for use there. It would have to be continuously purified and reused. Still, inevitably, some was lost. Charley knew that the French were drilling into the lunar surface searching for ice formed when meteors struck, or even older ice that crystallized after the moon was torn from proto-earth by a meteor billions of years ago. If they found a significant amount of ice, the lunar base had a bright future. If they didn't, it would never be more than a research outpost, one that would only be manned from time to time when political and financial realities allowed.

Artois believed the ice was there. Indeed, he had publicly guaranteed it to the French people. If it couldn't be found he was going to be embarrassed and French taxpayers were going to get the shaft—which is what taxpayers had been getting since the dawn of time, so they sort of expected it.

After she wriggled into her clean flight suit, Charley went exploring again, working her way aft and glancing into every compartment. Most of the other crew members were asleep, including Claudine Courbet. The adrenaline high that had carried everyone through launch and the first twenty-four hours in space had finally worn off.

Charley carefully inspected the ship's batteries, looking for acid leaks. All the ship's power right now was coming from batteries and solar panels. Electrical power was one of the absolute requirements for space travel; without it the rocket engines couldn't be restarted, and the ship would fly forever on a voyage into eternity.

Even the chef was asleep. Charley sampled some bread, cheese and wine, hummed a few bars of something romantic, then moved on.

Floating along the passageways was very cool, she thought. This small vessel of steel and aluminum reminded her of a seed pod. Filled with air and water, it carried its tiny blobs of protoplasm from one small island in space to another.

The coolest way to shoot the passageways was with the minimum motion of hands and feet, she decided, sort of like a seal slipping through an ice tunnel under the Arctic. Just push off with a flip of the wrist to start moving, then sweeten the trajectory when necessary with a touch of the bulkhead or deck or ceiling.

There was no one in the cargo bay. Charley flippered along the narrow passageways, checking tie-downs. When she found herself in front of the large container that Claudine and the male technician had been looking into, she paused. The container wore a key-actuated padlock.

She pursed her lips, then began examining the other containers more closely. None was locked. In fact, five minutes of inspecting revealed that there was only one padlock in the bay. Perhaps on the ship.

She went back to look again.

Now she was curious. Why would anyone lock a cargo container? It made no sense. Everything in the compartment was on the manifest.

Or was it?

She idly reached for the lock and gave an experimental tug. It opened in her hand. She stared at it dumbly for several seconds before she realized that it hadn't been locked. Whoever put it on hadn't squeezed it hard enough, so the lock failed to catch.

She took it off and began opening the six latches. Bracing herself, she lifted the container door.

And found herself staring at a symbol spray-painted in red onto a steel container.

She looked for five or six seconds, then shut the hatch, closed all the latches and installed the padlock.

Should she lock it, or leave it as she found it?

She decided that leaving it as she found it was the better choice. She glided on out of the compartment and shut the hatch behind her.

Charley had seen the cargo manifest, actually looked through it, a week or so ago. She didn't recall anything on the manifest that was radioactive. Nor should there be. Power at the lunar base was supplied by generators, batteries and solar panels. In fact, several solar arrays were in the cargo bay.

Isotopes? For running down drill holes in the search for water?

In the small compartment they shared, Claudine Courbet was zipped into her hammock fast asleep. She had tied the arms of her flight suit around one of the hammock hooks, so the legs and body were floating in midair, swaying to and fro as the moving air stirred them.

Charley Pine eyed the sleeping woman, then felt the flight suit. Something hard in one pocket. She reached in and pulled the object from the pocket to inspect it. Yep, a radioactivity safety badge. A few seconds later she found the key to the padlock. She checked the leg pockets. Eureka! A digital Geiger counter, about the size of a fountain pen.

She returned the objects to the flight suit pockets and headed for the cockpit. When she reached the door she saw Pierre Artois in the copilot seat. He and Lalouette were engaged in earnest conversation. They ceased the instant they glimpsed Charley.

Very curious, she thought.

3

Two hours into her watch on the flight deck of *Jeanne d'Arc*, Charley Pine learned the subject of Artois' and Lalouette's conversation. The French pilot was sick. She listened in on the three-way radio conversations between Artois, the physician at the lunar base and Mission Control. Although she didn't understand the French medical terminology, she understood the diagnosis well enough. Lalouette was suffering a gall bladder attack.

Artois sat beside her in the pilot's seat on the flight deck wearing Lalouette's headset during this discussion. Aborting the mission and returning to earth was one possibility weighed by the decision makers. The other was to proceed to the moon. The physician at the lunar base was equipped to operate, and could as soon as Lalouette arrived.

This development meant that Charley Pine was now in full control of the ship. She would have to pilot it into lunar orbit and thence to the surface without Lalouette's help. Artois asked her bluntly, "Can you do it?"

"Of course," she said firmly.

"Safety is paramount. If you prefer, we can skip the lunar

landing, slingshot around the moon and return directly to earth." Both she and Artois knew that reversing the ship's course without the use of the moon's gravity would take more fuel than they had. "As the pilot, you are responsible for the lives of everyone aboard," Artois continued. "The decision to land or return immediately is yours to make."

She had flown the entire mission in the simulator numerous times; the computers and autopilot were working perfectly. Charley, Lalouette and the controllers monitoring telemetry data had only identified seven gripes on the spaceplane, none of them major. If the spaceplane were experiencing serious mechanical problems, she would not be as confident as she was, but she was in no mood to share that thought with Artois.

"I can hack the program," she told him now. "I can fly this bucket anywhere we have the fuel to go. You know the state of the medical facilities at the lunar base, not I. If you feel Lalouette will get adequate care there, then we can go on."

Wearing a trace of a smile, Artois asked, "Did you know that the simulator instructors referred to you as Captain America?"

Her look of surprise widened his smile. Apparently satisfied, he keyed his headset microphone to tell Mission Control and the lunar base physician of his decision. "We continue," he said. "Our destination remains the moon." With that pronouncement, he gave Charley a nod and flashed another smile, then left the headset on the top of the instrument panel and went aft to check again on Lalouette.

Charley Pine took a deep breath and exhaled slowly. Whew! Double whew! She was going to have to be on top of her game—she had certainly been *there* before—and she was going to walk on the lunar surface. She would be the first American to do so since the Apollo astronauts left their footprints in the lunar dirt thirty-two years before. No doubt the footprints were still there. "Hot diggity dog," she muttered, and smiled broadly.

All alone in the cockpit, she took off and stowed her copilot's headset. Although it would function perfectly if plugged into the pilot's radio jacks, she wanted Lalouette's. She transferred to the pilot's seat and retrieved the headset from its glare shield bracket. She settled it on her head.

It fit perfectly.

She punched up a navigation computer display. The ship was within a minute of crossing the invisible boundary that separated the pull of earth's gravity from the pull of the moon's. Alone, covered with goose bumps, she watched the seconds tick down. Then they were across. As it crossed this invisible boundary, the ship had coasted to its slowest speed of the journey; now under the pull of lunar gravity, it would accelerate. Just for grins, she began monitoring the speed on the navigation readout. Within a minute it began to respond, picking up a few dozen feet per second with every passing minute. Only fourteen hours to go to lunar orbit insertion.

The voice of the mission controller crackled in her ears. "If you are going to go it alone, we need to begin now on the systems function tests and checklist items." His name was Bodard. Charley had spent many hours with him during training. He had a paunch and always smelled of garlic and tobacco.

Charley's mood instantly shifted to all business. "Let us begin," she said.

"ARE YOU READY?" EGG CALLED. HE WAS STANDING IN front of the hangar aiming a video camera mounted on a tripod.

"I guess," Rip Cantrell answered, loudly enough to be heard over the sound of the idling truck engine. He was seated in Egg's old Dodge in the center of the grass runway. He had removed the batteries from the truck bed and installed two large generators in the engine compartment of the pickup, with sheaves and belts to power them from the fan-belt takeoff.

"Any time," Egg shouted, and bent to his viewfinder.

Rip wiped the perspiration from his forehead, so it wouldn't get into his eyes, and tightened the belts in his three-point harness. His stomach was tied into a knot. He goosed the engine a couple of times with the accelerator, watching the amp meter rise and fall. Oil pressure okay, radiator temp okay. He did it one more time, allowing the engine RPM to rise. The truck rose a few inches, then settled back onto the tires as he let the RPM drop.

He had a small control box he had salvaged from a model airplane radio-control unit mounted on a piece of metal, a joy stick, protruding from the dash to the right of the steering wheel. He moved the stick back and forth, left and right.

"Here goes nothing," he muttered, and jammed the accelerator to the floor.

The truck rose into the air as the electrical power from the generators energized the antigravity rings under the pickup. The truck began to tilt backward. Rip moved the small control stick forward, lowering the truck's nose and stopping rearward movement.

The truck rose until it was about a dozen feet in the air. The natural gravitational field of the earth and the man-made one he had induced in the truck were repelling each other. As the engine under the hood roared at full power, Rip kept the pickup level and stationary by using the stick.

Ha! Satisfied he had control, he moved the stick ever so slightly to the right. The truck tilted and began drifting in that direction.

Now he leveled the truck, then tilted the nose down a trifle for forward movement. The truck obediently began moving. Slowly at first, then faster and faster. He jockeyed the stick to control the rate.

After he had gone a hundred feet, when he was doing perhaps fifteen miles per hour, he laid the truck into a left turn. He had enough room. The nose of the truck obediently swung around, turning back toward the hangar.

He had just gotten it stabilized when a cloud of steam rose from under the hood. Water and steam sprayed on the windshield. The radiator temp gauge needle pegged right. Rip let up on the accelerator.

Not quickly enough. He heard a loud bang, then the engine noise stopped dead.

Still slightly nose down, the bottom fell out and the truck dropped toward the earth.

The shock of impact snapped his head forward and stunned him.

In the silence that followed the crash, he became aware of his uncle leaning in through the window. He had trouble focusing his eyes. Part of the reason was the dirt in the air— he seemed to be sitting in the middle of a dust cloud.

"You okay, Ripper?" his uncle shouted, only inches from his head.

"Yeah. Sure."

"Let's get you out of this thing. I smell gasoline. You may have fractured the fuel tank."

Soon Rip was sitting in the grass fifty feet from the wreck with his uncle seated beside him. As his head cleared, Rip stared at the smashed Dodge. Gray smoke and white steam wisped from the engine compartment. There was no fire.

"Blew the engine, I guess," he said to his uncle. "Seemed like the radiator blew. Before I could react the crankshaft froze."

"Locked up tighter than the hubs of hell," Egg said, nodding vigorously. "You were at least ten feet in the air."

"Sorry about your truck."

"I'll take it out of your allowance," Egg said, then laughed. When he laughed his belly quivered.

Rip joined in. He lay back in the grass and laughed and laughed.

"It's good to be alive, isn't it?" Egg said when they finally calmed down.

"Yeah, Unc. It really is."

"So what are you going to do now?"

"Gonna put that system on the Extra. The airplane engine is designed to turn at high RPM all day. Won't blow it like I did the truck engine."

"Need any help?"

"Well, sure. But let me lie here another five minutes. And I want to see that video."

THE MOON WAS A GIANT ORB HANGING IN THE BLACK SKY when Charley turned the spaceplane and lined it up for the lunar orbit injection burn. When she had it perfectly aligned according to the computer display, she ran through the checklist again, studying the items, fingering switches, assuring herself for the tenth time that they were in the right position. It would have been comforting to have a second pair of knowledgeable eyes examine each switch, yet the eyes she was burdened with were Artois'. He sat beside her in the copilot's seat, watching everything, knowing nothing.

Both wore space suits complete with helmets, just in case Charley blew the landing and crashed on the moon, cracking the pressure hull. A sudden depressurization wouldn't kill them. Assuming they survived the crash.

Jeanne d'Arc was closing rapidly on the moon. Even though this was the dark side, it was a massive presence, only sixty-five miles from the spaceplane. For the first time since they had left earth orbit, the presence of the world off the left wing gave her the sensation of motion.

The pilot checked the navigation display again, ensuring that the low point of the trajectory would be at precisely sixty miles, exactly at the point of the burn, which would occur on the back side of the moon, the side opposite the earth. All was as it should be.

She cracked her knuckles in anticipation, a gesture that startled Artois.

Poor devil, she thought. He had signed up an American female pilot to fob off the demands of French politicians, and now Charley was all he had. She couldn't see his face inside his helmet, but she sensed his concern. She flashed him a grin that he couldn't see.

"Nothing to sweat," she said. "The program is working perfectly. There is nothing for us to do but sit and watch."

"So anyone could fly these planes?" he said acidly.

"As long as all the computers work perfectly," she replied carelessly. "If they don't, then you hand-fly it." Of course, Artois knew this already. He had been intimately involved in the design and engineering of the spaceplanes that made the lunar base possible. "That's why you spent the money for the very best sticks you could find, isn't it?"

Artois didn't answer that rhetorical question.

"Fifteen seconds to loss of telemetry," Bodard said from Mission Control. At ten seconds to go he began counting, and his voice faded at two. *Jeanne d'Arc* was no longer in communication with anyone on planet Earth. She would be out of communication for sixteen minutes, until she swung out from behind the moon.

Charley keyed the intercom and announced, "Everyone in their seats, strap in and report, *si'l vous plaît.* The lunar orbit injection burn will occur in seven minutes."

All six of the people not in the cockpit reported within the next five minutes. Claudine Courbet reported for Lalouette, who had been strapped in for hours and sedated. All were ready. They would remain in their seats until *Jeanne d'Arc* was on the surface of the moon.

The waiting was the hardest part, Charley Pine thought. She sat watching the display, her thoughts totally absorbed in the piloting problem.

Pierre Artois rubbernecked out the window at the moon. Since the spaceplane was hurling backward through space at the approaching burn point, the lunar surface slid by from rear to front. It was disconcerting, to say the least, to people used to viewing the earth from the window of an airplane.

The sun line appeared suddenly on the lunar surface, and reflected light filled the cockpit. Charley glanced at the lunar surface, adjusted the brightness of the displays and said nothing.

The seconds ticked down. The spaceplane dropped closer and closer to the lunar surface. Right on cue the rocket engines ignited, pressing Charley and Artois back into their seats. The Gs felt good after three days of weightlessness.

But the middle engine was not firing. Only the four smaller, outboard engines had ignited. Charley Pine instantly punched up a display that gave her a percentage of planned power. Only seventy percent. This meant that she would have to burn the engines thirty percent longer to get the required deceleration. She disconnected the autopilot, taking manual control of the ship and the burn. One of the engines was producing just slightly less power than the other three, which was to be expected. No four engines would produce exactly the same amount of power. Without conscious thought she adjusted the controls to hold the ship in the proper attitude.

The seconds ticked down, and she stopped the burn as the clock read 0:00. She didn't even notice the absence of G, so intent was she on checking the orbit. It would be a few moments before she knew precisely how well the burn had gone, how close to the desired lunar orbit they actually were.

The sensors were still locked on their guide stars. The distance to the moon from the radar seemed correct. She had only to wait for the computers to calculate the trajectory, which took time. The numbers were sorting themselves out, the display was moving, stabilizing . . . yes. They appeared to be within half a percent of the desired orbit, which was presented as a maximum and minimum distance from the planet. Now the graphic display stabilized.

She checked to ensure the orbit would take them to the desired burn point to begin the descent to the lunar base.

"We're going to need another small burn," she muttered, pointing at the display. "There. At that point." She looked at her watch. "In eighteen minutes."

"How long?" Artois asked, which was his first comment since before the orbit insertion burn.

"Two seconds."

"That is very good. Congratulations."

Charley didn't have time. She keyed the intercom. "Florentin," she said, calling the flight engineer by name, "the main engine refused to start. Please check it out."

Artois tried to remain as calm as she was. "What if it won't start for the descent burn?"

"We'll just burn for a longer period."

"And the ascent from the moon's surface?"

Charley was stunned that he asked that question. "The moon only has a sixth of earth's gravity," she answered. "We need all our power to get off the earth's surface, not the moon's."

He should have known that, she thought dispassionately.

RIP CANTRELL WAS ASLEEP IN THE OLD CONTROL TOWER near Egg's hangar when he heard his uncle's heavy tread upon the stairs. "You awake up there, Rip?"

"Yeah, Unc." Rip rolled out and reached for his jeans.

The little room with windows on all sides was a nice private bedroom. It contained a narrow bed, one chair, a bookcase and a small desk. The restroom that Egg had installed years ago was on the ground level. When Egg topped the stairs he lowered himself heavily into the only chair and sighed. Rip was seated on the bed. The moon was five days old and still above the western horizon. Moonlight filled the small room when gaps occurred in the low clouds racing overhead.

"Been watching television," Egg reported as he regained his breath. "The French pilot is sick. Charley flew the space-plane into lunar orbit."

"Good for her." Rip meant it.

"They're also having trouble with the main engine. The news is on all the channels."

Rip found himself staring at the moon. "Shouldn't be a problem," he said. Since Charley left for France, he too had been reading everything he could find on the French space-planes. "Still, something's wrong."

"I THINK IT'S THE HEATERS," FLORENTIN SAID TO CHARLEY. They were in the crawl space forward of the engines, between the engines and the fuel tanks. "Looks to me as if the heater circuit got a short and the temp is too low in the engines for the igniters to fire."

"Terrific."

"If that is the problem, sitting on the surface of the moon

should thaw the engines. The surface temperature during the day is about 107 degrees Centigrade."

"How about the other engines?"

"The heaters seem to be working."

"Okay," Charley said, and flippered backward out of the tunnel.

She regretted ever agreeing to a hurry-up training schedule. Eighteen hours a day for forty-two days, and it didn't seem nearly enough. Sure, if Lalouette were not sedated, she would merely be backing him up. Now she was the pilot in command and she had no backup at all, no one to tell her to slow down or rethink a problem. The pressure to get it right the first time was building inexorably, and it was beginning to take its toll. For the first time since that overwhelming first day in the simulator, she wished she hadn't agreed to do this.

True, she had been working for this day all her life. If she screwed up and the error cost her life, so be it. She had come to terms with that risk the very first time she went up alone in an airplane. Pilots' have to believe in their own abilities and come to grips with their own mortality. That goes with the territory. Yet there were seven other lives at risk here. *If I get there, they will too, but if I don't, I will have killed them.*

On the flight deck she committed the spaceplane to another orbit while she read the mission-planning manual again and talked the situation over with Bodard in Mission Control. In her mind's eye she could see his intense eyes, revealing the fire and intelligence he brought to his job.

"We think the problem is the heater," Bodard said finally. "You can reprogram the flight computers to compensate for your seventy percent power capability. Once that is done, we will check your data."

"Roger."

Charley began programming the computers. In five minutes she had finished. The solid-state computers readily took the new parameters, but the spaceplane was now out of radio contact behind the moon. Both the parameters and the navigation solutions would be automatically relayed to Mission Control when radio contract was regained.

She had been awake for twenty hours and was tired, so she rechecked her entries twice, keystroke by keystroke. If she screwed up the approach to landing she would have to abort. There was only fuel for one shot. Landing too far away from the lunar base was not an option, not if she expected to have the fuel remaining to get back to the fuel tank in earth orbit. Crashing on the surface was not an option, either.

Artois offered her an insulated bottle of coffee. She accepted it gratefully, stuck the straw through the port in her face mask and sucked gingerly. Ahh. Then she sat looking through the windshield at the lunar surface sixty miles below. She could see the lava flows and craters quite plainly, stark places that didn't resemble any terrain on earth because there had never been any erosion. Without the eternal erosion of wind and water, the land was jagged, the mountains taller and steeper than any on earth, their relief exaggerated by the stark brilliance of the unfiltered sunlight.

Artois maneuvered himself into the copilot's seat and said nothing. Charley ignored him. Her thoughts were occupied with the task before her, and with thoughts of Rip.

"We have telemetry again." Bodard's voice sounded in her headset, ending her reverie.

Five minutes later he told her, "Looks good. You are go for landing."

"Roger that." Her voice sounded flat, she thought. She was very tired.

AFTER CHARLEY MANUALLY ALIGNED THE SPACEPLANE FOR the approach burn, the autopilot refused to engage. She punched the button futilely. The ship was again behind the moon in the radio dead zone, so there was no one to complain to except Artois, sitting in the copilot's seat, and he would be no help.

"It's enough to piss off the pope," she muttered in English. She reached behind her on the overhead and found the circuit breaker, recycled it, then tried again to engage the recalcitrant device. Nope. Well, she would just hand-fly this garbage scow.

At least all three flight computers were in perfect agreement. Thank God for modern computers! How the Apollo astronauts did it with the primitive junk they had was a mystery.

The clock ticked down. "Here we go," she said over the intercom, and punched the button on the yoke to start the engines. The four small engines fired off, pushing her into her seat. Yeaaah! She concentrated on keeping the crosshairs centered on the display in front of her. *Flying backward takes some getting used to.*

On the completion of the burn, she waited impatiently for the new trajectory data to become reliable.

"*Très bien,*" Bodard said when the spaceplane came out from behind the moon. He was looking at the telemetry data on the trajectory.

Satisfied that she wouldn't need another burn, she waited. *Waiting is the hard part,* she thought.

The ship was descending at about a thousand feet per second. She had fifty more miles of altitude to lose. She checked the three-dimensional display on the trajectory computer and ensured that the remote cameras were on—she would need them in the final phase of the landing—and that the radar and laser backups were functioning properly.

The base site was still over the lunar horizon, nearly six hundred miles away.

The nose was well up now, the ship flying backward down the glide slope. Through the windshield she could see only stars. The earth was behind her, over her head. Now any burst of engine power would slow the descent. What she needed was the ability to finesse the power, so she selected a lower level of engine power, just thirty percent, so that the timing on the burns would be less critical.

The ship plunged on toward its rendezvous with the moon. The engines had to fire now when she asked for power or the ship would crash into the surface at this rate of descent.

Another burn was coming up. Fifteen seconds . . . ten . . . five . . .

She waited. And lit the engines. They fired. A two-second burst. Too much would shallow the descent and carry the ship far beyond the target landing area; too little would require more power later on and screw up the trajectory. She adjusted the ship's attitude to keep it perfectly aligned.

So far, so good.

Two minutes later she gave the engines another burst. The trajectory was almost perfect, just a little shallow.

The rate of descent was still a thousand feet a second, only twelve miles up now. She checked the altitude on the radar, cross-checked with the lasers. Due to the irregularities of the surface, the readings were merely averages.

Coming down, coming down . . . bringing the nose up as the speed over the surface dropped, using power to slow the descent rate, coming down . . .

Now the landing area came into view on the radar. It didn't look as she expected. The land was all sunlight and long, deep shadows; the mission had been timed to arrive just after the lunar dawn.

Cross-checking everything, she was shocked to realize that

the computer had somehow mislocated the target landing area. Or had it?

She had an instant decision to make. Was the trajectory right or wrong?

Still flying the bird, she punched up the landing zone's coordinates. They looked right. The trajectory looked right. She looked again at the radar picture and keyed in the camera that was slaved to the radar's point of sight. Yes, the landing area looked as she had seen it in the simulations.

She was overthinking this, she decided. *Rely on your instruments! Don't panic!*

Later she couldn't remember the exact sequence of the final phase of the landing. She used the engine, monitored the displays, kept the ship's nose rising toward the vertical while she monitored her ground speed. The objective was to zero out speed, drift and sink rate at touchdown—and land at the proper place. And use as little fuel as possible doing it.

With a final burst of power she slowed the descent to fifteen feet per second. Now she was glued to the television cameras. There was the mobile gantry for unloading cargo, the radio tower and the bank of solar panels for charging the base's batteries—*don't hit them!* Still moving forward at twenty feet per second, no drift, three hundred feet high . . . two hundred, engines on low, just ten percent power . . . dust began to rise . . . one hundred feet, fifty . . . zero groundspeed.

At fifteen feet Charley killed the engines and let lunar gravity pull the ship down. It contacted the surface sinking at one foot per second. The shock absorbers in the landing gear had no trouble handling this descent rate.

As the dust slowly settled on the television monitors, she keyed the intercom and the radio. She had to clear her throat to speak. "*Jeanne d'Arc* has landed."

Beside her Pierre Artois exhaled explosively. "*Très bien,*" he muttered, then decided that phrase didn't describe his emotions. "*Magnifique!*"

RIP AND EGG WERE GLUED TO THE TELEVISION IN MISsouri, even though the time was a few minutes after three in the morning.

They heard Charley Pine's words two and a half seconds after she said them, which was the period of time it took a radio signal to reach earth.

Rip's shoulders sagged. He looked at Egg and saw that he had tears streaming down his cheeks.

He patted his uncle on the shoulder and wandered out into the night. The clouds had cleared somewhat. The moon was well below the horizon now. He blew Charley a kiss at the sky anyway, then walked down the hill toward the control tower and bed.

4

THE PASSENGERS AND CREW HAD TO WALK FROM THE
spaceplane to the base air lock. The fact that *Jeanne d'Arc* was
sitting on her tail complicated matters somewhat. Base personnel maneuvered the cargo gantry alongside so that the
people could be lowered to the surface on the cargo elevator.

While Charley Pine and Florentin went through the post-
flight checklists, the other members of the crew maneuvered
the sedated Lalouette toward the ship's air lock. Two people
from the lunar base came into the ship to assist.

The pilot was near the ragged edge of exhaustion. It took
intense concentration to work through the checklists with Florentin. The checks took over an hour to complete, and by that
time Lalouette and the others were gone. Florentin exited
through the air lock, leaving Charley alone in the spaceplane.

The lunar base would have to wait, she decided. She was
about to sign off with Mission Control when Bodard passed
her a message for Pierre Artois from the French premier.
Congratulations, the glory of France, and all that. She
copied it down, promised to give it to him and signed off.

"Another day, another dollar," she muttered as she maneuvered herself out of her seat.

The descent of the main passageway was not difficult in the weak gravity of the moon. After shedding her space suit, she made a pit stop to answer nature's call, then proceeded to the bunkroom she had shared with Courbet. She crawled into her hammock. In seconds she was fast asleep.

SHE AWOKE TO THE SOUND OF HATCHES OPENING, METAL scraping against metal. She knew what the noise was—base personnel were unloading the cargo bay. Who had done the checklists, to ensure the bay was properly depressurized and that the rest of the ship was maintaining pressure?

Galvanized, she struggled from her hammock and made her way to the flight deck. Florentin was in the pilot's seat, which he had tilted forty-five degrees so that he wasn't lying on his back.

"*Bonjour,* Sharlee," the flight engineer said.

Charley muttered a *bonjour.* For the first time since waking, she looked at her watch. She had been asleep for five hours. Not enough, but she felt better. And hungry and thirsty.

They spent a few minutes talking about the main engine and what Florentin and the engineers from the base were going to do to check out the malfunction; then Charley lowered herself down the passageway.

In the weak gravity of the moon, getting into her space suit was easier than it had been on Earth. Actually the suit consisted of two pieces, an inflatable full-body pressure suit and a tough, nearly bulletproof outer shell that protected the pressure suit and helped insulate the wearer from the extremes of temperature present in a zero-atmosphere environment. Air for breathing and to pressurize the suit was provided by a small unit worn on a belt around the waist.

The unit hung at the small of the wearer's back and was connected to the suit by hoses.

Donning the suit alone was strenuous. Only when Charley had triple-checked everything did she enter the air lock. With the pressure suit inflated, she felt like a sausage.

When the exterior door opened the light blinded her. She remembered her sun visor and lowered it with her eyes closed. After her eyes adjusted she got her first real view of the lunar surface. She had seen the photos many times, yet the reality was awe-inspiring. The land baking in the brilliant rising sun under an obsidian sky—she had never seen a place more stark, or more beautiful. And the day was going to be two weeks long!

The cargo gantry was alongside, so she used that for a ladder. Standing on the surface, she bent and examined the impressions her boots made in the dirt. Then she turned and looked for Earth.

There it was, behind the spaceplane. She bounded several paces away and looked again. Should have brought a camera, she thought. Mesmerized, listening to the sound of her own breathing, she turned slowly around, taking in everything. She saw the air-lock entrance to the lunar base, an illuminated bubble that looked like a large skylight, a radio tower, the gantry and the jagged horizon. In the absence of an atmosphere, the visibility was perfect.

"Yeah, baby!"

Charley Pine pumped her fist and headed for the air lock, which was in the side of a cliff. She promptly fell. It was a slow-motion fall, at one-sixth the speed that she would have toppled on earth. Instantly she was all business. Impact with a sharp stone might tear the outer shell and damage the interior pressure suit. If the interior suit lost pressure, her blood would transform itself into a gas; death would follow in seconds.

She had come too far to die in a freak accident between the spaceplane and the base air lock. Adrenaline pumping, she caught herself with her gloved hands, then pushed herself back erect.

Concentrating fiercely, taking care not to overcontrol, Charley walked—or leaped—toward the air lock and entered it. She had to wait for a forklift to bring a container from *Jeanne d'Arc* into the lock; then the door closed and the operator on the other side of the thick glass began pumping in air.

THE AIR LOCK LED INTO AN UNDERGROUND CAVERN THAT had been carved from solid rock. Supplies in containers were stacked along one side of the capacious corridor. Charley stopped to remove her helmet and looked the containers over as she walked toward the locker room. The containers were stacked with their numbers facing out. She was looking for a specific four-digit final number, and didn't see it. The reactor was still on the plane.

After wriggling out of her space suit—one of the base personnel helped her and chatted freely while she did it— Charley got directions to the mess hall.

Just moving along the corridors took a great deal of getting used to. Too vigorous a step would send her to the ceiling; a misstep would send her crashing into a wall. Clearly the lunar gravity was going to take some getting used to. The people she met seemed to have adjusted well, so perhaps the learning curve would be steep.

In the mess hall, which doubled as a lounge, she filled a tray made of superlight, composite material with a judicious quantity of food—better keep an eye on the figure. The food was French, and yet it wasn't what she had eaten in France. One of the cooks, or chefs, was replenishing a warmer, so she asked, "How do you cook in this gravity?"

"It is difficult," he replied with a grin. "The food is not

pressing down. We use a pressure cooker for most things, except the sauces. The sauces are difficult."

"I suppose so."

She stood looking around. There were several televisions; they seemed to be running programs from French television, likely sent to an earth satellite and rebroadcast. In one corner of the room was a camera, mounted so that the background was the entire room, which was probably the largest on the lunar base.

She saw Claudine Courbet at a table with two other women and joined them, carefully. Tossing the contents of her tray on the diners would be a poor start to her visit.

One of the women was a geologist, the other an electrical engineer. Both welcomed her and smiled when they heard her accent. Before long all four women were chatting merrily about their voyages to the moon and life at the lunar base.

"I know you have been drilling for water," Charley said to the geologist. "Have you found any?"

"Yes and no. There are ice crystals well below the surface. Not huge chunks, but crystals. We have extracted some and recovered perhaps a hundred liters. To become self-sustaining and build up a surplus we must mine the material in quantity and bake it to extract the water."

"It must be really old stuff," Charley said. "Is it any good?"

The geologist grinned and removed a small bottle from a pocket. She handed it to Charley. "Try it."

Charley hefted the bottle, swallowed hard, then unscrewed the cap and took a tentative sip. The water was cool and delicious. A look of relief crossed her face, and the other women laughed.

"That first sip is always an act of faith," the geologist said as Charley handed back the bottle.

"How did the water come to be there?"

"That is another question," the geologist admitted. She

was deep into the various possibilities when a runner came looking for Charley.

Pierre Artois wanted her for a televised news conference in the communications room, which, in addition to sophisticated computers and transmitters, contained a small television studio with a moonscape mural on the rock wall as a backdrop.

Madame Artois was there, off camera. She was at least ten years younger than Pierre, a beautiful woman with a figure that her jumpsuit didn't hide. She shook Charley's hand and murmured something Charley didn't catch; then the cameras came on and the pilot was ushered to a seat.

Reporters in Paris asked her numerous questions, about the flight, the lunar base, and her initial impressions of the moon. She answered as best she could, regaled them with an account of her klutzy fall and bowed out of further questions. Artois smoothly interceded. As soon as she was off camera, Charley found herself standing beside Julie Artois, who listened intently to every question and answer.

Every now and then Pierre glanced at his wife, and Charley realized with a start that Julie was giving Pierre subtle clues on how to frame his answers through the use of body language. When she thought an answer had gone on long enough, she made a tiny circle with one finger, once against her cheek, once with her hand by her leg.

Pierre was still answering questions when Charley wandered away to explore. As she left the room Henri Salmon, the base commander, followed her out. "Welcome to the moon, Mademoiselle Pine. I trust you have found our accommodations agreeable?"

"Like the Ritz."

Salmon didn't grin. He was a wiry, fit man with close-cropped blond hair, togged out in the blue jumpsuit that all the lunar base personnel wore. His was not as tight fitting as the others', Charley noted.

"If you will permit, I will give you a tour of our facilities," Salmon said.

"Lead on," Charley replied.

Salmon went into a monologue about the base and its systems, explaining with the pride of ownership. Charley reflected that Salmon had arrived on the very first spaceplane to the moon and never left. He had been here over six months and had personally supervised every phase of construction. In truth, he practically owned the base.

"The lunar base is lit during the clock day with metal halide lights, which as you see generate entirely white light, artificial sunlight, if you will, which provides us with vitamin D. During the twelve-hour clock night, we illuminate the base with red light to keep people on a proper night and day cycle."

The underground base reminded Charley of a hard-rock mine she toured once on a geology lab field trip. The rock from which it had been quarried was hard lava that lacked cracks or faults. Still, air did leak in minute amounts, Salmon said, so there were some imperfections in the stone. Fire and general emergency alarms were located side-by-side every fifty feet along the corridor walls, alongside emergency oxygen bottles.

She watched the well drilling, looked in the generator room, watched sewage being recycled to extract the water, spent a few minutes in the atmosphere room where the air was scrubbed and enhanced with oxygen and hydrogen as required, and visited the gymnasium.

"A sixth of earth's gravity is insufficient to maintain the muscle tone required to keep the human body healthy over long periods," Salmon explained. "Everyone at the base is required to spend an hour a day exercising in this room, regardless of other duties." He demonstrated the gym equipment for Charley. "Transporting weights to the moon would have been outrageously expensive, so we brought these machines that rely on spring tension to supply the resistance. The amount of effort involved is unrelated to gravity." Salmon moved the heaviest weight without much apparent effort, Charley thought, which proved that he did spend his hour a day here.

There was also a set of barbells in the room, but the weights on the ends of the bars were huge rocks. Salmon saw her inspecting one and urged, "Pick it up. Carefully."

Charley set herself and jerked the bar. It seemed to weigh about a hundred pounds, she estimated, so on earth it would weigh six times that much. When she set it down she laughed. "I wish I had a photo of me lifting that. I would look like Superwoman."

"We'll see what we can do," Salmon said, deadpan. Charley wondered if he ever smiled.

Salmon led her to the science lab and explained some of the experiments as the technicians worked.

"We have found water on the moon," Salmon said, "and we will find more. But the primary purpose of the lunar base, its real justification, is this laboratory, where our scientists are working on creating complex organic compounds."

Charley stood looking at the computers, ovens, test tubes, retorts and other lab gear. "Trying to make food, I suppose."

"Precisely," Salmon said. "Has someone told you about our research?"

"No. But one of the main problems with interstellar space flight, and to a lesser extent bases on the moon or other planets, is going to be food. The astronauts are going to have to make food from waste products, including human wastes, or they'll eventually starve."

"Precisely," Salmon admitted grudgingly. "Our laboratory is already manufacturing more complex organic molecules than can be made in earth's gravitational field. We progress."

"Think of the possibilities," Charley enthused. "Throw some old newspapers and ratty jeans in the microwave, and half an hour later out pops a soufflé covered with a delicate sauce."

Salmon eyed her suspiciously and led her from the lab.

They visited the medical bay. Lalouette was out of surgery and recovering, although he was still asleep. They casually inspected the sleeping quarters. All the women were in one dormitory room. Oh, well, she was only going to be here about ten days, then she was going back to earth with Lalouette, assuming he had recovered enough to stand the G forces.

On one corridor they found a large dust curtain. Entering, Charley and Salmon saw a crew busy quarrying rock, enlarging the base. Powerful air scrubbers captured the dust. Two men in hard hats ran the machines that ate at the rock. Joe Bob Hooker was standing beside one of the roaring air scrubbers smoking a green Churchill cigar. "This is the only place they'll let me smoke," he explained loudly to Charley as Salmon conferred with the workers. "They say the smoke will set off the fire alarms."

Charley met people everywhere and heard more names than she could ever remember.

She and Salmon were traversing a corridor that penetrated deeply into the cliff when they passed a door marked NO ADMITTANCE TO UNAUTHORIZED PERSONNEL. The door had a keypad that allowed access. Power cables penetrated the metal bulkhead in which the door was set along one wall, as well as ducts to pipe air in and bring it out.

"What's in there?" she asked her guide.

"More experiments. We must keep the room scrupulously clean."

Charley didn't argue. And she didn't believe him.

So what was behind the door? Was that the destination of the reactor? Why in the world did Pierre Artois need a nuclear reactor on the moon? Electrical power was the only possible answer, but why so much?

"Why are you here?" she asked Salmon.

"I make it all work," he replied casually.

"That is what you do. But why are you here?"

He stopped, turned and scrutinized her face. "You are the first person who ever asked."

"Oh."

Salmon took a deep breath as he thought about the question. "Most people have little dreams, with small goals. They lead small, unimportant lives. Pierre's dream is huge, and he has devoted himself to it body and soul. Do you understand?"

"I think so."

Salmon was intense. "Even if he ultimately fails, he has tried mightily. And the attempt has made him great."

"Like Don Quixote, perhaps."

Salmon didn't think much of that analogy. He merely grunted and resumed walking.

"And your dream?" Charley asked.

"Pierre's dream has made him great. And if we believe, he will make us great, too."

The messiah on the moon, Charley thought, although she didn't say that to Henri Salmon. He had his dream and she had hers, which was to fly. *My dream is big enough for me,* she told herself.

In the mess hall Salmon bid her a curt good-bye and walked away. "Interesting," she muttered aloud. His jumpsuit bulged under his armpit. Henri Salmon was wearing a pistol. Whatever for, she wondered.

Her lack of sleep was catching up with her. She made her way to the women's dorm and leaped into her bed, which didn't collapse.

CHARLEY PINE WAS SITTING IN THE DINING AREA AFTER her long nap when Florentin found her. He sat down beside, her with his tray. "It was the heater in the main engine," he reported. "It froze up. I've reset the circuit breaker. Seems fine now."

"Why did it freeze?" Charley asked between bites.

"That I don't know. I've inspected everything I can inspect, and I can't find anything wrong."

"Could not duplicate the gripe," Charley muttered in English, then smiled at Florentin. He was the expert on the spaceplane. If he couldn't find the glitch, no one else at the lunar base would either. Some problems a pilot simply has to live with. Fortunately they wouldn't need the main engine to get back to earth. The main burns would be longer, but the computer could arrive at the proper trajectory to account for that.

"How are they coming on getting the cargo unloaded?" she asked.

"Another twenty-four hours or so. Then, Salmon says, they will begin loading the science experiments for the trip back."

"Terrific."

"So how do you like the moon?"

"Reminds me of a cave."

"Yes," he said with a grin. "We call it Cave Base. Do not say that to the press, though. Monsieur Artois is selling the glamour."

"Speaking of glamour," Charley said as Joe Bob Hooker came over carrying a tray and sat down with them. "Hello, Mr. Hooker."

"Call me Joe Bob. Well, whaddaya think?"

Florentin mumbled an excuse and took his tray to another table, where he sat with a collection of technicians.

"What this place needs is a golf course," Charley said to Joe Bob, just to make conversation.

"My sentiments, exactly. I've brought a driver and a box of balls. Been outside hitting a few, figuring out just how far they go. Can't get a real good swing in a space suit, and Artois will have to keep that in mind. He had a designer lay out a course and asked for my opinion. He knows I have a ten handicap."

Charley Pine's opinion of Pierre Artois' public relations skills soared. If he could keep the Joe Bobs of the world happy, there were no limits on what he could accomplish. Too bad the worker bees around here assiduously avoided the Texan.

As Hooker chattered about his golf experiences at deluxe courses around the world, Charley finished her meal. The lunar base personnel who entered the dining area avoided their table.

Money can buy the adventure, she thought, *but it can't buy camaraderie.* Joe Bob would always be a tourist. And he knew it. He eyed the technicians in their one-piece jumpsuits and concentrated on his food.

She made her excuses and left.

Life at the lunar base was regulated by the clock, almost as if the people were in a submerged submarine. Charley worked out in the gym, then spent the rest of the clock day sitting on an inflatable couch that didn't weigh five pounds in front of a television playing French and Italian movies. She watched people come and go from the cafeteria section of the room while scanning European newspapers that *Jeanne d'Arc* had delivered. Around her, off-duty base personnel chattered among themselves. They had engaged her in conversation, then turned to subjects that interested them—problems with the base, professional challenges, gossip and games. Several computers sat on a table against a wall and were set up to play games. Chess sets were nearby and were always in use.

People were the same everywhere, Charley thought ruefully. Even on the moon. People needed intellectual stimulation as well as physical exercise to stay healthy.

The adrenaline rush of the flight had worn off, leaving her depressed and lethargic. With no duties to engage her, she was bored. And blue. She wasn't yet ready to throw herself into computer games. Yeah, this was an adventure of a lifetime, but when it was over, then what?

Yawning and tired, she tossed away the newspapers and sat musing about Rip. Finally she gave up and headed for the women's bunkroom.

IN THE MONTHS THAT HE HAD HAD THE COMPUTER FROM Rip's saucer, Egg Cantrell had devoted much time and thought to try to learn how it worked. Yet he could not ignore the contents of the database. He had converted his office into a computer center so that he could transfer the contents of the saucer's computer to his own, where he could manipulate the data, attempting to organize it and make sense of it.

At times he felt like a man sampling books in the Library of Congress, knowing that reading them all would be impossible. At first he had tried to be systematic. The problem was that all knowledge is interrelated, so no matter where he began, threads to other interesting things led away in all directions. Finally he realized that systematic exploration of the storehouse of information contained in the computer would take thousands of years, and he only had a fraction of one lifetime left. So he abandoned system and, when he wasn't working on the programs that made the computer think, he followed any interesting thread anywhere it led. If he crossed another pathway that looked more interesting, he followed that.

The real problem was that he couldn't read the language. Much of the information was in the form of text, which he spent several months trying to decipher. Finally he realized the task was beyond him. With the help of several academics he knew, he located a young linguistics scholar and gave her a huge sample of the text and the graphics that were embedded around it. That was several months ago. She was still searching for a key, a Rosetta stone, that would give her an opening.

In their last conversation she said, "I am assuming that this language was the parent of all the eart\h's languages. That is a huge assumption and may prove to be wrong. There has been much theoretical work done on the so-called first language, and it's just that, theory. All that said, I guarantee you that I can crack it with a computer."

"When?" he asked.

"I don't know."

"What if it isn't a language but computer code?"

"It's not computer code. Computer languages are cake. I had to eliminate that possibility first."

Today he was examining the design of an interstellar spaceship. It contained a cargo hold for transporting two saucers. The ship reminded him of a giant Ferris wheel, with an outer ring that housed the passengers spinning slowly around an interior axis that held the ship's nuclear engines and fuel. The exterior ring was large enough to hold several hundred people. It also held hydroponic gardens, which were used to grow plants for the humans to consume, and a lab for manufacturing food from recycled organic compounds.

He was tracing the power and life support systems when Rip came into his study.

"Look at this," Egg said. "It might be the ship that brought the saucer people to earth."

Rip stared over his shoulder at the computer screen. "They assembled it in space."

"They certainly didn't bring it into the atmosphere," Egg agreed. "See the hold for the saucers, which must have shuttled people and cargo up and down to a planet."

After a bit Rip said, "If all the people came down to earth, where is the starship?"

"Perhaps some of the crew flew it on to another star. Or if everyone stayed on earth, perhaps they left it in orbit."

"It's not up there now."

"No, it wouldn't be. If it were left in low earth orbit, sooner or later it would have fallen into the atmosphere and been destroyed."

Rip sighed and turned away. He sagged into the only easy chair in the room and stared at his toes.

"You must be patient," Egg said. "Life always works out. Give Charley a chance."

"Umm."

"Give life a chance, Rip. If you are the man for her, she'll figure that out."

"I *am* the one," Egg's nephew replied. "How could she not see that? How could she doubt it? She's not blind."

"She'll have to discover that truth for herself."

"And if she doesn't?"

CHARLEY PINE AWOKE FROM A DEEP SLEEP KNOWING someone was in the room. She lay perfectly still for several seconds, trying to remember precisely where she was. Someone was shaking a person in the next bed. Ah yes, that person was Claudine Courbet, who had gone to bed an hour or so after Charley.

It was a man—Henri Salmon. Now he whispered something in French. He left the room, and Claudine Courbet bestirred herself. Charley pretended to be asleep.

Courbet dressed in the darkness; then Charley heard the door open and close. She opened her eyes and sat up in bed. There were two other women in the room, both apparently asleep.

Charley sat up, pulled on her flight suit and her boots, then pulled her hair back and put a band on it.

The corridor was lit with red light during the base night hours in an effort to help the humans regulate their internal clocks. And it was empty. She walked carefully along, past the doors to several workshops, toward the steel door that had been locked yesterday. *I'm getting accustomed to the moon's gravity,* she thought wryly. *A few more days and I'll look like a native.*

She approached the last bend in the corridor with care. Two men were wrestling a dolly loaded with something heavy. The reactor! They punched in the code; then one man held the door while the other maneuvered the dolly through the entrance.

As they disappeared into the space, Charley bounded toward the door—and caught it just before it closed.

She waited several seconds, then pulled it open and followed them through.

A FEW FEET PAST THE LOCKED DOOR SHE PASSED THROUGH an air lock, both doors of which stood open. Beyond the air lock the corridor opened into a commodious cavern. The two men with the dolly were off-loading the reactor. Claudine Courbet was hovering nearby, apparently supervising. None of the three noticed her.

A control console sat facing a large window. Beyond the window, which appeared to be thick, bulletproof glass or plastic, three large objects were visible.

One of them looked like an optical telescope, a huge one,

at least ten feet tall. The largest machine, if it was that, stood at least twelve feet tall and was covered with opaque plastic. Against the wall was another object, a giant cube about six feet high. Power cables three inches thick ran from it to the machine under the plastic.

Charley recognized the cube—it was a giant capacitor. The solar panels on the surface over their heads would never fully charge it, but the nuclear reactor, if used to generate electricity, certainly could.

Above the machines beyond the glass was a large metal roof, one that apparently consisted of panels that could be moved by a complicated arrangement of hydraulic rams. This roof must be the object she had seen from outside and thought was a skylight.

On this side of the window the control console dominated the room. There were four raised chairs, the usual emergency equipment and, against one wall, hangers that held at least a half dozen space suits and helmets.

The place looked like an observatory. Yet the orientation was wrong. When the roof was opened, the telescope wouldn't be pointed at deep space; it would be pointed toward earth.

Now Claudine saw Charley. She looked startled, then approached her.

"What are you doing here?"

"I heard you leave the dorm and wanted to see you set up the reactor."

Claudine blinked once. "Henri gave you the door code?"

"Of course."

Claudine seemed to accept that. She turned and gestured grandly. "What do you think?"

"Wow," Charley Pine said, and meant it.

5

CHARLEY WALKED TO THE CONTROL CONSOLE AND EXAM-
ined the presentations. Computer screens, track balls for
maneuvering cursors, LED readouts, a few analog gauges for
voltages . . .

*What is the purpose of this room? What is that large piece of
equipment under the plastic cover? Claudine knows, and she expects
me to know. An optical telescope, a reactor to generate large amounts
of electricity, a giant capacitor, and . . . ? Is this an observatory? Or
a weapons platform in high earth orbit?*

"How long will it take to get the system operational?"
Charley asked Claudine, trying to sound as matter-of-fact as
possible.

"A week or so, I imagine. If we don't have any unforeseen
problems."

"Aren't there always unforeseen problems?" Charley
turned so that she could see Courbet's face.

"Let's hope not. We tested the entire system extensively in
the laboratory, worked out the bugs, then brought the components here one by one. The testing phase took three

months." Claudine smiled confidently. "It'll function properly."

Looking through the glass, Charley carefully examined the metal plates and hydraulic rams that formed the ceiling above the machinery. Then she glanced again at the space suits arranged on hangers against one wall. When the roof opened, this window would be the pressure barrier—hence the space suits. If the glass cracked or air leaked past it, the people in this compartment would need space suits to survive. The air lock in the passageway was designed to prevent a sudden depressurization of the entire lunar base.

Claudine bit her lip, then went over to supervise the technicians unpacking the reactor, which was easy to manhandle in the weak lunar gravity.

A laser? Could it be?

Charley tried desperately to remember everything she knew about lasers. The light beams were most effective at short distances. They were degraded by moisture in the atmosphere. Firing a beam through a cloud was impractical. The earth, at which this device seemed to be aimed, was swaddled in a heavy atmosphere laden with moisture; clouds obscured huge portions of the earth on a regular basis.

Claudine was glancing at her from time to time. Charley studied the control console, looking for any clue. And failed to find any.

The pressure door to the equipment bay was standing open, so she went through it, out under the dome.

The telescope was mounted on a conventional stand. The larger device was mounted on a massive support structure that sat atop a round titanium base at least twelve feet in diameter, which looked as if it could support a tremendous weight. But why? Even if the device were made of pure steel, it couldn't weigh over a few hundred pounds here on the moon.

Obviously the engineer who designed it thought it would thrust downward against the lunar rock, and the base was designed to transfer the load, much like a bridge support.

A gun? To shoot a projectile at targets on earth?

She glanced around, looking for anything that might be ammo for such a gun—and saw Courbet walking toward her. The technicians who had unloaded the reactor were leaving. They disappeared through the air lock, taking the dolly with them.

"Is this base really strong enough?" Charley asked.

Faced with a technical question, Claudine found her confidence. "Oh, yes. Actually it is twice as strong as it needs to be. And the base is twice as large—the underlying rock may have a hidden fault."

"Of course," Charley said carelessly. Then it hit her. For every reaction there is an equal but opposite reaction. This thing was going to push hard against the rock that supported it. If it wasn't a gun, it was something that affected the lunar gravitational field.

She reached for the plastic cover, which was merely draped over the device, and jerked it off. A system of gears sat above the base, apparently to aim the device. Above the gears were metal rings arranged around a cone, the largest at the base and the smallest at the tip. Heavy cables led to them.

It was an antigravity beam generator!

Egg Cantrell had publicized the antigravity technology from the saucer just two months ago, with misgivings. The weapons potential of the technology was obvious. Egg knew that every advance in human knowledge could be misused, yet he believed the possible benefits outweighed the risk. Risk-benefit decisions are part of life; they have been routinely made by man ever since cavemen weighed the benefits of eating cooked meat against the risk of getting burned.

Were French scientists this far ahead of everyone else?

"Where did this technology come from?" Charley barked at the French engineer. "Where did you people get it?"

A look of surprise froze Claudine's face. "You . . . you . . ." she stammered, "you didn't know! You're not authorized to be in here."

"Has the French government gone off its nut?"

Fear registered on Claudine's face.

"So you're going to plug in the reactor, charge the capacitor, roll back the roof and zap the evil bastards for the greater glory of France."

"Nations are obsolete," Claudine explained with all the fervor of a true believer. "Pierre is going to combine the nations of the world into one kingdom. He is going to end war, starvation, epidemics, hatred and fear. He is going to feed the hungry, heal the sick, lead the peoples of the world into a glorious future."

"By threatening to kill them with that?" Charley gestured toward the beam generator.

"Few revolutions are bloodless. The greater good will require some sacrifices."

Charley Pine whistled silently, then said, "If he could manage to raise a few people from the dead, he could get himself elected messiah."

"I'm going to get Monsieur Artois," Claudine cried, then whirled and started for the door. She didn't get far. Charley grabbed her arm and jerked. As Claudine spun back around, Charley flattened her with a right to the chin.

And felt ashamed of herself. Violence is so tacky.

Claudine did a slow, languid backflip and slid to a stop in a crumpled heap. Her pulse was steady, and all her head bones seemed intact. Charley decided Claudine was just out cold.

Pierre was going to be peeved when Claudine recovered enough to give him the bad news. Any way you cut it, Charley had worn out her welcome on the moon.

She took a last long look at the beam generator and waiting power cables. "Been nice knowing you, lady," Charley said to the comatose Claudine. "See you around."

Then she strode out, trying not to bounce off the ceiling in her haste, went through the open air lock to the personnel door and opened it a crack. No one was in the hallway. She made sure the door latched behind her.

She found Joe Bob Hooker sitting by himself in the cafeteria nursing a cup of coffee. Florentin and two technicians were eating breakfast three tables away. Florentin saw Charley and nodded. She smiled at him, then dropped into a seat beside Hooker.

"Couldn't sleep?"

"Huh-uh. You?"

"Nope."

"How's the java?"

"Strong enough to stick a fork in. The frogs can't make decent coffee. Here or in Paris."

"How about showing me how to hit a golf ball?"

"Outside?"

"Yep."

He was surprised. "Now?"

"Why not? You got something better to do?"

"In this hole in the ground? You gotta be kiddin'!"

"Well, let's go." She stood.

He eyed her. "Okay. I'll swing by my room and get my sticks. Got about a dozen balls left." He dumped the coffee in the food bin to be recycled, left the cup in the dirty dishes rack and followed her out into the corridor.

In a few minutes he joined her in the locker room. As they suited up, he said, "You ever play golf?"

"Never had time."

"Worst game known to man. Gotta do it in Dallas with the

bankers and dealership managers, you know. Need to know who's who; which ones are screwing me and which ones want to. I watch 'em play for three hours and I get a pretty good idea what's in their heads."

"That the way you run your business? Figure out who's honest and who isn't?"

"That's the only way."

When they were completely suited up, they checked each other's suit, made sure the oxygen systems were charged and functioning properly, then headed for the air lock. Joe Bob carried the clubs. In the air lock both of them dropped their sun visors.

The instant the air lock opened, Charley checked the spaceplane. *Jeanne d'Arc* was standing on her tail with the sun gleaming on her. The gantry was still in place.

Joe Bob showed her how to hit a ball. Although their helmets contained radios, they talked back and forth by touching their helmets, freeing up their hands. Natural movement was impossible in a space suit. Still, with practice, one could approach some degree of dexterity.

Hooker was critiquing Charley's swing ten minutes later when the gantry elevator came down with a container on it. One man rode it down. The other operated the lift from the ground.

Once the elevator was down, the man on the ground crossed the surface to a modified forklift. Together he and the other man drove it toward the air lock.

The instant the door closed, Charley put her helmet against Hooker's and said, "Come with me. Into the space-plane."

She didn't wait for his response. He might have thought she wanted to fool around—she didn't care.

They rode the gantry elevator up to the open cargo bay. It was empty. That container the men had just off-loaded was the last one, Charley thought. She lowered the elevator to the personnel air lock. The door stood open.

She banged her helmet against Hooker's. "Get in," she said. "Go up to the cockpit and strap yourself into the copilot's seat. Don't use the radios."

"Want to tell me what's going on?"

"You and I are outta here."

He looked around, then looked into her visor, trying to see her face. She saw his shoulders rise in a shrug. He gave her a thumbs-up and walked into the lock.

Down she went on the elevator as the air lock door closed.

The gantry was battery operated, of course. There were feet to stabilize it, and they were extended. She retracted them, put the transmission in reverse and released the parking brake. Nothing happened.

She looked around for another control. There was a pedal on the floor. She pushed on it with a foot. The gantry began creeping away from *Jeanne d'Arc.*

She had to get it far enough away that it could not fall against the tail fins when hit by rocket exhaust. She jammed the pedal in as far as it would go, and the speed did not increase. This was all there was.

She had no idea how long Claudine Courbet was going to stay unconscious. She was sure, however, she didn't want to be on the moon when Pierre Artois and his disciple, Henri Salmon, found out that she knew about the reactor and antigravity beam generator. She was very certain of that.

Finally the gantry seemed far enough away from the ship. The thing stopped when she stepped off the pedal.

Charley bounded toward the ship, stopped under it and looked up at the open cargo bay. She was going to have to leap up to it. If she blew this and tore her space suit, she was dead.

She coiled herself and leaped. She soared up at least ten

feet but was a foot or more short of grasping the lower lip with her hands—then fell slowly back to the lunar surface. She cushioned her fall with her legs, and bounced.

Okay, she needed a running start.

Thank God she had played basketball in high school and at the academy.

As she went away from the ship, she saw the base air lock door opening. Two men came running out. They must have seen her on the television monitors moving the gantry.

One, two, three mighty leaps toward the gleaming white ship, then she launched herself upward. This time she grasped the edge of the bay.

Dangling there with her weight on her hands took little effort. She summoned her strength, then pulled hard. Up she went into the bay.

The lights in the cargo bay were lit. The ship's batteries were still supplying power to essential systems.

Once inside she went immediately to the door controls. Silently, majestically, the doors moved. The electro-hydraulic servos could move them in earth's gravity, so they had no trouble here. The doors snapped shut with authority. She inspected them to ensure the latches had engaged. Yes. She pushed the toggle to pressurize the cargo bay and waited. The gauge on the wall began to register air pressure.

She watched it until it equalized with the normal pressure inside the ship, then turned and climbed to the pressure door. It was difficult to open. She pried with all her strength on the bar. It refused to yield.

Godzilla must have cranked this puppy shut.

Urgency washed over her. The adrenaline magnified her strength. With one mighty heave the door opened and swung inward with a bang.

Too much pressure in the bay. That was the trouble.

She closed the door behind her and, using the bulkhead handholds, hurriedly climbed up the corridor to the cockpit.

HOOKER WAS STRAPPED INTO THE COPILOT'S SEAT, JUST AS she had requested. She glanced outside as she unfastened the latches on her helmet and removed it. The two men who had rushed outside were standing there looking up.

She could hear their voices coming over the radio, which was set to the base circuit. They were talking to Artois.

Hooker already had his helmet off.

"Want to tell me what's going on?"

"I'm leaving. Might be quite a while before another ship shows up. Didn't want to leave you stranded."

"That's mighty sweet of you. Only had a dozen balls left, and I can't stand French television. Want to tell me why the rush?"

"Later."

"You've seen one lunar base, you've seen them all," he said philosophically.

"Maybe you can get a partial refund on your money."

Charley dropped into the pilot's seat and brought up more power. She began running through the lunar launch checklist on the small computer as Artois squawked on the radio. Systems looked okay—no time to run the built-in tests—

Charley flipped the switch to turn on the intercom and donned the headset.

"If anyone is aboard this ship, better sing out."

There was no reply.

She began selecting options on the main flight computer. Fortunately it knew the exact Greenwich time, where the spaceship was on the moon, the location of the earth—directly overhead—and the location of the guide stars. It took three minutes for the star finders to lock on and the flight computer to recommend a trajectory that would take them toward earth.

Joe Bob watched in silence.

"Pierre's getting pissed," he said, jerking his thumb at the lunar base.

"Everyone has those days."

She began working through the start checklist. Electrical power on, power levels set, fuel, temps at the fuel controllers, pressures in the fuel tanks—everything was within normal limits.

She reached behind her and pulled out the circuit breaker for the radio telemetry data. Screw Mission Control.

"Mademoiselle Pine," Artois pleaded on the radio. "What are you doing? Please talk to me."

She motioned for Joe Bob to put on the copilot headset.

"We're leaving, Pierre," she said in English. "You better tell these two dudes standing out here to take cover or they're going to get fried."

Thirty seconds of silence passed while she checked systems; then the two men outside turned and began clumsily running toward the air lock.

"If you fly that ship without authorization, it will be theft," Artois said. "You will jeopardize the lives of everyone at this base. I will have no choice but to report this mutiny."

"Do what you gotta do."

"Will you tell me why?" Artois was persistent, you had to admit.

She was ready to start engines. She checked that the power level was set at the recommended value, fifty percent. That should be sufficient. All that remained was pushing the ignition button.

"I had a little chat with Claudine Courbet," she said.

Silence.

"She showed me your antigravity beam generator, Pierre.

Either you have been lying to the French government, or they have been lying to everyone."

"Mademoiselle—"

"Ruler of the universe. Should I call you Your Majesty? Or perhaps Your Supreme Gloriousness? Better get that figured out. Pick something that sounds really cool in French. Claudine is a couple of cards short of a full deck, but you're one crazy son of a bitch, Pierre."

Hooker touched her arm to get her attention. He pointed toward the door lock. The door was almost fully open. The forklift came buzzing out, accelerating, heading straight toward the spaceplane. The two empty spears were at the top of their rails. She could see the helmeted figure hunched over the controls.

"That fool may try to ram us, damage the ship."

Charley didn't wait. She reclined her seat and punched the ignition button.

Hooker hurriedly reclined his as the rockets ignited. From the corner of her eye Charley saw a blast of dust.

The Gs hit her in the back.

Charley Pine made one last radio transmission. "*Adios*—" Over the intercom, she asked Hooker, "What's Spanish for 'asshole'?"

Hooker barely got his words out against the accelerating G. "*Gringo*, I think."

6

PIERRE ARTOIS AND HENRI SALMON FOUND CLAUDINE
Courbet stretched out on the floor beside the BEAM generator. A half-full bottle of water sat on top of the control console. Artois squirted some in Claudine's face. Her eyes
opened.

Salmon lifted Claudine to a sitting position. Artois squat-
ted and examined the engineer's face. Her jaw was severely
swollen. He was still looking her over when his wife, Julie
Artois, came in.

She knelt beside Pierre, who tersely filled her in on the
situation.

"What did you tell Pine?" she snarled at Claudine.

Courbet's eyes swam. Julie Artois slapped her. That
focused her eyes.

"What did you tell Pine?" she repeated.

Claudine took a few seconds to collect herself before she
spoke. "She knew about the reactor. Came in here to see
what it was going to be used for."

"How did she get in?"

"Followed the men who wheeled the reactor in on a dolly, I suppose. I thought she knew. I thought she was one of us."

"You were told that she wasn't."

"But she was here, and she knew so much." Claudine really believed this.

"You know my rules."

"She jerked the covering off the beam generator," Claudine explained. "Recognized it for what it was."

Pierre rose and walked around aimlessly.

"Hiring her was really stupid," Claudine continued. She struggled to her feet. Once erect, she glared at Julie. "She flew in a saucer, knows what's in the computers. And she can add two and two. Of all the pilots on the planet you people could have hired—"

"Enough!" Julie commanded with a chopping gesture. "What's done is done. How long before you can get the generator operational?"

"We'll have to hook up the reactor and test the system. Can't run it to full power without serious testing, not unless you want this cave to glow in the dark for the next ten thousand years."

"How long?"

"A week. Perhaps a day or two less."

"You have three days," Julie said, staring at Claudine. "And if you don't make it work, I have people who can. We'll put you in the air lock without a space suit and watch you die. Do you understand?"

Claudine Courbet appealed to Pierre, who turned his face away. She turned back to Julie. "You are really sick, madame."

"The future of mankind is at stake," Julie Artois said. "I'm not going to let you or anyone else stand in our way."

Julie looked at Salmon. "Have someone with her every

moment. Don't leave her alone," she said coldly.

Then she walked out. Pierre followed.

They went to their private suite and made sure the door was locked behind them before they spoke.

"Years of work, a decade of planning, billions of euros invested, the future of mankind at stake, and one foolish woman allows another to sabotage everything!" Pierre stormed.

His wife took a deep breath, closed her eyes momentarily, then opened them again.

Pierre rubbed his eyes, tried to steady his breathing.

Illogical, stupid, venal, selfish people he understood. He had certainly met enough of them through the years. Those people he could handle. On the other hand, the Charlotte Pines of the world were a different breed.

He had counted on the spaceplane, which was a guaranteed ride back to earth when the time came. Without it, he and everyone else on this rock were marooned until another spaceplane made the trip.

"Can we force the French to send a spaceplane?" he asked Julie.

"Nothing important has changed," his wife said curtly. "Key people in the government are with us, as they have always been. Under our leadership France will assume its rightful place in the world. Our friends want us to succeed— they will bring Europe with them. France, Europe and the world. The glory of France will shine as it never has before."

The pitch and timbre of her voice rose as she spoke, mesmerizing Pierre. She had always had the ability to show him the grandeur that lay just beyond the shadows. He believed, and he knew others would too.

Still . . . "What of the British, the Americans?" he asked now.

"Their day is done. The world will speak French. If they refuse to see reason, we will bring them to their knees." She made a fist. "And destroy them."

AFTER ROCKET ENGINE SHUTDOWN, WHEN THE THREE flight computers all agreed that the spaceplane was established on course to an earth orbit rendezvous with the refueling tank, Charley checked the ship's habitability systems one more time, leaned back and sighed.

Without the background chatter from Mission Control and people in the ship talking on the intercom, the cockpit was unusually quiet. The only sounds that could be heard were ship's noises, the hum of air circulation fans and an occasional thumping from a pump that kicked in for a few seconds.

She yawned. "What say we see if there's anything aboard this garbage scow to eat, then grab a few winks."

"Maybe you had better tell me why we did an unscheduled boogie without people or cargo," Joe Bob Hooker said. "Sorta curious, I guess."

"Over food. I haven't eaten"—she looked at her watch—"in fifteen hours."

She unstrapped and headed for the locker where the space suits were kept. After she had properly stored hers, she went to the kitchen, where she found Joe Bob floating around.

"There isn't much," he said. "Gonna lose a few pounds on this flying fat farm."

He extracted some tubes of pureed goo from a refrigerator and tried to read the French labels aloud. "What's *cheval?*"

"Horse, I think."

"I forgot that we're dealing with gourmets. Here's something green."

"I'll take it. Nuke it to warm it up."

"This red stuff looks good to me. I'm a real sucker for red goo; can't get enough of it."

There was wine. With a squeeze bottle of vino each and their goo, they headed back for the flight deck.

The earth was visible through the windscreen, off to the right. They were on course for the point in space where the planet would be in three days. Behind the left wing, a sliver of the sunlit surface of the moon was visible. On the right, the surface of the moon was still in shadow, a dark presence.

As they squeezed and squirted, Charley told Joe Bob about finding the reactor on the outbound voyage, her inspection of the observatory and her conversation with Claudine Courbet.

When she ran down, Joe Bob said, "Pierre Artois, ruler of the universe. Not very catchy."

"Yeah. He's not a corporal with a cool name, like Hitler."

"I see your point. So what do you want to do?"

"I'm inclined to do nothing for a while. We have about seventy hours before we rendezvous with the fuel tank."

"Is the French government behind Artois?"

"Beats me. The politicians put up a huge chunk of the cost of the lunar project. Either he's betraying them or he's acting on their behalf. But that's neither here nor there. I get on the radio with this tale and no one will believe me. You can bet Pierre is telling as big a lie as he thinks he can get away with right now."

"We could listen in. Don't the radios pick up the base frequencies?"

"We could listen," she acknowledged. "But I don't want to. He'll think I'm listening and threaten me. I don't need the aggravation. I want to sleep and think."

"So what happens when he starts firing this antigravity beam at the earth?"

"Assuming the reactor generates sufficient power, the

polarity of the earth's gravitational field will be reversed in the area of the beam, so objects on the surface will be repelled by the planet."

"You mean . . . ?"

"Stuff will fly off into space," Charley Pine said, and squirted the last of her wine into her mouth. "Buildings, ships, people, cities, everything."

"You can bet someone will launch a rocket with a nuclear warhead at the moon. Squash the lunar base."

"Not if Pierre zaps the rocket before it's ready to fly."

Joe Bob thought that over before he said, "Do you really think he'd kill people?"

"I think Pierre Artois is a Looney Tune. If Henri Salmon and Claudine Courbet are fair samples, he has surrounded himself with people just as crazy as he is. There is no way to predict what crazy people will do."

"Unless you're a shrink."

"I'm a pilot. Flying is my gig."

"What if he fires the beam at this ship?" Joe Bob asked softly.

"He'd have to know precisely where we are. We're not flying a straight line; we're flying a parabola. I don't think he has a radar that can pinpoint us. Space is a big place."

"Even bigger than Texas," Joe Bob admitted.

PIERRE ARTOIS SAT IN THE BASE COMMUNICATIONS ROOM collecting his thoughts as the radioman on duty played dumb with Mission Control. They had heard the exchange between Artois and Charley as she took off and were demanding an explanation.

He stared at the radio. All his plans, all his dreams, the very future of the human race, jeopardized by that woman! She wasn't talking on the radio to Mission Control, but she could come on at any time.

She had gone crazy. That was it. The stress of training and the flight—she was unsuitable, had become extremely paranoid, accused them of horrible things, then, when they tried to sedate her, escaped and stole the spaceplane.

He tapped the operator on the shoulder. The man moved from his chair. Pierre sat down, arranged the microphone in front of him and called Mission Control.

RIP CANTRELL WAS INSTALLING ANTIGRAVITY RINGS ON the bottom of the Extra when his uncle Egg came down the hill and called, "Hey, Rip. Better come look at the television. Something has gone wrong on the moon."

Rip dropped his tools and trotted past the hangar. "What?"

"Come watch."

Soon they were in front of the television watching one of the twenty-four-hour news channels. A reporter was interviewing one of the spokespersons for the French space ministry.

"According to these guys," Egg said, summarizing, "one of the pilots has taken *Jeanne d'Arc* and left the moon, presumably headed back for earth. The flight wasn't authorized."

"You mean somebody stole the spaceplane?"

"An unauthorized flight, they called it."

"Same thing."

"So who is the pilot?"

"They haven't said. This happened six hours ago, according to the spokesman."

"So is Charley stranded on the moon or flying the plane?"

"Rip, I don't know."

The story unfolded slowly. *Jeanne d'Arc* had been the only spaceplane on the moon, so the passengers and scientific experiments that were to return aboard her were still there. Another spaceplane would be ready to launch in two weeks. Food and supplies at the lunar base were sufficient to sup-

port the people who were there for months, perhaps as
many as six. The people—they implied there was more than
one—aboard *Jeanne d'Arc* were maintaining radio silence.
She had insufficient fuel to orbit the moon, return to the
lunar base, then return to earth, so the experts believed she
was heading for earth now.

The press conference raised more questions than it
answered, yet the spokesperson refused to give additional
information.

"They've gotten the when, what and where," Rip
grumped, "and left out the who and why."

"Yeah."

"So what do you think, Unc?"

"Something weird happened on the moon."

As the sun set and night crept over the earth, they sat watching television, hoping for more information. None came.

PIERRE ARTOIS CONSIDERED HIS OPTIONS. HE HAD, OF
course, told Mission Control and the French space minister
that Charley Pine had gone insane and stolen *Jeanne d'Arc*. As
he sat watching Claudine Courbet run tests on the reactor
and slowly power it up, he examined the moves on the
board.

Pine had said nothing on the radio to anyone so far, and
perhaps she would not. With women, one never knew. On
the other hand, what could she say that would hurt him?
Well, she could stir up such a mess on earth that the people
here at the lunar base might refuse to obey orders. Or try to
refuse. Once he gave the governments of the earth his ultimatum, what she had to say wouldn't matter. Oh, she would
undoubtedly wind up on television and tell what she had
seen, but so what? That turn of events would be at worst only
a minor irritant, Pierre concluded.

What he really needed was a way to get back to earth if the

unexpected happened, as the unexpected was wont to do.

It didn't take much noodling to arrive at a method that might work. Pierre returned to the communications center and tuned the radio to a private frequency. Then he removed a notebook from his pocket and consulted it. When he found the code he wanted, he dialed it into the voice encoder. After the encoder timed in, he keyed the mike and began speaking.

CHARLEY TOSSED AND TURNED AND DOZED A LITTLE IN HER hammock, but she couldn't get to sleep. She couldn't relax knowing that no one was in the cockpit. Finally she gave up, took a shower and put on the clothes she had just taken off. She went to the galley to make coffee. Without gravity, the process was a chore. After the coffee grounds and water were heated together, you pushed a plunger that forced the hot liquid into a squeeze bottle while trapping the grounds. At least it was hot.

She went to the cockpit and strapped herself into the pilot's seat. She spent fifteen minutes checking ship's systems and the flight computers while pulling gently on the coffee. Satisfied that all was well, she sat staring at the earth, a black-and-white marble against a sky shot with stars. She could perceive deep blue hues amid the swirls of clouds. The planet appeared slightly larger than it had been when she went to bed. When they reached it, of course, it would fill half the sky.

She toyed with the controls of the radio panel. Did the French government know about Pierre's antigravity beam generator? Were the people at Mission Control on Artois' team, or was he a French traitor, an adventurer with an agenda? What were his plans?

She didn't know any of the answers. She put little faith in anything Claudine Courbet had told her. The woman defined "flake." On the other hand, the reactor and beam generator had been the real McCoys, despite the fact that lunar project managers had repeatedly assured a nervous public through the years that no nuclear material would be carried aloft from French soil.

She got out of the pilot's chair and went aft to the main communications room, where the video cameras and lights were stored. Artois had filmed a cell phone commercial from orbit. Did he leave the phone here?

After a one-minute search she found it. It had a sliding cover. She opened it and turned it on. No service, but the battery charge was good. She turned it off and pocketed it.

She was working on her second bottle of coffee when Joe Bob Hooker joined her. He hung his coffee squeeze bottle in midair, strapped himself into the copilot's seat so he would stay put, then rescued the bottle.

"Sleep okay?" he asked.

"No. You?"

"No. So what do you think we should do?"

"Can't decide."

"Me either."

They sat looking at the earth.

"I never met anyone like you," Joe Bob said.

Charley eyed him suspiciously. "Oh?"

"Yeah. You're a smart, take-charge, capable lady who isn't afraid to do what you think right. Aren't many of those around. Not where I've been hanging out, anyway."

"Don't get any big ideas."

"Heck, I'm a married man. You realize, though, that down in Texas there's folks who would say that we're shacked up."

Charley Pine couldn't help herself. She laughed. "Hoo boy."

"Honestly," he said. "Man and woman, all alone for three days. Long enough to fall in love or raise the dead."

"There went my reputation."

"So, you married?"

"No."

"Fool around?"

"Listen, Mr. Hooker. Joe Bob. I have a boyfriend. I think it might really lead to something. I want it to lead to something. You're a nice guy, but let's leave it there, shall we? Stifle yourself until you get home to your Junior Leaguer."

"We could be the first couple to do it in space."

"Wow, we'd be a footnote in the history books. It's tempting, but no thanks."

"Fair enough," he said. "Had to ask. You're mighty nice, and I wouldn't want to go on down the road not knowing. Owed it to myself."

"I understand. No hard feelings."

"So who we gonna call?"

"Damn if I know."

THE NEWS THAT CHARLEY PINE HAD STOLEN *JEANNE d'Arc* was a bombshell worldwide. Within ten minutes of the announcement by the French ministry, she was one of the most famous women on the planet, right up there in the pantheon with Britney Spears and Madonna.

The premier of France watched the media circus on television sets in his office with great misgivings. The accusation that Pine was mentally ill was met with media skepticism. Two hours after the announcement, CNBC had a clinical psychologist on camera pointing out that if she were really bonkers, she probably couldn't fly *Jeanne d'Arc*.

Of course, no one knew the spaceplane's exact location, so the talking heads had a lot of fun with the possibility that a crazy woman pilot and a Dallas car dealer were on a doomed voyage into the sun, or out of the solar system. Or perhaps they were going to immolate themselves in a spectacular fiery reentry to the earth's atmosphere.

It was great television, the biggest thing to hit the tube since the great saucer scare last year. And Charlotte Pine had been involved in that! What was Artois thinking?

The premier had never really trusted Artois, but had hitched his wagon to Pierre's lunar base scheme anyway. The spending had kick-started the French economy and made France the acknowledged leader of Europe. With 350 million people and the world's largest economy, the European Union was a superpower, and the premier was in the driver's seat.

That is, he was until Charley stole *Jeanne d'Arc*. The television announcers' uninformed speculation gave the premier a queasy feeling. In truth, the minister had known next to nothing when he briefed the premier via telephone before he announced the theft. The minister had grabbed at the straw proffered by Artois: Charley Pine was a deluded paranoid who had snapped.

Watching the story unfold on television, the premier felt like a man on a runaway train. He had no control, no way to stop the thing, no idea where it was going or what was going to happen when it got there. Except that the wreck was going to be bad. After an adult life spent in politics, he had a sixth sense about unexpected events. Artois could have gotten a German test pilot, or an Italian, but no, Pierre had to assert his independence, not to mention thumbing his nose at the premier, and bring in the American woman who flew the saucer last year.

The premier didn't think Charlotte Pine had gone crazy. He had met her once, and he came away thinking her a competent professional. If she hadn't gone crazy, Artois was lying.

By craning his neck, the premier could see the moon in the evening sky over Paris through his office window.

* * *

IN WASHINGTON, THE AMERICAN PRESIDENT WAS ALSO watching television, and he was in a fine mood. It was nice to watch a crisis unfold that would not cause him grief regardless of how it ended. No one was going to snipe at him. No one was going to demand legislation to right a wrong, an investigation to fix blame, new statutes to ensure it didn't happen again or a cabinet officer's head on a platter.

The president poured himself a diet soft drink and put his feet up on his desk. Aaah!

Amazingly, the woman involved was Charlotte Pine, who had caused him so much angst with the flying saucer scare a year ago. Thank heavens, this time she was picking on someone else.

She had had a boyfriend, he recalled, the saucer guy, ol' what's-his-name. Rip. Rip Something. That's the kid who found a flying saucer in a sandstone ledge in the Sahara and scared everyone on the planet. What a piece of work he was!

At least Rip was out of it. Now, if Pine would just keep that spaceplane out of the U.S. Let the French sweat for a change.

The president belted down a big swing of Diet Coke and belched loudly.

"You go, girl!" he said to Charley Pine, wherever she might be.

CHARLEY SLEPT IN THE PILOT'S SEAT OF *JEANNE D'ARC* ON the trip back to earth. She tried sleeping in the hammock she had occupied on the flight out and found that with no one in the cockpit monitoring the ship's systems and the navigation computers, sleep was impossible. So she went back to the flight deck, strapped herself into the seat and promptly dozed off. Every few hours she awakened and checked every system. Satisfied, she would allow herself to drift off again.

When she was fully awake, she thought about the situation. She discussed it with Joe Bob Hooker, who had no strong opinions. After all, she realized, he had only her word that Pierre Artois was a maniac. Anyone she talked to would have only her word, until such time as Artois and Claudine Courbet began zapping the earth with an antigravity beam.

In fact, she even doubted herself. What if Courbet had pulled a grotesque practical joke on her? If that thing wasn't an antigravity beam generator, then what was it? Why the reactor? And where, pray tell, had Artois and his minions learned how to build an antigravity beam generator? If Artois didn't need the reactor to power the beam generator, what did he need it for?

Try as she might, she could come up with no other explanation for the use of the reactor. The lunar base didn't need the kind of electrical power that reactor was capable of generating unless they really did have an antigravity beam.

She had been convinced then and she still believed. Pierre Artois, Henri Salmon and Claudine Courbet were rats. Even if she could feel a little worm of doubt gnawing at her.

From time to time she fingered the radio controls. No. The French wouldn't believe her. They would declare her insane before they admitted that Artois was a venal traitor who had duped the government and all the scientists associated with the lunar base project. After all, if they stood by him and he changed his mind and didn't use the beam generator, they would be vindicated. The presence of the reactor and generator on the moon could be hushed up, with no one able to prove anything.

But would Artois give up his dreams of glory? The man wanted to be emperor of earth. He had spent the family fortune preparing for this moment—what were the odds that he would chicken out now?

Perhaps the wise thing to do was wait for Pierre to hoist his flag. She lost nothing by choosing to wait, she decided.

Perhaps that was her only choice.

Charley Pine sat watching the cold, hard, immovable stars and the living earth as gravity accelerated *Jeanne d'Arc* toward the waiting planet. From this distance she could actually see the motion of the planet and the sun line moving across clouds and mountains and oceans. Mesmerized, she watched by the hour.

When Joe Bob came to the flight deck wanting to talk, she chatted with him about inconsequential things, and kept her own counsel.

7

EGG AND RIP SPENT THE MORNING PUTTING THE FINISH-
ing touches on the antigravity ring installation in the Extra
300L. The problem was not the rings or converter, which
were simple to install, but the aircraft's engine. When it was
being used to power the generators—there were two—the
prop had to be disconnected somehow so all the power of
the engine would be available to make electricity.

"You need a transmission that allows you to disconnect the
propeller from the crankshaft," Egg said. "That is going to
require some serious machining at a properly equipped
shop."

"For now, let's just take the prop off the plane," Rip said.

Egg continued thoughtfully, "The saucer has enough electrical power to keep the rings activated until the rockets pro-
pel it to flying speed. Even with a transmission, you'll lose
electrical power when you engage the propeller. You'll be in
a fully stalled condition and will drop like a stone."

"I've been thinking about that," Rip said. "This airplane
will never fly like the saucer."

"Then why the experiment?"

Rip tossed his wrench in the dirt. "What else am I going to do?" He hugged himself and glanced at the moon, which was still visible. "I'm spinning my wheels, I know. But I don't know what to do. Charley and I needed a challenge and we didn't have one."

"Making a living is a challenge for most folks. If you don't have that, you need to find another to make life worthwhile."

"Umm," Rip said, and patted the fuselage of the Extra. "Well, let's get the prop off. A scientific experiment, just for the heck of it."

Two hours later they were ready. Sitting in the cockpit, Rip started the airplane's engine while Egg stood by the hangar watching. He watched the voltage meter he had installed on top of the instrument panel as he revved the engine, let it drop to idle, then revved it again.

When the oil and cylinder head temps were in the green, he smoothly took the engine up to redline. With the engine roaring sweetly, the airplane rose smartly into the air.

He stabilized at fifty feet, using the control stick, which varied the voltage to various portions of the ring system, to keep the plane level. By easing the stick forward he could induce forward motion. Pulling it backward stopped the plane in midair, and continued rearward deflection made it move backward.

He was experimenting, getting the feel of the controls, when two cars pulled up to the hangar and four men got out. Rip saw them from the corner of his eye. When he turned to look, he realized one of the men was holding a pistol on Egg.

What—?

Two of them grabbed Egg by the elbows and hustled him toward one of the cars. Rip turned the Extra and nudged it toward them. One of the men stopped, aimed a pistol at the airplane and began shooting. The muzzle flashes of the pistol were plainly visible.

Rip jammed the stick forward. He felt bullets thumping into the plane as the gunman disappeared under the nose. He knew what would happen—the gunman would be lifted up and trapped in the zone between the plane and the ground.

He kept the plane moving forward.

The car with Egg in it peeled out, leaving muddy streaks in the grass in front of the hangar.

Should he fly over the car, see if the antigravity system in the plane could lift it from the ground? If he did, Egg might be injured. Or killed.

Reluctantly he veered off at the last second and went after the other car, whose driver was attempting to follow the first. Glancing back, Rip saw the gunman fall to the ground. He lay motionless with his stainless steel pistol on the ground beside him.

Rip flew in a circle, his eyes on the two cars, which had circled the hangar and headed for the road that led to Egg's gate. Coming out of the turn he shoved the stick as far forward as it would go and began closing on the second car.

As it disappeared under the nose he pulled back on the stick, stopping the plane over the car. After a few seconds, he eased the stick sideways. The first car, with Egg in it, was speeding toward the gate.

Well off to one side, he looked back. The second vehicle was lying on its side with its rear wheels spinning.

Perhaps he should follow the fleeing car. One glance at his cylinder temp gauge nixed that idea—without the flow of hundred-plus mile-per-hour air over the cooling fins of the engine cylinders, the engine was overheating. Oil temp near the red line, too. He set the Extra on the ground a hundred feet from the hangar, let the engine idle for thirty seconds to cool it, then turned it off.

The gunman crumpled near the hangar never moved.

Blood oozed from his mouth, nose and eyes, which stared fixedly at nothing. From the way he lay, it was obvious that his neck was broken.

Rip left the body and walked to the car lying on its side. The engine was still roaring, the rear wheels spinning. The man at the wheel had not fastened his seat belt, so he had been thrown partially out of the car. His head was under the driver's door. The windshield was shattered, glass fragments strewn everywhere.

Rip reached inside and turned the ignition off. He pulled the key far enough out of the switch to silence the beeping and left it there.

He thought of Egg's good pickup, sitting near the house. Egg always left the key in it. He could jump in it and follow the car that held Egg.

Yet he didn't move.

If he caught it, what then?

The kidnappers were armed. If they knew they were being followed, they might kill Egg.

The dead gunman had a wallet in his hip pocket. Rip flipped through the contents. A French driver's license—Maurice Neri, an address in Nice. French credit cards. He put the wallet back in the man's trousers, felt his other pockets and found something stiff . . . a passport. French. He returned that to the pocket where he found it.

The Extra was leaking fuel. He inspected the belly of the plane. Fuel was dripping from two bullet holes in the bottom of the right wing.

Then he remembered the guard at the gate, a retired local farmer named Ike Pingley. Rip began to run. It was five hundred yards through scrub forest to the gate; he saw Pingley sitting beside the guard shack while he was fifty yards away. As he got closer he could see that Pingley was bound with gray duct tape. He even had a strip across his mouth.

Rip jerked it off.

Pingley groaned. "Are my lips still on?"

"You okay, Ike?"

"Sorry, Rip. They pulled pistols and got the drop on me. There was nothing I could do. Taped me up. Didn't say doodley."

"They kidnapped Egg."

"I saw them go by. Get this tape off me, will ya?"

As Rip jerked tape, Pingley said, "I heard gunshots. And the plane. What was that all about?"

"Guy opened up on me with a pistol. Shot a couple holes in the plane. He and one of his pals are dead."

"You want me to call the law?"

"Yeah."

Rip walked back toward the house as Pingley made the call from the guard shack. They must want the saucer's computer, he thought. Or money. At least there were two of them who would never see another dime.

He was halfway to the house when the cell phone in his pocket vibrated.

"Hello."

"Rip, it's Charley."

Rip was stunned. "The French said you went off your nut. It's been on every television news show on earth. Where are you?"

"I'm a hundred miles above you in orbit. Won't be able to talk long."

"Four French dudes with guns kidnapped Egg. Two of them are dead, but the other two snatched him and drove away about five minutes ago. They probably wanted me too, but I was flying the Extra."

Charley said a cuss word. "I need your help, Rip. Let me tell you what's going down." And she did. After three minutes of nonstop talking, she said, "I'm going to lose you any second. Call you back on the next orbit, in about eighty minutes."

The phone went dead.

He stumbled along, trying to think. Thirty minutes ago he was strapping into the airplane, with Egg watching. Now there were two dead men lying near the hangar, and Egg was gone.

Pierre Artois!

CHARLEY PINE HAD FORTY MINUTES TO STEW IN THE COCK-pit of *JEANNE D'ARC* before the moon came over earth's horizon. Joe Bob Hooker was sitting in the right seat, where he had listened as she used Pierre's cell phone.

"Want to tell me about it?" he asked finally.

"Pierre sent some thugs to kidnap my boyfriend's uncle. Probably my boyfriend too. Two of the thugs are dead, but they managed to grab Uncle Egg. Pierre is sending me a message. Don't make waves, or else."

"How do you know it was Pierre?"

"The gunmen were French. They came to Egg's farm in Missouri. They snatched him. You figure it out."

"Oooh boy!"

"Yeah."

"So where you gonna land this thing?"

"I dunno."

"DFW would be nice. I'll take a cab home." DFW was Dallas–Fort Worth International.

"Hold that thought." The moon was coming over the curvature of the Earth, so she reached for the radio, flipped it on and dialed in the primary lunar base frequency. This was also the freq that Mission Control used to talk to the base.

"Hey, Pierre, this is Charley."

She waited.

"*Jeanne d'Arc,* Mission Control." It was a male voice, one she didn't recognize. He paused for a moment to give her time to respond. When she didn't, he began spouting questions in French anyway.

When Mission Control paused for air, Charley repeated her transmission in English. "Pierre, this is Charley, over."

This time she heard his voice. "I'm listening, Charley."

"Some French thugs just kidnapped my boyfriend's uncle in Missouri. You want to tell me about it?"

"You stole a spaceplane, and you ask me about a crime in Missouri?"

"So what's the deal here, Pierre? I assume you want to threaten me. Mission Control and probably half the news networks on the planet are listening, so go ahead."

"Mademoiselle Pine. I know nothing about Missouri. I do know that you stole our spaceplane. I suggest you land it at the spaceport in France as soon as possible."

"Or?"

"We'll get you the medical help you need. That I can promise."

Charley took a deep breath, then said, "I already have medical insurance, although I appreciate the offer. Since you are so kind, I'll tell you how it went up there before I boogied. Courbet showed me the beam generator and told me your plans."

A long silence ensued while Artois decided how to respond. Obviously he wasn't yet ready to turn on his beam generator and make demands.

She keyed her mike. "How much longer are you going to wait, Pierre, before you give them the bad news?"

"Mademoiselle, I don't know what you are talking about."

"Soon, I think," she said, and flipped the radio off before Pierre or Mission Control could reply.

* * *

"Was that wise?" Joe Bob Hooker asked, his voice deadly calm.

"So you think I'm crazy too."

"Charley, I don't know what to think. Frankly, I find it hard to believe that the man running a huge French expedition to the moon—the biggest space program in history—is off his rocker. All I have is your word for it."

She riveted her eyes on him. "Can you fly this thing?"

"Uh, no."

"Then I suggest you fix us some goo for dinner and stay out of my way. If I'm crazy, there's no telling what I might do."

Joe Bob opened and closed his mouth several times but decided that he didn't want to say anything. He removed his headset and unfastened his seat belt. He floated up and out of his chair and used the back of the copilot's seat as a launching pad.

In Mission Control, the French space minister listened to a replay of Charley's conversation with Pierre Artois. He didn't understand what they were discussing, and it was obvious they did not intend that he should. It was a private conversation with the whole world listening.

"*How much longer are you going to wait, Pierre, before you give them the bad news?*" What did that mean? What bad news? Certainly not the fact that Pine took the spaceplane—she knew that everyone knew about that. And what the devil was a beam generator?

The minister picked up the secure telephone and called the premier.

And was two minutes too late. The premier had heard the entire conversation on CNN.

"What is a beam generator?" the premier asked the minister.

"I do not know, sir."

"You are the man who is supposed to know. Find out and call me back."

THE PRESIDENT OF THE UNITED STATES WAS HAVING A QUIET afternoon in front of his television, sipping Diet Coke and munching barbecue potato chips. The White House pooch was asleep on the floor. The president had asked his staff to jiggle the schedule around so he could concentrate on the French crisis—he had told the press secretary to use precisely that phrase when talking to the working press: "the French crisis." You must admit, the phrase had a wonderful ring.

The president had his shoes and tie off when the television network began playing its tape of Charley and Artois' conversation.

When it was over he sat staring at the idiot box. He picked up the telephone. One of the secretaries answered it. "Get O'Reilly, the secretary of state, the director of the CIA, and the national security adviser. As soon as possible in my office."

"Yes, sir."

P.J. O'Reilly, the chief of staff, was the first man through the door. The dog growled, then went over to a corner to rearrange itself well out of O'Reilly's way. Brilliant, arrogant, utterly devoid of humor—and humanity, some said—O'Reilly was the most intensely political creature the president had ever had the misfortune to meet. No one liked him, not even the current Mrs. O'Reilly. One of his many enemies had said he had the soul of a lizard. With a résumé like that, the president thought, he was perfect for the job of chief of staff.

"I had the television on as background noise," O'Reilly told the president. "I heard it."

"Be nice if our spies knew what was going on in France."

"They don't," O'Reilly said bluntly. "And I don't think the French government has a clue either."

"Boy, I certainly would enjoy being a spy in France. It would beat the heck out of this job. Nice climate, great food, wonderful wine, beautiful women . . ." The president sighed wistfully. "Oh, well. What is a beam generator, anyway?"

"A searchlight would be my guess."

"Mine too. Or maybe a laser."

The president wriggled his toes and popped a potato chip into his mouth. After he swallowed it, he said, "Glad I'm not the premier of France." And he chuckled.

WHEN THE TELEPHONE IN HIS POCKET RANG AGAIN, RIP was on the porch with one of the state police lieutenants. "Excuse me a moment," he said. "I must take this call." He walked to the end of the porch and opened the cover of the phone.

"Hello."

"It's me."

"The police are here. We're certain the two dead kidnappers are French. One of them even had a French passport in his pocket."

"Pierre Artois sent them."

"How in hell did you get mixed up with that bastard?"

"I made a mistake. All right? Rip, I need your help."

"So does Egg."

"Have the police check bizjet flights to France. I can't see two Frenchmen holed up with Egg in a hideout in the Ozarks."

"Okay," he said briskly.

"Are you willing to help me?"

"This isn't Rent-a-Hero."

"I need you, Rip."

"Okay."

"And I need to hear you say it about me."

Rip Cantrell took a ragged breath. Well, there it was. Yes or no. *Do we go forward or rehash the past?* "I don't need someone who wanders off every time she gets bored or someone makes a better offer."

"I deserve that, I suppose."

"On the other hand, if I'd worked harder at being someone you wanted to be with, maybe you wouldn't have been bored."

"Yes."

"What say we get Egg back? When we get out of jail, we'll go on from there."

"Deal! But let's try to stay out of jail, for a little while, anyway. This is what I want to do." And she told him.

THE WARM GLOW OF TRIUMPH SUFFUSED JULIE ARTOIS AS she stood watching her husband and Claudine Courbet completing the final preparations for the testing of the antigravity beam. Henri Salmon stood beside her. There were three other men in the chamber, all engineers. The men had the dust covers off the telescope and beam generator; the reactor was producing power, and the computers calculating aimpoints and angles. Signals from the computer were gently moving the telescope and beam generator, aiming them. All the personnel were wearing space suits, although they had yet to don their helmets and pressurize the suits, and would not do so until they were ready to depressurize the chamber and roll back the roof cover.

Years of dreaming, scheming and planning were coming to fruition in the next few moments. The antigravity beam had been the final piece in the puzzle. A beam generator on the moon that could strike any spot on planet Earth was the ultimate weapon, against which the nations of the earth had no defense.

Finally, after eons of war, strife, starvation and disease, the rule of might makes right was going to be used for good. Henceforth she and Pierre were going to right the wrongs, cure the sick, feed the starving . . . lift mankind from the eternal struggle for every morsel to the enlightened benefits of a new civilization, one built on compassion for the needs of all.

Of course it would not be easy. Many would resist. Yet in human affairs the truth was indisputable: The ends do indeed occasionally justify the means. On the bright side, this would be the last great struggle. She and Pierre would lead mankind into a new and brighter tomorrow. Lead them kicking and screaming, but they were going—or they would die.

She was up to the task. *This* was her destiny.

Pierre, of course, thought it was his. Suffused with testosterone, the males of the species needed to believe in something, and being simple-minded fools, they usually believed in themselves. Every woman with a lick of sense understood that reality and worked with it. Pierre did as Julie wished him to do and believed it was his own idea. Watching Pierre now, Julie Artois smiled.

Her gaze switched to Courbet, and the smile faded. These engineers were true believers, but they lacked judgment. They would obey orders; they would have to, the stakes were too large. If they didn't— She became acutely aware of Salmon standing beside her. The man had an animal presence.

If they didn't obey, she would tell Salmon. He would fix things.

Julie Artois did not believe in heaven or hell or life after death. *This existence is all you get,* she mused. *This one short life is all you get to make your mark, to make life better for those who will come after.*

She was about to create an inferno that would forever change the nations of the world. Once the people of the earth saw the benefits of the new world order, it would become the new paradigm. National pride, war and the all-consuming, eternal quest for the all-mighty dollar would become ancient history. World peace would be her monument, and it would outlast the pyramids.

Her reverie came to an end when Pierre announced, "We are ready."

Claudine Courbet nodded her concurrence. She had helped design this entire installation. She seemed absorbed in the technical minutia and had personally supervised the connection of every cable and the testing of every component in the system. The success of the beam generator would be her triumph, Julie believed, against all those people who believed women were good for only one thing.

The people in the chamber donned their helmets, then pressurized their space suits and checked each other's suits. Pierre checked Julie's and he checked hers. Julie saw that he was smiling inside his helmet. He touched his helmet to hers and whispered, "This is the moment."

Men are truly amazing, she thought. He saw himself as Napoleon and her as his Josephine, when in reality she was Joan of Arc.

When everyone was ready, the depressurization of the cavern began. It took about five minutes to pump all the air out. When the pumps had extracted all the air they could, the overhead door was cracked open, allowing the last of the air to escape. Then the doors began their mechanical journey to the fully opened position. As they rolled back, sunlight at a low angle flooded one corner of the cavern. It was so bright that those who had forgotten to lower the sun visors on their helmets were dazzled by the brilliance.

Julie took two long steps to the beam generator and looked up. The earth hung in the black sky above like a round blue jewel, although one side was shaded in darkness.

With the door fully open, Pierre announced, "Let us begin."

One of the engineers manned the console that controlled the telescope. He brought up the picture on the monitor as Julie and Pierre watched. They found they were looking almost straight down at a brown landscape, a desert. The engineer used the computer to zoom in on the center of the picture. A square object was there, slightly off center. Even using star locators, the orientation of the telescope was not perfect, which was due to the inevitable manufacturing tolerances present in the gears and drives that aimed the device. Now the engineer aimed the telescope by hand, centering the square object, a building, in the crosshairs.

"Full charge on the capacitor," Courbet announced from her position at the main control console. Her voice was carried over an intercom system to each helmet by a wire. The transmissions from even a low-voltage radio system could have been picked up on earth, so the intercom system was hardwired.

Courbet slaved the beam generator to the signals from the telescope's servo drive, verified that it was aligned, then ordered everyone in the chamber to take a safety position. All involved moved behind the antimagnetic shield that had been erected between the beam generator and the main control console.

Pierre personally inspected the readouts, then gave the order. "Fire."

Courbet jabbed the red button on the console, discharging the capacitor to the beam generator.

Every person in the cavern felt the electrical charge, which tingled their skin and made the room glow with a blue light for several seconds. Then as suddenly as it had begun, it was over.

Claudine Courbet and Pierre Artois dashed to the telescope monitor and stared at the picture. The building in the crosshairs, a quarter million miles away, was not there anymore.

THE PRIVATE JET TOUCHED DOWN AT THE TONOPAH, Nevada, airport and taxied to the far end of a huge, crumbling concrete parking mat. Two four-wheel-drive vehicles drove up beside the airplane. Egg didn't recognize the airport, but he was fairly certain they were someplace in Nevada. A few old hangars were visible. From the size of the parking mat, he concluded that this was an old military base.

He had little time to look around before he was hustled straight into one of the vehicles. His hands were bound in front of him with a plastic tie, not too tight; no one had put a blindfold on him. Obviously they weren't worried about what he might tell law enforcement officials at some time in the future, if he had one.

The men who had kidnapped him had made several telephone calls while the jet was in flight, but they hadn't spoken to him. There were two of them, both fit men of about thirty. When they had something to say to each other, they said it in French, a language that Egg didn't speak. If they were grieving over their two colleagues who had died on the farm in Missouri, they hid it well. Occasionally they talked to the flight crew, but mainly they watched the news on a television monitor. They did share some food and offered Egg a glass of wine, which he accepted.

A few minutes after they snatched him, the kidnappers patted him down. They found his cell phone and threw it out a car window. Once they found it, they stopped searching. They apparently didn't expect him to have a concealed

weapon—and he didn't. Each of them did, however. Not that
Egg had much of a chance against two fit men twenty-five
years younger and seventy-five pounds lighter than he was.

One of the men sat in the backseat with Egg and the other
took the wheel of the SUV, which was, Egg thought, a
Chevrolet Tahoe. In seconds the Tahoe was under way with
the second vehicle following. As they drove away from the
airport on the access road, Egg saw the jet taking off.

The Tahoe was soon on the hard road, cruising at least
seventy-five miles per hour. Egg looked out the window a
while at the empty desert landscape and the distant mountains. Finally he slumped over, exhausted, and fell asleep.

The bumping and bouncing of the Tahoe over a dirt
road woke him. It was night. Egg announced he had to take
a leak, and the SUV stopped immediately. The man in the
backseat merely watched his back as Egg urinated beside
the car.

He was somewhere in the desert, he thought. There was a
decent breeze, and he could smell juniper, perhaps. Something with a dry, gentle scent. He glanced at the headlights
of the vehicle sitting behind his, then zipped up and climbed
back in the seat.

Thirty or so minutes later the Tahoe came to a gate in a
fence. The driver used a handheld radio, and soon a vehicle
approached the wire from the other side. The driver of Egg's
vehicle got out, went to the gate and talked. He came back as
the person on the other side opened the gate. The Tahoe
drove on through, then was again lost in the emptiness.

After another hour of this, a building loomed in the head-
lights. It was huge, with plain walls. An aircraft hangar. An
old one, from what he could see of it, with only a little paint
remaining on weathered boards.

The men got out of the car and gestured for Egg to do so
too. One of them led the way through a personnel door at

one end of the hangar that took them into an office of some sort. There was a man there, sitting behind a desk. He was in his forties, perhaps, with short red hair, faded freckles and a splotchy tan. He looked lean and ropy, as if he were too nervous to keep on weight or too busy to eat.

He stared at Egg Cantrell. "So you're the man, eh?"

Egg merely looked around at the wooden hangar walls, which hadn't seen paint since World War II. The desk was gray metal with a scarred top, the chairs metal and equally worn.

"Cut his hands loose," the man said to one of the Frenchmen, who took out a knife and did so. Apparently they spoke English after all.

As Egg massaged his wrists, the man pointed to a chair. "No, thanks. I've been sitting for hours."

"Yes. Well, I'll get right to it. We need your help. Last year you flew the flying saucer with your nephew. You've made quite a name for yourself since as an expert in saucer technology. We've got a saucer, and we want you to fly it for us."

Egg couldn't believe his ears. "*You* have one?"

"That's right."

"And who are you?"

The man said nothing.

Egg looked around, scrutinized every face, then pulled one of the chairs around and lowered himself onto it. "Maybe I should sit, after all. Where, may I ask, is your saucer?"

The man jerked a thumb over his shoulder. "In the hangar."

"Why the kidnapping? I think two men may have been severely injured—" He made a gesture. "If you had just sent me an e-mail I would have come charging out here as fast as the horses would run to take a look."

"There are a few complications," the man said dryly, "which we'll get into later, if you like. Suffice it to say that the need is urgent and there was no time to waste."

"I see."

"If you wish to look—" The man rose from his chair. He was tall, with large hands. He held one out to shake. "My name is Newton Chadwick."

8

THE OVERHEAD LIGHTS OF THE HANGAR WERE PINPOINTS in the accumulated dust on the saucer's dark skin. The floor was naked, cracked concrete covered with caked dirt and ancient oil stains. The windows high up on both ends of the building were coated with black paint. A few of the windows were broken, with panes missing. The lighting system was probably as old as the hangar; the entire place was poorly lit.

Egg Cantrell stood for a while taking everything in, then walked over to the saucer. He ran a hand along the top of the leading edge, wiping off dust. The skin was cool and smooth underneath and appeared black as the desert night.

His first impression was size. This saucer was larger than the one Rip had found in the Sahara, yet in all other ways it seemed identical. Same style legs, three of them, same canopy, same shape. He walked around it, examined the four rocket exhausts, looked at the maneuvering jet ports, ran his fingers along the leading edge, searching for dents or cuts or imperfections. And found none.

When he had circled the entire machine, he turned to face Newton Chadwick. "Want to tell me about it?"

Chadwick crossed his arms on his chest, then reached a hand up to feel the stubble on his chin. Finally he said, "It was found in New Mexico in 1947. The army moved it here. It's been sitting here ever since."

"You work for the government?"

Chadwick put both hands on the saucer and stood staring at it.

Egg lost his temper. "Come on, Chadwick. You aren't with the government—I know that. You had me kidnapped, two men are injured or dead, and you've had plenty of time to decide on your story. Get on with it or let me go. I've got better things to do than stand here in this filthy old hangar in the middle of the night surrounded by thugs."

"I was here in 1947 when they brought it on a train. Was working for the government evaluating Nazi rocket research. I was young then, just a kid. They only let us in the saucer for a day, one lousy day, before the cowards in Washington ordered us back to Florida and the saucer sealed and stored. I stole a computer out of it."

Egg laughed, a harsh bark. "You expect me to believe that? 1947 was fifty-seven years ago. Man, you are at least thirty years too young!"

Chadwick turned to face Egg and grinned wolfishly. "You've been looking at the database on that computer you took out of the Sahara saucer for at least a year. You know what's on it. Don't tell me I'm too young."

Egg stared at the man before him.

Chadwick took a step closer. "And don't tell me you weren't tempted. I *know* you were. How do you suppose people lived through a voyage across interstellar space?" He laughed long and loud with his head back as the French thugs stood and watched, then answered his own question. "They injected themselves with a drug that stopped the aging process, of course. It took years, but I finally got the manufacturing process right. I've been taking it for thirty years." His voice rose in pitch and volume. "I'm seventy-nine years old," he shouted, and slapped the saucer in glee.

"All these years I tried to sell technology from that computer. The American government listed me as an international fugitive—they even sent men to kill me. Don't deny it—I know it's true. So I couldn't just walk into a drug company and say, 'Hello, my name is Newton Chadwick and I have discovered a youth serum.' Oh, no! I couldn't walk into Boeing or Grumman or Aerospatiale and say, 'I'm John Doe and I have discovered how to reverse the polarity of gravity.' I couldn't walk into the University of Heidelberg and say, 'I'm Albert Einstein's bastard son and I have discovered the Grand Unified Theory, the theory that combines relativity, quantum mechanics and gravity, the theory of everything, the theory that explains the entire physical world.' Oh, nooooooo!"

His howl filled the hangar, startling a bird from its roost among the rafters.

Chadwick paused to breathe deeply and calm himself as the bird squawked and flapped its wings above their heads. Finally, in a normal, conversational voice, he leaned toward Egg Cantrell and said, "So I went to Pierre Artois, who was dreaming of building a base on the moon, and showed him what I knew. He believed me. He had faith. He *understood!* No one else ever had! But Pierre did." He paused, nodding, and added, "Yes, he did." He stared into Egg's eyes. "You believe me too, don't you?"

"If the government had this saucer squirreled away, how'd you get to it?"

"With money. Someone always wants money. The amazing thing is how little it takes to get what you want."

Chadwick nodded, turned back to the saucer and put his hands upon it. "So," he said. "So, that's where we are."

"And that is?" Egg asked.

"You have flown a saucer," Newton Chadwick said as he caressed the saucer's cold, black skin, smearing the dust. "I haven't. You and I and several of these men are going to fly this saucer to the moon."

"I don't know where you got your information, Chadwick, but you are wrong. I haven't flown a saucer—I've flown in one. I've flown in airliners too, but I never flew one. Surely even a man as full of it as you are can understand the distinction."

Chadwick faced Egg again. "I sent these incompetents to get your nephew, Rip, but they brought you back instead. You'll have to do. You and I are going to the moon in this saucer or you're going to hell—real soon."

Egg took a deep breath. "Sounds as if you want to go to hell with me."

"The moon, Mr. Cantrell. We are going to the moon."

IT WAS THE EVENING OF THE FOLLOWING DAY IN PARIS when Pierre Artois made his announcement. He broadcast it over an open frequency, where it was heard and recorded by the world's news organizations and immediately rebroadcast worldwide on television and radio.

On the moon, Artois announced, he had the ultimate weapon, an antigravity beam generator, which he would use for the betterment of all mankind. World peace was not going to arrive someday; it was here now, and he intended to enforce it. Henceforth the governments of the world would serve only at his pleasure, following policies of which he approved. Weapons of war were obsolete and would be destroyed. All nations would live in peace, their differences arbitrated by a commission that he appointed. Criminals and enemies of mankind would be dealt with summarily.

As evidence of their good faith, all the governments of the world must, within forty-eight hours, renounce their sovereignty and swear allegiance to the new world order, which Artois and his lieutenants would enforce.

As his proclamation circled the globe electronically, governments around the world met to confer. In Paris the premier had some choice words for the minister of space, whose incompetence had allowed this Artois maniac to transport himself, his henchmen and his weapon to the moon at the expense, primarily, of French taxpayers. The minister submitted his immediate resignation and stalked out of the premier's office. The premier found that the minister's departure did not improve the situation a detectable amount, but it made the premier feel better.

After an emergency meeting of the House of Commons, the British prime minister stood resolutely in front of television cameras and defiantly told Pierre Artois to "bugger off." Ten minutes later the Tower of London rose swiftly from its foundations in a cloud of stone and brick that was lifted almost a thousand feet in the air; then the fragments rained down on the city of London and the Thames. Fifteen minutes after that one wing of Buckingham Palace was destroyed in a similar manner.

While these spectacular feats of demolition were playing on television, the American president huddled in the Oval Office with O'Reilly, the secretary of state, the director of the CIA, the national security adviser, the secretary of defense and the Joint Chiefs of Staff.

"What can we do to thwart this maniac?" the president demanded. He looked at the uniformed generals, scanning each face.

The chairman of the Joint Chiefs, an army four-star, pulled at his tie. "Uh, in the short term, nothing, sir. Given enough time, we can mount a nuclear warhead on a rocket and shoot it at the lunar base. If Artois doesn't destroy it with his beam weapon before it gets there, it should do the trick nicely."

"How long would that take?"

The chairman's eyebrows rose while he considered. "Oh, six months or so, I would imagine."

"Six months?"

"Maybe more."

In the disappointed silence that followed that comment, the secretary of state said, "Actually a world government isn't such a bad idea."

O'Reilly looked at her in stupified amazement.

She continued, "Someday we'll have a world government, with or without Pierre Artois. Why not start now? Artois won't last forever. In fact, one suspects he won't last long." She rubbed her hands and continued enthusiastically, "We can tackle global warming, third world starvation, universal medical care, the equitable redistribution of the world's wealth—"

"Holy moly!" O'Reilly said, interrupting. "You're suggesting we rescind the Declaration of Independence and tear up the United States Constitution. If I may indulge in understatement, I don't think the electorate is quite ready for that bold step, Madam Secretary."

"I don't think that Artois intends to give the American electorate a choice in the matter," the lady retorted tartly.

"And you want to take advantage of that happy fact. You remind me of a bystander watching a robbery who decides to help himself after the clerk is tied up."

"That's outrageous," the secretary shot back.

While she and O'Reilly squabbled the telephone rang. The president picked it up, listened a moment, grunted, then put the instrument back on its cradle. After silencing the pugilists, he announced, "Artois has just zapped one of the space shuttles at Cape Canaveral. It rose five hundred feet in the air and fell back to earth. NASA thinks they may be able to salvage some of the smaller parts."

"We should probably evacuate the White House," the national security adviser advised. "Artois will undoubtedly target it too."

The president frowned. "Artois isn't going to go after this government until he learns we have no intention of surrendering. We have a few hours yet."

The secretary of state was plainly appalled. "You intend to let this maniac hurt innocent people?"

"I have no intention of surrendering the United States to anyone or anything, madam. Not now, not ever. At my inauguration I swore to support and defend the Constitution of the United States, and I intend to do just that. If Artois harms a single American, that is his choice, not mine."

The president shifted his gaze to the Joint Chiefs and national security adviser. "Presumably Artois doesn't intend to rule earth from the moon. As I recall, there are only four spaceplanes capable of making round trips. Charley Pine stole one from the lunar base, and the other three are in France. Target them. I want bombers aloft, over the Atlantic, twenty-four hours a day, ready to cross into French airspace and destroy those spaceplanes on ten minutes' notice. Place submerged submarines off the western and southern coasts of France. Have them target the spaceplanes with cruise missiles. Those spaceplanes are not to leave the ground."

"You're going to attack France?" the secretary of state asked disbelievingly.

The president didn't answer right away. He was apparently taking the time to choose his words carefully when the secretary of state, unable to wait for his answer, broke the silence.

"I strongly suggest consulting with Congress before we do anything rash."

"We try to never do anything rash," O'Reilly shot back, obviously miffed.

The president didn't let those two get into another squabble. "Artois may be a tool of the French government," he said. "He may actually be following orders." The president toyed with a pen on his desk. "Even if he is a rogue, he must have many allies in the French space agency. In any event, it is plain that he thinks the French government will cave. I suspect he's right."

The president cast a cold eye on his audience. "Regardless of what happens anywhere else, the British will never surrender, and of course we won't. Artois may cause a great deal of havoc, but he isn't getting any supplies from earth or a ride home from the moon without my permission."

The president smiled. The secretary of state had never liked his smile, and she didn't like this one.

The president glanced at the Joint Chiefs. "Let's not waste any more time, gentlemen. I want those bombers armed and airborne as soon as humanly possible. I want a plan on my desk within the next two hours that tells me precisely how many hours it will be before we have the bombers and subs in position to destroy those spaceplanes."

"Yes, sir!"

"Madam Secretary, I suggest you pop over to the State Department and work the phones. Keep me advised." He shooed her out.

When only the president and O'Reilly were left in the room, the president stood and stretched. "After the military destroys those spaceplanes, I'll make a televised address to the American people. We'll dither until then. In the meantime get the congressional leaders over here and consult with them. Have the speechwriters do a draft of the speech."

He started for the door before adding as an afterthought, "After the speech Artois may zap the White House. Better get the staff and the valuable paintings out. Don't let the television people see you doing it."

"Yes, sir. What should the press secretary tell the press in the interim?"

"We're consulting with allies, congressional leaders, talking to the UN, all that stuff."

"In other words, nothing."

"That's usually best."

"Where will you be if we need to find you?"

The president looked at his watch. "I think I'll go to the gym and work out. Call me when you have a draft of that speech ready for me to look at."

O'Reilly looked at his watch, then his notebook, which he carried everywhere. "You have an appointment in ten minutes with a *Sports Illustrated* reporter who wants to know if you think baseball should reinstate Pete Rose."

"Ah, the burning question of our time. Tell him I'm meditating on the matter and reschedule."

"May we say cogitating or ruminating?"

"Meditating. It makes me sound smarter."

NEWTON CHADWICK AND THE FRENCHMEN HUDDLED around a radio in the dilapidated hangar in the Nevada desert, listening to the news of Pierre Artois' announcement. They had rigged an antenna on top of the building and were tuned to a station in Reno.

Egg listened from his perch on a crate of canned food in the back of the room.

An antigravity beam weapon! On the moon. Egg scrutinized Newton Chadwick, who was hanging intently on every word from the radio. Yep, without a doubt, Chadwick gave or sold Artois the technology, which was right out of that saucer in the middle of the hangar—Egg would have bet every last dollar he ever hoped to get on that proposition.

And Artois intended to conquer the world. Egg knew he was the only person in the room to whom that was news. Chadwick and the Frenchmen were excited, intense. They looked like athletes on a team that was several touchdowns ahead.

So what else did Chadwick give Artois? The youth serum?

It wasn't a serum, really, but a gene blocker. The chemical latched on to the aging gene that was present in every human cell and inhibited its functioning. When he had first discovered it in his saucer computer, Egg had been so excited he couldn't sleep. Medical researchers were today attempting to find a formula that would affect the aging gene so that they could come up with some way to attack the diseases aging caused, diseases such as Alzheimer's, senility, diabetes and Parkinson's. Egg was ready to call them up, give them the formula.

Yet the more he thought about it, the less he liked the idea. Someone would undoubtedly realize the economic value of such a drug, and the vision of fantastic wealth would be irresistible. Listening to the announcer translate Artois' demands and the reaction of governments around the world to them, Egg thought about the impact upon human life—upon all life on this planet—that the ready availability of such a drug would have. The demand for the drug would distort the world's economy, the death rate would plummet, and the population would explode in a Malthusian nightmare that would crowd out other life forms and destroy civilization.

When Egg added it up, the human conquest of death didn't seem like a red hot idea. So he had said nothing to anyone about it, not even Rip or Charley. Nor had he been tempted, like Chadwick, to make a small batch of the drug for himself. He had perhaps two or three decades of life left, and that was enough. When his time came, he would be ready for the next adventure.

So Chadwick wanted to go to the moon. That figured. Charley Pine had stolen the only spaceplane on the moon; the other three might be destroyed or damaged at any moment, leaving Artois and his crew marooned high and dry. Obviously Artois was betting that Chadwick could deliver, that he could get the saucer there.

Egg shook his head, trying to clear his mind of extraneous thoughts. If he didn't take Chadwick where he wanted to go in the saucer in the hangar, this crowd would kill him and go after Rip. Artois had to have a ride home, and no doubt he would do whatever he could to get one.

He had inspected the saucer carefully. It looked intact, as well preserved as the one Rip had found in the Sahara. Larger than Rip's saucer, it had more capacity to carry water. Of course, it also weighed more. Still, rough calculations indicated that it should be able to reach the moon and land there. Once there, however, it would have to be refueled with water to make the return trip to earth. Was there enough water on the moon?

Egg had asked Chadwick that question and had received a curt nod. Yes.

Well, Chadwick had better be right or there were going to be more people stranded up there, Egg included.

The reactor seemed intact; it wasn't leaking radiation. Egg had checked with a Geiger counter. The main flight computer was installed, the headbands were there, the hatch seals seemed intact—he had checked everything that he could. As far as he could determine, the saucer was ready to fly.

He hadn't told Chadwick that, though. He had more things to check, he had said, which gave him more time to think, to come up with the right course of action.

Could he fly the saucer?

He knew how Charley and Rip had done it, but Charley was a highly skilled test pilot, and Rip was—well, he was fearless and a quick thinker, and he had flown repeatedly with Charley before he gave it a try. Egg had had exactly one ride.

Hoo boy!

CHARLEY PINE CRACKED HER KNUCKLES AFTER SHE FINished programming and checking the navigational computer. She ran through the program twice to make sure she had it right, went over the checklist one more time, then stowed the checklist, sighed and cracked her knuckles.

"You'll give yourself arthritis doing that," Joe Bob Hooker said. He was sitting in the right seat, watching.

"Doing what?"

"Cracking your knuckles."

"Oh," she said, vaguely surprised. "I've been trying to stop that. Bad habit."

Jeanne d'Arc was in low earth orbit, and had been for two days. The television monitor behind the pilots' seats picked up broadcasts as the spaceplane came over the horizon and lost them about ten minutes later when the stations sank behind the orbiting ship. Sometimes the signal faded just as the commercials came on, but it seemed that most of the time Charley and Joe Bob got all the commercials and lost the signal in the middle of some significant pronouncement by a political leader.

The snatches of news were clear enough; Pierre was causing havoc with the antigravity beam and making demands. France was in meltdown, it seemed. A great many Frenchmen were ready to march behind the Artois banner; they were loudly demanding the government accede to Pierre's demands. The small nations of Europe, with token military forces without any real combat power, were making noises, but not threats. Charley Pine got the impression that a lot of the elected persons were merely wringing their hands, waiting.

Everyone was waiting on the United States, which so far had taken no official position. The press secretary said the government was "studying" the matter. Indeed, the press reported that everyone who was anyone in official Washington had trotted over to the White House for consultations, but no one was saying anything for the record to the press. Oh, sure, there were the usual leaks and rumors, but nothing official.

"Where is the president?" one commentator asked rhetorically.

Joe Bob Hooker thought the political theater very entertaining, and watched by the hour as *Jeanne d'Arc* circled the earth and Charley Pine catnapped in the pilot's seat. But now the waiting was over. Charley had programmed the navigation computer for reentry and made a last inspection tour through the ship ensuring all gear was properly stowed, and now the minutes were ticking down.

The autopilot turned the ship, lining it up so that it was flying backward with its rocket engines pointing dead ahead. Charley wondered about the main engine. If it wouldn't start, the computer would automatically fire the other engines longer and adjust the reentry flight path accordingly. As long as the other four rocket engines worked!

"I want to thank you," Joe Bob said, "for the adventure of a lifetime."

Charley smiled. "I had nothing to do with it. Write a letter to Pierre Artois."

"Seriously, flying with you is the adventure of a lifetime. Selling cars will never be the same."

All four of the smaller engines ignited on cue, to

Charley's intense relief, and the deceleration Gs mashed her back into her seat. Joe Bob Hooker abandoned his attempts at conversation.

When the burn was over, the autopilot gently turned the free-falling spaceplane 180 degrees, until she was pointed along her trajectory like a large arrowhead. As Charley and Joe Bob sat watching, *Jeanne d'Arc* plunged silently downward toward the Earth's atmosphere.

THE FIXED-GEAR, HIGH-WINGED CESSNA 182 BUZZED LOW over the tops of the mountain ridges. In the pilot's seat Rip Cantrell scanned the sky, and occasionally glanced at the instruments to ascertain the health of the single piston engine. High clouds obscured the sky to the west, the pre-cursors of a front that was moving eastward, yet the sky over-head was clear except for a high, thin, gauzy layer of cirrus.

Rip glanced at his watch again and checked the fuel. He had been airborne for an hour and had plenty remaining, yet—

He had been cruising north along the ridge; now he turned south. He throttled back even more and leaned the mixture a tad, trying to save another gallon.

There, in the sky to the west, under the clouds a speck. He watched it intently. He had already been fooled twice, once by an airliner and once by a jet fighter.

The speck was high and descending.

Rip turned eastward, toward the stupendous expanse of salt flats that lay west of the Great Salt Lake, and rapped the mixture and throttle controls forward.

The spaceplane was ten or fifteen thousand feet above him when it passed overhead, descending steeply in a power-less glide. He had the nose down, the throttle and prop con-trols full forward as *Jeanne d'Arc* broke her long glide ten miles ahead of him and, with the nose well down, turned 180 degrees and lined up for a landing to the west, into the wind.

The spaceplane leveled its wings, descended steadily and flared just before the wheels touched the salt. A plume of dust rose behind it and tailed away to the east—Charley Pine had guessed right on the wind. *Jeanne d'Arc* rolled and rolled until she came to a complete stop.

INSIDE THE SPACEPLANE'S COCKPIT, CHARLEY PINE looked at Joe Bob Hooker and said, "Welcome back to earth."

Joe Bob threw back his head and laughed. "Oh, man, have I got a tale for the grandkids! If you ever get to Dallas . . ."

Charley was the first out of her seat. She almost fell on her face after the days of weightlessness, broken only by the weak gravity of the moon and occasional bursts of rocket power. Hanging on to whatever she could reach, she carefully made her way aft. The door that she had entered on the moon was the one she wanted, so she set to work releasing the pressure on the seals and opening it. It opened with a hiss.

The cool autumn air enveloped her. It smelled of salty earth and cooked brake pads—well, she did push vigorously on the brakes after she touched down. Wispy contrails floating in that high autumn sky made streaks in the gauzy cirrus. She filled her lungs and exhaled slowly. This certainly wasn't Kansas, but Dorothy Gale was right: There is no place like home.

By leaning out slightly and bending down she could see one of the right main landing gear's wheels. It hadn't sunk more than an inch or two into the salt. She had been worried about the salt's consistency—if it had been too soft, it could have torn the landing gear right off *Jeanne d'Arc*, which would have skidded to a quick stop on her belly, shattered beyond repair. She knew it was hard enough the instant she touched down, yet visual confirmation of her pilot's sense was nice.

Satisfied, she didn't waste any more time. She went to the locker room where the space suits were kept and brought hers back to the door. She tossed it out. There were three extra suits stored in the ship, just in case one of the fitted suits sprang a leak or was damaged during use. She threw them out the door onto the growing pile.

Joe Bob Hooker was there at the door when she made her last trip. "Why the suits?" he asked.

"You never know when you'll need a space suit," she replied, and tossed the air compressor and suit-testing equipment on top of the pile.

He went back for his and threw it out too. "Paid for it," he explained. "I'll strut around in it at Lions Club."

She had to help him down, then tossed his small bag of personal items to him. Then she jumped. She fell heavily and bruised herself.

She arose, dizzy and hurting, and brushed the salt from her sleeves and rump as the wind from distant mountains played with her hair. Eight days away from the earth's gravity and she was weak, as if she were recovering from a long illness.

Charley heard the Cessna before she saw it. It came out from behind the wing, already on the salt, and taxied up. Rip grinned and waved.

"Here's my ride," she said to Joe Bob. "You're going to have to wait for a while, but someone will be along pretty soon."

"I reckon somebody saw us land," Joe Bob said, scanning the seemingly endless expanse of empty, flat salt.

Rip killed the engine of the little plane and jumped out. He rushed over to Charley and enveloped her in his arms. When he came up for air, he whispered, "Missed you, lady."

"Oh, Rip—"

"Here comes someone now," Joe Bob said, pointing. A plume of dust was rising from the vast dirty-white expanse, still miles away. It looked as if it might be a car, or perhaps an SUV.

"Let's load the suits and get out of Dodge," Charley said to Rip.

They were in the Cessna taxiing when a police car rolled to a stop beside the spaceplane. Charley waved at the officer, a woman, while Rip reset the trim and eased the throttle in. The plane gathered speed and lifted off. Rip turned to the southeast.

Charley sat looking at *Jeanne d'Arc* as long as she was visible. As they flew away, the ship seemed to shrink on the endless expanse of salt, under the huge, high autumn sky. She looked small, almost toylike. Hard to believe she had flown to the moon and back.

The Cessna hummed loudly and bumped along in light turbulence. It was certainly real enough. Charley reached for Rip's arm, felt the firmness of his muscles. Rip grinned at her. "Welcome home," he said over the song of the engine.

She kissed him again.

9

JEANNE D'ARC'S FIERY PLUNGE INTO THE EARTH'S ATMO-
sphere was monitored by Space Command, which projected
that the ship's flight path would impact at the Bonneville
Salt Flats in Utah. The news was flashed to the Pentagon and
the White House while the spaceplane was still miles high,
descending. The news should have made a huge splash at
the White House, but today, of all days, the government of
France was in chaos. The news of the spaceplane's return
didn't even reach the brain trust that surrounded the president.

In Paris the cabinet ministers were in conference behind
closed doors. The networks had live feeds featuring
reporters in front of the doors with nothing to report but
speculation and the hourly communiqué from Pierre Artois,
demanding responses to his nonnegotiable demands. The
CIA had no idea what was going on in Paris. If the British
knew, they weren't telling.

The U.S. ambassador to France was huddled with his mistress, who had a brother who worked as a janitor in the

French parliament building. Every now and then one of the politicians visited the men's room where the brother was pretending to work and commented on this or that. The brother telephoned his sister, who told it to the ambassador, who flashed the comment to the State Department in Washington, where it was passed to the White House for the president and his advisers to ponder.

Periodically news of another French municipal or national monument rising abruptly into the sky, only to return to earth in ruins, was announced on television by breathless reporters. Enterprising producers ordered camera crews to set up in front of likely monuments in the hope that they could broadcast an attack from the moon as it happened. Pictures of rubble after the event had less dramatic impact.

In various places around the world the crisis was denounced as a hoax. The ayatollahs in Iran refused to discuss Artois' demands or allow news about them to be aired on television. Much of the Islamic world followed suit and buried their heads in the sand. On the moon, Pierre didn't have time just now to whip the little countries into line. He would get to them later. His priorities were France, then Europe, the United States, Japan and China. If he could get the big nations to fall into line, the rest, he thought, would have to follow.

Pierre had done his homework. He began making promises. Universal health care, universal employment, free care for the sick and elderly, free drugs (the medicinal kind), and free food for everyone on the planet were some of the major benefits that would accrue to all who followed his banner. "Together," he said, "free from the petty squabbles that have embroiled mankind since the dawn of recorded history, we can solve the world's problems and build a better life for people all over the globe." Needless to say, Pierre didn't talk about the messy details that he would have to handle to deliver his utopia, nor where the assets would come from to fund the free goodies.

Public debate broke out all over the English-speaking world. In Great Britain and across America political outcasts, conspiracy theorists, religious zealots and crackpots of every stripe accused the government—always their own government—of manufacturing a crisis to cover up something. The political opposition in every democracy on the planet was having a field day. Every spy agency in the world had overlooked a virulent, malignant conspiracy embedded in the French space agency. Even worse was the possibility that the spymasters had detected it and the governments involved failed to act, or were now reacting inappropriately. Political rivals postured, investigations were called for, resignations demanded, jail terms threatened.

All this was marvelous public theater and played out against a backdrop of antigravity beam strikes from the moon, with which Pierre Artois tried to silence the critics and extort capitulations from the various governments.

The French government decided to surrender when the first cathedral went up in a beam and came back to earth in a rain of stone and rubble.

The secretary of state rushed into the Oval Office to deliver the news to the president and the assembled national security types. "The premier says he has no choice," she reported. "Artois is threatening to destroy Paris."

"Buildings and monuments are just stone and mortar," the president replied, "even cathedrals. They can be rebuilt."

"Paris is the soul of France, its legacy to all the generations to come," the secretary of state explained. Talking to the president was always difficult, she knew all too well, because he was so obtuse. The voters had a lot to answer for.

She forced herself to say calmly, "France is not like other

countries. France is . . . inhabited by the French. Don't you understand? Innocent people might be killed, Paris—the most beautiful city on earth—destroyed, laid waste. The French government has no choice, none at all."

The president's tone never changed. "If the premier surrenders France to that madman, we'll nuke Paris. For the next thousand years the only living things in the rubble will be radioactive beetles. Tell him that."

All conversation in the room came to a dead stop.

The secretary was horrified. "My God! I can't believe you said that! Surely you wouldn't!" She stared at the president, who returned her scrutiny without expression.

"Get on the phone," he urged, finally, to get her moving. "Tell the premier what I said."

She dashed from the room. Conversation slowly began again.

"Uh-oh," O'Reilly whispered to the president. "We're in real trouble now. She thinks you would really do it. She'll repeat that comment to every reporter she knows. It'll be the headline in the *Washington Post* tomorrow."

"Explain to me again why she is the secretary of state."

"You wanted a bipartisan cabinet, and State was the only office she would accept."

"In a country infested with politicians, I picked that one. Sometimes I dazzle myself with my own stupidity."

Twenty minutes later the television had a live feed from Paris of the premier surrendering to Artois.

"That tears it," the president said to O'Reilly. He wadded up the latest communiqué from the men's room of the French capital and threw it into the wastebasket beside his desk. "How much longer until we can whack those space-planes?"

"It will be at least another twenty-four hours, sir. We don't have any carriers in position, and the submarines are still well out of range."

"How about a B-2 strike?"

"It's already dark in France," the chairman of the Joint Chiefs replied. "We can't get B-2s there until tomorrow night unless you want to send them in daylight, in which case the French may shoot down one or two."

The darn B-2s cost over a billion bucks apiece, the president knew, but were defenseless against enemy fighters and vulnerable to them during the day. Taking a chance that the French air force might drop a few into the French countryside didn't seem wise. "Tomorrow night," the president agreed reluctantly, "unless the Brits can do it sooner. Ask them."

"Do we really want the British to fire the first shot?" the national security adviser asked. He was thinking of the reaction of Joe Six-Pack out there in the American heartland. Joe would want America to lead the charge.

The secretary of state returned to the Oval Office in time to hear that exchange. "This entire discussion is outrageous," she declared heatedly. "The French are our oldest allies. They have been forced to surrender to a terrorist; now you intend to stab them in the back. If you attack France, I must resign my office. I'll have no part in this."

"We'll be sorry to see you go," O'Reilly shot back. "But before you leave, please tell us: Did you deliver the president's ultimatum to the French premier?"

"I did, and of course he refused to believe me." She made a dismissive gesture. "He said you would never destroy Paris, but Artois would."

The president sighed. Unfortunately he had recently announced that he would run for reelection. He realized that he should probably reconsider. He flipped listlessly

through a marked-up copy of his speech, which the leaders of Congress were demanding he deliver right now, if not sooner. His eyes went to a photo of a Montana trout stream that hung upon the wall. Sunlight glistened upon the water, and distant mountains wore a crown of snow.

"Why me, Lord?" he muttered.

"YOU'VE BEEN STUDYING THIS SHIP'S COMPUTER FOR FIFTY-plus years," Egg Cantrell said to Newton Chadwick. "Why don't you fly it?" They were in the saucer's main machinery space checking the integrity of fittings.

"I'm not a pilot."

"Nor am I."

"Each of us has his gifts, Cantrell. Mine isn't—I couldn't do it. I know that. I don't have the disposition for it. I'm impulsive and tend to get excited about things."

"I've noticed that."

"You're going to do the flying. If you get there, we will too."

"There's faith for you," Egg muttered, then changed the subject. "Do you really think enslaving the world's population is a good idea?"

"Most people are sheep," Chadwick replied flippantly. "They are better off if they do as they're told."

"This freedom thing sorta passed you by, I see."

"We don't need to waste time on philosophy, Cantrell. Starving people need food, sick people need medicine, everyone needs clean water and air. Freedom works great for the rich, not so good for everyone else."

"The fervor of your humanitarianism surprises me. I thought the only person you cared about was Newton Chadwick."

"I don't care what you think."

"Nor what anyone else thinks, apparently."

"Pierre Artois and I are going to give everyone a shot at a decent life."

"Give?"

"We're going to rearrange the social order, Mr. Cantrell. Call it what you will. Everyone will be better off."

"Including you."

"Including me," Newton Chadwick agreed. "Now let's top off the water tank and fly to the moon."

"I haven't finished preflighting. Crashing and dying in this big Frisbee would be a tragic waste of all that work you put into making youth serum."

"You've got one hour," Chadwick said. "Not a minute more." He crawled out of the space. Egg heard him drop through the main hatch to the hangar floor.

He looked though the open hatchway at the man sitting in the pilot's seat, who was looking back at Egg. He was one of the men who kidnapped him. Today he was wearing a pistol on his belt and had a short submachine gun draped over his shoulder. Terrific!

Egg moved out of the man's sight and sat contemplating his rounded middle.

IT WAS LATE AFTERNOON AT THE AIRPORT IN GRAND JUNC-tion, Colorado, when Rip and Charley landed and taxied to a stop in front of the small general aviation terminal. He and Charley Pine stood under the awning near the building wrapped in a serious embrace, getting reacquainted, while the line boy fueled the Cessna 182 from a truck. Rip had wanted to do this ever since he saw her, but the little plane lacked an autopilot.

Charley had talked for the entire two hours of the flight to Grand Junction, telling Rip of her adventures on the moon. At one point, after describing Artois' antigravity beam generator, she said, "I can't believe French scientists invented it. It's a derivation of the antigravity technology in the saucer you found, but they've been working on theirs for several years, at least."

"There must be another saucer somewhere," Rip said. "One we don't know about."

"That's the most likely explanation," she agreed. "But where?"

They left that subject and discussed her decision to escape. It seemed important to have Rip tell her she had done the right thing. He did that, but still, she thought, it wasn't enough. The people on the moon were stranded. It would cost a large fortune to fly *Jeanne d'Arc* to France, then back to the moon, and the French space ministry would probably sue her for every dime. The world had only her word for it that Pierre was a megalomaniac—and guess who the reporters would believe.

She had Rip, and he sure knew how to kiss, but boy oh boy.

They followed the line boy into the one-story building after he finished fueling the Cessna. Four men and a woman were huddled around a television in one corner of the room watching the news. The woman reluctantly left the set and came over to the counter to ring up the sale and process Rip's credit card. She was in her forties, wearing a no-nonsense sweater and jeans.

"Anything new?" Rip asked, referring to the international situation.

"The French have surrendered to Pierre Artois. He is the new emperor of France. Now they're trying to persuade the rest of Europe to also surrender."

A beatific smile split Charley Pine's face. Suddenly the load felt a hundred pounds lighter. She wasn't going to have to prove to anyone that Artois was crazy; now everyone on earth knew it. The smile faded, though, when she realized that if he became emperor of the world, she might have to look for a way to get off. He hadn't impressed her as the forgive-and-forget type.

"And the Americans?" Rip asked.

"Nothing out of Washington. I think they're hunkered down, waiting to see which way the wind is blowing." The desk person looked at the one-piece flight suit that Charley was wearing and said, "Isn't that something like the French astronauts wear?"

"I think so," Charley replied innocently. "I ordered it over the Internet. They said it was very authentic."

"Probably made in China," the desk lady said languidly, and glanced at the name on Rip's credit card. "Cantrell. Same name as the saucer guy. Don't you wish you were?"

"Oh, you bet," Rip shot back. "Money, hot women, fame— I don't know how he stands it."

The woman waited until the credit card machine spit out the slip, then slapped it on the counter for Rip to sign. "Too bad he gave that flying plate to the Air and Space Museum. If he had it now he could go after that clown on the moon."

"Umm," Rip Cantrell said, and signed the credit card slip.

When they were walking out to the plane, Charley said to Rip, "How *do* you stand it?"

"My low IQ is the only thing that keeps me sane."

She squeezed his hand.

"The whole world is going nuts," Rip said, "so it's up to us to rescue Egg."

"I just hope he's okay," Charley Pine replied. She was so tired, it was difficult to concentrate. She yawned. "You fly this leg, Rip." She crawled into the second set of seats and stretched out as Rip preflighted the plane, ensured the fuel caps were on tight and pulled chocks.

EGG CANTRELL AND NEWTON CHADWICK STUDIED A MAP of the moon that they had spread on the leading edge of the saucer. Egg noted that it was published by National Geographic. "The lunar base is right there," Chadwick said, marking the map with a pen. He put a dot on the base and drew a circle around it.

Then he brought out a Nevada highway map, one distributed free by the state. He studied it a bit and put an ink mark smack inside a federal prohibited area. "We're right here."

"Okay," Egg said, folding the maps and placing them in his hip pocket. "I guess I'm as ready as I'll ever be. This is your last chance to back out and live to a ripe old age."

Chadwick ignored that last comment. "Open the hanger door," he told one of the flunkies, then repeated the order in French. The two men who had kidnapped Egg were already in the saucer.

Egg got down on his hands and knees and crawled under the saucer to the personnel hatch. A less bulky man could just bend over and walk there, as Chadwick did behind him.

Once everyone was inside, Egg closed the hatch and ensured it was latched, then checked that the food cartons the Frenchies had loaded were properly stowed against the rear bulkhead of the passenger compartment and secured with bungee cords. Cartons of full water bottles, squirt lids, plastic baby bottles full of pureed goo. Bet the Frenchmen had fun shopping for this stuff! There were even four space suits, flown in from France. Egg had tried on the largest—it was a tight squeeze, but he got in it.

Fortunately this large saucer contained a head, one designed to be used in zero gravity. And there was plenty of room in the passenger compartment—although if all the people on the moon tried to return in this ship it was going to be impossibly crowded.

The moon! Here we go!

Egg climbed into the pilot's seat, which was on a pedestal in front of the instrument panel. Chadwick stood beside him, watching the men struggling with the hangar doors, which consisted of a half dozen very large panels on rollers.

"They haven't been opened in many years," he muttered.

While the men were struggling with the doors, Egg pulled the red knob on the panel to the first detent. The computer displays in front of him came to life, just as the displays had in Rip's saucer. He studied them. The displays looked as he remembered them, but it had been what, thirteen or fourteen months?

He picked up the computer headband and placed it on his head, adjusting the strap so that it would stay there.

He said *Hello* to the computer, and asked for the launch display.

This part, at least, was familiar. He had spent much of the past year talking to a computer just like this one.

Relieved, he wiped the perspiration from his brow with his hands, then wiped his hands on his trousers.

"They can't get the door open," Chadwick said. Egg looked. The two men working the door had the first large panel open about ten feet, but the wheels were rusty. The door panels seemed to be stuck.

Do we have enough fuel? Egg asked the computer.

The display appeared before him. Yes.

Hull integrity, reactor temp, hydrogen pressure, oxygen?

The displays flashed before him as quickly as the thought passed through his mind.

He glanced outside. The men were hooking up one of the vehicles to the door with a towing chain. They were going to drag it open.

Egg waited more or less patiently, concentrating on the computer displays. He touched the rotating earth on the navigation display, putting his finger on Nevada. The view zoomed in on the selected area. Cities and highways weren't in the computer's memory—oh, my! Yes, they were. This saucer must have flown after the cities and highways were built! Perhaps 1947, as Chadwick suggested.

The display of Nevada grew and grew, but it was post–World War II Nevada, the West as it had been in 1947. Highways but not superhighways, small airports. After consulting the map again, Egg put his finger on the place on the computer display that corresponded to Chadwick's mark. The airport should be there. *This is where we are,* he told the computer.

Just by thinking about it, he brought up a display of the face of the moon and went through the exercise again. He designated the location of the lunar base with the touch of a finger. *This is where we wish to go.*

The SUVs managed to drag open the panels of the hangar door, one by one. They were struggling with the last one when a helicopter crossed the visible swatch of sky.

Chadwick was beside himself. "I told them to cut the door alarms," he roared. "They must have forgotten to cut the ones on the hangar doors."

"Guess that bribe wasn't big enough," Egg remarked to no one in particular.

The last door seemed to be out of the way.

"Let's go, right now," Chadwick said, slapping Egg on the back.

Up about a foot, Egg told the computer. The ship rocked once, then rose slightly and stopped.

Gear up!

He heard the whine of the landing gear coming in, felt it thump home. Three green lights on the instrument panel disappeared.

Forward, slowly.

The saucer crept toward the open hangar door. Egg looked right and left. The opening seemed to be wide enough.

Safely outside, he looked around for the chopper.

There it was, some kind of gunship, in a hover on his left, facing the saucer. The nose turret gun was tracking.

Dear Lord . . .

Go, Egg urged the computer. *Full power.*

The rocket engines lit with a roar and the G came on instanteously. Newton Chadwick, who had been standing beside Egg, tumbled aft. Out of the corner of his eye, Egg saw muzzle flashes from the helo's machine gun, but only for an instant.

The ship accelerated in a gentle climb, faster and faster, gathering speed as at least four Gs pushed Egg aft into the seat. When it was several thousand feet above the desert, traveling at least five hundred knots, the nose of the saucer began to rise.

On the computer presentation before Egg a pathway appeared, one that led up, up, up from the earth in a long, gently curving path off to the east.

Go, go, go, Egg told the computer as the exhilaration of flight filled him with laughter. Oh, yessss.

RIP WAS ABOUT TO GET IN THE CESSNA WHEN HE HEARD the deep, low rumble of rocket engines at very high altitude. He looked up into the evening sky—and saw the twinkle of rocket exhaust. The dot of fire was well to the east when the sound arrived, and it disappeared eastward into the night sky more quickly than any jet as the rumble from the heavens washed over Rip. The sound was lower in pitch than jet noise, and stronger. It seemed to engulf him. Charley heard it too, and got out of the little airplane to listen.

Rip knew what it was. A saucer, going into space. Perhaps the one he and Charley had speculated about just two hours ago. Or a spaceplane, like *Jeanne d'Arc.* Where it had come from he didn't know, but he knew as well as he knew his own name who was in it. Egg Cantrell. That was why the frogs had kidnapped him.

Holding hands, he and Charley stood listening to the low rumble until it had faded completely. It was one of those sounds that you think you still hear long after it has gone, so even after it faded he stood frozen, straining for the last whisper.

Rip shook himself, finally, then leaned against the side of the plane for support and thought about what they should do. He and Charley discussed their options.

They got into the Cessna and Rip started the engine. Charley was exhausted, feeling the effects of eight days in zero or low gravity. She lay down again on the rear seat and immediately drifted off to sleep.

It was a clear, windless evening over the Rockies. The sun set as Rip flew eastward up the valley of the Colorado River. The moon was well above the horizon and about three-quarters full. Its light illuminated the ridges and peaks. Rip left the Colorado River at Eagle and made for Vail Pass. Safely through, he flew over Dillon Reservoir while climbing to fourteen thousand feet.

He was aware of the magic of this moment—the hum of the engine, the mountains at night, the stars and moon above, and Charley asleep in the backseat. He turned and looked. She was sacked out with her flight jacket around her shoulders.

If only those bastards hadn't kidnapped Uncle Egg . . .

The interstate was illuminated by a steady stream of head-lights. Flying above it, he crossed the Divide over Eisenhower Tunnel and immediately saw the lights of Denver gleaming in the darkness sixty miles away. He eased the throttle out an inch, dialed the RPM back a hundred, and retrimmed for a gradual descent.

*   *   *

SAFELY IN ORBIT, WITH THE ROCKET ENGINES SHUT down, Egg Cantrell sat strapped to the pilot's seat while he swabbed the perspiration from his face with his shirttail. Ohmigawd! He had done it! Flown a saucer into space. Actually, he had done nothing but talk to the computer via the headband, and the computer had flown the ship, but *wow!*

Newton Chadwick floated near him, white as a sheet and unable to speak. Chadwick looked through the canopy at the earth, then turned his head to look into the infinite void of deep space. Egg could see that Chadwick's hands were still shaking.

"I have never—" Chadwick began, then gave up.

Egg put the headband back on and asked the computer for a flight path. He studied it. The computer had planned two orbits of the earth and, on the second one, a burn that would accelerate the saucer on a course that would loop it around the moon. On the back side another burn would decelerate the saucer, placing it in lunar orbit.

Fine, Egg told the computer. *That's the way we'll do it.*

Regardless of how this adventure turned out, Egg felt as if he had reached the zenith of his life. Nothing he ever did in the past or would do in the future could compare with the rush he got flying this saucer into space. Now he knew how Charley Pine felt, and why she took the job Pierre Artois offered.

If NASA ever calls me, I'm signing up, Egg told himself, and laughed.

THERE WAS A TELEVISION CREW WAITING AT THE CENTEN-nial Airport executive terminal when Rip taxied up. Charley had awakened on final approach. Now, seeing the camera-man and female reporter waiting with her microphone, she groaned. "This isn't going to do your uncle any good," she said over the intercom.

"Just don't say anything that will set Pierre off."

The television crew charged the plane the instant the prop stopped.

"Mr. Cantrell, Mr. Cantrell," the reporter called breathlessly, "what can you tell us about Charley Pine? Why did she steal the spaceplane?"

Then the reporter saw Charley. She elbowed Rip out of the way and jabbed the microphone at her.

"Get that thing out of my face," Charley snapped.

Rip hurried into the terminal and squared around in front of the desk person, another woman. "I thought you people promised customers some privacy."

"Oh, my heavens," the woman said, fluttering her hands. As Rip well knew, celebrities and business bigwigs didn't want the press lurking when they departed or arrived in their bizjets. "We didn't think you'd mind. The reporter is the spouse of one of our executives. He thought—"

"Get that camera crew out of here now or I'll make a formal complaint to the president of the company."

The woman snapped her fingers at one of the line boys, and in less than a minute the camera crew was marching through the lobby toward the parking lot. The reporter scowled at Rip, who ignored her. Charley trailed the media into the building and followed the signs toward the women's room.

"Did you have a nice flight?" the woman at the desk asked Rip with a frozen smile.

"Great. Now we need to charter a jet to take us to Washington. We'll leave as soon as you can get a crew." He tossed the keys to the rental Cessna on the counter.

It took the crew of the jet an hour to get to the airport and file a flight plan. Charley Pine took a shower and ate a sandwich from the vending machine while they waited. Rip watched a little television. European camera crews had managed to capture an Italian cathedral in Rome being zapped by the antigravity beam from the moon. Joe Bob Hooker, home from the moon, was the hottest man on the planet. A battery of reporters were questioning him about the lunar base, his conversations with Pierre Artois, his thoughts on Pierre's demands.

Charley joined Rip in front of the television. After she had watched some of the interview, she said, "I told him most of that stuff."

"He referred to you as the most beautiful woman alive, and the finest pilot."

"Joe Bob is a discerning individual," Charley said, and squeezed Rip's hand.

"He's going to be in big trouble with his wife when he gets home," Rip replied.

Then a newsflash.

"This network has just learned that a flying saucer went into orbit from an unknown site in Nevada several hours ago. It is now in orbit. Here is the announcement from the White House."

Charley watched in frozen silence as Rip squeezed her hand.

"Oh, Rip. You know Egg was in it."

"Flying it, probably."

They talked in whispers. They were still head to head in one corner of the room when the desk lady came to tell them their jet was ready to depart.

An hour and fifteen minutes after they landed in Denver, Rip and Charley were on their way to Washington in a Citation V. The space suits and air compressor were stacked in the empty seats.

10

"Artois' antigravity strikes only occur during periods of good atmospheric visibility, usually during the sunlight hours," the astronomer said. "We believe he is using some type of optical instrument to aim the antigravity beam."

"Why can't he use city lights to target his weapon?" the president asked.

"It's certainly possible," the astronomer said, "but probably technically difficult. Yet Artois has struck several times during the night hours. As you know, just now the earth is moving between the moon and the sun—"

"How do we know that?" O'Reilly demanded.

The astronomer gaped, then said, "Don't you look out the window occasionally? The moon is almost full. When the earth is between the moon and the sun, as it is now, the surface of the earth facing the moon would appear very dark when viewed from 238,000 miles away, which is its average distance from the earth. The more magnification his optical instrument has, the darker the surface would appear. And behind the earth is that huge bright light, the sun."

"Doesn't the relationship change daily?" someone else asked.

The astronomer couldn't believe her ears. "The moon appears to move across our sky every day because the earth is spinning," she explained. "The moon actually takes twenty-nine days, twelve hours and forty-four minutes to complete one revolution around the earth, as measured against the sun. The moon also revolves on its axis, but at the same rate that it circles the earth, which is why we always see the same side of it."

"And when will the moon be overhead today?" the president asked.

The astronomer almost shook her head in amazement. The weather had been fantastic in Washington this past week—as usual, this autumn had the best weather of the year—and the night of the full moon was three days away. The Hunter's Moon, for those with a romantic bent. "At about thirty-eight minutes past ten P.M., sir."

The president looked at his watch. It was almost midnight. He tossed his pencil on his pad with a sigh. "So if Artois doesn't zap Washington tonight using the city lights, he can't do it until tomorrow night."

The leaders of Congress were demanding that he publicly reject Artois' demands, the sooner the better, but he didn't want to trigger Artois' wrath—at least until all the spaceplanes had been permanently grounded. So he had a little breathing room. Just enough, perhaps.

The president was counting hours on the wall clock, figuring when the attack on France would happen, when a messenger scurried into the room with a piece of paper. He handed it to O'Reilly, who read it and passed it to the president. The president scanned it and tossed it on the table.

"Aha! An ultimatum from the moon. Surrender within forty-eight hours or Artois will flatten Washington."

That remark set off the president's advisers. Everyone wanted to talk at once. The president used to insist they talk one at a time, but he didn't anymore. Now he merely tuned in to snatches of each speech and got the gist of it. One voice hammered on public safety, someone fretted about paying people not to work, several were horrified at the cost to rebuild public buildings, and the attorney general remarked on the government's liability if anyone were injured or killed by flying debris. Evacuation would look bad to voters, everyone agreed. Tourists would flee Washington, the local economy would be devastated, government workers would refuse to commute into the city, essential government services would be disrupted, Social Security checks wouldn't go out on time, the homeless had noplace else to go . . .

"Now you understand why the French surrendered," the secretary of state said smugly.

The president couldn't resist. "We'll rebuild the capital in Kansas," he told her. "The climate there is better, and it's closer to Texas." Then he shooed them out.

O'Reilly, the national security adviser, and the chairman of the Joint Chiefs remained when the others had left. "Have the director of homeland security make sure every government building in Washington is empty from moonrise to moonset tomorrow and every day after that," the president said to O'Reilly. "Things may get nasty if we don't whack those spaceplanes tomorrow night."

"We'll have to evacuate the White House."

"*Are* we going to whack those spaceplanes?" the president asked the national security adviser.

"The submarines are in position to launch cruise missiles now, sir," the adviser said. "But I suggest we wait for darkness to fall in France, then launch a coordinated strike. That will maximize the chances of catastrophically damaging the targets. And the incoming cruise missiles will be perfect cover for the B-2s. Under no circumstance should we risk having the French capture a B-2 crew."

"What do you think?" the president asked the chairman.

"If they move the planes while the missiles are in the air, the missiles will miss. We have a better chance of hitting the birds with B-2s."

"The spaceplanes could fly away while we are waiting," the president objected. "If they're ready to fly. Are they?"

"CIA doesn't know. But if we shoot cruise missiles and miss, I guarantee you that the pro-Artois French will shuffle those planes all over. The B-2s are already in the air. They'll refuel twice on the flight to France and twice coming home."

The president went to the window. The moonlight was so bright the trees in the lawn cast shadows. He looked up. He could see the moon by leaning close to the glass. The seas, really dark areas caused by ancient lava flows, were quite stark.

When he was small someone told him about the man in the moon, frightening him. He had hid from the moon's sight, afraid of that man up there. Now a whole generation of kids might grow up afraid.

That egomaniac Artois!

He looked again at his watch. It was a few minutes past six A.M. in France. "Okay," he said. "Wait until darkness in France." The national security adviser and the general left the room.

O'Reilly turned on the television. The president wasn't paying much attention until the announcer said breathlessly, "Earlier this evening a reporter for our Denver affiliate attempted to interview Charlotte Pine, the American pilot for the French space ministry, who stole the spaceplane that took Artois to the moon. Tonight she was a passenger in a private airplane that landed at a general aviation airport in

Denver. She refused to be interviewed." The network then played fifteen seconds of footage of Charley Pine snarling at the reporter.

So she was back, and in the United States!

"Have the FBI detain her and bring her here," the president growled at O'Reilly.

He was back at the window, looking at the moon, when a military aide came into the room and handed him a slip of paper. A saucer or rocket had gone into orbit from Nevada.

The president's eyebrows rose toward his hairline. He knew about the saucer that the Air Force had stashed in Area 51, had learned about it the hard way last year. Surely no one had flown that artifact away. That thing had been guarded day and night and locked up tight since 1947!

More than likely this report was another false alarm. Boy, there had been plenty of those. People were edgy, defenseless and ready to stampede. Rumors swept from coast to coast as quickly as telephone switching equipment could handle long distance calls.

Tomorrow night. With the spaceplanes destroyed, Artois would have to reexamine his cards.

"Better check on this report," the president said, and handed the slip of paper about the Area 51 saucer to O'Reilly. "Sounds as if someone in Nevada panicked big time. And find that spaceplane that Pine flew back."

Then he smiled one of those smiles the secretary of state hated.

AFTER ARRIVING AT REAGAN NATIONAL, CHARLEY PINE and Rip Cantrell rented a car, loaded the space suits and air compressor in the trunk and went looking for a motel room. They found one near the Potomac, south of the city on U.S. 1, which had been the main drag south back in the dark ages before the interstates were built. The motel dated from that era, although it had been painted three or four times since.

Charely Pine washed her clothes in the sink of their room and hung them up to dry. Rip gave her a toothbrush and some other personal items that he had brought in a small tote bag from Missouri. When Charley put her clothes on the next morning they were still damp. She complained to Rip, who had just returned from the small diner next to the motel with coffee.

"You gotta be tough this day and age," Rip said, and kissed her good morning.

"I am tough, but wet panties—" Charley shivered.

Charley already had the television on and had watched a replay of her vignette with the Denver reporter. As she and Rip sipped coffee, she flipped back to CNBC and turned the audio down.

"So do you still want to do it?" she asked Rip.

"Artois snatched Egg. If he hadn't, I'd vote to find a hole and crawl in. But we can't."

"You're right. And I owe Pierre. If he wins, he's going to squash me like a bug."

A half hour later, as they ate breakfast in the diner, the news broke that the three spaceplanes in France had just taken off, and had presumably gone into orbit on the first leg of their journey to the moon.

Charley and Rip sat frozen, watching the film clip of the spaceplanes taking off, a minute apart, on the television at the end of the counter.

"They have to get fuel at the orbiting tank," Charley remarked thoughtfully. "I didn't think there was enough there for three spaceplanes."

"What if there isn't?" Rip asked, speaking softly so no one seated at the counter would hear them.

"One of the spaceplanes may have carried up excess fuel for the other two. The crew would pump the excess into the tank, then the receivers would take it out. Much easier than rigging hoses between orbiting bodies."

They soon paid the tab and drove away in the rented car, with the space suits and accessories in the trunk. They stopped at a convenience store and purchased six bottles of water and three bags of jerky. Then they drove to the parking lot of the old RFK football stadium, which was empty. They parked, locked the car, and walked to Independence Avenue, where they found a bus stop and waited. When the local came along, they climbed aboard.

"Going to be a pretty day," the bus driver said to Charley after she smiled at him.

Rip and Charley took a seat and rode into the heart of the city.

THE NEWS THAT THE THREE SPACEPLANES IN SOUTHERN France had taken off from their base hit the president hard. He had let the military professionals talk him into waiting to attack, and now it was too late. He said three or four cuss words.

While he waited for his blood pressure to return to normal, he thought about the situation. Due to the fact that the moon was overhead during the middle of the night when public buildings in Washington—such as the Capitol, White House, Supreme Court Building, Pentagon and Treasury—were empty, the government didn't yet have to panic the electorate by evacuating those buildings during the day, in effect shutting down official Washington. During the day the government could continue with business as usual. For a week or so.

Across the street in Lafayette Park several thousand demonstrators were cavorting in front of television cameras. They were demanding the United States surrender to Artois. His promises sounded pretty good, they said. A handful of film stars were there with the demonstrators, telling everyone watching on television that the man in the moon was a better deal than the United States Constitution.

What the heck, the president thought, *I might be dead in a week.* There might be a revolution, a meteor might strike the earth, Yellowstone might explode, or California might slide off into the Pacific. A whole week . . .

STANDING OUTSIDE THE NATIONAL AIR AND SPACE Museum on the side that faced the Mall, the northern side, Rip examined the huge glass facade. Just beyond this wall of windows were the most important treasures the museum possessed, the Wright Flyer, the *Spirit of St. Louis,* the Bell X-1, and the saucer Rip had found in the Sahara. Behind him Charley Pine was purchasing sunglasses, baseball caps and sweatshirts from a pushcart vendor.

She donned her sweatshirt, cap and sunglasses and offered Rip's to him. Her sweatshirt sported an American flag on the front and the Capitol dome on the back. Rip's sweatshirt had a likeness of the president on it. "This the only one they had?" he asked.

"It was the cheapest," Charley replied.

"If they took the reactor out of the saucer," Rip said, "you and I are going to spend the next ten or twenty days in the city jail." One of the conditions Rip had put on his donation of the saucer to the museum was that the reactor be removed, rendering the saucer incapable of flight.

"You know they didn't," Charley said. "They don't have a place to store nuclear materials."

The lack of adequate storage was the reason the museum had been sued by local antinuclear activists, who had obtained an injunction against removal of the reactor from the saucer.

"But if they did . . ." Rip said.

The sunglasses were plastic wraparound mirrors that cost

three dollars a pair. With glasses on and ball caps pulled down, they joined the queue for the security checkpoints at the north entrance. There weren't a lot of tourists here today—most folks were probably huddled around a television somewhere, trying to catch the latest news—so Rip and Charley breezed through the metal detectors and soon found themselves inside the museum.

The saucer was on the main floor, with the *Spirit of St. Louis* hanging from the ceiling above it. They walked to the velvet rope that surrounded it. Rip could see that the hatch in the belly of the saucer was closed.

"What do you think?" he whispered to Charley, who was looking at the armed security guards. They had to get into the saucer and close the hatch before the guards could react.

"Check to see if the reactor is there."

Well, why not? The light from the wall of windows fell directly upon the saucer's skin; that electrical current should be enough to maintain a minimum charge on the battery.

Saucer, power up! Last year, when Rip flew the saucer, the computer memorized his brain waves. If it had enough electrical power to pick them up now . . .

He thought he heard a faint whine from the direction of the saucer, but he couldn't be sure. It would take a moment or two for the reactor temps to rise enough to begin generating electricity. In the interim, *Saucer, flash the interior light.*

He saw the blink inside the dark cockpit.

So did Charley, who squeezed his arm, then said, "I think you should pull the fire alarm in the men's room while I open the hatch."

"I've got a better idea. You pull the fire alarm in the women's room while *I* open the hatch."

"Too late," Charley told him. "I suggested it. Go do it, Ripper."

"You sure about this?" Rip whispered to Charley. He knew

it was the right thing to do, but still . . . "If you thought stealing *Jeanne d'Arc* got them in an uproar, wait until you see what happens after we fly out of here."

"Are you going to stand here all morning talking, or are you going to get on with it?"

The man beside Charley tapped her on the shoulder. He was in his forties and balding, wearing baggy shorts and a sweatshirt. "Say, aren't you Charley Pine, the saucer pilot?"

"Uh—"

"Well, if that don't beat all!" the man loudly exclaimed. "I recognized you right off. You're a mighty pretty woman, and I knew you were somebody. Matilda, come over here. There's somebody I want you to meet. Here she is, Charley Pine, the woman that swiped that spaceplane from the moon and left that idiot Frenchie high and dry."

Everyone within earshot turned and stared at Charley.

"ARE YOU TRYING TO SAY SOMEONE REALLY STOLE THE AIR Force's Roswell saucer out of its hangar in Area Fifty-one?" the president demanded.

"Yessir," the aide stammered. "That's what they said."

"Area Fifty-one is a top secret base. How in the world did thieves get in there?"

"They drove through a gate, sir."

The president eyed the aide without affection. Young, with a terrible haircut and baggy pants, the aide had to be the dullest of the first lady's cousins, the president thought. Then he remembered that last family picnic he attended. Perhaps not. "Who let them through the gate?" he asked with more patience than he felt. "Why didn't the security forces find the thieves and arrest them before they flew away?"

"I don't know the answers to those questions, sir. The Air Force and FBI are investigating, Mr. O'Reilly said."

"So where is the saucer now?"

The aide jabbed a thumb at the ceiling. "Up there."

When O'Reilly came in a few minutes later, the president had his feet on his desk and his chin on his chest. O'Reilly had two Secret Service types with him. O'Reilly pointed, and they began taking paintings down from the wall. The president watched morosely as each agent carried two from the room, one in each hand, and then returned for more.

THE TOURIST HAD A VOICE LIKE A CARNY BARKER, Charley Pine thought. Or a leather-lunged politician. A dozen people were staring at her. "We're from Ohio," the man brayed, "just here visiting, you understand, staying with my brother's in-laws—they're retired from the government—and taking in some of the sights. The White House people wouldn't let us take a tour with all this craziness going on, so we came to the museum this morning. Terrorists, demonstrators, idiots on the moon, and look who we run into! If this isn't something—"

The wail of the fire alarm cut him off.

As everyone looked around for smoke or flames, Charley ducked under the velvet rope and scooted under the saucer. She put her hand on the latch to warm it, trying not to hurry.

"Hey, you, get out from under there!" The shout could be heard even above the howl of the fire alarm.

Now. The latch rotated in her hand. The hatch dropped open and Charley shot up through the hole.

Rip was right behind her. So was one of the guards.

"Sorry, pal, you didn't buy a ticket," Rip said, and slammed the hatch shut in his face. In seconds he had it latched.

Charley Pine was already in the pilot's seat. Through the canopy she could see horrified tourists and running guards. In front of her the computer displays came vividly to life.

She tore off the ball cap and sunglasses she was wearing

and tossed them away. The computer headband lay on the console before her; she placed it on her head. *Hello,* she said to the computer.

Lift us up about a foot.

She felt the motion as the computer gave the necessary commands to the flight computer and the ship responded.

Gear up!

She heard the whine as the three arms retracted into the body of the saucer, and the final thump as the gear doors slammed shut. Now she turned the saucer, pointing it at the wall of windows.

Do we have any water in the system? she asked the computer.

A graph appeared on the main screen before her. Rip had brought the saucer here a year ago with some water in it, and the staff had apparently never drained it out. The ship was about thirty percent full, she estimated.

Outside the saucer, the crowd was backing away, panic-stricken. A steady stream of people were forcing their way out the main entrance. A half dozen uniformed guards stood in front of the saucer with their pistols drawn. They seemed unsure of what to do.

Charley lowered the saucer to within a few inches of the floor to ensure no one would be crushed under it in the antigravity field. Then she began moving the saucer forward. She thought the command, and the flight computer altered the current to the field just enough to move the machine.

She could still hear the fire alarm sounding, although the sound was muffled. She ignored it and concentrated on moving the saucer.

The guards scattered. A tourist information booth was shoved out of the way, as were several crowd control stanchions and a sign that explained how Rip Cantrell had found the saucer in the Sahara Desert, as the saucer moved slowly toward the window at about half the speed a man could walk. Staring, pointing people lined the walls, including some parents with fierce grips on their kids.

With the saucer inches from the windows, Charley Pine stopped forward motion and caused it to rise until it was about halfway up the glass. She was a little concerned about nudging the *Spirit*, which was someplace behind and above the saucer, but the higher she hit the windows, the easier they would be to break.

Now the saucer contacted the glass. *Forward!*

The window directly in front of the saucer shattered, yet the framework stayed intact.

"Better back up and whack it," Rip suggested. He was standing right beside her.

"I really don't need suggestions from the peanut gallery," she muttered, and backed the saucer up about a yard.

"Just trying to be helpful," Rip said, not a bit apologetic.

She drove the saucer forward as hard as she could. The framework cracked and buckled in a shower of glass. Still it held, preventing the saucer from passing.

She backed up, smashed the wall again. This time the saucer shot through.

No one under her on the patio outside. The shower of glass from the window had moved everyone away.

The saucer was only fifty feet from the building when Charley lit the rocket engines and turned it to the left so she wouldn't fly over the downtown. The fire from the rocket exhaust nozzles of the accelerating saucer was subdued since she had only asked for a little power, but the noise was awe-inspiring.

It was heard all over downtown Washington.

In the White House the president heard it and wondered, *Now what?* He went to the window of the Oval Office just in time to see the saucer accelerating toward the Lincoln Memorial trailing a sheet of fire.

*   *   *

CHARLEY TURNED HARD OVER GEORGETOWN AND CAME back down the Potomac. She passed the Pentagon, still low, only about a hundred feet above the river so that she wouldn't interfere with airline traffic into and out of Reagan National, then turned and headed for RFK Stadium. The rockets were silent as she coasted toward the lone car parked in the empty acres of asphalt. She used the antigravity system to lower the saucer onto its landing gear beside the car.

Rip went out the hatch like a jackrabbit. Two minutes later he had the space suits and compressor loaded. The food and water in bags on the backseat took another two minutes, then he popped back up through the hatchway.

"Check the fuel cap to ensure that it's open," Charley said. She had told the computer to open it, but it wouldn't hurt to check.

Rip leaped back out.

A police car roared across the empty parking lot with lights flashing and siren howling. It was still fifty yards away when Rip scampered back up through the hatchway, shouted, "It's open," and pulled the hatch shut behind him.

"The cops are coming," he called to Charley, who was still busy with the computer displays. "Whenever you're ready."

She lifted the saucer, retracted the gear and headed back for the Potomac. At the confluence of the Anacostia and Potomac, she stopped all relative motion, then lowered the saucer into the river. Brown water covered the canopy. A gurgling could be heard as the water flowed into the open neck of the fuel tank.

"This water is pretty bad," Rip said nervously. "Lots of mud in it."

Charley didn't respond to that comment. She concentrated on the computers, plotting their journey.

When the tank was full of water, Charley lifted the saucer

from the river and flew along two hundred feet above the Potomac using the antigravity rings. Several miles downriver she saw a golf course on the east bank and landed on a fairway. Rip dropped through the hatchway to check that the fuel cap had indeed latched shut.

Two golfers drove up in a golf cart and stopped a hundred feet from the saucer. They sat frozen with their jaws hanging open.

"It's on tight," Rip reported when he was back inside, with the hatch shut. "But before we go, hadn't we better check the antiproton beam?"

"Good idea," Charley admitted. When Egg analyzed the systems aboard the saucer, it took him a while to realize that the power that generated the antigravity force was coupled into some weird-looking heavy-duty electrical conductors that he originally thought were part of the lift/control system. It turned out, though that the power was routed to drive an antiproton beam weapon. Antiprotons are forms of antimatter and are manufactured on earth today only in giant accelerators in particle physics laboratories. The creators of the saucer, however, equipped it with a small accelerator, which generated an antiproton beam.

Charley lifted the saucer ten feet in the air and stabilized in a hover. At her command, crosshairs appeared in front of her on the canopy. She turned the saucer to line it up on a large oak tree on the edge of the fairway. The trunk appeared to be about three feet in diameter.

Rip was right beside her, his head at her shoulder.

Fire!

A smoky beam of fire, almost like lightning, shot from a point on the leading edge of the saucer and reached out for the oak. Some of the antiprotons were striking ordinary protons in the molecules that made up the air, destroying them and releasing gobs of energy, hence the lightning.

The lightning went completely through the oak tree and out the other side, since there was so much space in and between the molecules of the tree that some of the antiprotons could survive their trips through it and emerge out the other side. Pieces began flying from the tree.

"Better stop—" Rip began, just as the tree trunk exploded from the release of energy.

Charley stopped the beam. The stub of the trunk smoked as the top of the tree crashed to the ground and fragments of wood showered down.

"Holy cow," Rip said, and whistled.

"Let's get outta here," Charley Pine muttered, and told the saucer to go.

Two seconds later the rocket engines ignited, blasting the saucer forward over the carcass of the devastated tree. Charley held the nose down as the ship accelerated. When the speed had reached several hundred knots, she commanded the computer to lift the nose and follow that holographic pathway on the display before her.

THE PRESIDENT WAS ON THE SOUTH LAWN OF THE WHITE House as the saucer shot above the treetops, going almost straight up, on its journey into space. When he saw the saucer fly over the Mall a half hour ago, he suspected it would soon go into orbit, so he ran out here to catch the show. Although he was now at least ten miles from the saucer, the president had to squint against the glare of the white-hot rocket exhaust rising into the sky.

The noise was a loud, deep, bass roar that overwhelmed the senses.

Without realizing he was doing it, the president shouted in frustration. His shout was lost amid the thunder of the saucer.

11

Pierre Artois felt that sense of sublime satisfaction that comes to those who dare great things, run tremendous risks and win. A deep calm descended over him. He was
standing on a mountain peak with the world at his feet.
Actually he was standing on the moon, looking up at the
earth, but the folks on earth were looking up at him. *All* of
them.

Indeed, he reflected, he had *won*. Three spaceplanes were
in orbit, one of which carried extra fuel to recharge the orbiting fuel tank; the other two would top off and journey on to
the moon. In the unlikely event anything went wrong with
the spaceplanes, Newton Chadwick and Egg Cantrell were on
their way to the moon with the Roswell saucer, which Chadwick had managed to steal from under the nose of the U.S.
Air Force. Most important, the government of France had
surrendered, renounced the republic and proclaimed Pierre
Artois emperor, pledging loyalty, honor and obedience.

First France, then Europe, then the world.

"Fame, fortune and power," he said to his wife, Julie. "Life
doesn't get better than this."

"We haven't won yet," Julie pointed out. "The British are just across the Channel, their moat, and they can be so tiresome."

"That little ditch won't save them this time," Pierre said confidently. "We can handle the British."

"Then there are the Americans. The U.S. president is a Neanderthal—I don't know why they elect such men."

"Probably couldn't find any better," Pierre said, and made a gesture of dismissal. He didn't want to fret about the Americans today. He felt like music, a banquet, champagne and, afterward, Julie in a large, soft bed. He eyed her speculatively.

"Forget it," Julie told the emperor of France. "We don't have time."

ABOARD THE ROSWELL SAUCER, COASTING TOWARD THE moon, Newton Chadwick and his two French friends were nearly as ecstatic as Pierre Artois. The news of the French government's surrender came to them via a battery-powered radio that Chadwick had brought aboard. Egg sat listening, saying nothing.

Later Chadwick locked himself in the saucer's head. He wore a small fanny pack at all times, and it contained, Egg suspected, his antiaging drug. Egg wondered if the drug took the form of a pill, a liquid that must be injected or some kind of cream. Egg also wondered about how much of the drug Chadwick had with him. Hmmm . . .

When he tired of plumbing the depths of the Roswell saucer's memory, Egg Cantrell amused himself by frequency surfing on the saucer's radio; he listened to taxi drivers in Rio, police calls from Moscow, ships at sea, soldiers on maneuver and air traffic controllers talking to airplanes. And he caught part of the great debate over the demands made by Pierre Artois. Amid the babble he could hear a steady, hard drumbeat of voices insisting that while Pierre's promises were very nice, the ability to vote out unpopular governments—the freedom to choose—was more important.

Egg paid particular attention to American news reports. Charley Pine was in America; he concluded that the space-plane she stole from the moon was probably also there. The three spaceplanes in France had taken off, presumably on their way to the moon. Finally, someone had stolen the saucer from the National Air and Space Museum in Washington and flown it into space.

Chadwick and his friends were asleep when Egg heard the flash about the other saucer, and still asleep when the reporters figured out that apparently Rip Cantrell and Charley Pine were the guilty parties.

So the equation had changed, Egg mused. He had agreed to fly the saucer for Chadwick because he feared for Rip and Charley's safety, and his own. Chadwick and his thugs certainly weren't above using force if he failed to obey Chadwick's demands. Yet if they disabled or killed Egg, Chadwick would have to fly the saucer—if he could. If he couldn't, he and his two pals would also die in this thing.

Egg wasn't ready to die just yet. He enjoyed life and wanted more of it.

And now wasn't the time to play the hero. The best way to get back to earth was to continue on this trajectory, which would slingshot the saucer around the moon and start it back for earth unless he fired the engines to slow it and put it into lunar orbit.

He turned the saucer so that earth filled the canopy. He searched the jeweled darkness around the planet, trying to spot the twinkle of rocket exhaust that would indicate the presence of a saucer or spaceplane. A saucer or spaceplane accelerating for a journey to the moon. He saw nothing of the kind, of course. The distances were too vast, the exhaust plumes far too small.

Egg grinned widely. Rip and Charley, a real pair of aces.

He loosened the safety belt that held him in the pilot's seat, leaned back and drifted off to sleep thinking about his nephew Rip and the beautiful Charley Pine.

THE RIDE INTO SPACE WAS EVEN MORE EXCITING THAN RIP remembered it. He wanted to sing, but managed to stifle himself.

Charley Pine was all business. When the rocket engines stopped, signaling that the saucer had achieved orbit, she began tuning the radio that she remembered from her previous adventure in this ship. Like the one Egg was listening to in the Roswell saucer, this radio was also capable of receiving and transmitting on an extraordinarily wide band of frequencies.

She knew the one she wanted: the spaceplane's orbital refueling freq. She had to play a while with the radio, then finally found it.

The spaceplanes were already in orbit and were now rendezvousing with the fuel tank. The problem was that she didn't know where the tank was. Oh, she knew it was orbiting the earth at a height of about a hundred miles, more or less, but where above the earth was it?

As she listened to the French pilots chat back and forth between themselves and their controller on the ground, she tried to reason her way through the problem. When she and Lalouette had launched in *Jeanne d'Arc,* the launch was timed so that when the spaceplane reached orbiting velocity, it would be in the vicinity of the fuel tank. She suspected the French had done the same thing this time. Indeed, if they hadn't, the spaceplanes would waste prodigious quantities of fuel and time maneuvering for a rendezvous.

She and Rip hadn't timed their launch, of course. They had to find and rendezvous upon the spaceplanes before

they successfully refueled and began their lunar orbit insertion burn. Once they did, she and Rip would never catch
them in the saucer; it didn't have enough fuel.

She examined the radar display, running it out to what she
hoped was maximum range. The only way to determine what
that range was would be to find a target and let the computer figure a course and burn to intercept. She could make
an estimate based on that.

Which was beside the point, because the display was
empty.

If the radar was working.

But why wouldn't it be working? Everything in the saucer
had worked as it was supposed to from the day Rip and his
friends hammered it from a sandstone ledge in the Sahara.
Assume that it is working, Charley told herself.

"How are you going to find these dudes?" Rip asked. He
was watching over her shoulder.

"I don't know that we can." She gestured toward the radio.
"They're already rendezvousing with the fuel tank. We don't
know when they launched, so they could be anywhere above
the planet."

"Let's ask for help."

She looked at him. "Who from?"

"How about Space Command? Bet they know where that
tank is." Space Command was a branch of the U.S. Air Force
charged with monitoring the position of satellites, among
other things.

Charley Pine thought about it. "The duty officer will refer
the request to Washington, and they'll have to staff it, which
could take a day or two. We have a few hours, at best. And if
the U.S. government helps us, Pierre will be most unhappy
with them. They will suspect that."

"Life's full of trade-offs," Rip remarked. "If Pierre gets
those spaceplanes, he'll be sitting in the catbird seat. Most

Americans must be very unhappy with him right now. The worst that Space Command can do is say no."

"And make a lot of threats."

"I don't figure we're winning any Citizen of the Year Award points now. Oh, I know, I don't have any more faith in politicians than you do, but at some point you have to throw the ball in their direction and see if they can catch it."

Charley began tuning the radio. She certainly didn't know what frequencies she might use to contact Space Command, but no doubt the U.S. air traffic controllers did. Charley tuned to that portion of the VHF band where she thought air traffic controllers might be, and sure enough, there they were, working airliners into and out of . . . Miami.

She waited until there was a moment of silence, then said, "Miami Approach, this is Saucer One with a request, over."

The controller didn't miss a beat. He must get calls from flying saucers every day. "Saucer One, Miami, you have a flight plan on file?"

"That's a negative. We have a request, though. We need a frequency that we can call Space Command on. Can you recommend one?"

"Where are you, Saucer One?"

"In orbit."

"Stand by."

THE CONTROLLER'S SUPERVISOR SOON APPEARED AT HIS shoulder. Trying to keep his voice as dry and matter-of-fact as possible, the controller said, "Saucer One says she's in orbit and wants a freq for Space Command."

The supervisor had just returned from her break, where she had been watching news coverage of the saucer's theft from the Air and Space Museum, a story that had been sandwiched between the latest bulletins from Paris and the moon.

"Just another day at the office," she said, and picked up the military hotline telephone.

A MOMENT AFTER SHE WAS GIVEN THE SPACE COMMAND frequency by Miami Approach, Charley Pine lost radio contact with North America. She figured out the conversion and dialed in the frequency. Even the ancients had classified frequencies by the number of cycles in a given time span. Although they didn't use seconds, Egg had figured out the conversion formula long ago, and both Charley and Rip remembered it.

As they rode over the Sahara and the Red Sea, Rip and Charley sat in silence, each lost in his own thoughts. Over the Indian Ocean Charley finally spoke.

"You know that they're going to want us to destroy those spaceplanes."

"If we pop the refueling tank, we don't need to destroy them. They can't get to the moon without more fuel than they can carry aloft. It'll take a while to get extra fuel into orbit."

"It's already in orbit."

"Okay, we pop the cow."

"Rip, I know these people. I trained with them in France. Blowing up the tank will kill some of them."

"Hey, I didn't talk Pierre Artois into trying to conquer the world. I didn't give the order to kidnap Egg. His Royal Moonness Emperor Pierre the First gave the order."

"Not the weenies in the spaceplanes."

"They signed up to be soldiers in Pierre's army. If you don't want to pull the trigger, get out of the pilot's seat," Rip said. "I'll do it."

"I just want to make sure you know what we're getting ourselves into."

"Little late for second thoughts, don't you think? Maybe

we should have had this conversation outside the Air and Space Museum, before we walked through that door."

"Maybe, but we didn't, so we're having it now."

"Outta the seat. I'll do the shooting and I'll live with it afterward."

"We'll both have to live with it," Charley Pine said, and stayed in the pilot's chair. She was thinking of Marcel, who had stolen a kiss one evening in the simulator. Was he aboard one of those spaceplanes?

THE PRESIDENT WAS IN THE CABINET ROOM AT THE WHITE House as the duty officer at Space Command, an air force two-star general, relayed Charley's comments via telephone. Around the table were the leaders of Congress, who were here to find out exactly what was in the president's speech to the nation, which he had yet to give.

"The French spaceplanes rendezvoused with the fuel tank twenty minutes ago," the general said. "They may have finished refueling and have made their lunar orbit insertion burn by the time the saucer gets there."

"Give Cantrell and Pine all the help you can," the president whispered into the telephone. Of course, every eye in the room was upon him, yet he didn't want his side of this telephone conversation on the news shows during the next hour. As he waited while the general passed the order to the supervisor, who passed it on to the operators monitoring the progress of the various craft orbiting the earth, the president toyed with the idea of leaving the cabinet room to finish the conversation. He decided to stay put because there wasn't much else to say.

When the general got back to him, the president said softly, "Tell me again about this weapon Pine says is on board the saucer."

"Sir, she didn't explain anything about it. Her only comment was that the saucer had a short-range weapon that she could use to attack the spaceplanes. We asked what kind of weapon, and she said, 'Antimatter.'"

"And that thing sat right down the street in a museum for over a year without our wizards learning that it had a ray gun on it?"

"I couldn't comment on that, sir," the general said diplomatically.

The president dropped the telephone into its cradle and stared without enthusiasm at the legislators sitting around the table.

"Well, sir?" Senator Blohardt prompted.

"Gentlemen—and ladies, of course," the president said, "the fact is that I haven't decided precisely what I want to say to the citizens of the country about this matter. Since you are here, I'd like to hear your views. Perhaps you could lead off, Senator Blohardt."

"In the first place, Mr. President, you couldn't cede or surrender an iota of this nation's sovereignty to a foreign power without an amendment to the Constitution, which you'll never get."

"Treaties often cede sovereignty," a senator from the other party shot back.

After sex and violence, there is nothing Americans love more than legal wrangles, which is why football, which combines all three, is so popular. Naturally most of the legislators were lawyers, so away they galloped, arguing the case. The president sighed and slipped off his shoes. If Artois could figure a way to balance the budget and pay off the national debt, the president thought, turning the country over to him would be an idea worth discussing.

He kept the telephone close at hand.

* * *

THE REFUEL TANK WAS A THIRD OF AN ORBIT AWAY, behind the saucer.

Charley Pine attacked the saucer's flight computer. This was the first time she had attempted to program it to compute a maneuver more complex than a reentry profile. She couldn't figure it out on the first attempt, and said, "Rip, you're going to have to help me with this."

On the third attempt, there it was, a loop that took the saucer high into space and dropped it down on the predicted rendezvous point.

"My Lord, do we have fuel for that?" Rip murmured at Charley, who was already examining the quantity indications.

"It's going to be tight," Charley Pine said, "really tight. We won't have any fuel left to maneuver with when we reach the rendezvous—if the tank and spaceplanes are really there. Not if we ever expect to return to earth."

"I was sorta counting on getting down. One of these days."

"I was too."

"Well, hot woman, what do you want to do?"

Charley turned the saucer, pointed it in the direction recommended by the computer and came on smoothly with the power. The saucer leaped forward.

THE MANEUVER THE FLIGHT COMPUTER RECOMMENDED sent the saucer over the top of a giant loop after a twelve-minute climb. Rip and Charley were no longer weightless in the saucer, which was now traveling in a long arc. They were pushed toward the floor of the saucer at perhaps a tenth of a G. Mild as it was, the acceleration force gave them a sense of up and down. The blue, green and gray earth was above them, over the canopy as they went slowly, lazily over the top and started down the back side of the loop.

Charley checked the flight display, upon which the radar target should be presented. It was empty. The spaceplanes and refueling tank were still somewhere to the west and far below, speeding along at eighteen thousand miles per hour toward that invisible point in space where they would rendezvous with the saucer. That is, if the designation of the spaceplanes' position was even in the ballpark.

The saucer hurtled downward on the back side of its prodigious loop as Charley and Rip waited, their eyes on the flight display. Seconds turned into minutes.

"Space Command, Saucer One, where are they?"

"Our computer shows you are four minutes from target merge."

Rip and Charley were looking straight at earth as the saucer accelerated toward it. Rip gave a gentle jump and did a somersault in midair, then landed on his feet. "Four minutes," he said, his voice dripping with disgust.

"I really admire your endless patience," Charley remarked. "It's one of your better traits."

"Hold that thought." Rip did another flip, but faster. "I always wanted to be an acrobat, but earth's gravity was just too much."

"Held you down, did it?"

After three more somersaults, he tired of it and decided to take advantage of the G to relieve himself in an empty water bottle. "Don't look behind you," he advised Charley Pine.

"I never do," she said. He was back at her side when she murmured, "Here they come."

The spaceplanes were slightly to one side, ahead, moving upward on the display. The displacement from dead ahead was, Charley knew, a graphic presentation of the inaccuracy with which she input the target's position. But she had come close enough. Maybe.

The nose of the saucer continued to rise toward the earth's horizon.

Charley Pine, jet fighter pilot, knew the rendezvous was going to work out.

They didn't see the spaceplanes until they were about twenty miles away. They appeared as tiny dots of reflected sunlight.

The saucer still had a speed and angular advantage, which caused it to close the distance. Ten miles out Charley Pine took over manually and used the saucer's maneuvering jets as a brake to reduce some of the overtaking speed. Her experience as a fighter pilot visually judging closure rate was very helpful here.

At about ten miles she could see all four objects. There was the tank, with one of the spaceplanes nestled to it. But was that the donor or a receiver craft? The other two spaceplanes were nearby, within a few hundred yards of the ship that was joined to the tank.

The saucer's computer read Charley's brainwaves, and the optical crosshairs appeared on the canopy.

Perhaps, she thought, she had braked too much. The spaceplanes and the tank were growing larger, but the closure rate seemed slow. She glanced at the flight display, trying to judge the distance. Now she could have used a radar screen calibrated in miles or kilometers or whatever, but she didn't have it.

She maneuvered slightly to put the crosshairs on the fuel tank.

Still closing.

"What's the range of the shooter?" Rip asked.

"How would I know?" Charley said, her voice so tense she had trouble getting the words out.

"No atmosphere to siphon off antiprotons," Rip mused.

"Why don't you give 'em a squirt now, just to see what happens?"

She thought of the Frenchmen she had trained with—and nothing happened. *No!* She shouted, "*Shoot! Goddamn it, shoot!*" Instantly the weapon began discharging a steady stream of antiprotons. As it did so, a small warning light appeared beside the optical crosshairs.

As Rip had implicitly predicted, without an atmosphere, there was no chain lightning effect. The only visible evidence that the antimatter weapon was working were the sparkles that appeared on the side of the tank.

The saucer was now less than a mile from the other ships. "Better stop your forward progress," Rip urged, "before that thing—"

The tank exploded in a blinding flash. Fire shot away in every direction.

The concussion rocked the saucer. Dead ahead, the brilliant red and yellow fireball, expanding rapidly, grew larger and larger and rushed toward them, engulfing the saucer.

As the saucer bounced in the turbulence, Charley Pine ripped off the headset and shut her eyes. She didn't want to collide with anything, if indeed there were anything left to collide with, yet she didn't want to coast out of the area.

Seconds ticked by, and finally she opened her eyes. The expanding gases were still glowing, as if a new universe had been born. Her eyes slowly adjusted to the glare.

"What do you see?" Rip asked, his hand hard on her shoulder. She reached for his hand, grasped it hard.

The incandescent gases gradually burned out. Where the explosion had occurred, nothing remained. "Oh, God!" Charley moaned. "I think we killed them all."

"There, to the left!"

Charley looked left. A spaceplane, perhaps two miles away,

pointed almost at the saucer, was moving perceptibly away from the epicenter of the blast. The burning, expanding gases must have pushed on the side of it, like a sail, imparting a velocity vector. It wasn't stationary, but was in a slow, flat spin, like a Frisbee. Of course; the blast pushed harder on the vertical tail, less so on the nose.

Rip grabbed at her arm. "Up there, to the right!" There was the other one, also moving away. Its nose pointed up and farther right.

One or both might have completed refueling and be capable of flying on to the moon. But which one?

The spaceplane on the left spun through one more revolution, the spin visibly slowing; the motion ceased when the nose pointed west in relation to the planet below, a direction over Charley's left shoulder.

"Maybe that's the tanker," Rip said, "and it had finished filling the tank. Maybe—"

Before he could speak again, the rockets in the tail of that westward-pointing spaceplane ignited. It began accelerating in the direction it was pointing.

"Maybe it's going—" Rip shouted as the ship crossed Charley's left shoulder.

"Going to reenter the atmosphere," Charley muttered. The rocket burn must be decreasing the spaceplane's velocity in relation to the spinning planet below, which would send it into a lower orbit. If the deceleration burn was long enough, the spaceplane would reenter the atmosphere.

As the ship shot out of sight behind her, she looked again at the ship high and to her right. The distance was probably three miles. Its orientation had also changed. Now it was pointing more along the vector in which it and the saucer were orbiting, and the nose was up above the horizon, about ten degrees. If the rocket engines fired, it would accelerate and climb. If the engines burned long enough, it would reach escape velocity and, perhaps, be on its way to the moon. To Pierre and Julie, for conquest and glory.

She turned the saucer, pointed it toward the spaceplane and asked the engines for power.

As the saucer's rockets responded, the high spaceplane's rockets burped to life.

"It's going to the moon!" Rip shouted. He didn't even know he was shouting.

Charley came on hard with the juice and turned to parallel the other ship's course. Both ships were accelerating, but if she deviated from her victim's course, she would drop behind.

"Get him, get him, get him!" Rip urged.

She was at full power now, trying to close that gap, the Gs pressing her backward into her seat. Beside her Rip held on for dear life.

She didn't have the fuel for much of this nonsense, not if she hoped to ever return to earth. Even as that thought crossed her mind, the computer displayed the fuel remaining. Less than ten percent.

By God, she didn't have enough now!

The gap didn't seem to be closing. Desperate, she fired the antiproton weapon and swung the nose to the right, intending to rake the antimatter beam across the fleeing spaceplane. This would work or it wouldn't.

The crosshairs projected on the canopy in front of her crossed the spaceplane, and she kicked rudder, trying to hold it there as the French ship widened the distance between them.

A second passed, then two. Three . . .

And the three smaller rocket engines on the underside of

the ship went dark, leaving only the main engine and the two small engines above it still firing.

Instantly Charley cut off her rockets to save what water she had for a reentry attempt.

Ahead of her the spaceplane's nose dropped as the asymmetrical power took effect.

Still accelerating, the nose fell through the planet's horizon and continued down.

The ship was far ahead now, the white-hot rocket exhaust all that was visible.

The angle of that falling star continued to steepen—it dropped lower and lower and began to move aft in relation to the saucer. Charley rolled her ship so she could see the white pinpoint of exhaust.

Deeper it went, down into the darkness, down toward the waiting atmosphere that enshrouded the massive planet.

Finally, far behind and below the speeding saucer the exhaust plume twinkled out, and there was nothing more to see.

"I hope they're dead before they hit the atmosphere," Rip said softly.

"Yes," she said, thinking of Marcel, with the black eyes and the shy smile. "If God is merciful."

JACK HOOD WAS A FARMER IN KENT, ENGLAND, ONLY A FEW miles from the white cliffs of Dover. It was after midnight when his wife awakened him. "There's something out there, Jack. Listen to the cows."

Hood blinked himself awake and listened hard. The cattle were bawling loudly. Hood glanced at the bedside clock: It was at least an hour before dawn.

"I'd better go check," he said, and rolled out of bed.

He had a gnarled shillelagh standing in the corner, and after he dressed and stomped into his Wellingtons, he reached for it, just in case. He made his way to the front door of the house without turning on any lights and went out.

It had rained last evening, so the earth was pungent and sweet. During the night the wind had moved out the clouds and now the sky was clear, ablaze with stars, with the moon low in the west. Standing on the porch in the moonlight, Jack Hood remembered the flashlight in the kitchen and went back for it.

The moon gave enough light that he didn't need the flashlight to find his way to the barn. Last night Hood and his wife had watched all the latest news from capitals around the world on the telly and heard the demands of the man in the moon, so as he walked he flashed Pierre the finger.

The cattle stopped bawling when they sensed his presence, yet still they milled about, looking toward the pond. Actually the pond was a small lake, almost two acres in size.

Hood let himself through the gate and walked toward the water. He flipped on the flashlight and swept it around the shore. Nothing out of the ordinary here. A few bushes, lots of mud churned up by cattle, here and there a small tree.

"Out here," a voice called.

Elmer turned the flashlight toward the center of the pond—and saw a man standing there. In the pond. In only to his ankles. What the—?

"Hope you don't mind treating us to a fill-up," the man called. He had an American accent, which Jack Hood recognized from the movies. "We ran out of water and missed North America. We were skipping and hopping and hoping, and this is where we wound up."

Hood went down right to the water's edge. Now he could see that there was a shape, something dark, mounding up out of the water. Aha, the man was standing on something!

"Name's Rip. Bet we woke you up, huh?"

Jack Hood didn't know what to say. He simply stood and stared.

Now the man bent over and rapped on the thing he was standing on. It rose slowly and gently out of the water. The thing was a saucer! A bloody flying saucer!

It was big! Ohmigosh, it was big, maybe sixty or seventy feet in diameter. As it came completely out of the water, the water level in the pond dropped, perhaps as much as a foot. The saucer moved gently over the pasture with the man still standing on its back. Its legs snapped down, and it settled onto the grass.

The man jumped down and strolled over. He was in his early twenties, clean-cut and lean. He reached for the flashlight and turned it away from his face, then grasped Hood's hand.

"Rip Cantrell. Glad to meet you."

"Righto," Jack managed.

"Have a good night," Rip said, and turned back to the saucer. He went under it and disappeared into the belly.

Seconds later it lifted and the gear retracted.

It moved out over the pond, accelerating, then a small flame burst from a series of rocket nozzles on the trailing edge.

When the saucer was perhaps two miles away, traveling at several hundred knots, the exhaust became intense and all the noise on God's green earth washed over Jack Hood. The fireball rose almost straight up and kept going and going, shrinking to a pinpoint as it drifted toward the east. Finally it disappeared among the stars.

12

THE DISASTER THAT HAD CLAIMED THE THREE FRENCH spaceplanes was the topic of considerable conversation between Mission Control in France and Pierre Artois on the moon. Newton Chadwick listened on the battery-operated encoded radio in the Roswell saucer and passed on what he heard to his two colleagues. All of the conversation was in French and unintelligible to Egg Cantrell. From Chadwick's reaction, he could tell that the news was bad.

When the radio had finally fallen silent, Chadwick and his colleagues discussed what they had heard for half an hour, and finally Chadwick shared what he had learned with Egg.

"A disaster. The orbital refueling tank exploded when the second of the two ships bound for the moon was refueling. The explosion was actually seen over Japan in the hours before dawn. The tank and that ship were destroyed. The crew of the tanker, which had carried the fuel aloft, thought they saw another ship in the vicinity, but they couldn't be sure. It was black and saucer-shaped. They immediately fired their engines for a reentry, and talked to Mission Control before they entered the atmosphere and lost radio contact.

That ship crashed somewhere in the Pacific, Mission Control believes."

He sighed. "No one knows what happened to the third ship. There were several garbled radio transmissions, which the agency is studying, trying to decipher. An oil tanker in the western Pacific reported a large object—they thought it was a meteor—penetrating the atmosphere at a steep angle and burning up a few minutes before dawn."

"Saucer-shaped?"

"A saucer!" Chadwick made a face. "The American news media reports that the saucer housed in the National Air and Space Museum in Washington was stolen in midmorning, several hours before the disaster aloft. An extraordinary coincidence that must somehow be explained."

"Stolen?" Egg said, his disbelief evident in his voice.

"Of course not!" Chadwick replied acidly. "The American government obviously sent that saucer aloft to attack the spaceplanes while they were still in earth orbit. What kind of weapon the saucer used is unknown." He stared into Egg's eyes. "Is there a weapon on this saucer?"

Egg blinked and managed to look surprised. There was the antiproton beam on the saucer from the Sahara, of course, but— Naw! Certainly not! No one knew of it except Rip and Charley. No one in the government—

"Don't be absurd," Egg said sharply. "Do you really think the government converted this saucer to a weapons platform? If they did, where is it?" He made a show of looking around the compartment. "This thing has been sitting in an abandoned hangar in Nevada for how many years?"

Chadwick was thinking—Egg could see that. Obviously he hadn't learned of the antiproton beam in his exploration of this saucer's computer or he wouldn't even have asked the question. In fact, Egg had only discovered its existence from studying the schematics. Chadwick wasn't an engineer; he just wanted to get rich and live forever.

"How could the American government install a space weapon on a museum artifact in a few days?" Egg asked. "Do you think they bolted it onto the belly? Or put it inside here and cut a porthole in the leading edge to shoot through?"

"I think you know something you aren't telling me," Chadwick said, still gazing intently at Egg's face.

"Think what you please," Egg grunted, and floated toward the toilet facility.

As soon as he had the door closed he put his hands on his face, trying to compose himself.

He didn't know if this saucer had a weapon on it—he hadn't asked the computer. He wondered if Chadwick would. All he had to do was put on the headband and ask. If he knew enough to ask. In his explorations of the computer's memory, Egg had spent months wandering along, poking here and there, completely on his own, before one day the thought occurred to him to ask the computer for the information he wanted. Then data spewed forth like an Oklahoma gusher.

What if this saucer did have an antimatter weapon of some sort and Chadwick learned of it? So what? They were on their way to the moon.

Given a moment to think about it, Egg put two and two together. If Rip's saucer had indeed flown again, Rip and Charley Pine were in it.

Were they still alive? Were they safe?

If anything happened to them . . .

When he had himself completely under control, Egg opened the door and floated out into the main compartment. Chadwick had strapped himself to the pilot's seat and was wearing the headband.

*   *   *

THE NEWS OF THE LOSS OF THE SPACEPLANES HIT PIERRE hard. He had bet his quest—indeed, his life and Julie's life—on the fact that his friends could get control of the French spaceport and continue to fly the spaceplanes to and from the earth. He was sure the French government would fold—he knew most of the ministers personally. They weren't gamblers, they were politicians. They read the papers, were acutely attuned to the public mood and strove mightily to stay in front of the parade so they would appear to be leading. If the public could be persuaded, the politicians would go along, and Pierre knew how to sway the French public. Honor, glory, for the good of all mankind, which would be united under a French banner. The appeal would be irresistible.

And, *mon Dieu!* It worked.

Except for that Charley Pine. Stealing the spaceplane from the moon, stranding them.

He wondered if she had flown the saucer that attacked the three spaceplanes in orbit. His gut told him yes. She would do that.

It would take at least two years to build another spaceplane and test it, even on an expedited schedule. Then another fuel tank would have to be placed in earth orbit and filled with fuel before a spaceplane could make a trip to the moon filled with supplies.

The lunar base was not self-sustaining, as he well knew. Oh, there was indeed water, but the hydroponic gardens would not sustain the forty-two people who were here. Make that forty-six, for four more were coming on Chadwick's saucer. Nor were the complex carbon-based compounds being created in the lab yet edible.

Somehow, some way, Chadwick's saucer had to be used to carry critical supplies back and forth across the chasm.

He was musing thus when Julie came into the com center. He told her of the disaster to the spaceplanes. She took the bad news well, he thought, although obviously it was a blow. They discussed how Chadwick's saucer would have to be used.

"Even with the saucer, it will be difficult to sustain forty-six people," she remarked distractedly.

Pierre nodded. "We will send as many as possible back to earth on the saucer."

"Yes. We must lower the number somehow."

The radio crackled to life. It was Mission Control reporting that the French space facilities were under attack. "Hangars are exploding, the fuel dump just detonated—" He was cut off in midsentence.

"The Americans," Pierre said heatedly.

"Or the British," Julie said. "We'll give them a taste of their own medicine. They want war, and they shall have it! And I'm going to enjoy pulling the trigger!"

IT WAS STILL DARK IN WASHINGTON WHEN CHARLEY PINE drifted the stolen saucer to a stop ten feet in the air outside a large hangar at Andrews Air Force Base. One of the huge doors began opening, revealing a brilliantly lit interior and dozens of people. The saucer slipped through the open door. Inside, the gear snapped down; then the ship settled to the shiny, reflective white concrete beside Air Force One, a huge Boeing 747 that dwarfed saucer and people. Behind the spaceship, the door was already closing.

Rip and Charley dropped through the open hatch. The first person they saw was the president of the United States. He walked over with a hand out.

He pronounced their names as he shook their hands, but

didn't say his own. After all, Rip thought, any American who didn't know the name of the president was in danger of being involuntarily committed.

Charley said, "Hi," to the president, then asked, "Where's the ladies?"

Surprised, the president looked around for a sign. One of his aides pointed, and Charley headed that way, leaving Rip and the president standing in front of the saucer.

"She's had a rough night," Rip explained. "She knew the spaceplane crews, trained with them in France."

"Sure," said the president.

"Sorry about smashing up the window over at the Air and Space. I'll pay for the damage. We didn't have time to get permission," he finished lamely.

The president's eyebrows rose. "The director told one of my staff that he figured it would cost ten million to repair the side of that building."

"We've been doing okay licensing the propulsion technology. When I get back to Missouri, I'll write the museum a check."

"I've never been inside your saucer," the president said. "How about a tour?"

Once inside, the president climbed into the pilot's seat and looked at the blank computer presentations. Rip pulled out the power knob to the first detent, and the presentations came vividly to life. After Rip's cursory explanation, the president said, "Tell me about the spaceplanes."

So Rip told it, about going into orbit, calling Space Command, doing a huge loop and dropping down onto them, blowing up the refueling tank with the spaceplane attached . . .

When Rip ran dry, the president said, "One spaceplane blew up with the fuel tank, one burned up in the atmosphere, the third came down in the Pacific. The survivors were picked up by a freighter. One crewman dead, four injured. The fourth ship, which Ms. Pine flew, is parked on the Bonneville Salt Flats under armed guard."

"Guess that's the inventory."

"Then there is the saucer that we kept in Area Fifty-one. Top secret and all that. It was stolen and is on its way to the moon, presumably under the command of Artois' colleagues."

"With my uncle Egg flying it."

"Space Command said that you believe this saucer can make that trip."

"Yessir. If we put bladder tanks here in the cabin, plumb them into the water system, we can increase our fuel capacity by two hundred percent. Charley and I figure that will be enough to get us there and back."

The president wiggled the controls. "And this saucer has a weapon?"

"Yessir. An antiproton beam."

"What's an antiproton?"

"Antimatter. When an antiproton hits a regular proton, it destroys it, releasing a lot of energy. A whole lot. $E = mc^2$."

"Your uncle will be at the lunar base. That will complicate things."

"We're going to need a couple of assault rifles and some grenades. They'll work the same there as they do here."

"Want to take a couple of marines with you?"

"It's sorta cramped in here now. When we add the water tanks, there won't be room."

"Okay." The president stirred the stick, kicked the rudders and took in the displays one more time. "Before you go, can I get a ride in this thing?"

TO GET TO THE RESTROOM CHARLEY WALKED THROUGH A large office and along a hallway. When she came out, she

paused to examine the framed photos of World War I avia-
tors hanging on the hallway wall. There was Georges Guyne-
mer, with lean cheeks and haunted eyes, wearing a coat with
a fur collar; Charles Nungesser standing in front of his plane
in a leather coat, his hands in his pockets; Albert Ball in profile, only nineteen, in the cockpit of his Nieuport; the wild
man, Frank Luke, with his arms folded across his chest, leaning against the lower wing of a Spad; Mick Mannock bending
down to pat a dog . . . ahh, and Billy Bishop seated in a Nieuport, with his head turned, looking at the camera.

She wiped at her tears, trying to see clearly. Bishop's eyes
bored into hers. Bishop, the consummate aerial warrior, was
the only one of the group to die of old age. *Seventy-two con-
firmed kills, Billy, and you lived with every one of them the rest of
your days.*

So was she feeling sorry for the men she killed, or for
herself?

"ARE YOU THE SAUCER PILOT?"

Charley Pine looked up. The questioner was a girl, perhaps ten years old, with yellow hair pulled back in pigtails.
"Yes," Charley said. "I'm the pilot."

"Why are you crying?"

Charley was sitting in a chair with her legs drawn up in the
office off the main hangar floor, amid a dozen desks, each
holding a computer and printer. The walls were lined with
filing cabinets. She swabbed at her eyes. "People do, you
know. Cry sometimes."

"Sometimes it helps," the girl said, very grown up.

Charley used the sleeves of her flight suit to dry her eyes,
then tried to smile. It was a miserable effort, she thought.

The girl took a chair nearby. "I'm Amanda. I'm eight."

"Charley."

"That's a funny name for a girl."

"It's actually Charlotte. My dad started calling me Charley because I was a tomboy, and it stuck."

"I like being a girl," Amanda said.

"I do too."

"Boys are so icky."

"Sometimes," Charley agreed, and hugged her legs.

"What's it like to fly the saucer?"

"Sometimes it's pretty cool. Other times . . ."

"I mean, what's it *really* like?" Amanda leaned forward, her eyes shining. "When you go zooming up and fly off into space and see the world from way out there, with a billion stars shining and the moon so bright and the sun hanging there on fire."

"Way cool," Charley admitted, remembering.

"Tell me."

Charley searched for words, which had never been her long suit. She could fly it and live it and savor it, but she had never tried to tell anyone about it, except for one female reporter, who turned out to be more interested in Charley's sex life than her flying experiences.

Looking at Amanda, she started talking. She told about the G forces, the rush of acceleration with empty heaven ahead, the way the sky turned dark as the saucer climbed above the atmosphere, how the clouds looked from twenty, fifty, a hundred miles high looking down. She explained about the oceans, the million shades of blue, the mountains with snow, windstorms over the deserts, cities twinkling at night . . . told it to Amanda with the shining eyes.

RIP BENT DOWN AND KISSED CHARLEY'S CHEEK. "HEY there, lady. How you doing?"

"Visiting with Amanda."

"I see you met my granddaughter," a man said from behind Charley. She turned to see who it was. The president.

"She's going to be a pilot," Charley Pine replied, winking at Amanda.

"They're going to install the water tank, get us some new clothes and underwear and provide some MREs." MREs were Meals, Ready to Eat. "Can you think of anything else?"

"A couple cases of water to drink, and I want two flight suits with an American flag on the shoulder. I'm tired of wearing this French flight suit."

"Done," the president said.

"Uhh," Rip said, leaning close and whispering. "While they're getting bladder tanks ready to install, the president wondered if you could give him and Amanda a ride in the saucer. You know, sort of an out and in to see the sights and stuff. Will you?"

Charley Pine winked at Amanda. "Want to try it?"

"Sure," the youngster replied. "If you're going to fly it. I only ride with women pilots."

"She's a true believer," said the president, grinning broadly, and rumpled the girl's hair.

"Let's put some water in it and light the fires," Charley said. She led the way out into the hangar bay. The hangar door was already open. Through it she could see the dawn.

SUSPECTING THAT ANDREWS AIR FORCE BASE HAD ITS share of neighbors who complained about noise and wanting to go easy on her passengers, Charley Pine used the rocket engines sparingly after takeoff. Amanda sat on her lap, the president stood on her left, and Rip stood in his customary place on her right. Rip had briefed the president about hanging on; each man had a death grip on the underside of the instrument panel and the back of Charley's seat.

Once over the Chesapeake, Charley pulled the nose up to thirty degrees above the horizon and tweaked on more juice.

She was flying with just the headband, using both arms to hold Amanda.

The saucer soared through forty thousand feet, now fifty. The morning sky darkened; the rim of the earth became a vivid, unbroken line. She gently banked the saucer, let the nose fall to the horizon and reduced the rockets' thrust until they became a murmur behind her.

Here the spaceship was safely above the airliners, and above the high cirrus layer that was coming in from the west. In that direction the cloud formed a bright, gauzy sheet between earth and sky, almost luminescent in the morning sun. Charley Pine thought the sky very beautiful. Gorgeous in all its moods, she reminded herself.

Charley glanced at Rip. He was grinning widely. He leaned over and kissed her on the cheek.

Rip, Rip, Rip, you are the one.

The president was also smiling. "Thank you," he told her. "And you, Rip."

She looked for the moon, then remembered that it was below the horizon at this time of day.

Enough. Pierre was waiting, with his plans for world conquest.

She silenced the rocket engines and let the nose drop toward the earth below.

AS THE SHIP CAME DOWN THE POTOMAC, AMANDA WAS full of giggles and comments. She entertained the adults royally with her observations and her mood. "I'm going to be a saucer pilot when I grow up," she announced.

"You go, girl," Charley said, and the men seconded her.

Charley flew the saucer straight into the open hangar and set it on the concrete. As Rip opened the hatch, someone handed up a message for the president. He read it, then handed it to Charley.

Golden Gate and Bay Bridge in San Francisco destroyed. Artois demands your answer. On the next pass he will reduce Washington to rubble, he says, unless the United States surrenders.

"Time to go back to work," the president said sadly, and read the message aloud. He looked at Charley, then Rip, searching their faces. "If you can destroy the other saucer or render it inoperative, Pierre Artois and his friends will be marooned up there. I think they'll listen to reason then. This saucer will be their only ride home, and we've got it."

"We're going to the moon to get Egg," Rip said.

The president opened his mouth to reply, thought better of it and slapped them both on the shoulder. He turned to his granddaughter.

"Say good-bye, Amanda. I've got to go to work. These folks need to get some food and sleep while the mechanics work on the saucer."

He shook hands with both of them and pushed Amanda toward the hatch. When they were all standing in front of the saucer, Amanda told Charley where she lived and her telephone number and asked for another ride for herself and her girlfriends. Finally she bounded away, her grandfather urging her on, her pigtails flying.

13

"THE EUROPEANS ARE COMING AROUND," HENRI SALMON reported to Pierre Artois. "All but the British and Dutch, who are being obstinate."

"As usual," Julie remarked.

She and Pierre had just seated themselves in the lunar base com center to listen to the president of the United States, who had asked for network time to make a speech to the nation. That speech was, of course, being broadcast worldwide. Salmon and his department heads were also there, standing because there were not enough seats.

When he appeared, the president started with a brief exposition of Pierre's demands, which amounted to a world government that Pierre would rule by fiat. The president even repeated some of Pierre's stated goals for that government, such as solving the world hunger problem, and so forth.

Then he went into a summary of the history of democratic government as it had evolved through the centuries, taking it from the Magna Carta to elected parliaments to the American Revolution to universal suffrage.

"Representative democracy is not perfect," the president said, "but I am absolutely convinced that it is the best method yet devised for making the public decisions that affect our lives, liberty and property. Similarly, the rule of law is the best method mankind has yet come up with for arbitrating personal and business disputes and resolving legal issues. The rule of law is also not perfect. Still, both institutions have grown and taken root in Western civilization and are, I believe, our legacy to the generations of mankind yet to come. Both institutions are being slowly adopted, and adapted to local conditions, in fits and starts by developing nations all over the globe. I stand before you today as an elected official of our constitutional democracy; like every president before me, I have sworn an oath to uphold and defend that Constitution."

The president continued on for a few minutes more, but Pierre pushed a button to silence the audio. He had gotten the message.

"We've been too gentle," Julie said. "We've been attacking things, trying to minimize the loss of life." She managed to imply that choice had been an act of humanitarian kindness. A cynic might have disagreed, but there were no cynics in the com center, only true believers. "It's time to take off the gloves," she added flatly.

"SOME REPORTER HAS GOTTEN WIND OF YOUR SAUCER ride," P.J. O'Reilly told the president after his speech. "He called my office minutes ago to see if we wanted to comment."

The president pondered a bit before he answered. "No comment," he said finally.

O'Reilly was horrified. "But, sir, the press will think we have something to hide. The congressional opposition will demand an investigation."

"Let 'em investigate. We've got other things to worry about."

Sensing that he was not getting through, O'Reilly attacked from another direction. "The press will imply that you've launched the saucer on a military mission to the moon."

The president brightened. "I did."

"They'll want to know specifics."

The president thought about it. Rip Cantrell and Charley Pine—they were sure nice young people. He took a deep breath. A rescue mission, Rip said. Well, he and Charley were bright enough and courageous enough to do the right thing.

"No comment," the president said, "about the saucer or anything connected to it. Pierre can sweat a little."

THE TRIP TO THE MOON IN A FLYING SAUCER WAS, EGG Cantrell thought, the high point of his life. During his waking hours he sat in the pilot's seat wearing the headset that allowed him to talk to the saucer's computers. Looking through the canopy into deep space, watching the moon move against the stars, glancing over his shoulder at the spinning earth while exploring the wisdom of the ancients— it made him feel as if he were sitting at a window that allowed him to look at the eternal. He was beginning to get a glimmer of the how and why; it felt as if he could see the springs and gears that made the universe turn.

When he took off the headset and sat silently looking, he found himself thinking of the people and events in his own life from a different perspective. His parents and his childhood friends and experiences seemed to become part of the warp and woof of life. His personal and professional triumphs and failures—he had had his share of both—seemed somehow less significant. Now he saw life as a grand, glorious adventure, and in some mysterious, almost mystical way, he was a part of all of it and it was a part of him.

Egg didn't get to spent all his time lost in thought. Chadwick used his satellite radio to check in with the men in the moon on a regular basis, and to chat with the people at Mission Control in France. That was how he learned of the president's upcoming speech, which he, Egg and the two Frenchmen, whom Egg referred to as Fry One and Fry Two, listened to as it was broadcast.

"Politicians are ambitious, venal and selfish," Chadwick said as the president talked about representative democracy.

Egg couldn't resist. "And dictators aren't, which is probably why people all over the planet are ridding themselves of them as quickly as they can."

"Pierre Artois isn't," Chadwick asserted. "He's a friend of all mankind."

Egg let it drop. He consoled himself with the thought that reasoning with fanatics was a fool's errand. And Chadwick was a fanatic, he well knew, a dangerous one.

After the speech, they listened to news commentary from "experts" and a report that a saucer had been seen flying around Washington, D.C., earlier in the day and was now thought to be outfitting for a flight to the moon.

Chadwick discussed that tidbit with Artois on the moon using the encrypted radio. Both men spoke in French, but Egg didn't need to understand their words to know they were worried men. He could see the strain on Chadwick's face and on the countenances of Fry One and Two, who whispered back and forth.

Egg sighed and tried to keep a poker face. It was difficult. Rip and Charley must be planning to come to the moon, no doubt in an attempt to rescue him. It would be exceedingly dangerous, he thought. In addition to the length of the journey in a craft not designed for it, a battle on the moon held little appeal.

Someone was going to die. He prayed it wouldn't be Rip or Charley.

EGG WENT BACK INTO THE COMPUTERS, WHICH WERE VERY similar to the one at his house that he had been studying for a year. As near as Egg could determine, each computer had four programs devoted to analyzing data and attempting to collaborate with their human creators by generating and testing new ideas, new hypotheses. When a computer was given information, it would assimilate it, generate a theory, test it against known physical laws and then look for connections between this new theory and others.

To perform these feats the computer used four programs running simultaneously. Egg had named them. Franklin had a short attention span and jumped off in a new direction with each piece of data, brainstorming into areas that at first appeared implausible. Jefferson was pickier and only toyed with novel or interesting ideas. The Professor was more pedantic, exploring ideas only when they conformed to its preconceived concepts and rules. Einstein, more thorough, explored different shades and implications of ideas from any source, including his three colleagues, and occasionally arrived at a profound insight.

Egg lived for Einstein's insights, when he understood them. He communicated with a computer by watching it work and trying to understand the reality that it was exploring. The medium wasn't language; it was thoughts. He saw the thoughts, felt them and watched his four horsemen continuously mold and shape them, trying them out.

Egg found that he wasn't in the mood for computers. Nor did the games they contained interest him. Normally he had to ration himself on the games, which were interactive intel-lectual exercises presumably designed to stimulate the minds of interstellar voyagers. He couldn't stop thinking of Rip and Charley.

A few hours later Chadwick had another long conversa-tion with Pierre. When that was over he said to Egg, "In about four hours, when the moon is over Washington, Pierre will teach the Americans a lesson they'll never forget."

"He's a friend of all mankind," Egg murmured.

"Eggs must be broken—"

"Ah, for the lunar omelet."

"They will thank him someday. Few revolutions are bloodless."

"Nor conquests, as I recall."

"The people of the earth must learn to obey, for their own good. Fear will teach them that lesson."

"Let's hear it for fear," Egg muttered, but Chadwick appar-ently decided that he had argued enough and ignored the remark. As he floated away he unconsciously adjusted the fanny pack.

Two hours later Egg was the only one in the saucer awake. The sleeping men were suspended in makeshift hammocks, which merely kept them from floating into something—or each other—while they slept.

As Egg sat staring at Newton Chadwick, he realized that Chadwick had forgotten to snap his fanny pack in place on his last visit to the head. He could clearly see the snap, and it was unlatched. A portion of the pack hung through a gap in the hammock netting that held the sleeping man.

It appeared one could merely pull the pack another few inches though that hole and open it.

If the deed were done quietly enough, Egg mused, per-haps Chadwick wouldn't awaken.

* * *

RIP AND CHARLEY MISSED THE PRESIDENT'S SPEECH. THEY were too busy supervising the installation of the water bladders and checking for leaks. A leak on the ground would be a gusher under four Gs of acceleration. Going to the moon waist deep in water didn't seem like a good idea.

When they had the new bladder tanks full and all their gear stowed, Charley and Rip shook hands with the air force personnel and climbed aboard. Outside the hangar, the moon had risen just as night fell. This was the night of the full moon.

Charley and Rip both found themselves taking long looks at the moon as the saucer sat bathed in moonlight outside the hangar while Charley programmed the flight computer.

Six minutes after Rip closed the hatch, the saucer rose from the earth on a cone of white-hot fire. The fireball appeared like a rising sun to many on the south side of the metropolitan area.

The president was packing papers in the Oval Office— which was probably going to go up in a cloud of splinters in just a few hours—when the saucer's deep roar rattled the windows and chandeliers of the executive mansion. He stood frozen, listening intently, until the noise of the saucer had faded completely. Then he smiled.

WHEN THEY HAD COMPLETED THE LUNAR ORBIT INSERTION burn and were coasting on course for the moon, Rip checked the plumbing for leaks. It was difficult moving in and out of the tight spaces when weightless. He felt like a worm crawling around the pipes and pumps. Finally he wiggled clear and reported to Charley, who was still sitting in the pilot's seat working with the flight computer.

"Everything is dry," he said.

When he reached her and got a look at her face, the grimness he saw surprised him. "Charley . . ."

"Pierre is going to trash Washington," she said bitterly.

"He was going to do that sooner or later. You know that."

She finished with the computer and sat staring at the moon, which was well off to her left.

"How far do you think these antiprotons will travel in a vacuum?" she asked Rip.

He glanced at her. She was staring at the moon. "I don't know," he said. "Want to try an experiment?"

"Why not," she muttered, and turned the saucer so that the moon was directly in front of them.

"We don't even know how fast the antiprotons go," Rip said. "So we don't know whether it will take seconds or minutes or hours for them to get there. The chance of a hit is mighty small."

"Infinitesimal," Charley agreed.

The crosshairs of the optical sight had appeared on the canopy as she spoke. She looked to see where the lines intersected, then directed the computer to fine-tune the saucer's position, which moved the crosshairs slightly. Of course, they were so thick that at this distance the junction covered miles of the moon's surface.

The lunar base was . . . there, on the edge of that sea, to the south of that mountain range, which could only be seen at this great distance as a fine shadow line.

Fire!

The small light appeared on the sight. The antimatter weapon was discharging.

She tweaked the crosshairs in the direction the moon was traveling in space as the weapon continued to fire a stream of antiprotons into the vacuum.

After thirty seconds, when the crosshairs were on the edge of the lunar orb, she stopped the discharge.

"Well," Rip said, his disappointment audible, "that was a nonevent. It's not like I expected the moon to blow up, but still . . ."

"Sort of like tossing a pebble into the Atlantic," Charley said, and sighed. She was still thinking of those spaceplanes. She rubbed her face.

"I'm so tired," she murmured, and unfastened her seat belt. Rip reached for her, and she floated into his arms.

TRAVELING AT HALF THE SPEED OF LIGHT, THE ANTIMAT-ter particles shot through the vacuum of space, across the empty two-hundred-thousand-mile gulf that separated the coasting saucer and the moon. As they did they dispersed slightly, so by the time the particles reached the moon they fell like rain across a ten-mile swath of the lunar surface.

Still moving at half of the speed of light, each particle shot through the dust and rock of the lunar surface until it encountered a proton speeding in its orbit around an atom's nucleus. When they collided, the two particles spontaneously obliterated each other, releasing a colossal burst of energy. Sometimes the detonation took place with inches of the surface; sometimes, depending on the density of the material, it happened much deeper, at a depth of several feet.

Although each explosion was quite large in relation to the size of the particles involved, the particles were indeed very small, so the explosions resembled large firecracker detonations.

The vast majority of the particles fell across the empty wasteland, and no living thing was there to witness their self-destruction. The wave marched across the lunar surface, and by sheer chance, one edge of it crossed the French lunar base. Most of the antimatter particles detonated harmlessly, although one did pass through a solar power cell. It met its opposite particle six inches deep in the rock underneath, and the shards of rock blasted upward by the explosion destroyed the power cell. Since there were hundreds of power cells, the loss of one was undetected by the voltage-monitoring equipment.

Those two dozen antimatter particles that impacted the soil over the lunar base met their positrons in the rock, before they reached the caverns underneath, and the explosions rocked the base. Dust fell from the overhead; people felt the triphammer concussions, which triggered the seismic and air-pressure-loss alarms. As alarms clanged throughout the base, people dove frantically for their space suits, just in case.

Two of the particles penetrated the cover above the anti-gravity beam generator and telescope. One detonated a foot deep in the rock floor, showering the room with dust and bits of rock, while creating a nasty small crater. The other went off simultaneously six inches under the surface; the resulting explosion severed a data cable between the telescope and the main computer.

Julie and Pierre Artois and Claudine Courbet were at the console, inputting the coordinates for the major buildings they planned to pulverize in Washington, D.C., during the next hour. They looked around wildly, trying to understand what was happening, as the gong and wail of the alarms sounded even while the debris slowly settled from the explosions.

"What was that?" Pierre demanded.

No one answered. When it became clear that the base wasn't losing air, and the alarms had been reset and were once again silent, he and Julie and Claudine took stock. That was when they discovered that the telescope was inoperative. Seconds later Claudine found the severed cable.

"A meteor shower," Pierre said dismissively. All his life he had minimized difficulties and then plowed his way through.

Julie, however, was made of different, more paranoid, stuff. With no evidence at all, she leaped to a completely different conclusion. "It's a weapon of some kind! That Pine woman! She must have used it on the spaceplanes."

Pierre snorted. After all, *he* was the emperor of France. "It was in Washington just hours ago. Even if it is headed for the moon, it is three days away. A weapon with a range of 238,000 miles? Preposterous!"

Yet the fact remained that something had struck the lunar base. Just what it was, no one could say.

As the United States spun under the lunar base, the emperor's technicians worked to rig a new cable.

In Washington the president and an expectant nation waited . . . and nothing happened. The absence of the promised disaster stunned the experts, who debated the nonevent on television, explaining their different visions of what it might mean and arguing bitterly among themselves.

"Pierre Artois," the secretary of state said hopefully in an interview, "must have come to his senses." She listed the possible reasons why, dwelling heavily on the sanctity of human life and Pierre's progressive goals, but the network cut away midway through her exposition to air a Viagra commercial, depriving the public of the benefit of her views.

Coasting toward the moon, oblivious to the media frenzy on the mother planet, Rip and Charley slept in each other's arms.

14

THE ROSWELL SAUCER, WITH EGG CANTRELL IN THE PI-
lot's seat, looped around the back side of the moon. Egg
positioned the saucer so that it was flying backward, and,
while still behind the moon, fired the rockets to begin a
descent to the lunar base on the side facing earth. When the
burn was completed, he turned the saucer 180 degrees so
that it was again aligned with its trajectory, which he could
alter slightly, as necessary, with the saucer's maneuvering
jets.

He had weighed the possibility of using the antimatter
weapon on the lunar base when it hove into view, but he was
unsure how to fire it or how much damage the weapon
would do. As the saucer descended toward the lunar surface,
crossing from the darkness into the light, soaring over stupendous mountain ranges and dark lunar lava flows, Newton
Chadwick was hovering on his right side and Fry Two on the
left. At the most, he thought, a two- or three-second burst
was about all he could hope for before Chadwick and the
Fries throttled him.

Egg also considered crashing the saucer, power-diving the

moon to make a new crater. That would quickly and pain-lessly kill him and his three passengers and permanently maroon Pierre Artois and his disciples. Egg thought about it for about two seconds and decided he didn't have it in him. He wasn't suicidal. Nor, he decided, was he warrior enough to pull the trigger on Chadwick, the Fries and the French astronauts, even if there were a way he could live through the experience. Maybe he should have had the courage, if that was what it was, but he didn't and he knew it. As that great American philosopher Dirty Harry Callahan once said, a man has to know his limitations.

Eventually, as the saucer descended and slowed, the lunar base appeared, right where it should be. The solar power panels were an unmistakable landmark. Egg snapped down the landing gear and sat watching as the flight computer used the maneuvering jets and the antigravity system to bring the saucer gently into a hover outside the entrance to the base. Now he saw the lunar dune buggy and the forklift, parked near the main air lock.

Talking silently to the flight computer, he allowed the saucer to settle toward the lunar surface. It touched down almost imperceptibly on its three legs, and all motion stopped.

Egg found that he had been holding his breath. He exhaled convulsively and pushed in the power knob to the first detent, which retained electrical power on the saucer but killed the reactor and propulsion system. Then he used a shirttail to swab the perspiration from his face.

Only then did he look at Newton Chadwick. Chadwick's face was devoid of color. The man had been hanging on with both hands, a death grip he was unable to release, even now.

"We're here, Chadwick," Egg said, pointing out the obvi-ous. He was surprised how cool and calm his own voice sounded. *Yeah, man, I'm Egg Cantrell, saucer pilot. I do this every day.* As he mopped his brow again he noticed that his hands were trembling.

"SO, YOU ARE THE BRILLIANT CANTRELL," PIERRE ARTOIS said in lightly accented English. He said that as if Egg's reputation were somehow disreputable. They were standing inside the com center.

Egg had managed to wriggle into a space suit without ripping it, but it was a close call. He needed to lose at least twenty pounds to lessen the strain on the zipper. Maybe thirty. He was out of the space suit now, trying to take in everything, see how the lunar base was laid out.

He concentrated on Pierre. Of medium height, erect, charismatic, with what some might term good looks, Pierre radiated control. "That's right," Egg said slowly, shaking his head. "The brilliant Cantrell."

"We have experienced a new phenomenon I wish to ask you about, Cantrell. The effects are unknown to science. Suddenly, all in the same moment, a series of minor explosions rocked the base. Two were in our observatory. I wonder if you might be able to shed some light on this unique experience."

"Sorry. This is my first trip to the moon." Egg thought that a rather witty answer.

"I thought perhaps this phenomenon might be the end product of some kind of weapon. On the other saucer, perhaps, the one your nephew stole from the Air and Space Museum in Washington just a few days ago, the one he used to shoot down three French spaceplanes and murder the crews."

"I know nothing about the other saucer. I have been an unwilling guest of Mr. Chadwick. Perhaps you can enlighten me—in this new utopia that you will lead, will kidnapping be illegal?"

"I haven't the time to split the hairs, as you Americans say." He nodded at Henri Salmon and turned back to the radio mike. Salmon placed his hand on Egg's arm.

"If you will come with me, sir. We'll show you to your quarters."

"I need food and a bath," Egg shot back. He made eye contact with Julie Artois, who was standing against one wall frowning slightly, as they led him out.

WHEN EGG WAS OUT OF SIGHT, PIERRE TURNED ON THE charm for Chadwick and embraced him. "Your arrival in that saucer has saved us, saved our great quest. Our debt to you is large."

Chadwick beamed. The terrors of the flight were over, and he was on the winning team—it doesn't get any better than that.

"Would you like to see the saucer?" he asked Pierre, who readily agreed.

As they were donning space suits for the walk to the parked saucer, Chadwick said, "Cantrell lied to you. There is a weapon aboard the saucer, a generator that fires antiprotons in a continuous stream."

"Antiprotons?"

"Antimatter. When an antiproton strikes a regular proton, they annihilate each other. I don't know if the Sahara saucer has this weapon, but the Roswell one does. And it sounds from your description as if you were showered with antiprotons."

"Charley Pine," Pierre said grimly. "She and young Cantrell are presumably headed this way. The press reported the saucer going into orbit from Washington about six hours ago. Four hours ago we experienced the attack." He was silent as he zipped himself into the suit, then said, "Now that Egg Cantrell is here, I doubt if they will again shower us with antimatter. But Pine and young Cantrell are coming, so we must arrange a suitable reception."

He pushed the intercom button on the wall and spoke to the duty officer in the com room. "Ask Jean-Paul Lalouette and Henri Salmon to come to the suit room. They will enjoy seeing the saucer."

WHEN THE FOUR MEN WERE INSIDE THE SAUCER, CHADWICK closed the hatch and repressurized the interior. He had watched Egg depressurize it, so he reversed the process. When the pressure had stabilized, he removed his helmet and gestured for Pierre, Salmon and Lalouette to do likewise.

"This is it," he told them. "Roswell, New Mexico, 1947. What do you think?"

Pierre looked at everything, stared at the holographic displays on the instrument panel, touched this and that, before he finally spoke. "I confess, Chadwick, when you first approached me with your antigravity device, I did not believe you. If you had not had a working model that proved that the antigravity theory could be put to practical use, I would have thrown you out of the office."

"As everyone else did," Newton Chadwick said with a gleam in his eye. "No one else believed. Not one."

"And so, this is where your journey led. To the moon, eh?" Artois was jovial. He slapped Chadwick on the back. After all, he *was* the emperor of France. "Show us how this saucer works."

Newton Chadwick gave them the tour, explained the propulsion system, the antigravity rings, gave summaries about the various computers and let each sit in the pilot's seat wearing the headband.

A long hour later, Artois asked Chadwick, "This saucer has a weapon?"

"Oh, yes." Chadwick put the optical sighting crosshairs on the canopy and ran through what he had learned of the system from his explorations of the computer.

Artois listened intently. "With this weapon we can prevent the saucer that is on its way here from Washington from hurting us."

"True," Chadwick admitted.

"Can you fly this ship?"

Chadwick took a deep breath and held it while he studied the instrument panel. He had watched Egg do it, of course. Watched intently. Wearing the headband, one merely asked the computer for the appropriate maneuver and it manipulated the various propulsion, control and navigation systems. And yet . . .

Newton Chadwick exhaled. "No," he said forcefully. He glanced at Jean-Paul Lalouette, then looked Artois in the eyes. "I could teach him, though. He is a pilot. He has the . . . the confidence, the judgment, the experience . . . that I do not."

Artois looked expectantly at Lalouette, who was not thinking of the saucer but of Charlotte Pine. She would be flying the saucer that he was supposed to attack. She had become famous last year by flying it, and now she was at it again. He had gotten to know her fairly well during the training cycle for the spaceplane mission. A U.S. Air Force Academy graduate, Pine served a tour in F-16 fighters before she went to test pilot school. When Artois had hired her to fly the spaceplane, Lalouette was very skeptical. He didn't believe anyone could learn the ship in the short time available. And she had. Not only had she learned to be a copilot, she had flown it solo back to earth and landed in Utah. She was, he thought now, perhaps the finest natural pilot he had ever met.

Lalouette cleared his throat and examined the various displays on the instrument panel. There was no book that explained all this. One had to intuitively grasp the significance of what one was seeing or . . . or else.

He looked again at Artois. "You want me to shoot down the other saucer?"

"Yes."

So there it was. Lalouette rubbed the stubble on his jaw. He found that Salmon was staring at him, his face expressionless.

When Salmon captured Jean-Paul's eyes, he said, "If you don't fly this ship, the other saucer may destroy or hopelessly damage it. The only other ship on earth capable of reaching us is in the United States. The American president will probably order it destroyed. The lunar base will be our burial crypt. Do you want to die here?"

Still Lalouette hesitated. When he was younger he spent three years flying Super Entendard fighters. He fingered the throttle grip on the antigravity lever. The water necessary to refuel this saucer was here, at the lunar base, but without a radar or GCI controller, intercepting the other saucer at altitude was impractical. The interception would have to be made low, near the lunar base, while the other saucer was on its final approach with the antigravity system. Yes, he decided, that was the best way to do it.

"Chadwick will fly with you," Artois said. "He knows the systems. He doesn't want to die." He turned his gaze on the redheaded American. "Do you?" he asked.

There was something in the tone of his voice that sent a cold chill up Chadwick's spine.

"BILLIONS AND BILLIONS OF STARS. DO YOU EVER STOP and wonder what's really out there?" Rip said to Charley Pine. Head to head, they were staring through the canopy at the Milky Way, that huge splash of stars that streaked the heavens, our galaxy.

"Our species will be exploring it until the end of time,"

Charley replied. She too felt the magic of the moment. Hurling though space toward an uncertain rendezvous, with life hanging in the balance, still there was time to look at the eternal . . . and wonder.

"Like Egg, I've spent time this winter and spring surfing the saucer's computer," Rip said. "But the people who built the saucer stopped making entries 140,000 years ago. What have they learned since then?"

"If they still exist?"

"Oh, they're out there," Rip replied thoughtfully. "Someplace out there, amid all those stars, are people just like us. Professor Soldi was right, I suspect—they are our cousins. And they are probably looking our way and wondering about those colonists that went bravely forth into the great unknown a hundred and forty millennia ago."

"If you look into the abyss long enough, the abyss stares back. Didn't someone smart say that?"

"Speaking of the abyss, how are we going to go about rescuing Egg when we get to the moon?"

WHEN JEAN-PAUL LALOUETTE DONNED THE HEADBAND that allowed the saucer's computer to read and respond to his brainwaves, he felt as if he had walked through a doorway into another world, another dimension. He could see—

Frightened, he ripped off the headband. He was in the pilot's seat of the saucer, the panel was there . . . he fingered the controls, reassuring himself with their tangible solidity, the texture and sensuous shape of their surfaces. Yes, this was real.

He looked at the headband, fingered it, then placed it back upon his head.

Oh, now he understood. He was living in two worlds, that of the cockpit and, superimposed over it, that of the computer.

He decided that the first command would be to lift the

saucer from the lunar surface where it rested, and he instantly felt a tiny lurch as the ship rose until it was absolutely level, then severed its contact with the moon.

He was up; he could see the change in perspective. *Now forward*—and the saucer began to move.

Stop!

Aft!

Right!

Left!

Higher—oh, it was magic!

"See how easy it is," someone said. Chadwick's voice. Chadwick, one of life's spectators, one of those who lacked the courage to put his own lips to the silver cup.

Lalouette snapped up the landing gear and let the saucer accelerate away from the base, out across the vast dark lava flow that stretched away to the south and east. It accelerated slowly, no doubt because the lunar gravity was so weak. Yet it was accelerating, faster and faster, until on just the antigravity system alone the saucer was doing about two hundred knots, which appeared to be terminal velocity unless he lit the rockets. He did—and the saucer accelerated abruptly.

After a few moments he tilted the saucer and used the controls to turn and head back for the base, maneuvering freely to get the feel of the machine.

With the rockets off near the lunar surface, he tilted the saucer to sixty degrees and used the antigravity system and a squirt from the ship's maneuvering jets to turn a sharp corner. The G came hard and, after two weeks away from the earth's gravitational field, almost blacked him out. He strained against it, fighting to stay conscious.

He straightened out and raced back across the lava flow toward the lunar base, its solar cells marking its position. Behind the base was the first of the ridges. He climbed progressively higher and higher, aiming for the tops of the crags on the highest ridge, which towered fifteen thousand feet above the flat lava bed below.

The ridges were knife edges, sheer and steep, untouched by the forces of erosion in a place without wind or rain, although they did bear the scars of weathering caused by the fierce temperature extremes between sunlight and shadow. The stark sunlight and deep purple, almost black, shadows made the jagged formations seem even more severe. The French pilot worked the saucer up the slopes and ridges, barely clearing the high points, turning first one way, then another, tilting right and left, staying just a few feet over the rock.

He slowed the saucer and brought it to a halt, finally, above the highest peak—stopped it above that apex as if it were mounted on an invisible pedestal.

Now Lalouette took off the headband and looked around. Both Artois and Chadwick were unconscious on the floor. They had succumbed to the G forces. Salmon was conscious, however, strapped into one of the seats. He looked grimly at Lalouette.

Jean-Paul snorted and shook his head, then donned the headband again. He looked up at the earth, which was merely a black spot against the sunlit sky.

Pierre Artois thought he was the emperor of the earth, but oh, how little he knew!

Jean-Paul dumped the saucer's nose and let it accelerate down the slope. It accelerated slowly, pulled by the weak lunar gravity, as if life were being lived in slow motion.

On the crest of a lower ridge he saw a sharp promontory, a spire of rock that had stood upright since the ridge was made. Even as the thought crossed his mind, the crosshairs of the antimatter weapon appeared on the canopy before him. The saucer turned slightly, pointing precisely at that rock finger, superimposing the crosshairs over it.

Fire!

Flashes from the rock. Shards and dust flew off as antiprotons found protons and the particles obliterated each other in bursts of pure energy.

The spire was obscured in an opaque cloud of rock fragments when he stopped shooting at the last instant and pulled the saucer up just enough to avoid smashing into it. Accelerating downward toward the lava sea, the saucer quickly left the shattered spire behind.

Lalouette's face wore a terrible grin.

15

THE MOON WAS JUST ABOVE THE WESTERN HORIZON THE next morning when the sun rose in North America. The weather was magnificent across most of the continent on this autumn day. As the earth spun in the sky over his head, Pierre Artois used his antigravity beam on the White House, then the arch in St. Louis, and finally, the Rose Bowl in Pasadena.

Some California sports fans became positively giddy when the Rose Bowl was reduced to rubble. Perhaps, they thought, the feds could be induced to build a new stadium to replace it, one that might attract an NFL team.

Pierre could have zapped a lot more places—the weather was perfect, the sunlight at a low angle gave the telescopic picture excellent contrast, and Julie was urging him to—but he refrained, preferring to pretend he had been forced to violence by a recalcitrant president who refused to listen to reason.

The president of the United States had problems of a different sort. Millions of Americans watched the White House being reduced to splinters as they ate their breakfast. It was not a pretty sight, and the reaction was immediate. A delegation of infuriated senators and representatives called upon the chief executive at "an undisclosed location" and urged war on France.

"That idiot Artois is the emperor of France, according to the French government, and he is waging war on us," Senator Blohardt said forcefully. "We must deliver an ultimatum to the frogs—renounce Artois or suffer the consequences."

"And the consequences would be . . . ?"

"Nuclear war," said a senator from the Deep South, smacking a fist into his palm.

"No, not that," a California congressman replied. "Conventional explosives only. Surgical strikes. Radioactivity would poison the water and spread through the food chain."

"A blockade of all French ports," another urged. "We'll shut down their industry."

"I might support a boycott of French products," the secretary of state said tentatively. "We might be able to get the UN to go along with a boycott, as long as there was a wine-for-food provision so that the French wouldn't starve."

"Hmm," said the president, and sent the delegation off with the secretary of state to argue the issue.

"So what *are* we going to do?" P. J. O'Reilly asked the president when the legislators had been ushered out.

"Nothing," said the president, "until we hear from Rip and Charley."

"The latest polls say the public wants action," O'Reilly reminded him. He gestured toward the television, which was replaying a video of the destruction of the executive mansion one more time. "You're sitting on a volcano of outraged voters. You cannot remain passive."

"If you have any suggestions, trot them out."

O'Reilly thought hard, but he couldn't come up with anything. The president couldn't either, so he went to the gym to work out.

"WHY CAN'T WE SEE THE SAUCER THAT IS COMING TOWARD us?" Pierre demanded of Claudine Courbet. He was standing at the telescope controls staring at the computer-enhanced image as he scanned the scope slowly back and forth, trying to find a single tiny dot of light that moved in relation to the background stars.

"You are looking for one grain of sand on a very large beach, monsieur," Courbet said respectfully.

"If only we had a decent radar!" Pierre declared. A radar unit that they could use to aim the antigravity beam or scan the sky for incoming spaceplanes would have been impossible to justify to the French politicians; Pierre had used all the excess lift capacity he had transporting unmanifested items that he absolutely had to have. Now that he was emperor he could get anything he wanted on a manifest, if only he had a way to get it here.

He gave up on the telescope and glanced over his shoulder at Egg Cantrell, who stood between Henri Salmon and Fry One against a wall. Pierre had had Egg brought here to watch the recalcitrant Americans being zapped in the hope that he would be suitably impressed. A videotaped appeal from a humbled Egg might be useful at some point.

"So, you see how futile is the American resistance, eh?"

"Did the thought ever occur to you that you might have killed people in those buildings you destroyed?"

"Your president has chosen to sacrifice American lives rather than doing the proper, honorable thing, which is to submit. I do what I must in the interest of all mankind. If lives have been lost, it is his responsibility, not mine."

Pierre was a megalomaniac so far around the bend he was

out of sight, Egg concluded. Reasoning with him was a waste of time.

Egg looked through the thick, bulletproof glass, if that was what it was, at the chamber beyond, with the antigravity beam generator in the center and the telescope and capacitor slightly offset, at the scaffolding against the wall, at the plates and hydraulic rams that could seal the chamber from the vacuum of space. The chamber was lit by brilliant sunlight, which was not streaming straight down through the hole in the roof but was coming in at a slight angle. Yet through the opening one could see stars in the dark sky.

A remarkable engineering triumph, Egg thought. Quite remarkable.

As Pierre chattered on about his plans for the people of earth, for the future of the species in the utopia that he would build, Egg thought about Rip and Charley, who were coming to the moon in Rip's old saucer . . . to rescue him.

Finally Pierre tired of Egg's monosyllabic answers and turned to Claudine. "How is the weather over Japan?"

"Clear enough, I think. The sun will not be up for hours but I believe Tokyo is very well lit. Perhaps we can see it. Clouds will obscure the islands tomorrow."

Pierre rubbed his hands together. "Then we must discipline them now," he said, and turned to the control console.

Egg's thoughts shot down the road Pierre had inadvertently suggested. God rest you, Sigmund Freud. Julie Artois was standing at the console monitoring the reactor's output and checking computer readouts. She would enjoy wielding the whip, Egg decided. A bit embarrassed at the mental image, he flushed slightly.

So there it was. A megalomaniac and his dominatrix, shattering lives all over the globe because they knew what was best for everyone.

Egg closed his eyes and concentrated fiercely.

Power on!

He let ten seconds slip by, then ordered, *Rise from the surface, about fifty feet. Gear up.*

He was looking up toward the opening above the antigravity beam, into that brilliant sunbeam, when it momentarily dimmed, then brightened again.

Egg stared at the hole, concentrating hard.

Now he saw it, the leading edge of the saucer. He brought it over the hole, completely blotting out the sunbeam, and lowered it until it was about ten feet above the opening.

The dimming light instantly alerted everyone in the control room. They all stared upward at the stationary saucer suspended above the hole. As Egg's eyes adjusted to the lower light level, he could see surface dust and debris forming a layer in the repulsion zone halfway between the saucer and the floor of the chamber.

"WHAT?" PIERRE EXPLODED. "IS LALOUETTE FLYING THE saucer? Is he crazy?" He grabbed the microphone on the console and pushed buttons.

"Lalouette?" The name boomed over the public address system. "Where is he?" Pierre demanded in French. "If Lalouette is in the base, send him to the power chamber immediately."

Julie Artois stepped in front of Egg. Her eyes glittered as they stared into his. "You did this!" she said bitterly. "You foul little man." She slapped him as hard as she could swing. Egg staggered from the blow, caught himself and put everything he had into a return slap. Henri Salmon blocked Egg's arm; then he and Fry One pinned the American.

"What is this?" Pierre shouted at Julie. "Why hit him? Someone is in the saucer!"

"Who?" she demanded.

It took ten minutes to account for everyone at the lunar

base. Lalouette and Newton Chadwick rushed into the chamber while the count was being conducted. Chadwick and Julie huddled in one corner while the French pilot conferred with Artois.

The two men holding Egg didn't relax their grip, even though he wasn't struggling. Egg tried to keep a poker face. He should have refused to fly the saucer for Chadwick, should have crashed it into the moon, should have had more courage . . .

He was still berating himself when he heard Chadwick say, "Brainwaves are tiny electrical charges generated by the synapses in our brains. The saucer's computers read them through the tiny wires embedded in the headband that the pilot wears. Cantrell must have programmed the saucer's computer to perform certain maneuvers at designated times."

Julie whirled toward Egg. "That's it, isn't it? The saucer is under your control."

Egg nodded his head. They were all staring at him now, everyone in the control chamber. "You aren't going to zap anybody with the saucer parked over your hole. If you people lay a finger on me, I'm going to fly the saucer into the sun."

Pierre was the first to recover his composure. He was definitely emperor material. "You're bluffing. You'd be committing suicide."

Egg shrugged. "It'll be your funeral too, Artois. We'll sit around talking about old times and what might have been while we starve to death."

He jerked his arms free of the two thugs, then said, "I'm going to get something to eat." Everyone stood speechless as he carefully hopped toward the air lock. The Roswell saucer remained in position ten feet above the top of the chamber, so steady it seemed to be welded there.

* * *

THE BRAIN TRUST, PIERRE, JULIE, CHADWICK, SALMON AND Lalouette, huddled near the control console. Every now and then one of them glanced through the glass at the belly of the saucer.

"We can't just climb up on a ladder and open the hatch," Chadwick said. "The saucer is resting on an antigravity field, and anyone trying that would be crushed."

"If Cantrell fires the saucer's rockets, we're all dead," Pierre reminded them, quite unnecessarily. He was stunned by their proximity to the edge of the abyss. An entire fleet of spaceplanes was gone, either destroyed or beyond reach, and the only transport he and his followers had to get back to earth was an artifact stolen from the U.S. Air Force, an artifact of unknown age and condition, controlled somehow by a fat twisted genius they had had to kidnap. *Mon Dieu!* If that weren't enough to freeze one's blood, there was another saucer equipped with an antimatter weapon on its way here to destroy his saucer. Pierre put his hands to the sides of his head and pressed. *There must be a way out of this maze. There must be!*

Julie used a broadsword on Chadwick. "You had a computer from a saucer for over fifty years. Cantrell had one for a year and knows more about the ship than you do. I must say, I am not impressed, Chadwick."

"He and I have different interests," Chadwick answered, his anger showing. "Do you want my help or don't you?"

"You jump right in if you want to stay alive."

"It beggars belief that he programmed the saucer to fly to this cavern and park itself above the opening, blocking the antigravity beam. When we were on our way to the moon he didn't know the precise location of the lunar base, didn't know where the cavern was, didn't know where the saucer would be parked, didn't know the elevation difference between the parking area and the top of the opening, and he didn't know the bearing or distance from one to the other."

"Quite true," Pierre admitted.

"Go on," Julie prompted.

Newton Chadwick threw up his hands. At times the myopic stupidity of these people was truly amazing, and they intended to rule the world. "So if he didn't program the maneuvers into the computer on the way to the moon—and he didn't know enough to do so—then it follows that he is flying the saucer himself. Now. He is telling it what to do, even as we speak."

"But he wasn't in the saucer!" Julie exclaimed. "He was standing against that wall. He isn't in it now!"

"You are very quick, madam," Chadwick said. "That is precisely the point."

"So how do we get Cantrell to return the saucer to us?"

That *was* the question. They discussed it from every angle. He would never willingly turn over control of the saucer. If they killed him it would still be hovering where it was until the reactor malfunctioned or the core decayed, whichever happened first, and since the hatch was on the belly of the thing, in the midst of the antigravity field, the saucer might as well be back on earth—they would never get inside.

"Unless . . ." Newton Chadwick said thoughtfully. He turned his gaze upward, at the belly of the saucer hovering over the antigravity beam generator. He concentrated fiercely and asked the saucer to move. *Sideways a few feet. Please.*

Nothing happened.

So as long as Egg had control, the saucer would obey no one else. That seemed a reasonable conclusion, and Chadwick examined it in detail. He could see no logical flaw.

Chadwick explained to the knot of people around him. As he did, Henri Salmon thoughtfully rubbed his left armpit.

Pierre was dubious. "What if you're wrong?"

"What other explanation could there be? Give me one."

"I am not a genius like you or Cantrell," Pierre said without apology. "Yet in my opinion, we had better not do anything irrevocable until we're absolutely certain you're correct." He put his hand on Salmon's arm and said to him, "Cantrell is not to be harmed."

WHILE THE BRAIN TRUST EXAMINED THEIR OPTIONS, EGG sat sampling food in the cafeteria. The food was amazingly good, he thought. The French could be relied upon to eat well under any circumstances.

He thought about Rip and Charley, he thought about the saucer and its astounding treasure trove of information, and he thought about what he would do when he got home. He did not think about what the Artois gang might do now that he had scarfed their flying saucer. He refused to think about it. Anything but that.

The other people in the cafeteria were whispering among themselves and glancing at him from time to time. The news about the saucer he had parked over the antigravity beam generator must be spreading like wildfire, he thought. He lowered his gaze to the food on his tray. It was all very good, but he had no appetite.

Egg figured that sooner or later they would realize he was controlling the saucer, but he didn't think they would figure out how. He hoped not, anyway.

Lalouette, the French spaceplane pilot, came through the door and walked over to Egg's table. "Would you please come with me, Monsieur Cantrell?"

Egg shrugged. Might as well. He stood and followed.

There were five of them waiting in the com center. Pierre gestured to an empty chair that faced him. "Monsieur Cantrell, please. Let us discuss this matter like gentlemen."

Egg hesitated. Julie was there, Claudine Courbet, Chadwick and Salmon. Chadwick was propped against a wall with his arms folded across his chest. He met Egg's eyes.

Egg turned his gaze to Artois. "Have you told these people who is going to be left behind when you and Julie take the saucer back to earth?"

"That's not your concern," Pierre said smoothly.

"I'll bet they are wondering, since the saucer is not large enough to hold more than ten people. And if the saucer leaves, one doubts that it will ever return."

"Sit down, sir."

"I suspect you'll negotiate some sort of immunity for yourself in return for abandoning your attempted conquest. I'm sure you'll do quite well with a book or two and a movie about your adventure."

"You're quite the cynic—" Pierre began. He stopped abruptly when Henri Salmon grabbed Egg from behind.

Julie also leaped at Egg, and he felt a sharp pain in his arm. He looked down, saw the syringe—and felt himself falling as everything went black.

JEAN-PAUL LALOUETTE DONNED HIS SPACE SUIT AND exited the lunar base. Standing in the parking area where he could see the saucer, he ordered it to return to its parking place in front of the main air lock. As he thought about it, the saucer responded.

Soon he had it sitting on its landing gear in the spot where Egg had left it a few days before.

Lalouette looked up at the stars. They were clear and seemed very close. It was an optical illusion, he knew. The only thing close was death, and it was just inches away, waiting . . .

When he had the saucer shut down, he turned and walked back into the air lock.

16

THE 140,000-YEAR-OLD SAUCER RIP HAD DUG FROM A sandstone ledge in the Sahara Desert crept slowly through the mountains of the moon a hundred feet above the valley floors. Charley Pine sat in the pilot's seat wearing the head-band. The sight reticle of the antimatter weapon was pro-jected on the canopy in front of her. She saw it with every sweep of her eyes.

Rip stood beside her holding tightly to the instrument panel and the back of her seat. He too was looking, ahead, above, as far behind as he could see, and of course to the right and left.

The cliffs were jagged, sheer jumbles of rock and lava raised billions of years ago when the moon was born, torn from proto-earth and ejected into space by the impact of a meteor. The only weathering had been through differential heating caused by the sun's unfiltered rays, and here and there huge impact marks where ancient meteors had crashed.

Yet there were gullies and canyons, as if at some time in eons past water had rushed down these slopes.

Charley flew the saucer up a canyon, rose slowly to the top

of the ridge and paused there momentarily with just the canopy sticking up. She and Rip scanned carefully, looking. The sun was low in the sky, casting long, deep shadows. Mountains, ridges, cliffs in every direction. And far beyond, the lava sea.

"If he's hiding in one of these shadows, we'll never see him," Rip whispered. The only sound in the saucer was the faint, almost inaudible hum caused by liquid coursing through the reactor pipes. Beyond the saucer was a vacuum that would carry no sound. Still, Rip whispered. His palms were perspiring. Without thinking, he wiped each hand on his jeans.

Charley crossed the crest and began descending into a canyon that pointed toward the lava sea.

She and Rip had dropped from lunar orbit an hour ago and were wending their way through the mountains in the general direction of the lunar base using only the antigravity rings. On earth they were capable of lifting the saucer to a height of two hundred feet; on the moon, with its reduced gravity, they would hold the saucer twelve hundred feet above the surface, if Charley wished to keep it that high. She didn't. She was skimming the rocks, loafing along. They were still at least fifty miles away, an hour's flight at this rate of speed. Charley Pine was in no hurry.

Somewhere ahead was the other saucer, the Roswell saucer that had rested in a secret hangar in Area 51 since 1947. It would be waiting.

Jean-Paul Lalouette was probably at the controls. His job was quite simple. He had to shoot down the Sahara saucer.

Charley and Rip were absolutely certain that Pierre Artois intended to destroy the saucer they were in. His life and the lives of all his followers depended upon keeping the Roswell saucer intact, able to fly back to earth. Charley and Rip were a mortal threat.

After millions of years of evolution and thousands of years of civilization, the wheel had turned full circle. Once again the law was kill or be killed.

The saucer was still a mile or so away from the floor of the lava sea, only a hundred feet above the rock but perhaps a thousand feet in elevation above the lava, when Charley brought it to a stop in the shadow of a steep ridge that rose precipitously into the black sky.

"So where is the base?" Rip asked, still speaking softly.

Charley pointed. "About six or seven miles that way." She stared. Fortunately, in the absence of an atmosphere, the visibility was perfect. She could plainly see the base's solar panels. She could even see the radio tower. "I don't think it's there." She meant the other saucer.

"He's around," Rip said, thinking of Lalouette. He had never met the man, knew only what Charley had told him. Charley was certain, and Rip agreed, that Lalouette would be flying the Roswell saucer. Rip wondered if Lalouette had ever killed anyone.

They sat hidden in the shadow, watching and waiting. A slow hour passed, then another. Finally Charley climbed from the pilot's seat and used the makeshift toilet facility, then got something to eat and a bottle of water to drink. She stood beside Rip sipping water as the minutes ticked by.

"He's out here, somewhere," Rip remarked, "waiting for us, just like we're waiting for him."

RIP WAS ABSOLUTELY RIGHT, OF COURSE. JEAN-PAUL Lalouette was hiding in a shadow cast by a ridge, about five miles from the lunar base. He had the Roswell saucer inside a meteor crater with just the canopy protruding. He too was waiting.

Lalouette had more than his share of patience, but his passenger, Newton Chadwick, certainly didn't. Chadwick didn't know the meaning of the word. He had tried to read a book, tried to study the saucer's computer via a headband and tried to nap, all to no avail.

There was a shootout coming—perhaps soon. Newton Chadwick knew that someone was going to die. Despite Lalouette's sangfroid, Chadwick thought the odds excellent that the dead men might be Lalouette and . . . him. *We're two fools waiting for Wyatt Earp and Doc Holliday to come strolling along on their way to the OK Corral,* he told himself. It was not a happy thought.

After hours of waiting he sealed himself inside the tiny toilet compartment and prepared an injection of youth serum. The liquid was clear and colorless. He drew the proper dose into the needle, slipped it into his arm and pushed the plunger.

He studied his reflection in the shiny metal above the sink. It wasn't much of a mirror, but it was adequate.

He looked, he decided, about mid- to late thirties. Perhaps forty.

Talk about a miracle drug—the serum had indeed stopped aging. The drawback, of course, was that he had to take the drug at regular intervals for the rest of his life. Forever! Newton Chadwick smiled broadly. *Forever!*

Artois had insisted that he accompany Lalouette so he could answer any questions about the saucer. This flight was an unnecessary risk, of course, but if this saucer were destroyed, the people at the lunar base would be stranded. They would die when the food ran out, because the hydroponic ponds couldn't make enough, or when the chemicals that were used to generate oxygen and scrub the air were exhausted.

Even if the number of people were lowered to match the food supply—by whatever method—the chemicals were finite, and inevitably equipment casualties would take their toll. The machinery that scrubbed and purified the air and recycled human waste would eventually fail to work. The machinery in the lunar base wasn't like the machinery in the saucer, which had been built to essentially last forever without failure, or so it seemed.

Chadwick removed a comb from his pocket and used it on his hair. He tugged at a tangle—and lo, the whole tangled knot of red hair came out with the comb.

He stared at the comb and the wad of hair. He grabbed his hair with his free hand, tugged on it—and more came out.

God in heaven! He was losing his hair.

This wasn't supposed to be happening!

He leaned toward the mirror, blinked mightily—for some reason, his vision was a little fuzzy—and stared at the face that stared at him.

Crow's-feet around his eyes!

He backed away from the mirror a trifle—and the image blurred.

His eyes! His vision was deteriorating.

He turned away from the mirror and fumbled with the fanny pack. The serum was in two bottles. He jabbed the needle of the syringe into one, took the tiniest amount and squirted it onto his finger.

He tasted it.

Oh, my God! Water!

Chadwick's mind raced. Someone had stolen his serum, obviously. Who?

Any of them could have done it while he slept. Any of them. Including Lalouette.

Newton Chadwick charged from the head screaming and leaped across the saucer with his hands outstretched, going for Lalouette, who was still in the pilot's seat.

Jean-Paul heard the ungodly howl and turned in his seat

just in time to see Chadwick stretched out in midair, flying at him like a human missile. He deflected the outstretched hands and smashed at Chadwick's neck with his fist as the American flew by, right into the instrument panel. The collision with the panel, or perhaps the pilot's fist, knocked Chadwick out; he collapsed unconscious on the floor of the saucer.

"LET ME BACK IN THE SEAT," CHARLEY SAID TO RIP, WHO willingly changed places.

Charley fastened her seat belt, then aligned the sight reticle with the base radio tower.

"Let's let Pierre know we're here," she said.

"Okay," Rip said, and grinned.

Fire!

The light appeared beside the reticle. Sparks began to appear on the base of the radio tower. Thousands of antiprotons, perhaps tens of thousands, were passing through the metal of the tower every second. Some found protons in the metal; some continued on to burrow into the ridge a mile behind.

Fifteen seconds after she ordered the weapon fired, Charley noticed that the tower was no longer perfectly erect. It was leaning slightly. As the antimatter particles continued their bombardment, the tower slowly tilted and, in agonizingly slow motion, collapsed, raising a cloud of dust.

Cease fire!

"I hope you didn't ruin Pierre's day," Rip said.

PIERRE ARTOIS WAS IN THE COM CENTER DICTATING AN ultimatum to the United Kingdom when the radio tower collapsed. Pierre finished a page, released the transmission key to clear his throat and heard nothing from the operator on earth who was recording his words.

A long five minutes passed—a silent five minutes—before the radio technician gave him the bad news. Something was wrong with the base antenna, which appeared incapable of functioning. Engineers would go outside onto the lunar surface to inspect it, a chore that would take most of an hour.

Julie looked at Pierre. "Charley Pine. She's here with her saucer."

"So it would appear," Pierre said, trying to look calm and collected. He picked up the handheld radio. "Jean-Paul, our base radio antenna seems to have become inoperative. Ms. Pine may be in the vicinity."

One word came back, embedded in static. "Roger."

JEAN-PAUL LALOUETTE HAD SEEN THE FLASHES AS THE antimatter particles annihilated themselves inside the metal of the tower, and he had seen the tower fall. By sheer happenstance, he had chosen a location in which to wait that prevented him from spotting the impact point of those particles that went through the tower and failed to find positrons, so he wasn't sure precisely where the other saucer was.

That it was nearby, with its optical sight centered on the radio tower, was a given. But where?

He craned his neck, searching in every direction.

Newton Chadwick was curled up in a fetal position on a chair in the back of the compartment, apparently oblivious to Lalouette and his problems.

Chadwick had been that way for the last hour, ever since he regained consciousness. "Someone stole it," he muttered, looking wildly at Lalouette, reaching for him.

The French pilot pointed toward the rear of the saucer and raised his right fist threateningly. The American shrank away, still muttering. "It came out," he said mysteriously. "I'm aging quickly. I need more serum. God in heaven, how am I going to get it stuck on the moon?"

Lalouette didn't know what to say. Chadwick seemed to have come completely unhinged.

"My serum," the American shouted at him, "someone has stolen my serum."

After that he fell silent. He sat in a chair, and seemed somehow to shrink into it, becoming smaller and smaller.

Lalouette forgot about Chadwick.

Pine wasn't out on the lava sea. He would see her ship if she were there. No, she was somewhere in these mountains, either to the right or left, or perhaps above him.

He turned his saucer and began climbing the steep gully using only the antigravity rings, trying to stay in the shadow of the ridge as he did so. He had plenty of water on board—he had filled the saucer's tanks in the two days he had been waiting for Charley Pine to fly to the moon.

So he had the fuel to use his rockets whenever the tactical situation required. Pine couldn't, not if she planned to ever get back to earth. The surplus fuel gave Jean-Paul a huge tactical advantage, and well he knew it.

Every fighter pilot since Roland Garros had used every advantage they had to kill the enemy and avoid being killed themselves. Only fools liked fair fights, and Jean-Paul Lalouette wasn't a fool. Nor, he reflected, was Charley Pine. She would shoot him in the back without the slightest iota of remorse.

Unless he killed her first.

He intended to do just that.

CHARLEY LIFTED HER SAUCER FROM THE SHADOW THAT had shrouded it, lifted it until the canopy was just clear of the ridge line and she and Rip could see.

They watched expectantly. Sooner or later Lalouette

would come looking for them, and they intended to see him first. They *had* to see him first.

The minutes passed, one by one, agonizingly slow.

So where is he? she asked the computer. The holographic display was blank. The ship's radar and computer system had yet to detect the other saucer, and until it did, it could not answer the question.

There—a flicker of movement, on top of the ridge to the left. As fast as Rip saw it, it disappeared.

He pointed. "The other saucer just crossed the ridge there. Seconds ago. Going away from us."

CHARLEY STARTED UP THE HOGBACK USING ONLY THE antigravity rings. She thought the French pilot would silhouette himself somewhere on the irregular crest when he crossed back to this side, the southern side of the range. He had to know that she had just shot up the radio tower; Artois could be relied upon to pass that word along using a short-range radio of some sort.

Climbing the hogback, watching the crest for the flash of movement, Charley was ready. If Jean-Paul came over the crest to the right or left—and she saw him—she would get a quick squirt with the antimatter gun. Maybe that would be enough.

But where was he?

And why had he crossed over to the northern side of the range?

On a hunch, she moved laterally off the hogback, placing the crest of it to her left. Now she had some room to duck down, if necessary, or to dive away. Just in case—

The rock to her left began popping, as if bullets were striking it. Or antiprotons.

She jammed the stick forward as Rip shouted, "There!" and thrust out an arm. To the left.

She glimpsed the other saucer just as she sank behind the hogback. It was nestled in a deep V, a cleft in the rock. Jean-Paul had let himself be seen crossing the mountain crest so that she would follow and he could ambush and kill her.

The canyon she was in wound its way up the steep slope above and dropped quickly away toward the lava sea. Up or down?

She continued upward for a few seconds, then stopped the saucer, spun it 180 degrees and tilted it. Lalouette would be popping over that hogback, ready to pounce.

She didn't have long to wait. The larger Roswell saucer crossed the ridge banking sharply. What Jean-Paul didn't expect was that she was waiting for him. She jerked the crosshairs onto the bigger machine and shouted, "*Fire!*"

Most of the antimatter particles were deflected by the Roswell saucer's streamlined, stealthy shape. However, a few of the particles penetrated the saucer's skin, roaring ahead until sooner or later, inevitably, they encountered positrons buried in atoms' nuclei. One popped harmlessly in the saucer's water tank; another met its positron in the food bay, and the resultant small explosion scattered cans and plastic-wrapped goo willy-nilly. One of the particles hit the instrument panel and blew out a multifunction display, showering Jean-Paul with shards of a hard glasslike material.

He was already on the juice, trying to accelerate over the smaller ship using the rockets. As the G hit him he went over the small ship and pulled the nose up hard to avoid the rising slope of rock. Accelerating hard, the big saucer shot up the slope and across the crest before Charley Pine could turn her ship and send a river of particles after it.

Off the juice, turning hard in a 120-degree angle of bank while pulling four Gs, Jean-Paul whipped his saucer around and decelerated. He didn't think Pine had the water to maneuver with him; yet if he persisted in riding around her like an Indian riding around a circle of covered wagons, he was going to get shot out of the saddle.

He halted the saucer and waited to see if she was going to pop over the crest in hot pursuit.

His heart was pounding. He tried to get his breathing under control as he waited under the crest for Charley Pine, waited for his shot. For he knew he would get one. He would win. He would kill her and everyone else in the enemy saucer. He was good and he would live and they would die. It was as simple as that.

So where was she?

EGG AWOKE IN THE DISPENSARY, ACROSS THE CORRIDOR from the com center. The door was open, and he could hear the people in the com center gabbling in French. They were not happy—that was obvious from their tone. He tried to move his arm and found he was tied to the gurney. He was only half awake, and it took a few seconds for all of it to come back. Moving the saucer over the antigravity beam generator, Julie Artois and her syringe . . .

Augh! He blamed himself. If he had had more courage when Chadwick kidnapped him, he would have refused to fly the Roswell saucer. Would have told them to go to hell.

But he didn't. Now Charley and Rip were up there somewhere, risking their lives, and these fools were trying to take over the world.

As he came fully awake he began working on extracting an arm from the cloth ties that held it. His right was looser. He worked it, tugged, pulled and strained, trying to create some slack. The more he pulled, the angrier he got.

THE HOLOGRAPHIC DISPLAY PANEL IN FRONT OF JEAN-PAUL literally exploded. He was wearing the computer headband, so the rocket engines ignited as quickly as thought and the saucer was instantly accelerating—but not before he heard a series of bangs behind him as positrons and antipositrons detonated like firecrackers.

In seconds he was out of the antimatter particle stream, accelerating rapidly at six Gs, heavy on the juice. He began weaving, right, left, up and down at random. Finally he went into a turn and looked back over his left shoulder. By leaning left he could see almost dead aft.

There was the other saucer, moving slowly along the crest, not using its rockets. The distance was at least five miles, opening fast. Now it was turning toward him, barely moving.

He tightened his turn, put the other saucer over his head and pulled as hard as he could. The Gs began graying him out. He tensed every muscle, moaned against the weight, fought to keep his head erect, watched the nose come around and the enemy move slowly under the reticle. He was still on the juice, still accelerating.

Straighten out and fire!

Now the other saucer lit its rockets. He saw the fire from its exhausts, and it squirted out the bottom of the sight reticle.

He dumped the nose, trying to hold the crosshairs on it as the G threw him upward against the safety belt, tried to throw him out of his seat. He couldn't get the crosshairs on the enemy ship—and the dive angle was steadily increasing. Now he pulled hard, upward.

My God. His nose was well down. He was below the ridgeline, which filled his canopy. He was going to crash into it! No! *More G.* The lights began to fade as the G mashed him downward, six, eight, ten Gs . . . His peripheral vision came rushing in; he was screaming as his vision shrank until he could see only the rocks ahead . . . then everything went black.

The G was taking him out . . . With the last of his consciousness, he asked the computer for more G.

* * *

JEAN-PAUL RECOVERED CONSCIOUSNESS AS THE G EASED.
His saucer was still accelerating at about four Gs. He thought
about weaving to throw Charley's aim off if she was behind
him, and the ship automatically responded.

So where is she?

Even as he asked the question, the display in front of him
gave him the answer. She was diving down between two
mountain ranges, the one north of the base and the one
beyond it. *Jean-Paul, you fool! You should have been asking the
computer to track her all along. She is diving into that steep chasm.*

He brought his ship around in a wide, gentle turn, slowing
as he checked the display, matching it to the real world
beyond the canopy.

He would get her this time. With the system's help, he
would keep the stream of particles on her until something
vital blew apart or she crashed into the rocks.

Coming over the ridge he lowered the nose and let his
saucer accelerate downward. Yes, the symbol for the other
saucer was right there, ahead and low.

He was below the rock walls now, dropping swiftly, the
sun shining full upon his face. He had to squint to see the
display. He held up a hand to shield his eyes, kept zooming
down.

Shallow the dive, close the distance.

The valley was steep and narrow and twisty. He threw the
saucer right, left, then right again to avoid the steep walls.
They rushed past in a blur.

He glanced at the display—

And Charley's saucer was no longer there!

Of course not! She'd disappeared from radar. The computer—

As he rounded a turn the enemy saucer was only feet away

on his left, motionless. He glimpsed it as he shot across in front of it.

His left arm exploded. Blew apart at the elbow. The hand and forearm fell onto the instrument panel in a spray of blood.

The cliffs were right there, on either side.

Full power, nose up, Jean-Paul told the computer.

He grabbed at his stump as the nose began to climb and the G came on steadily, increasing.

He forced himself to lift his damaged appendage and hold it straight up so the G would help stanch the flow of blood.

He kept the nose rising and the juice full on. Ahead through the canopy he could see stars. And the earth.

Earth, he told the computer. *Take me home!*

17

Pierre Artois had stationed a man on top of the lunar base in a space suit to radio him firsthand reports of the saucer battle. Each suit had a radio in the helmet; the transmissions were picked up by a small antenna mounted on the top of the base air lock. With the base radio tower in pieces, these transmissions were not automatically rebroadcast to earth, nor could Pierre talk to or hear Mission Control in France on the com center radios. The man outside spotted the exhaust plume of the saucer leaving the moon. He reported it to Pierre.

"Which one is it?" Pierre asked, a question that revealed the depths of his despair, because even he knew that there was no way to tell one saucer from the other from a distance. And the distance was great, at least twenty miles.

"I don't know."

"Keep watching," Pierre ordered, trying to calm himself. He made a transmission on the handheld, calling Jean-Paul Lalouette.

There was no answer.

Julie strummed her fingers on top of one of the useless

large radio transmitters, which didn't help the emperor's mood. He called several more times on the small radio before he finally gave up and laid it on the plastic counter. Henri Salmon, Fry One and Claudine Courbet were also in the com center, so he weighed his words before he spoke.

"It must have been Charley Pine," he said. "Lalouette probably frightened her."

Julie said nothing as Pierre recalled his contacts with the American pilot. She never struck him as a woman who would frighten easily. He cursed under his breath.

Of course, Jean-Paul Lalouette wasn't a person who would turn tail and run from a fight either. He was French, after all, and he believed body and soul in the glory of Pierre's crusade.

"Or something went tragically wrong," he admitted aloud.

"Newton Chadwick," Julie said bitterly.

Ah, yes, Pierre thought. Chadwick, a man without a shred of honor. If something happened to Lalouette, Chadwick would abandon the fight, abandon the people on the lunar base, abandon the dream of world conquest, abandon everything to save his own skin. If something happened to Lalouette, Chadwick would run like a rabbit. He was that kind of man.

"Without a saucer, how are we going to get back to earth?" Claudine Courbet asked rhetorically. Pierre and the other two men stared at her.

"Putting Chadwick in the saucer with Lalouette was a mistake," Julie said, unable to resist a dig at Pierre's decision to send them both to shoot down Pine. "You fool!" she continued shrilly, addressing the emperor and unable to control the timbre of her voice. "You taught Pine to fly the spaceplanes, you allowed her to come to the moon when she knew nothing of our plans, you failed to prevent her escape with the spaceplane, and you sent a person of dubious loyalty with Lalouette in our only possible transport off this miserable rock."

Pierre sat frozen, unable to think, unable to analyze the situation. Never in his worst nightmares had he envisioned a situation like this. Marooned on the moon!

Julie unconsciously brushed the hair back from her forehead and eyes. In times past Pierre had thought the habitual gesture captivating, but he didn't now.

He watched mesmerized as Julie took several deep breaths and by sheer force of will brought herself back under icy control. "Fortunately all is not lost," she said. "We still have Egg Cantrell. Pine and her boy-toy will undoubtedly try to rescue him. They will land their saucer somewhere nearby. We *must* have that saucer."

She scrutinized the faces of her listeners, ignoring Pierre. Then she looked directly into the eyes of Henri Salmon and began issuing orders.

WHEN SHE FINISHED, JULIE ARTOIS SENT EVERYONE OFF TO make preparations. Pierre remained, listlessly staring at the useless radios.

She waited for him to meet her eyes, but he didn't. After a moment she walked out. Salmon was heading into the mess hall to address the assembled base personnel when she saw him. She caught his eye and motioned for him to follow her. They ducked into the Artois living compartment and shut the door.

"You saw him. Do you think he is still capable of leading us?" Julie asked bluntly.

Salmon considered carefully. He wasn't sure where she was going with this and didn't want to make a mistake. They needed the saucer, which had a limited carrying capacity.

Regardless of how the cake was cut, many of the base personnel would have to be left behind. Henri Salmon didn't want to be one of them.

"I don't know," he said after a pause.

"Oh, you know," she said, "and you are hedging." She moved closer, reached for his hand and placed it on her breast. "That's what you want, isn't it? I've seen the way you look at me."

"You are a beautiful woman," Salmon admitted.

"The conquest of earth was my idea," Julie said, holding his hand in place and staring into his eyes. "I thought Pierre was the man who could do it, but when major difficulties arose, he folded. You, I think, are made of sterner stuff."

Salmon said nothing. He was very aware of the ripe firmness of her breast. The rumors weren't true, he decided. She had not had surgical enhancement.

"If we take the saucer to earth, negotiate, then return, the antigravity beam generator will still be here. We can still force the world's governments to yield. Honor, power, glory, wealth—it can all be ours. You and I—we can rule a united earth!"

Salmon felt the power of her personality. And he wanted off the moon. He swept her into his arms and kissed her.

RIP CANTRELL AND CHARLEY PINE STARED THROUGH THE canopy of their saucer at the lunar base, which was about two miles away. The saucer was behind a ridge northwest of the base, with just the canopy protruding above the bare rock ledge. The only sign of man that they could see was the pile of rubble that had been the radio tower—and the tiny figure of an individual in a space suit standing near it. The sun reflecting off his silver space suit made him readily visible.

"So what do you think?" Rip asked.

"I dunno."

"We are going to have to go in there after Egg."

"I suppose."

"Can you think of another way?"

"Make them send him out."

"How?"

"That's the problem," she admitted, and inadvertently glanced upward. The other saucer had left an hour ago in a plume of rocket exhaust, on its way into orbit or back to earth. Or, perhaps, leaving the area so that it could reenter later and try to ambush her and Rip, one more time. She wished she knew which of the three possibilities was the fact.

Rip seemed to read her thoughts. "You must have hurt him badly," he said.

"Umm."

"Flying across the antimatter stream at point-blank range—something must have popped in that saucer. Telling the saucer to pull up and fire the rocket engines may have been Lalouette's last conscious thought. He might be dead. The saucer might orbit the sun forever, or eventually fall into it."

"I hope he's on his way back to earth," Charley Pine said, and meant it. She had liked Jean-Paul.

"I wish he'd crashed back there in that canyon," Rip shot back. "Then we'd know."

After thinking through the possibilities one more time, she said, "I think we should wait for a while."

"He may return," Rip mused. "An hour from now, a week, two weeks, whenever. He could be stalking us right now."

"If Lalouette comes back when we're out of this ship, he'll destroy it." Charley knew she could expect no mercy from the French pilot. "You and I and Egg will die here on the moon."

"That's right," he said, and turned his head to look at her.

She met his eyes. "So how long do you want to wait before we go get Egg?"

AFTER ANOTHER HALF HOUR, THE MAN STANDING BESIDE the carcass of the radio tower disappeared from view. Rip and Charley decided he had gone back inside the base. Charley was in the pilot's seat. She lifted the saucer, and they flew slowly, as low as they dared, toward the base. The sun was well down toward the horizon. In another forty-eight hours or so it would set and the two-week lunar night would begin.

They looked for the dome over the antigravity beam generator and didn't see it. Finally they saw the hole, several hundred yards away. The dome was open.

"That's my way in," Rip said.

"And what do you want me to do?"

They were discussing it when they saw a knot of six people in space suits walk out of the shadow of the base air lock into the sun.

"There's our reception committee." They quickly lowered the saucer out of sight.

After a brief discussion, they donned their space suits, each helping the other. That's when Charley remembered that Rip had never before worn a space suit. She made him finger every control and explained how everything worked.

"The outer shell is the protective cover, very hard to damage. But under it is the pressure suit, and it can be torn or ripped. The tiniest leak will kill you. Now here's the dangerous part—a fall that won't tear the outer shell may still damage the pressure suit."

"Oh, that's comforting."

"If the pressure suit is damaged, there will never be any little Cantrells."

"I'll keep that in mind."

"Remember the first time you and I crawled into this saucer and tried to fly it?"

"Sure."

"This is not that risky."

"I hate to tell you this, lady, but I'm older now, not as carefree and stupid as I was when I was young." A whole year had passed since he found the saucer. "I don't even buy lottery tickets these days."

"Right."

"Was that a Freudian thing, that mention of little Cantrells?"

"Well, I was thinking, maybe someday . . ."

He kissed her, gently and tenderly.

Charley found she had an eye that was leaking and swabbed at it, then clamped her helmet on her head.

With the helmets on and latched to the suits, they turned on the helmet radios. French sounded in their ears. Charley understood most of it. She touched her helmet to Rip's and said, "That's Julie. She's outside."

"What's she saying?"

"She's telling them to stand easy. We'll be along."

"I feel like a sausage in this thing," Rip said.

"That's good. When you don't, you're in big trouble."

Rip put three hand grenades in the small belly pocket of his space suit. Getting the pins out with his gloves on would be difficult, but it could be done. There were two M-16 rifles. Charley loaded them both, chambered rounds and put the weapons on safe. She showed Rip how they worked, then asked, "Are you ready?"

"Yeah. You?"

"Yes."

They pulled on their gloves and zipped them to the

sleeves of the suits. After each of them checked the other one last time, Charley told the saucer to extend its landing gear, then to land. It settled several feet and came to rest.

When all motion had stopped, she depressurized the ship. Air was pumped from the interior of the saucer into a pressure tank. Finally, when the interior of the saucer was at a near vacuum, Rip opened the belly hatch. He felt a tiny rush of air as the last of it escaped from the ship. He dropped though the open hatchway and stood in it.

Charley gave him a thumbs-up. He blew her a kiss, then closed the hatch behind him.

"Mr. President," P.J. O'Reilly said, "we've got audio from the moon. Apparently they are outside the base in space suits and talking to one another."

The president was still at the "secret, undisclosed location." He brightened. "I thought we couldn't hear anything from the moon." The folks on earth had heard nothing from the moon since the radio tower there went down. And they didn't know why.

"Space suit helmet transmissions are only a few watts. We can normally hear them only when they are picked up and rebroadcast by the base's transmitters, which are apparently off the air. We're getting these signals from the National Radio Astronomy Observatory's hundred-meter telescope in Greenbank, West Virginia. The moon is above the horizon now, and they have the telescope aimed at the lunar base."

"Let's listen," the president said.

O'Reilly picked up the phone. After a few words, he listened, nodded and punched the buttons so they could hear the audio on the speakerphone. Then he hung up the handset.

Voices speaking French filled the office.

"Get a translator," the president said. "I want to know what's going on up there."

RIP CANTRELL CAREFULLY WALKED AWAY FROM THE saucer. In the reduced lunar gravity the trick was keeping his balance, he decided. He had to work carefully at it. He was a hundred feet away from the saucer when it lifted off in a swirl of dust. He turned to look. He could see Charley's helmeted head in the pilot's seat. He waved and she waved back. After the saucer had moved off, he watched the dust settling. It sifted slowly down undisturbed by the slightest breeze.

He watched the saucer go around the base, pass over the remains of the radio tower and settle onto the lava bed in front of the main air lock.

Then he walked toward the gaping hole in the top of the cavern that held the antigravity beam generator.

He paused near the edge and approached it carefully. The cavern was lit—but he couldn't see if there was anyone in it. Nor did he know if the beam generator was in use. Better find out, he thought. He stooped, picked up a pebble, and tossed it across the hole. It sailed across like a baseball thrown from the outfield. *They're not using it,* he concluded. *If they were, that little rock would have soared up out of sight, like a pebble caught in a torrent from a fire hose.*

Now he needed to know if there was anyone in the control room. He laid the rifle down, got to his hands and knees and began crawling toward the edge.

THE SAUCER CAME INTO VIEW OF THE SMALL CROWD STANDing in front of the air lock from their right. It was low, only ten feet or so above the surface, and moved slowly, trailed by a cloud of dust.

They had been waiting for it, yet they were surprised when it appeared. "It's not Lalouette!" someone shouted into his helmet microphone. "The saucer is too small."

"*Oui,*" Julie agreed bitterly.

"THEY MADE IT!" O'REILLY EXCLAIMED TRIUMPHANTLY when he heard the translation. "Rip and Charley made it!"

"Umm," said the president.

O'Reilly couldn't sit still. He bounded from his chair and paced the small office. The president kept his gaze riveted on the speaker of the telephone, waiting.

18

RIP LEANED HIS HEAD OVER THE EDGE OF THE HOLE. THE floor of the cavern was at least twenty feet below. Right in the middle was the beam generator. Wow, it was big.

He felt for the hand grenades. They were there. He pulled the Velcro loose that held the pocket closed and reached for one.

French exploded in his earphones. At first he thought someone below had seen him; then he realized that the people outside in space suits had probably seen Charley.

He raised his head, just in time to see the saucer settling below his horizon.

No grenade! Dropping one on the beam generator wouldn't get Egg back. Better stick with the plan.

He lowered his head, trying to see what was on the opposite side of the cavern. And did. It was rock.

More French assaulted his ears. They were certainly excited. They had to have the saucer if they ever expected to see trees and grass again in their lives. He had emphasized that point to Charley, who had merely nodded.

She had brains and guts—more than he did, he thought—so he let it go at that. She could handle it.

He backed up, stood carefully and hopped around the edge of the hole ninety degrees, then got down on his hands and knees and crawled in for another look.

This time he saw the glass panels and the control console beyond. And there was no one there!

Rip moved and took another look. Finally he was satisfied that he had seen the entire layout and the cavern and control room were indeed empty.

He went back and picked up the rifle, checking that the safety was on.

Hoo boy.

The gravity was only one-sixth as strong as earth's. Charley had told him that. So a twenty-foot fall would be equivalent to a three-and-a-half-foot drop. *Heck, it'll be like jumping off a picnic table.* Only he was wearing this zoot suit, and if it tore— *Well, hell, nobody lives forever.*

Standing erect, holding the rifle in both hands, Rip shuffled to the edge of the hole, took a deep breath and jumped.

CHARLEY PINE BROUGHT THE SAUCER INTO A HOVER FIFTY feet beyond the six people standing in front of the base air lock. She pointed the saucer right at the air lock door.

One of the figures was rotund, wearing a space suit that looked to be under severe stress around the middle. Egg! There was a person immediately beside him on the right and left. Both held what appeared to be pistols in their hands.

Charley reached up to her helmet and keyed the mike.

"Is that you, Uncle Egg?" she asked in English.

The heavyset figure reached for his helmet. "It's me, Charley."

"Ah, Mademoiselle Pine, welcome back to the moon." That was a feminine voice in French. Julie Artois.

"English, please," Charley said.

"We must talk, Ms. Pine," Julie said, shifting languages.

"You people stay right where you are. Don't move."

She looked at her watch. She wanted to give Rip at least fifteen minutes to get inside before she landed. She looked carefully around, at the parked forklift for off-loading spaceplanes, at the small lunar ATV, at the rocks behind, anywhere that might conceal a man. And saw no one.

Which didn't mean no one was there.

RIP FELL WHEN HE HIT THE CAVERN FLOOR. HE HAD TRIED to catch himself by bending his knees, but he misjudged it and bounced in slow motion. Then he toppled sideways and was unable to right himself. He landed the second time on his shoulder, bounced again and this time used a hand to cushion the impact. He managed to hang on to the rifle. His motion was heavily restricted by the pressure the suit put on his limbs. He struggled to stand erect, then stood looking into the control room.

It was empty of people, thank heavens! Any semidangerous villain who witnessed his ignominious arrival would have died laughing.

The air lock to the control room was tempting, but he ignored it. He stepped over to the beam generator and inspected it carefully.

That was when he heard Charley and Egg speaking.

At least Egg wasn't dead or injured. That simplified the problem, he told himself. He wouldn't have to cram Egg into a space suit and carry him to the saucer.

EGG CANTRELL THOUGHT THE SAUCER LOOKED OMINOUS hovering stationary and motionless above the lava bed. The sun behind them gleamed off the dark surface and made it difficult to see through the canopy. Impossible, really.

Julie was on his right with her pistol in her hand, Fry Two on his left. These other people he didn't know. Pierre hadn't come out.

He felt terrible, hung over from the drugs they had given him to keep him sedated, and guilty because he had gotten Rip and Charley into this fix. Here they were, face-to-face with these murderous megalomaniacs.

Someone, Egg well knew, was going to die soon. He closed his eyes and prayed that it wouldn't be Charley or his nephew Rip.

"WHAT'S GOING ON?" O'REILLY ASKED IMPATIENTLY. HE found the radio silence difficult to endure. He directed the question to the translator, a young woman from an Ivy League university who didn't look the least impressed with her august company. She was chewing gum and occasionally running her fingers through her hair. She didn't answer O'Reilly's question, merely stared blankly at him. He resumed his nervous pacing.

The president sat behind his desk with his fingers laced across his tummy and his eyes closed. He couldn't fool O'Reilly—the chief of staff had seen him like this numerous times when he was digging deep for tact or patience. One of the drawbacks to public life, in O'Reilly's opinion, was the fact that politicians spent much of their time seeking votes from the ill-informed and the uninformed. Those unable to deal gracefully with fools never got into office or were soon voted out. In fact, the president had once confided to O'Reilly that he owed his political success to his ability to spend hours surrounded by idiots without biting one. O'Reilly was made of different stuff, a fact of which he was well aware. Still . . .

"It *would* be nice to know what was going on," the chief of staff remarked to a painting on the wall.

The painting didn't answer.

* * *

RIP CANTRELL EXAMINED THE BEAM GENERATOR CLOSELY. The panels on the base of the unit fastened with wing nuts; he quickly opened them and took a look. The major components he recognized. There was no doubt that this unit had been designed based on saucer technology.

The power cables that led into the unit were as thick as Rip's wrist and were clearly marked: positive and negative. They were attached with clamps, which were held on with nuts. He tried to turn one of the nuts with his fingers. Nope.

There must be a toolbox around here somewhere!

He scanned the cavern—and saw it, placed against the wall.

He had it open in seconds. Found a wrench that looked about the right size.

His earphones were silent. Ominously silent. As Rip worked on the nuts he nervously eyed the door to the control room, another air lock door.

The job took two minutes. It was simple, really. He undid both clamps and reversed the wires, then tightened the nuts and replaced the panel.

He replaced the wrench in the toolbox, closed it and went into the air lock.

"MADEMOISELLE PINE, WE ARE TIRED OF WAITING," JULIE Artois said firmly.

Charley estimated that she had been in position for about ten minutes. She had the antimatter reticle squarely on Julie's chest. She was tempted. If the clown on the other side of Egg hadn't had a gun, she would have zapped Julie then and there, splattered her all over, and told Egg to run for it.

She sighed. It wasn't going to be that easy. Yet it wouldn't hurt to make them sweat. She turned the saucer ever so slightly and let the reticle rest for fifteen seconds or so on the chest of each of the people with Egg. The maneuvering of the saucer was minute, but she thought they would see it.

Finally she stopped and lowered the saucer to the ground. Dust swirled up, almost obscuring her view of the people, but not quite. She waited until it settled, then opened the hatch and dropped through. She quickly scrambled out from under the saucer, then told it to lift off. It rose twenty feet in the air and stopped there.

She turned to face the reception committee.

THE AIR LOCK ADMITTED RIP TO THE CONTROL ROOM. HE wasted no time examining the control console but went straight to the air lock that led into the heart of the lunar base and stepped inside. He closed the door behind him, checked the pressure gauge on the bulkhead and carefully removed his gloves and helmet. He sniffed. The air smelled fine. With the gloves dangling from his wrists by straps and the helmet under his left arm, he checked the position of the safety, then pointed the rifle in front of him and pushed the button to open the inner door of the lock.

The opening door revealed an empty corridor with gray rock walls, one brilliantly lit by ceiling lights every few yards. He could hear the faint strains of an orchestra, classical music, coming over the loudspeaker system.

CHARLEY PINE LEFT HER RIFLE IN THE SAUCER. IT WOULD have detracted from the aura of confidence she was trying to project. She took a deep breath, then marched forward to the little group. She glanced back at the hovering saucer. As she thought it would, the sun glinting off the canopy prevented anyone from seeing inside.

She stopped a few feet in front of them, keyed the mike button on the side of her helmet and said in English, "I assume that none of you people are interesting in living out the remainder of your lives on this round rock pile. Correct me if I'm wrong."

Julie had no intention of letting Charley take charge of the conversation. "Permit me to clarify the situation, mademoiselle. Monsieur Cantrell is our hostage. We will kill him where he stands if you give us any trouble."

"Then you'll never leave the moon. Your choice."

"After we kill him, we will kill you."

"And Rip will splatter you all over this lava bed with the antimatter beam, then fly on home."

The other people in the group stirred uneasily, glancing at each other. The ones on the edge took a step away from the group, Charley noted with satisfaction.

"Alright, Julie," Charley continued. "Enough threats and bullshit. I have come to the moon with authorization from the president of the United States to make a deal."

WHEN HE HEARD THAT STATEMENT, P.J. O'REILLY grunted, then turned to the president. "You didn't—"

"Sssh!" the president hissed, holding up his hand.

O'Reilly glanced at the interpreter, who was checking her nail polish and looking bored, and held his tongue.

THE LIGHTS IN THE CORRIDOR WERE VERY BRIGHT. It took several seconds for Rip's eyes to adjust. He walked carefully down the corridor, pausing in front of each door to look into the rooms. He saw no one.

Well, where are they? It's a cinch they all aren't standing outside.

He eased along with the weapon at the ready. The com center—there was someone in there. Seated with his back to the door.

Rip walked in, making as little noise as possible, yet making some. The man didn't turn around. He jabbed the rifle barrel in the man's back. Still he didn't turn around.

Rip moved off to the side. It was Pierre Artois—he recognized him from his pictures. The man had even been on the cover of *Time* a month or so ago.

Pierre ignored Rip. He seemed . . . detached . . . disconnected somehow.

He was unarmed, apparently. No weapons that Rip could see. He left him seated there in front of the radios and television cameras.

The entrance to the mess hall was only a few steps farther along the corridor. Rip looked in the door. The place was full of bodies!

No!

The corpses lay contorted, frozen in death, under that brilliant white light. Blood was spattered everywhere; pools of it stained the floor. Amid the gore were glittering, empty brass cartridges. Rip went from body to body, looking. Not a one of them had a weapon.

At least two dozen people had been murdered here. Men and women.

Rip felt the vomit coming up his throat and managed to choke it back. He walked on, making sure that they were indeed all dead. Not that there was much he could do if he found anyone alive.

And he did. Find one alive.

Above the classical music background he heard a man groaning. He was lying behind the food service counter and wearing a white apron stained with blood. Rip bent and turned him over. The man was hugging his stomach, and blood was oozing around his fingers.

His eyes opened, focused on Rip.

"Easy there, fella. Who shot you?"

The man took a few seconds to process it. "Who you?" he asked in heavily accented English.

"Name's Rip."

"Reep?"

"Yeah. Now tell me, who shot you?"

"Salmon. Henri Salmon. He got all in here, then bang bang bang . . . He shot me in the stomach, and laughed."

Rip grasped the rifle and looked around the room again, checking the two open doors. "Where is he now?"

"I saw him go by . . . in suit. Space suit."

"He went outside?"

"Yes."

"Didn't come back in?"

"Not that I see. But I passed out. My stomach . . . the pain."

"There's nothing I can do for you."

The chef thought about that as he hugged his middle. He looked down at the blood.

"Bad way to die," the Frenchman said.

"Yes."

"You . . . have a pistol?"

"No. And I'm not going to shoot you either."

"Not for me. For *him*. If he comes back."

Rip looked the dying man in the eyes and made a decision. He reached into the belly pocket of his suit and pulled out a grenade. He held it so the chef could see it. "You know what this is?"

"*Oui.*"

"You pull the pin. It is perfectly safe as long as you hold the lever on. After you release the lever, you have eight seconds."

The man held out a bloody hand. Rip placed the grenade in it. He tried to think of something to say, couldn't, rose too fast from his kneeling position and almost fell, then hopped carefully from the room, avoiding the bodies.

"SO HERE'S THE DEAL, JULIE. A FRENCH CREW WILL BE admitted to the United States, and they will fly the spaceplane to France. It can take a fuel tank into orbit, refuel on earth, then launch for the moon. They can take you guys back to earth."

"That's it?"

"Yeah. We take Egg and leave, you get a ride home. They want you bad back there. Over two hundred people are dead in the States alone from your antigravity attacks. There are warrants in the U.S., Britain, Germany—"

"That was Pierre. He tried to minimize the loss of life."

"Good ol' Pierre, always thinking of others. I've heard that France and Germany are full of progressive thinkers who have abolished the death penalty. We're a little more backward in the States. Still, maybe the jury will give you folks life in the can instead of frying you. Get the best lawyers money can buy, cry for the cameras, and hope for the best."

"You certainly sugarcoat it, Pine."

"Or you can stay up here enjoying the scenic view until the air or food runs out, the machinery breaks down, whatever. Stay forever or wait for your ride, your choice. But Egg is going with us."

"What if we say no?"

"Then you die where you stand."

THE PRESIDENT GRINNED AT P. J. O'REILLY, THE SAME GRIN the secretary of state found so offensive. "That woman has style! We gotta appoint her ambassador to something."

"If she lives," O'Reilly said thoughtfully.

RIP CANTRELL HURRIED THROUGH THE ROOMS OF THE base looking for people while Charley laid out the options for Julie Artois. Didn't find anyone. The two grenades that remained in his pocket were on his mind. Perhaps he could booby-trap a couple pieces of equipment. Naw.

Satisfied that the dying chef and Pierre Artois were the

only living folks in the base—he looked in again at Pierre to make sure he was behaving—he went to the main air lock and stepped inside.

"YOU DON'T SEEM TO UNDERSTAND THE SITUATION," JULIE told Charley Pine. "My friends and I are leaving in the saucer. You, your friend and Monsieur Cantrell can accompany us. But we are all leaving together."

"You don't even have a pair of deuces, lady."

Julie didn't understand the poker analogy, but she correctly surmised that Charley was commenting on the weakness of her negotiating position. "I have Monsieur Cantrell," she said confidently, "and I have you. One bullet for him, one for you. Your friend in the saucer may make it back to earth, but I promise you that you won't. Are you ready to die, Charley Pine?"

Charley glanced upward, at a spot on the rock above the air lock door. *Aim and fire,* she ordered.

The place that she was staring at began to sparkle and pop. Pieces of stone flew off. Some of the chips struck the man beside Egg, and he looked around.

Smoke and dust and rock fragments poured from the stone.

Cease fire!

It took several seconds for the dust to slowly settle, revealing a hole the size of a bushel basket in the cliff.

Keeping her pistol jammed in Egg's ribs, Julie glanced over her shoulder as the last of the rock fragments fell like snowflakes around the little party.

When she turned back to Charley, the American pilot asked, "Are you ready, Julie?"

The man on the other side of Egg tossed his pistol away. It flew for ten feet, a long, lazy arc, before it hit the lunar surface and skittered along.

"Waiting for the spaceplane sounds like a good deal to me," he said on his helmet radio.

Julie stiffened. She looked around once, then looked at the saucer, the nose of which was tilted down and seemed to be pointing directly at her. "You win," she said, and dropped her pistol. It fell at her feet.

"Come on, Uncle Egg."

He walked forward toward Charley. She hooked her arm in his and walked toward the saucer. It descended slowly until the landing gear touched the ground. The hatch under it was still hanging open. Charley glanced back to ensure the Frenchmen hadn't moved, then bent to go under the saucer to the hatch. That's when she saw a space-suited figure with an assault rifle leveled at her approaching from behind the saucer. *Where has he been hiding?*

"Not so fast, Charley Pine," Julie said gleefully. "Stop right where you are or Henri Salmon will shoot you dead."

Charley glanced over her shoulder. Neither Julie nor her pals had yet retrieved their pistols.

She shoved Egg forward into the dirt and dove down herself. At the same instant the rocket engines of the saucer spurted out a blast of flame, several seconds' worth.

The saucer hopped forward a few feet. One of the landing gear pads struck Egg a glancing blow on the arm, but fortunately he rolled away from it and it didn't crush him.

Charley Pine lifted her eyes, looking for the man. He was flying above the surface away from the saucer, tumbling end over end, being carried along by the hot exhaust gases. He didn't have his rifle.

Charley scrambled up, dragging Egg. She grabbed an arm and jerked him off the surface, half lifted him into the yawning hole in the saucer's belly. He began scrambling too, and she pushed against his leg. He tumbled in and she leaped upward with so much vigor she struck the ceiling of the craft and almost fell back through the hatch opening. As she reached for the hatch a bullet spanged off it, making a spark. She grabbed the handle and pulled it closed.

Whew!

Charley Pine stood and looked through the canopy. The little knot of world conquerers in front of the air lock were milling around, collecting their guns, touching helmets together and probably asking each other, *What now?*

She climbed into the pilot's seat. Lifted the saucer a few feet and aimed the reticle at Julie.

"Where are you, Rip?"

"In the lock."

"Come on out."

Julie Artois heard the transmission, of course, and spun around. She was facing the lock as it opened. Rip stepped out with his rifle leveled and moved slightly to his left to go around the group.

"Drop the pistols!" Charley ordered over the helmet radio.

Julie turned her head to look at the saucer, then turned back to face Rip. She lifted the pistol ever so slightly, aiming, probably.

Fire!

The antimatter particles caught her in the right side. Most of them passed harmlessly through her suit and her body and exited out the other side, where they penetrated the cliff and annihilated themselves in the rock. One of them didn't, however. It exploded an atom in her lung. The pain was intense and sudden. She released the pistol as a second antipositron met its opposite number in her liver.

Cease fire!

Julie staggered. Blood flowed from her nostrils in a stream. She tried breathing though her mouth, and with every breath she gushed blood. Suddenly she was too weak to stand. She slowly toppled over.

Charley set the saucer down and rushed to the hatch. When it opened, Rip came scrambling in. He slammed the hatch shut and latched it, slapped her on the arm and whacked his helmet into hers. "You did great. Let's repressurize and get the hell outta Dodge."

"What about the antigravity beam generator?"

"I took care of it. Everyone in there is dead except for Pierre." He didn't take the time to tell her about the chef. "Salmon shot them all."

Charley climbed into the pilot's seat and began the pressurization process. The people milling around outside couldn't hurt them now. One of them was bent over, looking into Julie's faceplate.

Still, Charley had had enough of this place. She lifted the saucer on the antigravity rings, turned it and began moving across the lava plain to the southeast.

"WHAT'S HAPPENING?" P. J. O'REILLY ROARED AT THE speakerphone. The president, the translator and O'Reilly were staring at it. The president was holding on to the desk so tightly that his knuckles were turning white.

"There was some kind of shootout," the president muttered.

"God in heaven," O'Reilly said, and mopped his brow with his handkerchief.

When the radio remained silent, he pleaded at it, "Tell us something, please!"

HENRI SALMON CAME RUNNING IN HUGE LEAPING bounds toward the open air lock. He didn't even glance at Julie Artois, who was still lying on the lunar surface, unable to breathe, drowning in her own blood. He was the first into the air lock, and the others crowded in right behind him.

When the pressure was safe inside the lock, he jerked off his helmet and glared at the others. "Fools. Idiots! Our only hope of getting off this damn rock alive was that saucer, and you let it get away!"

"We still have the antigravity generator," Claudine Corbet said calmly. "We can force the Americans to send the space-plane back. Or the saucer. We aren't beaten yet."

As the air lock door opened into the interior of the base, Salmon nodded, staring at her. "You are right. First, however, I suggest we destroy the saucer. We must prove to those people we mean business or they will ignore us."

Claudine grasped at this straw. She didn't want to spend any more time on the moon than necessary, yet she certainly didn't want to die here. She rushed off along the corridor toward the cavern while she unfastened her helmet and pulled it off.

Salmon was right behind her. They charged into the control cavern, fired off the reactor and computers and were soon charging the antigravity capacitor. While the charge was coming up they heard the rumble of the saucer's rocket engines—except they didn't really hear it, since there was no air; what they heard and felt was the concussion of the rocket exhaust traveling through the rocks.

"The saucer will rise toward the earth," Salmon said. "We'll pick it up on the telescope and fire the antigravity beam at it. That will ruin their day. We can't let the Americans win a triumph."

An hour passed before they caught the glint of the sun reflecting off the saucer. The engines were secured, and it was coasting toward earth with sufficient velocity to escape the moon's gravitational field.

Holding it in the telescope was tricky. The telescope's drive mechanism wasn't designed to track a moving target, so the controls had to be adjusted manually. Courbet lost the saucer several times before she figured out the proper rate of traverse.

At her nod, Salmon fired the beam generator.

Since Rip had reversed the power cables, the generator no longer pushed against the moon; it repelled it. The generator shot away from the floor of the cavern, accelerating on its way into space. When it had risen to the length of the power cables, they tore out of their clamps, killing the power to the generator. Still, the velocity the unit had already attained was enough to carry it several hundred feet above the surface of the moon before it coasted to a stop and began to fall. When it arrived back in the cavern thirty seconds later it smashed itself to pieces on the floor. Flying metal cracked and crazed the bulletproof glass window, but didn't break it.

An amazed Henri Salmon and Claudine Courbet watched the entire debacle, including the crash at the end.

"*Mon Dieu!*" she whispered. "We are dead."

With shoulders sagging, she turned and walked slowly through the open air lock.

Henri Salmon kicked at the console in frustration. He shouted, he raged, but it did no good.

Finally, when the bitterness had ebbed to the point that he could again think, he sat on the stool in front of the controller trying to think of a way to save this situation. There was none. After an hour or so, even he had to admit it. He wandered through the open air lock doors into the interior of the base.

He looked into the com center at Pierre, who hadn't moved from his chair.

The bastard isn't worth killing, Henri thought. The damned fool sitting here out of his mind, his bitch wife outside in the dirt, everyone inside dead or going to die, all of this madness to the strains of classical music. Henri Salmon tried to laugh, but it rang hollow and died in his throat.

Out in the corridor he met a figure fully clad in a space suit, walking toward the air lock. Claudine Courbet.

"Where are you going?" he asked.

She ignored him, went to the main air lock and opened the inner door. It closed behind her. Salmon shrugged.

Two of the people who had been with him outside scampered from the mess hall when he went in. He glanced at the bodies as he walked toward the refrigerators—and felt nothing. Not remorse, not sorrow, not anything.

Salmon was looking into a refrigerator when he heard something solid hit the door. He half closed the door and scanned the floor.

A grenade! It had no pin, no safety lever. He glanced up. The chef was lying there looking at him, his face and stomach a bloody mess.

Then the grenade exploded.

COURBET FOUND JULIE ARTOIS LYING WHERE SHE HAD last seen her. Her helmet faceplate was covered with blood. She didn't seem to be breathing.

Claudine looked around, at the stark lunar mountains, the setting sun, the rubble of the radio tower, the earth hanging above her in the sky like a giant half-moon. Even at this distance she could see the riot of colors in the area still lit by the sun.

She lowered her gaze to the ground before her and began walking southeast, out into the vast lava sea that stretched away to the horizon.

TEN HOURS LATER THE LAST THREE PEOPLE ALIVE WHO had been outside with Julie Artois walked by the com center.

Pierre was still there, rocking slowly back and forth, muttering to himself. Dressed only in their base jumpsuits, they opened the inner air lock door and stepped inside. When the green light came on that showed that the door seals were properly inflated, one of them reached up and pushed the button that would evacuate the air from the chamber.

19

EGG'S LEFT ARM WAS BADLY BRUISED AND SWOLLEN, although the bone appeared intact. He used his right arm to hug Rip, then Charley, then Rip again. "I'm sorry you had to come," he said over and over, as Rip and Charley assured him getting kidnapped wasn't his fault.

"You did the right thing, Uncle Egg. You didn't get killed and you didn't kill yourself. We made it. In three days we'll be home."

"Still—" Egg found that his eyes were leaking and he couldn't stop the tears. Rip discovered he had the same problem, as did Charley Pine.

"You know," Charley said after a while as she swabbed at her eyes, "bad as it was, at least you guys got a free trip to the moon."

They had to agree. Rip didn't mention the ten million dollars he had agreed to pay for repairs to the National Air and Space Museum's glass wall, although the thought did cross his mind.

Finally, when they had their emotions under control, they told each other of their adventures on the moon. Rip's report of how he sabotaged the antigravity generator delighted his listeners. "They won't check it," he assured them. "They'll just turn it on and zot, it'll fly out of there and destroy itself. All the emperor's engineers won't be able to put that puppy back together again."

His report of how someone had shot all the people in the mess hall sobered them.

"I guess Julie was taking the people who were there with her, and to heck with the others," Charley said.

"Including Pierre," Rip mused. "I left him sitting in front of television cameras in the com center. I think he'd lost it. He didn't even look at me when I prodded him with the rifle barrel."

"Dreams die hard," Egg said thoughtfully. "Everyone needs dreams, or ambitions, if you will, but sometimes they get too big, grow out of control."

They didn't talk any more of the people left on the moon. They were doomed, and there was nothing anyone could do. Or wanted to do.

Egg said, "I'll bet the folks back on earth would like to know what happened up here. They can stop worrying about Emperor Pierre."

"Let the party begin," Rip muttered.

Ten minutes later Charley was talking to the president on the radio. She told him they were coming home in the saucer, just the three of them, and the antigravity generator on the moon was no longer operational.

"Can they fix it?" the president wanted to know.

"I doubt it," Charley said.

"That's very good news, extremely good news. When you get back, land at Andrews Air Force Base. The White House is in rubble or I'd have you land on the south lawn. I want to have a press conference with you folks so everyone all around the world can stop worrying."

Rip made a face. Charley frowned at him, then said, "Yes, sir," to the president. When she released the mike button, she said to Rip, "We have to do it and you know it. A lot of people won't believe a government announcement. Would you?"

"Nope," Rip admitted.

"See?"

"How many people are still alive on the moon?" the president asked.

Charley counted on her fingers. "Six or seven." She wasn't sure about the man she had blasted with the rocket exhaust.

"Was Artois one of them?"

"Pierre? When Rip last saw him, he was alive."

"When we have a private moment, I'd like to hear all about it."

"Roger that."

"By the way," the president added, "you can tell Rip that he won't have to pay for the damage at the museum. I think we can probably get a special appropriation from Congress to cover it. They'll undoubtedly want to pass a resolution thanking you for all your efforts."

The president said his good-byes, and the conversation was over. Charley turned off the radio.

"How badly did you damage the museum?" Egg asked his nephew.

"Ten million dollars' worth."

"They should be at least that grateful," Egg muttered.

Later, when Egg was asleep, Rip murmured to Charley, "That other saucer is around someplace."

"I've been thinking about that," she admitted.

WHEN THE RADIO CONVERSATION WAS OVER, THE PRESI-dent beamed at his advisers and cabinet officers, all of whom had listened to the conversation with Charley over loud-speakers. He aimed his smile at the secretary of state. "We didn't have to declare war on France after all. I hope you're pleased."

"A great many French people are very proud of Pierre Artois."

The president waved a dismissive hand. "That's the way it goes. Sometimes you eat the bear and sometimes the bear eats you. They'll just have to soldier on."

"As a gesture of goodwill, I think we should offer to return the spaceplane to France. They may wish to use it again in their space program."

"We'll address that request when they make it, if they do," the president said. He changed the subject. It took the group twenty minutes to reach a consensus on the best way to break the good news to the public, in America and world-wide. In deference to the feelings of the French, the assem-bled savants thought that the president should avoid the appearance of gloating.

"I don't gloat," he stated positively.

Still, he might smile or be erroneously perceived as gloat-ing, which wouldn't do, they assured him. The group finally agreed that the White House press spokesperson should pass out a flyer to the press and take questions. On that note the meeting broke up.

When the president and P. J. O'Reilly were alone, the pres-ident's smile faded. "What are the chances the French would launch a rescue mission to the moon if they got their hot hands on that spaceplane?" he asked O'Reilly.

"Pretty good. A lot of people in Europe and America will demand it, for very different reasons. Senator Blohardt is already talking about trying Pierre and his henchmen for a variety of felonies, including murder and extortion. If the French do indeed bring him back, things could get nasty."

"We'll all be better off if Pierre stays up there. Have the air force destroy the spaceplane. Burn it up in an accident. We leave that thing sitting around, some fool may be tempted to steal it."

"Yes, sir," said P. J. O'Reilly.

"People can tell their kids that the man in the moon is French."

O'Reilly liked it when the president did sneaky things that nobody could pin on him. He planned on telling all the secrets someday in a book about his White House years, a book that would make him rich. The possibility that the president wouldn't care what he said in his book never once entered his head. He strolled from the room with his lips pursed, whistling silently.

It was a foggy, misty night in Missouri when Charley Pine set the saucer in the grass in front of Egg's hangar. For the last two hours she had been running on the antigravity rings, rushing along above the treetops. The three of them had been fighting earth's strong gravity and were very tired. As the saucer touched solid ground, Egg swayed on his feet.

The fog was so dense that it obscured the trees behind Egg's house. "A hot shower would really be nice," Charley said wistfully as she stared at the building. "With clean sheets and a soft pillow afterward."

"A home-cooked meal wouldn't be bad either," Rip said, "but I think we should stick with the plan."

"Okay," Charley said, and pushed the power button in to the first detent. Rip opened the hatch as Egg kissed Charley good-bye. Then all three of them stood around the open hatchway inhaling the wet, foggy earth smell.

"I'd forgotten how good that smells," Egg said, and sucked in another lungful. He shook Rip's hand, then hugged him. "You two be careful."

"Sure, Unc. Sure."

They watched him lower himself carefully through the hatch and waddle away. Rip closed the hatch. "The pond," he told Charley as she remounted the pilot's seat.

They flew away as Egg stood waving with his good arm. They didn't fly far, a mere three hundred yards to a clear pond that Egg had created years ago by damming a creek. Charley submerged the saucer in the pond, and they filled up the main tank. They didn't bother filling the empty bladders in the main cabin.

Charley set the saucer on the edge of the pond so that Rip could get out and check that the cap on the tank had closed automatically. It had.

As he scrambled back aboard he told Charley, "Ooh, it smells so good, feels so good. The moon is cool, but there's no place like home."

"And this isn't even Kansas," Charley said as she lifted the saucer into the air.

Using a bit of rocket power, they headed east at ten thousand feet, well below the altitude at which the airliners flew. When they were cruising with the computer flying the ship, Charley announced, "I'm whacked. I've got to sleep."

Rip flew while she curled up with a blanket on the seats at the back of the compartment.

At this altitude the clouds were well below. The moon, in its last quarter, was resting right on the cloudtops. Rip turned the saucer so he could see it, then resumed course. As he watched, the moonlight on the clouds faded and the night grew very dark. Rip didn't notice; he was thinking about the other saucer.

Lalouette was a fighter pilot before he was recruited to fly spaceplanes. Sure, he had made a few foolish mistakes battling Charley on the moon, but if he was alive and wanted another go, the rematch could be vicious.

Surely he wouldn't be so foolish. If he had any sense,

Lalouette was probably lying on a beach in the South Sea islands, with the saucer hidden in the surf. As he flew eastward Rip fervently prayed that Jean-Paul did have some sense and had decided to become a survivor. Still, he scanned the sky ceaselessly, looking.

AFTER THE SAUCER DISAPPEARED SILENTLY INTO THE FOG, Egg Cantrell slowly climbed the hill to his house. He unlocked the door and began snapping on lights. In a night this dark there should be light.

He climbed the stairs to his room and took a long, hot shower. The days in low gravity and weightlessness had taken their toll. He was so tired. He was toweling off when he heard a faint, low rumble. Ah, the engines of the saucer! A smile crossed his face.

He put on his pajamas and fell into bed. Despite his fatigue, his eyes stayed open. He had this vague feeling that something was out there. With the lights in the house off, he went from window to window, looking out into the foggy night. And of course saw nothing. Finally he went back to bed, and slept.

TWO AND A HALF HOURS AFTER THEY LEFT MISSOURI, RIP glided down toward Chesapeake Bay under a clear night sky. He could see the vast sheet of water glistening in the starlight.

He brought the saucer to a hover, lowered the landing gear and let the ship slip gently into the water. The water lapped at the canopy as he steadied the saucer. He opened the cap on the water tank and let the water run in. He could hear it gurgling. When the noise stopped, he closed the cap and let the weight of the saucer carry it down. Finally, at least a hundred feet down, the ship contacted the floor of the bay. It came to rest at a slight angle.

They were safe here, he thought. There was no way Lalouette could find this ship under a hundred feet of water.

Rip pushed the power knob in to the first detent, climbed
from the pilot's seat, used the meager facilities, then curled
up beside Charley with a blanket. In seconds he was sound
asleep.

WHEN EGG AWOKE THE SUN WAS COMING OVER THE TREE-
tops and the birds were singing. A dove on the gutter just
above the window cooed repeatedly. Looking out, he could
see that the grass was covered with droplets of dew, which
reflected the light of the rising sun. The foliage was chang-
ing; splotches of red and yellow and brown decorated the
trees.

Egg rubbed his hands together, then donned clean
clothes from his closet. Soon he was in the kitchen making
breakfast. He turned on a network morning show and
watched the president's press secretary answering reporters'
questions—most of which, he said, he didn't yet know the
answer to.

Yet the news was good—very, very good—and the talking
heads were euphoric. The government said Pierre was no
longer a threat, and even the French admitted that they were
unable to contact the lunar base. Later today the heroes of
the hour, Charlotte Pine and Rip Cantrell, would be landing
the saucer at Andrews. The reception would be carried live
on this network. Happy days were here again.

Egg snapped off the television and hummed as he served
himself bacon and eggs, toast and coffee. He ate at the little
table where he always ate, with the morning sun streaming
through the window.

Ooh, boy, life is *good!*

After he had put the dishes in the dishwasher and started
the machine, he donned a sweater that was hanging on a peg

near the front door and went out onto the porch. A squirrel in a nearby tree scolded him. A cool little breeze rustled the autumn leaves.

Egg kept a sealed container of bird food in one corner of the porch; now he opened it and dribbled a scoopful of sunflower seeds along the porch rail. In less than a minute the large, fat gray squirrel leaped from the tree to the rail and settled in to dine, ignoring the man.

With his hands in his pockets, Egg strolled around his lawn, looking at this, examining that. He soon found himself at the entrance to his hangar. He opened the door, went inside and flipped on the light.

An old man was sitting on the couch by the refrigerator. His face was in shadow, but Egg could see his wispy white hair and the gnarled bony hands, one of which held a nasty little automatic.

"It's about time, Cantrell. I was getting tired of waiting."

Newton Chadwick!

"How'd you get here?"

"I've got the gun, Cantrell, so I'll ask the questions and you'll supply the answers." He wheezed a bit after he spoke, seeming to fight for air. "Come over here and sit so I can see you better."

Egg hesitated.

"Do as I say or I'll drop you where you stand. Don't have much time left, and I owe you a big one."

Egg walked over and took a chair eight feet from Chadwick, on his left side. Chadwick rested the hand that held the automatic on his thigh.

"That's better," the old man said. And he was old. From this distance Chadwick looked every day of eighty-five, perhaps ninety.

"Yeah, Cantrell, take a good look. My hair turned white

and most of it fell out, my teeth got loose and I lost half of them. I dropped twenty pounds just like that and got splotches all over my hands. Damn prostate swelled up so I can't piss, hands shake, can't see very well—I'm in a hell of a shape, and I got you to thank. You're the bastard that dumped my drug and replaced it with water, aren't you?"

"I did that, yes."

"And now it's too late," Chadwick said fiercely. "Even if I got more of the serum, it won't reverse the aging process. It merely retards it, puts it on hold. Who the hell wants to live for a hundred years in the shape I'm in? I ought to just kill you here and now."

"Why don't you?"

"I'm thinking about it. I want to watch you sweat before you die. Like I'm doing. Haven't got long left. My heart is also acting up." He paused for a moment, shook his head as if to clear it and coughed silently. "Lalouette dropped me here. The antimatter weapon on Pine's saucer blew his left arm off at the elbow. He was in no shape to fight anymore and headed for home. Lucky for us I managed to get a tourniquet on that stump or he'd have bled to death."

"So you didn't die and you're back on earth. Most of those people on the moon are dead, and the rest are doomed. Be glad you're here."

"But I'm dying, you fool! Dying of old age that's catching up to me all at once. Thanks to you. Hell of a thing, what you did to me."

"Oh, cut the self-pity," Egg roared. "I haven't got the stomach for it. You've lived a long, healthy life and worked hard at something you liked. That's more than most people get. Now here you sit like a toad in a well crying, 'Woe is me.' Pfft! It's time to stop the pity party. Get off your butt and go outside. It's a marvelous fall day. The birds are singing, the critters are fat, the sun is shining, and the world is turning."

Chadwick lifted the pistol and pointed it at Egg's middle, which was a large target. His hand shook. "Don't you understand?" His voice was high pitched, querulous. "I'm old and worn out and dying."

Egg lowered his voice and leaned forward. "You are the one who doesn't understand. If you only have a day or an hour or fifteen minutes left to live, you should spend it out there in the sun, savoring this day. The value of life isn't measured by the amount of time you get, but by how well you enjoy what you do have."

Chadwick couldn't hold the pistol up. He lowered it into his lap. "I was always too busy looking forward, scheming, wanting more of everything. Money, recognition, fame, respect—"

He paused, breathing in and out, put the hand holding the pistol up to his heart and pressed on his chest with his wrist. After a bit he lowered his hand back into his lap. He seemed to forget about the pistol. At least he didn't aim it.

"Come on," Egg said, and stood up. He held out his hand. "Let's get out in it."

Chadwick hesitated, then held out his left hand. As Egg pulled he pushed off with his right, which still held the pistol, and levered himself erect. He stood swaying, holding on to Egg. Finally he looked down at the pistol, seeming surprised that he still had it. He put it in his trouser pocket.

"Let's go," Egg said, and helped the old man walk. He took tiny, shuffling steps. Egg held the door open, and Chadwick shielded his eyes from the sun. It took almost a minute for his eyes to adjust.

Egg took him along the path beside the runway so Chadwick wouldn't have to climb the hill. The flowers were still out, bees were busy, and Egg pointed out a hummingbird. Chadwick looked as if he were seeing these wonders for the very first time. The gentle breeze played with his hair. He put up his hand, felt his hair moving around and smoothed it some.

"Was there ever a woman?" Egg asked.

"Yes," Chadwick said. After a bit he added, "She had dark hair, nearly black. Brown eyes."

A little farther along, Chadwick staggered. "Pretty tired," he gasped. "Let me . . . sit under that tree."

The old maple was at least twenty inches in diameter and had lost a major limb in the last big summer thunderstorm. The shattered limb lay beside the tree in the grass, still sporting its withered leaves. *Gotta cut that up for firewood,* Egg thought.

Chadwick eased himself to the ground and leaned back against the tree.

"Should have married her," he muttered. "Wish I had."

He closed his eyes. His breathing became regular, and he seemed to go to sleep.

Egg sat nearby and watched the treetops dance. The breeze must be stronger up there. Grasshoppers were singing, and before long a ruffed grouse came hesitantly from the brush to search for them. The bird ignored the men.

The similarity between his life and Chadwick's hit Egg hard. He too had never married, had submerged himself in work. Today he was acutely conscious of all the things he had paid too little attention to, such as family, friends, spring rains, summer thunderstorms—and women.

Maybe . . . There was an archaeologist at the university who had wanted to see the saucer computer. They had spent a day together at the farm. After she completed her article, she had called and asked him to dinner. He had refused. Now he remembered her smile, the way she held her head when she looked at him. Maybe he should call her up and accept that invitation.

The breeze was stronger now on his face; clouds were

forming overhead. As a boy he had liked to lie in the grass looking at clouds. He hadn't done it since junior high. *When I'm old, I'll wish I'd done it all my life*, he thought.

After a while Egg glanced at Chadwick. He seemed to have sagged a little. His chin was on his chest, which had stopped moving. Egg checked Chadwick's pulse. There wasn't one. The breeze was still caressing his white hair.

Egg stood, sighed as he took a last look at the old man, then slowly made his way along the runway toward the hangar and the telephone.

20

"WHERE THE DEVIL IS THAT SAUCER?" THE PRESIDENT asked the chairman of the Joint Chiefs after another look at his watch. They were standing on the reviewing platform that had been hurriedly erected in front of the huge hangar at Andrews Air Force Base, on the outskirts of Washington. Three days ago the president had specifically told Charley Pine eleven o'clock. She and Cantrell were twenty-two minutes late.

"Hard to say, Mr. President," the general replied. "We can't see the thing on radar—it's very stealthy. Every now and then the operators get a stray glint from a leading edge, but only on a sweep or two, and only occasionally."

The president was in no mood for technical explanations. The French spaceplane had burned to cinders in an accident yesterday at the Bonneville Salt Flats—a fuel leak, according to the press release—and this morning the French ambassador had delivered a note to the state department demanding reimbursement.

"A billion and a half dollars for a used spaceplane?" the

president exclaimed to the secretary of state. "Don't be ridiculous."

"They're very adamant," she retorted.

"Tell 'em we'll deduct a couple hundred mil from the bill we're sending them for a new White House, an arch in St. Louis, the bridges in San Fran and that stadium those folks in California want."

"You intend to bill France for a football stadium?"

"Damn right! Dirt, grass, skyboxes and everything, the whole works."

That conversation had taken some of the shine off the president's bonhomie. He looked at his watch again, glanced over at the press mob, which was restrained by a rope and a dozen military police, and tried to look relaxed even though he was worried. Twenty-eight minutes after the hour now.

The air force said two objects had reentered the atmosphere over California, one yesterday and one the day before. When he received the report on the first one he knew it wasn't Pine—she couldn't have made the trip from the moon that quickly. It must have been the Roswell saucer, the one Pine had fought on the moon, the one stolen from Area 51. He had tried to call Pine on the radio and give her a warning, but she never acknowledged. Probably had the radio off.

After it came into the atmosphere, the Roswell saucer had been spotted over Missouri by people on the ground, over Illinois by an airliner going into O'Hare, and by several pilots flying over Canada. The Canadian military had been searching for it ever since without success.

The president wondered if he should have canceled this event. He had decided not to because it had already been announced and publicized.

As he kept checking his watch, he fretted.

If he had only known that Pine and Cantrell were late because they had overslept, he would have been infuriated.

A passing ship, a freighter out of Baltimore, woke them from their deep sleep. They heard the screw noises; then the saucer rocked slightly as the disturbed water reached the bottom. Charley Pine looked around, blinked, then looked at her watch. Omigawd! Half past eleven.

"Rip! Rip! Wake up. We're late."

She stumbled over to the pilot's seat, wiping the sleep from her eyes. She donned the headset, pulled the power knob all the way out and lifted the antigravity control on the left side of the seat. The saucer didn't want to come out of the mud. She lifted the control a good bit, and finally the mud released its grip.

The heavy saucer rose slowly, lifting a column of water above it. Impatient, Charley shoved the stick forward while lifting the antigravity control. Instantly the spaceship began moving through the water, faster and faster as the saucer-shape began developing lift. She lifted the nose a tad and the ship planed upward toward the surface. The flying saucer accelerated nicely and shot out of the water in a ten-degree climb.

A fisherman in a nearby boat was nearly swamped in the mini-tsunami. He stared openmouthed as Charley lit the rocket engines and the saucer accelerated away in a long, sweeping turn to the north.

Aboard the freighter, a severely hungover sailor who witnessed the saucer's departure swore off booze. Never again, he vowed, as he squeezed his eyes shut against the glare of the rocket exhaust and belatedly clapped his hands over his ears.

JEAN-PAUL LALOUETTE WAS IN PAIN. THE STUMP OF HIS left arm was turning gangrenous, he suspected. He and Chadwick had bandaged it as well as they could, and then gradually loosened the emergency tourniquet to restore blood flow, but the bleeding had been so bad they had had to tighten it again or he would have bled to death.

During the three-day journey to earth he had fought the pain and shock, and watched in horror as Newton Chadwick aged before his eyes. The whole flight from the moon had been a living nightmare. He was already suffering the tortures of hell and he wasn't even dead. Yet.

Chadwick had wanted to go to Missouri so he could kill Egg Cantrell when he arrived, as he would sooner or later. Lalouette thought that request sounded reasonable. He wanted the sweet taste of revenge himself. He dropped Chadwick at Cantrell's farm, refilled his water tanks and left. If the other saucer didn't show up for a week or two, he suspected he'd be dead when it arrived. His time was running out. He needed to intercept the saucer as soon as it came back to earth.

Charley Pine. He was going to kill her before he died.

Then he would be ready to go. Not until then, though.

Listening to the radio, Lalouette learned of the welcome-home event planned at Andrews. *Then!* That would be the time and place.

He flew northeast into Canada, found a lake in the woods and refilled the saucer's tanks. And he lucked out. There was an empty fishing cabin on the shore of the lake, already battened down for winter. He parked the saucer under a canopy of trees near the cabin. He broke into the cabin, found a sheet that he tore up for a new bandage, prepared a meal from canned goods the owners left behind and spent a miserable thirty-six hours huddled by a fire, consumed with rage.

Jean-Paul Lalouette wasn't an evil man. Yet he had been beaten by a *woman,* and he was in severe pain and suffering from blood poisoning. He was no longer a rational human being.

Now he was gliding down toward Andrews from the northwest. The entire city of Washington lay under him. He ignored it, watching the sky for fighters. The Americans might try to intercept him, shoot him down.

He had timed his arrival for an hour after the event started. He would hover in front of the grandstand and kill everyone on it with the antimatter particles. Kill them all—Charley Pine, Rip Cantrell, the president, all of the bastards.

He saw airliners, but no fighters.

Despite the pain in his arm, he smiled grimly.

THE PEOPLE ON THE REVIEWING STAND HEARD THE LOW moan of the saucer's rocket engines before they saw it. People stood to get a better view; everyone scanned the sky. The president's granddaughter, Amanda, spotted the saucer first just above the horizon, coming swiftly from the southeast. She should have been in school today but demanded vociferously to see Charley Pine again, so her parents agreed that she could play hookey.

"There it is!" Amanda shouted, and pointed.

A wave of relief washed over the president, who collapsed back into his chair and mopped his brow.

The lenticular shape rushed toward them, its engines murmuring gently. Then the sound of the engines died away as Charley Pine put the saucer into a glide.

CHARLEY CONCENTRATED ON THE PARKING MAT IN FRONT of the huge hangar, trying to judge the closure rate. She could see the hordes of people, tens of thousands of them, the reviewing stand and the empty place in front where undoubtedly they intended her to land. Off to her right, on the northern edge of the mat, was the Goodyear blimp, which an enterprising television network had hired to obtain aerial shots of the saucer's landing.

Standing beside Charley's seat in the saucer, Rip Cantrell scanned the sky forward, right, left and as far aft as he could see on either side. So he saw the other saucer first, ninety degrees off the port beam, tilted at a seventy-degree angle, turning hard to come in behind.

"Nine o'clock high!" he shouted, pointing, then instinctively grabbed something to hold on to.

Charley Pine looked where he pointed and acquired the other saucer instantly. A surge of adrenaline shot through her. She twisted the throttle grip on the lever that controlled the antigravity rings wide open. The engines lit instantly. She shoved the stick left and began tweaking the nose up. The saucer laid over into a turn, its nose rising as it quickly accelerated.

THE ROAR FROM CHARLEY'S ENGINES HIT THE CROWD below like the fist of God. Everyone had been watching the approaching saucer so intently that no one had seen the second one, circling high and maneuvering to drop onto the tail of the first.

The FAA administrator, who was on the reviewing platform, instantly assumed that Charley Pine intended to buzz the crowd, and roared, "I'll have her license for this." The noise was so loud that no one heard this promise.

When the second saucer lit its engines and passed overhead immediately behind the first, its sudden appearance shocked the administrator, the hundred thousand spectators and the audience around the globe watching on television, the vast bulk of whom had not even known that *two* saucers existed.

Although he knew all too much about the second saucer, the president's reaction was typical. "Oh, my God!" he said, and the words were lost in the deep bass thunder that massaged flesh and made the earth tremble.

* * *

JEAN-PAUL LALOUETTE THOUGHT HE HAD CHARLEY PINE as he turned hard, descending, to come in behind her. He had the antimatter reticle projected on the canopy in front of him, and he was ready to kill.

Then she lit her engines and turned hard into him. He knew that with his speed and descent angle, there was no way he could turn inside her, so he shallowed his turn and leveled the saucer, intending to accelerate and extend out, then turn hard and come back in for another pass. This course took him right over the assembled multitude below. Unfortunately, he was looking over his shoulder at Pine, hoping she would keep her turn in, so he didn't notice that he was still descending. The roof of the hangar flashing under him caught his attention, however.

He automatically fed in back stick and glanced forward, ensured his nose was above the horizon, then looked left to reacquire Charley visually.

Still accelerating, his saucer headed straight for the Goodyear blimp.

THE CAMERAMAN IN THE GONDOLA OF THE BLIMP COULDN'T believe his good fortune. He had a flying saucer coming at him head-on. He engaged the autofocus on his camera and got a shot that mesmerized his television audience: the saucer boring in, the black lenticular shape framed by the halo of white-hot exhaust flames that shot from its engines.

His elation quickly turned to horror as he realized the saucer was coming precisely at the camera. At the blimp. At *him!* He closed his eyes and braced himself.

LALOUETTE SAW CHARLEY PINE REVERSE HER TURN, whipping the saucer over from an eighty-degree bank to the

left to a ninety-degree bank to the right. She was pulling
hard too—he could see the swirl of a cloud forming on top
of the turning disk and being swallowed by the exhaust
flame.

He glanced ahead—and saw the blimp. He was going right
at it. He was too close to avoid it. Even as the sight registered,
the saucer hit the inflated blimp dead in the middle. Nearly
supersonic now, the saucer cleaved through it in an eyeblink,
like a bullet through paper, and shot out the other side.

FORTUNATELY THE BLIMP WAS FILLED WITH HELIUM, A
nonflammable gas, so it didn't explode. It folded like a
ripped dishrag and felt straight down—into the base sewage-
settling pond that just happened to be immediately below.

Five minutes later the pilot, copilot and cameraman staggered from the shallow pond, coughing, spluttering and
uninjured. Lying on the bank covered in slime, the cameraman remembered the shot he had before his eyes slammed
shut and began thinking about a Pulitzer.

JEAN-PAUL LALOUETTE EASED BACK ON THE GO JUICE AND
laid the saucer into a climbing, high-G turn. He wanted to
get a shot at Charley Pine head-on or nearly so, and if the
antimatter particles didn't do the trick, he was going to ram
her. He didn't consciously think about it, but he knew that
was the way it would go.

He lost sight for a second in the turn, and when he reac-
quired the other saucer visually, it had turned somewhat,
making a head-on pass possible. He racked his ship around
hard to bring the reticle to bear and opened fire.

He hadn't thought about what would happen when his
weapon began squirting antimatter particles through a
gaseous medium, so he was surprised at the tracer bullet

effect as random particles annihilated themselves on positrons in the air molecules.

Charley Pine saw the streak of fire and smoke, and jogged to avoid it.

Lalouette suddenly realized that he could not bring the particle stream onto her ship as they closed, so he concentrated on ramming. He was pulling hard when his ship barely missed Charley's, passing immediately behind it, right through the rocket exhaust plume.

He immediately killed the rockets and began pulling back toward Charley, intent on getting behind her. The G killed his speed quickly, and indeed, Pine's saucer began to move forward on his canopy.

Yes! He was going to get her! Elation flooded him and he pulled even harder on the stick, forcing his speed to bleed off even quicker.

WHEN CHARLEY LOOKED OVER HER RIGHT SHOULDER AND saw the enemy saucer banking toward her without its plume of rocket exhaust, she knew precisely what Lalouette intended—to get behind her for a killing shot.

She almost instinctively cut her engines, which would have set up a low-speed scissors, but she rejected that option. Her opponent was already slower than she was, so had the advantage. Instead she opened her throttle all the way, twisting the grip to the stop. The Gs shoved her backward into her seat.

REGARDLESS OF WHAT ELSE HE WAS, LALOUETTE WAS A good fighter pilot. He knew he had been outmaneuvered when he saw the exhaust plume on Pine's saucer grow into a mighty torch, almost as bright as the sun. Too late, he ordered the computer to give him full power. Still, the enemy saucer began opening the range dramatically. He did manage to get Pine in his sights and fired. A river of sparks and smoke shot forward, but he sensed the range was already too great. None of the antimatter particles would survive to reach the target. Closer. He had to get closer.

AS IT HAPPENED, PINE WAS HEADING NORTHEAST WHEN she stroked the rockets, so that was the way she continued. With Lalouette well behind, the two saucers shot away in that direction and soon disappeared from sight.

The thunder of their engines continued to reverberate around the hangar and parking mats of Andrews Air Force Base for almost a minute, however, before it faded below the threshold of hearing.

As the roar diminished, people began removing their fingers from their ears. Amanda exclaimed, "I'm going to be a saucer pilot someday, just like Charley Pine!"

The president was a thoughtful man. If Lalouette succeeded in shooting down Pine, there was nothing to stop him from refueling and returning to the moon to rescue Pierre Artois, nor from carrying technicians and parts aloft to repair the antigravity beam generator. As the excited voices around him became a hubbub, he turned to the chairman of the Joint Chiefs and whispered, "Scramble every fighter on the East Coast. Shoot down that big saucer."

"There's no way for fighter pilots to tell those saucers apart," the chairman protested. "How will they know which is which?"

"Shoot 'em both down," the president ordered after a glance at Amanda, to ensure she wasn't listening. "The stakes are too high. We can't take a chance."

FLYING STRAIGHT AND LEVEL AT FULL POWER IN A CLEAR autumn sky, Charley Pine rapidly considered her alternatives as her velocity increased dramatically. She could zoom up into inner space, where the air was thin or nonexistent, turn at the top of her climb and take a head-on shot at Lalouette as she dove. Or she could turn hard and convert her airspeed advantage into an angular one, which if she played it right would eventually give her a shot at her opponent. Or she could combine the two tactics, climb and turn at the same time.

She was torn, unsure of how to play this, when she saw clouds ahead. Aha! A front; a line of cumulus with bases at several thousand feet, tops at perhaps ten.

At her speed, now approaching Mach 7, she was in the clouds in seconds. Off the throttle, she turned hard to kill some speed—a turn that covered seventy miles of New Jersey in seconds. She asked the computer for the radar presentation, and got it. Numerous returns appeared on the display; after all, this airspace over New Jersey was full of airplanes. Lalouette would be easy to spot because his saucer would be the quickest blip on the scope—if she managed to get him into her forward quadrant, and if the radar could pick him up.

Her speed dissipated rapidly with the G she had on. Just as she was beginning to suspect that her tightening turn might have worked, the saucer shot through a relatively clear area and she got a glimpse of an airliner, a twin-engine commuter turboprop. She cleared it by a few feet; at the speed she was traveling the encounter looked close enough to trade paint. The airliner was gone so quickly that when she realized what it was, she was already well past it.

That was good. If she hit an airplane at these speeds in these skies, the accident would be over before she even knew it was going to happen.

She wondered whether Lalouette was using his radar. If he wasn't, he had lost her in this wilderness of gauzy, puffy towers.

There he was! On the display. She had slowed seconds before he had, so could turn tighter than he could. He was trying to turn, which was a mistake. Although he had an energy advantage, hers was now angular, and it would be enough to give her the victory if he continued to play her game for a few more seconds.

Turning hard, flashing in and out of the clouds, she closed on her opponent, who was merely a blip on the three-dimensional holographic display on the panel in front of her. She was on his altitude, turning inside him with the range closing nicely. She centered the symbol on the reticle and glanced down in time to see the target sinking toward the bottom of the display, which was her saucer.

LALOUETTE HAD LOST PINE. WHEN SHE ENTERED THE cloud he had lost sight of her exhaust plume. Now she was somewhere in this soup thrashing around, no doubt maneuvering to kill him. He had the radar going and was busy trying to figure it out, which was difficult since he was flying and fighting the pain in his arm and the general malaise that came with blood poisoning.

He had entered a left turn in order to scan with the radar and backed off on the power. All this he accomplished merely by thinking about it, since he was wearing the headband. Without the band he couldn't have flown the saucer one-handed.

These clouds . . . He eased higher. He wanted to get above them, so he could see right, left and behind.

He had just topped the clouds when the first antimatter particle detonated in the saucer behind him. He automatically looked left, inside his turn, and aft. There she was, coming out of the clouds and closing, only a couple hundred yards away, a river of sparks and smoke vomiting from the front of her saucer, straight at him.

Triphammer thuds behind him. Then a horrible pain in his right calf!

Power! Full power!

The Gs shoved him into the seat and the hammering stopped. He was out of the particle stream, accelerating quickly.

His leg! Blood. He felt it with his good arm. A cavity, a horrible wound, bleeding badly.

He didn't have much time left.

The separation between the two ships was increasing, so he made a gentle turn to the right. He wasn't thinking clearly, but he remembered the buildings of New York. He could hide in the concrete canyons.

Behind him a trickle of water flowed from the saucer's damaged main tank.

THE TWO SAUCERS RACED TOWARD NEW YORK CITY AT full power. Lalouette dove back into the clouds, but he didn't maneuver, just ran flat out, and Charley couldn't close the distance. She tried a few squirts of antimatter particles when she got a firing solution on the holographic display. The particles had no apparent effect on the saucer ahead. Perhaps the distance was too great, perhaps the moisture in the clouds soaked up some of the particles, whatever.

She knew New York was in the direction that Lalouette was going, with her hot on his tail. There was nothing she could do about it; wherever he went, she intended to follow. If she let him escape now he would hunt her down and appear, probably, when she least expected it. She intended to follow him to the limit of her fuel unless she killed him sooner, which she was trying mightily to do. She and Rip would be at the bottom of a smoking hole at Andrews if Rip hadn't spotted the other saucer just seconds before Lalouette could open fire. A couple of seconds . . . the difference between life and death.

Other targets appeared on the display—airplanes. They were so slow they appeared nearly stationary. There were so many! Then she realized that Lalouette was embedded in the planes queuing up to land at Newark. And he was slowing.

The distance closed rapidly. Yet she dared not shoot; there were too many airplanes nearby.

She backed off on the throttle, felt the G ease up. She lowered the nose, feeling for the bottom of the clouds as she weaved to avoid the airliners.

She came out of the clouds at about fifteen hundred feet above the ground, still making at least Mach 2. Rip was right beside her, pointing out planes. She merely glanced, then resumed her concentration on the display on the panel.

Lalouette had to be the fast mover on the display. Now he was turning right, headed straight for Manhattan.

She tried to cut across his turn, shorten the distance. Yes. Closing . . . almost in range.

But beyond the saucer were buildings. People. If the particles were scattered by impact with the saucer's skin, or went all the way through it, they would hit those buildings and people. And if she succeeded in shooting down the saucer, it would crash into New York!

She held her fire and stayed high, just under the base of the clouds, which covered about half the sky. Visibility was excellent underneath.

Lalouette descended sharply, heading right for the Verrazano Narrows Bridge at the entrance to the bay.

"He's going to hit it!" Rip exclaimed with horror in his voice.

Seconds later Charley replied, "No, I think he wants to go under it."

And he did. The shock wave off the now subsonic saucer

rocked the bridge. As it swayed traffic stopped and people bailed from their vehicles.

The saucer continued up the bay, streaking past ships and ferries, only a few feet above the water. A roostertail of water rose behind it. From their perch Charley and Rip had a ring-side seat—which was perfect. If Lalouette turned and climbed, they would have a shot, if they had to defend themselves. If he didn't, they could attack him after he left the city behind.

Lalouette headed for the East River, which was spanned by several bridges.

"God in heaven, he's going to go under them all," Rip said in awe.

BLOOD WAS SOAKING THE LEG OF JEAN-PAUL'S JUMPSUIT. He was in severe pain. He was flying without a plan because he could think of no way to end this nightmare. No way to destroy the saucer that he knew was behind him, hunting him, no way to kill that Charley Pine.

The sensation of speed this close to the water was sublime. He avoided a ship and two smaller vessels, weaving slightly, and saw the bridges ahead. Unconsciously he asked the computer to back off on the power, and it did. The saucer was down to three hundred knots now.

In seconds the spans shot over his head.

He had to turn hard to stay over the river, and the Gs made his leg bleed more. He screamed in agony.

There was no relief from the pain.

Desperate to do something, he commanded a pull-up and turn to the left. The saucer responded to his thoughts.

NOW CHARLEY SAW THE ENEMY SAUCER RISING AND TURN-ing, cutting across midtown. This was her chance, her opening.

Yet she refused to take it. There was no way she was going to force Lalouette to crash in Manhattan. She racked her ship into a turn to preserve her angular and height advantage.

THE FRENCH PILOT SOARED OVER THE BUILDINGS IN A long, lazy turn that carried him across the island and out over the Hudson River, where he steadied out going south.

He was in too much pain to think, to look around for his opponent. He held on to his bleeding leg with his one good hand, trying to stanch the blood flow. To no avail.

When he saw the Statue of Liberty approaching his nose he turned again, descending.

"NOW WHAT?" RIP ASKED THE GODS.

The other saucer was in a descending turn. It looked for a moment as if it might go into the water. Then the nose came up and it skimmed the surface heading north toward the Battery.

LALOUETTE WAS AGAIN DOWN ON THE DECK. HE SHOT over Battery Park at two or three hundred feet and actually went between two buildings immediately north of the park's small splash of green. Charley Pine pushed her nose down, intending to get immediately behind the other ship. Yet she was afraid to go as low as the French pilot.

He was frightened, she realized. He must be injured.

"Jesus," Rip said as the saucer ahead flashed between buildings.

A jog on Broadway, then straight north up the Avenue of the Americas toward Central Park. She was only a few hundred yards behind, but the larger saucer was lower, below the plane of the antimatter weapon. She couldn't bring herself to dive down to his level. The buildings whipped past like fence posts.

* * *

AFTER THE SAUCERS FLED THE VICINITY OF ANDREWS, television producers were left without a main event. Talking heads took over as the producers ran replays of the footage they did have.

When it became probable that the saucers weren't going to return to Andrews, television stations in cities across the nation launched their traffic helicopters in the hope that the saucers would come their way. One of the networks now put on the air video of the two saucers racing along, one behind the other, between the buildings of New York.

In the presidential lounge off the main hangar floor at Andrews, the president and his advisers were called to the television by the president's granddaughter. "There they are," Amanda squealed, pointing at the set against the wall.

After watching for a few seconds, the president tightened his grip on the arm of the chairman of the Joint Chiefs. "Where are those fighters?"

"I don't know, sir," the general said bitterly. As if a Pentagon four-star knew the exact location of airborne airplanes. If they were airborne. The alert had gone out about fifteen minutes ago, plenty of time for the alert fighters to scramble. But without guidance from their ground control station, the general knew, the pilots would have no idea where to go to intercept their targets. The general also knew that now was not the time to explain the facts of life to the president, but he did pry the commander-in-chief's fingers off his coat sleeve as he concentrated on the television picture.

Man, the general thought as the saucers rocketed between the buildings, *those fools are just flat-out crazy!*

BLEEDING PROFUSELY, IN SHOCK AND SCREAMING WITH pain, the here and now—this moment—was all that mattered to Jean-Paul Lalouette. At some level he knew he would never live to see France again. He tried to ask the computer to fly him into a building, to end it right now, but he couldn't make himself do it.

She was probably behind him, closing in for the kill. Why didn't she shoot?

He got a glimpse of Central Park ahead, rapidly approaching, just a blur of green.

CHARLEY TOO SAW THE PARK COMING UP AND KNEW THAT this was her chance. Perhaps her only chance. She would try to drop the enemy saucer in the park. She would fly right over him, using the wash from her saucer to force his into the ground. She lowered the nose of her bird and dove, closing the distance.

As the southeast edge of the park flashed under them, Lalouette began a gentle turn to the left. The distance between the two ships was less than a hundred feet. Charley turned harder left and added more power as the enemy ship began moving under her nose.

At precisely that instant fate took a hand. A moment of clarity broke through the fog of pain that held Jean-Paul Lalouette in its grip. He didn't want to crash in the city, kill innocent people.

He reacted automatically. *Full power, nose up,* he screamed at the computer. And the saucer instantly responded. It pulled up directly in front of Charley Pine, rising in an eye-blink right though her flight path.

THE BLAST OF ROCKET EXHAUST AND THE WASH FROM THE saucer ahead flipped Charley's saucer ninety degrees onto its side as the enemy saucer did a maximum-G pull into the vertical.

She was on a knife's edge, a hundred feet above the tree-

tops of Central Park, doing about three hundred knots—
with no visible means of support. Her saucer was flying a
parabola into the ground.

Horrified, she slammed the stick sideways to right the ship
and pulled the antigravity collective up into her armpit. The
saucer responded, but not quite fast enough. It hit the top of
a tree, bounced back into the air and settled into another.
Clouds of leaves exploded behind her as the saucer once
again caromed into the air.

Power, power, power, she begged the computer. As the
engines responded, Rip Cantrell lost his death grip on the
panel and the back of the pilot's seat and tumbled aft.

THE LUCKY NETWORK THAT HAD CAPTURED IMAGES OF
the saucers had three helicopters over Manhattan: one over
lower downtown, one over Greenwich Village, and one over
midtown. Each broadcast its video in turn as the saucers
raced north. The last helo got the saucers in Central Park,
the lead saucer pulling up abruptly and the trailing saucer
gyrating wildly and smacking into the treetops. As the clouds
of leaves exploded skyward, the network lost the video feed
from the helicopter.

Back at Andrews, the president had his nose a foot from
the screen when it went blank. Forgetting the presence of his
granddaughter and the two dozen other people crowded
around trying to see, he swore a mighty oath and smashed
his fist down on top of the recalcitrant set. The picture
stayed blank.

THE ROSWELL SAUCER ROSE VERTICALLY ON A PLUME OF
fire. A severely wounded Jean-Paul Lalouette thought of
France, so the computer began to slowly tilt the saucer
toward the east, toward the North Atlantic.

Lalouette had lost a lot of blood, and the Gs of acceleration quickened the blood flow from the damaged area. His blood pressure dropped precipitiously. In seconds he lost consciousness. Twenty seconds after that his heart stopped.

The saucer continued upward, tilting slowly to the east, accelerating . . .

THE EXHAUST PLUME OF THE ROSWELL SAUCER WAS impossible to miss. Charley Pine stayed on the juice, trying to catch Lalouette. Unfortunately he was perhaps twenty seconds ahead.

The combined roar of the two saucers was the loudest noise ever heard in New York. It rattled windows all over the five boroughs and shook the buildings of Manhattan. Elevators jammed. In offices and apartments, restaurants and bars all over the island, floors and walls trembled; dust rose from gypsum drywall and settled from the ceiling light fixtures. People dove under furniture or ran for doorways as the pictures on their televisions finally reappeared, depicting two incandescent white-hot fireballs rising between the towering clouds.

RIP CLAWED HIS WAY BACK TO THE PILOT'S SEAT AND fought the Gs to stand erect. He took one look at the brilliant star that was Lalouette's exhaust plume and said, "There's no way. We'll never catch him."

Charley didn't reply. She was offset to the right of Lalouette's flight path so that she could avoid the turbulence created by his ship. This offset meant that she couldn't bring her antimatter weapon to bear.

They had been climbing for at least five minutes and were now above most of the earth's atmosphere. Above them the sky was dark. Stars began to appear. Below, the haze hid the sea.

"He must be badly injured," Rip said, struggling against the G. "Or dead."

Charley thought so too. She had refused to give in to her emotions since Lalouette attacked them over Andrews, but now the angst and remorse hit her like a hammer. *Why me, God?*

Finally Charley remembered to check her fuel. Less than five percent remaining!

She looked up, just in time to see the other saucer's exhaust plume wink out, then reappear, then cease altogether. One second it was there, then it wasn't.

Lalouette's ship was at least seventy degrees nose up, so it decelerated quickly. The distance between the two saucers closed rapidly.

At first it was just a tiny dot against a darker sky; then it became a lenticular shape, growing larger.

Charley pulled the power, letting her excess speed bring her up onto the other ship's tail. For the first time today the saucer cabin was deathly quiet, and she could feel her heart thudding in her chest.

Is he out of fuel? Why doesn't he drop his nose? If he holds that attitude much longer, he's going to run out of airspeed, and—

Even as she thought it, the big saucer stalled and the nose fell precipitously.

Charley rammed her nose down so she wouldn't stall too.

The nose of Lalouette's saucer fell and fell, and its trajectory became steeper and steeper until it was going straight down.

"He must be dead," Rip said again, with finality.

CHARLEY PINE STUFFED THE NOSE OF HER SHIP DOWN, pointed it at the sea below, and began a gentle, three-G spiral to hold the other saucer in sight. The larger ship raced downward into the haze toward the waiting sea.

They were still over a hundred thousand feet high, Charley estimated, perhaps twenty miles up.

Her speed, which had dropped dramatically since she cut her engines, began building. The radius of her spiral became larger and larger. As the distance to the other ship increased, it began to merge with the gauzy, bright, sunlit haze. *Don't want to lose it,* Charley told herself, and lowered her nose still further.

A minute passed, then two. Still the large saucer plunged downward.

There were no clouds. Now Rip and Charley could see the ocean below, a featureless blue plain. Lalouette's saucer seemed suspended above it, although it wasn't. Without a visual cue it was impossible for Rip and Charley to appreciate Lalouette's closure rate with the waiting ocean.

Knowing they were low and it wouldn't be long, Charley shallowed her descent rate even more.

Lalouette's saucer never pulled out. One moment it was there, diving toward the sea, and then it disappeared in a mighty splash, a ring of white. When the white circle began to dissipate, the Roswell saucer was gone.

SKEETER DUNN AND WARD CARROLL WERE OFF THE COAST of New England in F-16s, inbound for the Cape, when they got the call on the radio to look for and attack any flying saucers they saw.

"What's the world coming to?" Carroll asked aloud into his oxygen mask. Through the years he had developed a habit of talking to himself in the cockpit—and in the car and the shower and anywhere else he found himself alone. "Flying saucers!" He made a rude noise with his tongue and lips.

In the other fighter, out on Carroll's left wing, Skeeter gave him an exaggerated shrug, which in less politically correct days had been known as the Polish salute.

Not that Carroll thought that the world was being invaded. Like every other person in the world between six and ninety-six, he had read and seen video clips of the departure of Charley Pine for the moon in the saucer from the National Air and Space Museum and heard about the theft of a saucer from Area 51 in Nevada. One reporter claimed the government acquired the Nevada saucer in 1947 in Roswell, New Mexico, after they found the crew of aliens all dead inside. The truth of it, Carroll believed, would never be known.

Now the government wanted all the saucers destroyed. Ahh! Guess things didn't go so great on the moon, after all.

Not that these two F-16s, or any conventional fighters, were much of a threat to the saucer Carroll had gazed at in the museum. He and Skeeter had been over the ocean for a training exercise—practice interceptions—and now were inbound. As usual, both planes carried Sidewinder heat-seeking missiles on their wingtips and, since 9/11, a full load of ammo for their 20-mm cannon. And they were way below the fuel normally considered necessary for a combat engagement.

The trick, Carroll mused, would be to get the saucer to fly low and slow enough that the fighters could get weapons' solutions.

He was sitting in the cockpit watching his DME roll down as they tracked the TACAN inbound, and wondering if a Sidewinder would lock on a saucer, when he actually saw one plunge past him, going straight down. At first he wasn't sure, so he rolled up on one wing and looked.

Holy cow! There it was, going straight down. Straight into the drink. The splash was awesome, like a meteor might make.

"Skeeter, did you see that?"

"Yeah, I did. And do you see the saucer at your nine o'clock high?"

Carroll looked. *By all that's holy*—there it was, in a turn from left to right, maybe ten thousand feet above.

"Let's strap it on," Skeeter suggested.

Carroll glanced at his fuel gauges. "All the missiles together," Carroll told his wingman, "then we gotta go home or swim."

He advanced the throttle and lifted the nose.

WITH ONLY A LITTLE WATER LEFT IN THE TANKS, CHARLEY Pine decided not to use the rocket engines. She would coast down to the ocean and go back to Andrews on the antigravity rings. She had leveled out and was descending to the southwest when Rip took one more look at the widening circles where Lalouette had hit the ocean—and saw the two fighters in loose formation climbing toward the saucer.

"Uh-oh," he said. "Fighters. Coming at us from the right."

Charley continued to descend. She couldn't get Lalouette out of her mind. Crashing into the ocean . . . Was he dead when the saucer hit, or did he intentionally fly it into the sea?

"Missiles!" Rip shouted. "They shot missiles—"

Charley Pine rolled the saucer onto its back and pulled. She also lit the rocket engines.

WARD CARROLL HAD FIRED BOTH HIS MISSILES AND WAS watching them track when the plume of flame erupted from the engines of the saucer. He said a cuss word. The missiles would track the fire, a heat source a hundred times hotter than the jet engines the heat sensors in the missile were designed to guide upon. And they did. All four missiles shot through the saucer's exhaust plume.

With her nose well down and the engines on, Charley quickly went supersonic and outdistanced the fighters diving after her.

When she thought she was well ahead of them, she killed the engines. She was only a thousand feet above the water.

She hoisted the nose and used the antigravity rings as a brake. Rip was thrown toward the canopy by the sudden maneuver.

"What are you doing?" he demanded.

"I've had enough of this crap," Charley retorted, and lowered the saucer's nose toward the water.

She braked again, just above the waves, then let the saucer slip gently into the sea. It was ten feet under and descending when the two fighters came roaring over the splash site with their 20-mm cannons blazing.

21

It was drizzling rain when the saucer came over the treetops at four in the morning at Egg Cantrell's Missouri farm and landed softly in front of the hangar.

Rip pushed the power knob in to the first detent and climbed from the pilot's seat. He was whipped. Charley was asleep on the couch with a blanket over her. He kissed her and held her hand until she awakened.

"We're home," he said.

"Oh, Rip," she said, and hugged him.

"It's over, Charley."

"I hope." She kissed him one more time, then tossed the blanket aside and pulled on her boots. Her French space boots, she noted wryly. *Maybe someday I'll sell them on eBay.*

Rip opened the hatch, and Charley went through first. Rip followed. The gentle rain felt good on his skin. He closed his eyes and turned his face to the sky. After a long moment he followed Charley toward the hangar.

Egg was sitting on a folding chair to one side of the open hangar doorway.

"I've been worried about you two," he said, after the hugs.

"The news said that the military was ordered to shoot down all the saucers."

"I figured it was something like that," Rip said. "Lalouette crashed into the ocean, then we were attacked by two fighters, F-16s I think. They shot missiles at us. We put 'er in the water and stayed under until dark."

"Lalouette's dead?"

"Yes."

"And the Roswell saucer is destroyed?"

"Nothing could survive a plunge like that. It's history."

"We've got to do something to hide this one," Charley said. "They'll be after it."

"Maybe put it in a pond or something," Rip said.

"That trick has been used too often," Egg told them. "The government will look in every lake, fishpond and swimming pool in America. I've got a better idea. Been sitting here thinking about it."

"I don't want it destroyed, and I don't want the government to have it," Rip said heatedly.

"You two go up to the house, get baths and something to eat. I'll take care of it."

Charley reached for Rip's hand, looking into his face.

"Okay," Rip said slowly, and nodded.

He and Charley took one last look at the dark shape of the saucer, then walked around the corner of the hangar and took the path for the house.

EGG CANTRELL CRAWLED UNDER THE SAUCER AND CLIMBED up through the open hatchway. Inside he found blankets, food, a makeshift zero-gravity potty, rifles, ammo and the inflatable water tanks that had been installed at Andrews. He carried armload after armload to the hatch and dropped it through. There was still a half case of bottled water—that went too. When the interior of the saucer was free of foreign objects, he got out and began transferring the pile to a spot near the hangar. His sore arm was almost well now and didn't bother him much. Still, the task took a while and about wore him out. Finally he climbed back into the saucer, pulled the hatch shut and latched it.

The pilot's seat felt familiar, like an old friend. He donned the headband and said hello to the computer. First he asked for a fuel check. The ship was nearly empty of water—apparently Rip and Charley had burned it all getting here—but the saucer automatically captured enough hydrogen to power the control jets, even after it refused to give the pilot additional hydrogen for the rocket engines. There was a store of oxygen aboard, and Egg had the computer vent it to the atmosphere. The vent, he knew, was through one of the rocket engine nozzles.

Satisfied, Egg pulled the power knob completely out and waited for the reactor to come up to operating temperature.

Only then did he ask the computer to lift the saucer from the ground. He didn't touch the controls, merely asked the computer to maneuver the ship.

Staying below the trees, he took the tractor path toward his south forty. The trees were merely dark shapes under a layer of clouds in this rain, seen through a wet canopy. Fortunately he knew the ground perfectly, knew every tree and stone and bush.

Finally Egg set the saucer down. He pushed the power knob in to the first detent to ensure the antigravity rings were off. He climbed from the pilot's seat, took a last look around, touched this and that, then opened the hatch and lowered himself carefully through the opening. After closing the hatch, he crawled from under the ship on his hands and knees, soaking his trousers.

When he was standing in front of the ship, he looked around carefully. On the other side of his line fence was a huge high-tension tower, one that carried at least 150,000 volts. He found the tower, looked up and tried to see the wires. No. Well, they were up there and they were wet.

Egg turned to the saucer. The rain seemed to be falling harder now. He could feel rivulets coursing down his neck, feel the dampness in his shirt and jacket.

Power up!

He waited for ten seconds, then told the computer, *Lift off.*

The ancient saucer rose slowly and majestically into the air.

He flew it up above the wires, then brought it in over them. *A little lower. A little more.*

A continuous bolt of energy arced from one wire to the saucer, ran through it and went back into the adjoining wire. The arc was brilliant, like a huge floodlight. Egg squinted so that he could see.

After a few seconds there was a giant flash. The saucer seemed to shrink instantly to half its former size. Still the electricity arced from the wires and ran through it.

Three seconds, four—Egg was counting—and there was another huge flash. The saucer instantly shrank again.

After two more quantum jolts, Egg lifted the saucer off the wires. The juice stopped flowing. He flew the saucer over to the field and let it touch down on its extended landing gear.

It was now just less than four feet in diameter. In the dim light, after the brilliance of the electrical arc, he had difficulty discerning details. The ship was small—that was enough.

He ordered the ship to lift off, then turned and began walking along the tractor path, headed for the hangar. He looked back and ensured the saucer was following. It floated along like a metal cloud, six feet in the air.

The darkness was beginning to dissolve into dawn when Egg reached the hangar. He walked over to the old stone outcropping between the hangar and the control tower. Yes, it was solid enough. So solid that the Army Air Corps didn't bother blasting it out when they built this old base during World War II.

Egg set the saucer on the stone. He didn't like its first location, so he moved it to another. Then he decided to turn it slightly so that the rocket exhaust nozzles faced the forest.

Finally satisfied, he secured all power to the saucer.

Egg Cantrell's clothes were about drenched from the rain, but he didn't notice. *The saucer looks pretty neat sitting there,* he thought. He reached for it, pushed against it, tried to move it. Nothing doing. Its mass was still precisely the same as it was before he shrank it; the electrons in the atoms were simply running closer together.

Egg patted the saucer, then went into the hangar for several garbage bags so he could clean up the mess of items from the saucer. The day had completely arrived, a soggy rainy day, when he finished. He walked past the hangar and took the path to the house.

THREE DAYS LATER, ON A SUNNY FALL MORNING AS THE frost burned off the grass, Rip, Charley and Egg, bundled up in coats and blankets, sat on the porch sipping steaming hot coffee. Since they had arrived Charley and Rip had avoided talking about their adventures. The television was still chewing on the Artois story and replaying video clips of the great saucer battle over Washington and New York. Egg watched in the privacy of his bedroom, yet when Rip and Charley turned the television on, they immediately turned it off again as soon as the commercial was over and the talking hosts resumed chewing the rag. They didn't want to think about it.

But now, out on the porch, Charley tentatively broached the subject. "I can't get Jean-Paul Lalouette out of my mind," she said. "I want him to go away but he won't."

"You just gotta let it go," Rip advised.

"When he slowed down and flew under the bridges, I was

really worried he was going to fly his ship into something, end it all in a spectacular crash. I had visions of 9/11 all over again."

She paused, sipped coffee and thought about that moment. "I guess it was his slowing down that worried me. That meant that he was flying the saucer, either with the controls or by telling the computer what to do and when to do it. As you know, if you are physically manipulating the controls or telling the ship what to do, you can take the ship outside its performance envelope. Once you're out there, if you can't get back in you've bought the farm. On the other hand, if you tell the computer to fly the ship—in effect tell it merely where to go—it will use the radar and other sensors to learn what's ahead, then adjust your flight path and speed and so on to get you where you want to go safely, staying within the performance envelope. These two modes of operation sound similar, but they're as different as night and day. When he slowed down, I knew Lalouette was flying the saucer, not the computer."

"Why?" Egg prompted, to keep her talking.

"Because if he merely told the saucer to fly under the bridges, it could have done so at Mach Two. It would have come down sooner, kept the speed up, zipped under the bridges—the Brooklyn and Manhattan bridges are nearly side by side—then pulled up to avoid the next one or a ship or a turn in the river. But the saucer slowed down. That meant Lalouette was flying."

"And if he judged anything wrong, he would crash?"

"Precisely. At the time, I thought he might intend to crash. I wasn't sure. Especially when he flew around the island and dropped down onto the avenues. He was still flying his ship then. That was the scariest moment of my life. I thought he was going to kill a zillion people. Either intentionally or unintentionally. Whichever, they would still be dead."

"He must have been dying," Rip mused. "He stopped flying the saucer on that irrational climbout."

"I think he died right after he pulled up over Central Park and lit the engines," Charley said. "The ship tilting to the east must have been his last conscious thought. From that moment his saucer merely flew along until it exhausted its fuel."

"And you killed him," Egg said, eyeing her face.

Charley Pine hid behind her coffee mug. "Something like that, I guess."

"Was he a nice guy?"

"Just a guy," she said softly.

To change the subject, Egg asked, "How did you keep the saucer from sinking to the bottom when you put it in the ocean?"

Charley explained, "When we came out of the Chesapeake I found that the ship would plane under water if you used the antigravity rings for propulsion. When the fighters jumped us, we were about out of fuel and didn't want to shoot them down, so we hid in the ocean. Went under and began motoring southeast. Later we heard ships going over, probably headed to our splash location to look for wreckage. I'll bet ten bucks those fighter jocks reported that they shot us down."

"Indeed," Egg murmured. "That's precisely what they did. And they never found the wreckage." He had been watching television.

"Aren't looking in the right place," Rip said, and laughed. He stretched hugely—man oh man, it was good to be alive.

THE DAY WAS WARMING NICELY AND CHARLEY AND THE Cantrells were still on the porch chatting when four stretch limos pulled into the parking area by the old control tower. Men in suits piled out of the two front vehicles and the rear one and deployed around the cars. Several of these men carried visible weapons, small submachine guns. They also talked into their lapels.

"Oh, damn," Egg Cantrell said flatly.

The man in the right front seat of the third limo now hopped out and opened the rear door. As Egg suspected, the president of the United States climbed out of the back of the third limo, followed by another man Egg didn't recognize. The two of them crossed the lawn on the sidewalk and stopped on the porch steps.

"Mr. Cantrell?"

"Yes."

"Sorry to barge in on you like this, but I need to have a little talk with Ms. Pine and young Mr. Cantrell. Hope you don't mind."

"Please, come up and be seated. Would you like some coffee?"

"That would be very nice, thank you. I like mine with a spot of milk, and Mr. O'Reilly takes his black. Folks, this is P.J. O'Reilly, my chief of staff."

The president dropped beside Rip on the porch swing and O'Reilly pulled a chair around while Egg went to make another pot of java.

"Good to see you folks again," the president began.

"Likewise," Rip replied. He could bullshit with the best of them.

"Now, I know you folks are probably a little put out that the military tried to shoot you down, but things got mighty confusing and mistakes were made. These things happen, yet no harm was done."

"Umm," Rip said.

"Uh-huh," Charley agreed.

"So, anyway, figuring there could be some hard feelings, I thought maybe I should jump on a plane and zip out here to see you. The FBI checked and said you were here."

"You could have determined that with a telephone call," Charley said.

"God bless the FBI," Rip muttered.

The president ignored them both. "One of the reasons I came is the saucer. We want it back."

"We?"

"The government. *Your* government."

"You made a long trip for nothing," Rip said smoothly, without inflection.

"Now, son, you signed that flying saucer-thing over to the Air and Space Museum. You swiped it without permission, and they could sue you to get it back. Those facts are indisputable. Unless you turn it over PDQ with a smile on your face, I can pretty much guarantee you that they will sue."

Rip kept his cool. "One of the conditions of the gift was that the museum folks had to remove the reactor from the saucer, which they failed to do. Arguably they forfeited the gift by failing to abide by one of the essential conditions. I'm keeping it."

The president smiled the smile that the secretary of state found so loathsome. "Where is it?"

"I've heard about this Fifth Amendment thing," Rip said with his face deadpan, "and thought I'd give it a whirl and try to ride it. Seems like everyone ought to give that one a short ride every once in a while, don't you think?"

The president's grin faded. "Apparently they can't take the reactor out of the saucer and transport or store it because the design is unapproved. The regs are quite specific."

"Sorta seems like the prez oughta be able to cut through that kind of knot."

"Seems like, but he can't. Some federal judge would drop an injunction on me and that would be that. But we can't let that saucer just sit around. You stole it from the museum; anyone could. Surely you see the problem?"

"I'll hang on to it." Rip thought about that statement, and added, "If I have it."

Egg brought out a tray with five cups of coffee, sugar in a little bowl and milk in a small pitcher. The cups weren't china, but mugs bearing logos from the state university, the St. Louis arch and numerous other public attractions. Egg handed the president one from Dollywood.

The president slurped coffee without glancing at the mug, then addressed himself to Egg. "Mr. Cantrell, your nephew is refusing to return the saucer to the government. What do you think of that?"

"His mom told me he was difficult to potty train."

"Ms. Pine?"

"It's not my saucer," Charley said curtly.

After spending most of his adult life in politics, the president knew when to drop a subject and go on to something else. From a pocket he produced an envelope. He extracted three sheets of paper from it and handed one each to Egg, Rip and Charley. As they read he took three medals from another pocket. He handed them each one in turn. "From a grateful nation. Little bits of enameled metal and ribbon aren't much, I know, but you people saved a lot of lives and property. On behalf of the nation, I thank you."

Charley recognized the medal. "The Distinguished Flying Cross," she told Rip and Egg.

"Coolidge gave one to Lindbergh after he flew the Atlantic," the president told them. "You three deserve them."

On that note the president leaned back, crossed his legs and asked about the battle on the moon and the saucer battle over Washington and New York. After an hour of conversation, he rose to go.

"Sure you don't know where that saucer is?" he asked Rip.

"Pretty sure that if I knew I wouldn't tell" was the reply.

"Well, if you find it and change your mind, give us a call."

Egg accompanied the president and O'Reilly toward the

cars. The president was about to get into his limo when he saw the small saucer on the rock. He walked over to it for a look while Egg and O'Reilly trailed along. Once there, he even put on his glasses to examine the detail.

"Nice," he said finally. "Thing'll turn green out here in the sun and rain. Maybe you should put it inside."

"Outside seemed best," Egg said.

"By the way, the folks in western Missouri, Kansas and half of Arkansas and Oklahoma lost their electrical power for a couple of hours the other night. You know anything about that?"

"Read about it. We didn't lose power here."

"Heard about Chadwick passing away. The newspaper said he died an old man, of natural causes, right here on your property."

"That he did. Lalouette dropped him here. He died peacefully."

"Any connection between his death and the loss of electrical power?"

"Not that I know of," Egg said truthfully.

"Umm." The president leaned on the saucer, tried to push it. "Heavy thing," he muttered.

"It's welded to steel rods in the rock," Egg said.

The president glanced sharply at Egg, then said, "Just as long as it doesn't go anywhere."

"Yes, sir," Egg replied.

The president got into his limo and the Secret Service agents boarded theirs.

Egg waved as the entourage rolled off toward his gate, took a last look at the saucer, then walked up the hill to the porch where Charley and Rip were waiting.

EGG HAD JUST SETTLED INTO HIS CHAIR ON THE PORCH when the telephone in the kitchen rang. He rushed away to answer it.

"So what are we going to do now?" Rip asked Charley.

"You mean this morning?"

"In this lifetime."

"Oh," she said casually, as if the question were no big deal. "I've got an offer I'm weighing. Found it as an e-mail on the computer this morning."

She passed Rip a folded sheet of paper. He opened it and read: "Am divorcing the Junior League babe. If you're looking for someone to go flying with, I'm available. Joe Bob Hooker."

"Very funny," Rip said sourly. He folded the sheet of paper into an airplane and tossed it back.

Charley winked at him, but Rip noticed that she refolded the paper and put it in her pocket.

Egg came to the screen door. "You two won't believe this, but the Australians have found a piece of what they think is an ancient mother ship buried in the Great Barrier Reef. They've invited us down for a look. They're still on the phone."

"Mother ship? You mean an interstellar spaceship?"

"Precisely. Like the one that brought the saucer to this solar system. You two want to go?"

Rip and Charley glanced at each other; then Charley said, "Of course. We could catch a plane tomorrow morning in St. Louis for L.A. and cross the pond from there. You're coming, aren't you?"

"I'll come to Australia next week to see what they have. I have a date this weekend." Egg flushed and hurried away along the hallway.

Rip winked solemnly at Charley Pine, who threw back her head and laughed.